'A wickedly funny novel about love and loss (and man makeovers). Your best friend will thank you for it—and she'll laugh 'til she cries!'

—*Company*

'A witty yarn of love from a male point of view—you may want to lend it to your fella. Four stars.'

—*Hot Stars*

'Reading about [Edward's] journey is very funny, heartwarming, and enlightening…It gives a real insight into the different ways men and women think.'

—*Prima*

'Delightfully shallow and self-obsessed—that's the male psyche for you.'

—*Elle*

'Ed needs to learn how to make the ladies fancy him again, so he embarks on a journey of self-discovery. Most amusing. Four stars.'

—*Closer*

'Funny and witty, this is a great read that gives us a look into the workings of the male mind.'

—*The Sun*

Praise for Matt Dunn's previous novel, *Best Man:*

'Fast-paced, insightful and very, very funny.'

—*Heat*

'A well-crafted tale of when love goes wrong and love goes right—witty, astute but tender too.'

—Freya North

'Full of great one-liners, this book is a terrifying eye-opener into what men really think.'

—*Company*

'Frighteningly funny and sometimes just plain frightening. I suspect that Matt Dunn's *Best Man* is the most realistic perspective on the average man's world view most women will get without hanging around in a locker room.'

—Chris Manby

'Required reading for any woman contemplating marriage, this book provides an invaluable insight into the mind of your boyfriend's best friend.'

—*Irish News*

'A warm, open and damn funny book.'

—*Lads Mag*

'Both hilarious and touching.'

—*Best*

By the same author

Best Man
Ex-Girlfriends United
From Here to Paternity
The Good Bride Guide

THE
EX-BOYFRIEND'S
HANDBOOK

MATT DUNN

sourcebooks
landmark

Published by Sourcebooks Landmark, an imprint of Sourcebooks, Inc.

P.O. Box 4410, Naperville, Illinois 60567-4410

(630) 961-3900

Fax: (630) 961-2168

www.sourcebooks.com

Originally published in Great Britain by Pocket Books, 2006.

Library of Congress Cataloging-in-Publication Data

Dunn, Matt
  The ex-boyfriend's handbook / Matt Dunn.
      p. cm.
  1. Men--Conduct of life--Fiction. 2. Self-actualization (Psychology)--Fiction.
3. Dating (Social customs)--Fiction. I. Title.
  PR6104.U5449E9 2010
  823'.92--dc22
                                      2010032550

Printed and bound in the United States of America.
            VP 10 9 8 7 6 5 4 3 2 1

For Tina. For everything.

Acknowledgements

Thanks: to Patrick Walsh and the Conville & Walsh team, and Kate Lyall Grant, Digby Halsby, and everyone else at Simon & Schuster, without whom my ramblings wouldn't see the light of day. To the delightful Chris Manby, and the wonderful Freya North, for their self-lessness and generosity. To my family and friends for their continued support. To Tony Heywood, whom I can never thank enough. To John and Nuala, Carlos and Africa, Ann and Jim—*gracias, amigos*. To the Pavilion and Avenue Tennis Club social players—mine's a Nastro. To Dr Debs for the technical input. And lastly, to the Board, who have ensured I'm anything but. Thanks, Mike, for inviting me to the party.

Sunday 16th January

7 p.m.

'EDWARD. LET ME GET this straight. You've called me right in the middle of *Antiques Roadshow* just to tell me your girlfriend's gone to bed?'

'*Tibet*, Dan. Jane's gone to Tibet. She's left me.'

It's the first time I've said those words out loud, and my voice cracks a little down the phone line. My girlfriend of ten years, the woman who I've been sharing my bed, my flat, my *life* with, has gone. Vanished. Departed. Cleared out. And, by the looks of things, cleared me out as well.

'What do you mean, "she's left you"?'

'Dan, there's no clearer way of saying it. Jane's. Left. Me.'

I can almost hear the cogs turning in Dan's head as what I've just said sinks in. 'Stay where you are,' he says. 'I'll be right over. And don't do anything stupid.'

Don't do anything stupid? I put the receiver down, wondering what Dan's idea of doing something stupid would actually be. Wearing socks with sandals, possibly.

I stare disbelievingly around my flat, which appears to be almost as empty as I'm feeling inside. The place looks like it's been ransacked: wardrobe doors still ajar; drawers left open as if they've been rifled through in a hurry; and the CD rack empty except for a couple of dodgy rock compilations and my collection of digitally re-mastered Queen albums.

While I wait for Dan to arrive, I walk from room to room, compiling a mental check list of what Jane's taken. The chairs and dining table set she bought from IKEA: gone. The red imitation leather sofa her mother gave us which made obscene noises whenever you sat down too quickly: missing. The breadmaker that she won in a competition and then used just the once: well, I won't miss that, I suppose. Even the Picasso poster she bought as a souvenir from that exhibition we saw five years ago in Barcelona has been neatly removed, leaving just the faintest outline on the kitchen wall where it used to hang. At least she's left me the bed, although most of the rest of the furniture seems to be missing. All *her* things, now I come to think of it.

I'm amazed at how clinical Jane's been; how effectively she's managed to excise herself from this flat, and my life, without leaving so much as a trace of the ten years we've been together. The only hint of anyone else ever having lived here is the photograph I find on the floor in front of the bookshelf of the two of us, taken at college, when we first met. Jane and I always used to smile when we looked at it, remembering the time it was taken, and just how happy and carefree we were back then. She'd even bought a special frame, and given it pride of place above the fireplace. But as I prop it up on the mantelpiece I realize she's taken the frame but left the picture, and I'm not smiling any more.

I retrieve Jane's note from where I've screwed it up and thrown it into the fireplace, smooth it out, and read it through one more time, even though I can already remember it word for word.

Dear Edward,

By the time you get this letter, I'll be on a plane to Tibet. I'm going away for a while because I need to sort some things out, and while I'm gone, I suggest you do the same.

Let's face it, Teddy, you've let yourself go, so I'm letting you go too.

I'd tell you not to think about following me, but I know that a romantic gesture like that would never even occur to you. And that's part of our problem.

As I'm sure you've noticed, I've taken my things, although I've left you the bathroom scales—you might want to use them for something other than stacking your old newspapers on.

I'll be back on April 16th, so perhaps we'll talk again then. Meanwhile I suggest you use this opportunity to take a long hard look at yourself in the mirror.

Jane

P.S. I realize at this point I'm supposed to say something like 'it's not you, it's me', but in actual fact, it is you.

As I finish reading, my hands are shaking. I fold the note carefully and place it in my pocket, then light a cigarette and inhale deeply, longing for the calming buzz of the nicotine, hoping it will take the edge off the pain I'm feeling.

It doesn't.

7.59 p.m.

I'm smoking my fourth cigarette, and wondering where on earth Dan's got to, as he only lives in the next street, when he finally rings my doorbell. I buzz him in impatiently; a swirl of cold Brighton air follows him in through the door, adding to the chilly atmosphere already in my flat.

Dan takes one look at my miserable expression. 'How are you?' he asks.

When I can't seem to answer, he doesn't know how to react. We stand there for a second, and then begin an awkward dance as he tries to give me one of those male hugs where you touch at the shoulders while ensuring no body contact below the nipples, but I don't know what he's trying to do and instead lean forward to try and shake his hand. We end up accidentally bumping heads, which digs my glasses painfully into the bridge of my nose.

As he lets me go, I jab a finger at my watch.

'That's what you call "I'll be right over", is it?'

Dan's my best friend, although there are times I could gladly punch him in the face. He's one of those annoyingly good-looking guys, with almost model features, and a smile that could get him off a murder charge. Trouble is, he knows this.

'Sorry, mate,' he says, grinning sheepishly. 'Had to get ready. Make sure I looked OK.'

'Looked OK? Just to come round and see me?'

Dan shrugs. 'Never know who you might bump into. Paparazzi and all that.'

'Dan, you're a daytime television presenter on a rubbish antiques programme. I hardly think you're going to have photographers camping outside your front door.'

Dan doesn't reply, but just taps the side of his nose in that annoying way. I sigh with exasperation and show him through into the front room.

'Jesus, Edward. It looks like you've been done over,' are his first sensitive words.

'At first I thought I had been,' I say, wistfully. 'And then I wished I had.'

Dan examines the space where the hi-fi used to sit, then inspects the near-empty CD rack. He walks into the kitchen, then through to the bedroom, silently taking in the scene, then turns to look at me, a puzzled expression on his face.

'At the risk of asking a stupid question…'

'That's never stopped you before.'

'You are sure you haven't been? Burgled, I mean.'

I nod. 'Pretty sure. Burglars don't normally only take half your stuff. Especially not just your girlfriend's half—'

'Or your girlfriend,' says Dan, peering inside the near-empty wardrobe.

'Thanks for reminding me.'

'Sorry,' he says, following me back into the front room. 'Shame, though. At least then your insurance would have replaced everything. And with some decent furniture.'

'Yes, well.' I remove Jane's letter from my pocket and wave it in front of him. 'Things kind of fell into place when I found the note. Burglars don't usually leave a note.'

Dan stares at it for a second or two, as if it might be infected. 'What does it say?'

'What do you think it says? The usual "Dear John" stuff.'

Dan looks a little confused. 'Er…Which is?'

'Sorry, Dan. I forgot the concept of the woman actually doing the dumping would be alien to you.' I unfold the piece of paper and speed-read it in front of him. '"Dear Edward, you've let yourself go, it's over, I'm off." That about sums it up.'

Dan takes it from me and reads it through slowly, his lips moving as he does so. Eventually, he hands it back to me with a grimace.

'That's terrible.'

'I know. How could she do it? Just end it like this?'

'No. I mean the fact that she calls you "Teddy". Yuk.'

Dan takes his jacket off and looks around for a place to throw it, a task made somewhat difficult by Jane's recent removals. Eventually, he just puts it back on.

'Well, look on the bright side,' he says. 'At least you don't have to go through that painful "sorting out who gets what" time.'

'Thanks, Dan. That really makes me feel better.'

He punches me playfully on the shoulder. 'Don't mention it. Anytime.'

'I was being sarcastic.'

'So was I. Anyway, how on earth did she manage to get it all out without you knowing?'

'Yeah, well, I'd been away visiting my parents for the weekend—my mum's birthday—it'd been planned for months, and then at the last minute Jane hadn't been able to come. Emergency at work, she said.'

Dan sticks his lower lip out and nods appreciatively. 'Ah, the old "emergency at work" line.'

'She said that she might be out when I got back. I didn't realize that she meant out of the country.'

'And out of your life, by the looks of it,' he says, taking Jane's note back from me and reading it once more. 'What are you going to do?'

I take my glasses off and rub my eyes wearily. 'I don't know. I just…She…I mean…'

Worried that I might start crying, a look of panic crosses Dan's face. He puts a reassuring hand on my shoulder.

'Edward—before you go any further, we need to sit down and talk about this. And we can't do that here.'

'Why ever not?'

Dan points to the space where the sofa used to be. 'Well, mainly because there's nowhere to sit.'

'Ah.'

I look up at him, and he smiles, and utters those immortal words, his cure-all for any situation.

'Come on. Drink.'

Dan slips Jane's note into his jacket pocket and marches off down the hallway. I stare at him for a moment, then pick the photo up off the mantelpiece, slide it into my wallet, and follow him out of the door.

8.15 p.m.

Our local, the Admiral Jim, is perched on the border between Brighton and Hove in a quiet mews that runs between our respective streets. It's typical of the new wave of Brighton pubs: beer-stained carpets replaced with bare wooden floorboards; traditional ales swapped for the latest Czechoslovakian lagers; and brightly coloured alcoholic mixers with names like 'Psst' and 'Rekd' lining the shelves behind the bar. We like it not only because it is extremely local, but also because it's one of the few places around here that doesn't need a bouncer on the door, which is mainly due to the fact that it's off the usual Brighton stag and hen party routes. Most weekday evenings, it is full of office workers sniggering, 'I'm just at the Jim' into their mobiles. As is customary on a Sunday evening, however, the place is a little quieter.

'Hold on,' says Dan, nervously peering in through the window. 'Just let me check the coast is clear.'

This is a necessary precaution at most of the venues we visit because Dan, King of the one-night stands, has an unfortunate habit of regularly bumping into his exes. Most of them are, shall we say, less than pleased to see him due to the abrupt manner of their dismissal, and aren't afraid to tell him so, sometimes quite forcefully. With a last relieved look, Dan pushes open the door, and I follow him inside.

'Tibet, eh?' he says, as we head towards the bar.

I make a face. 'Yup.'

Dan whistles in that 'ohmigosh' kind of way, and then his expression changes into a frown. 'Where exactly is Tibet, anyway?'

'You know, near India. Where Mount Everest is? In between China and Nepal.' Sometimes he's not the sharpest pencil in the box.

Dan starts to snigger. 'Nepal?'

'What's so funny?'

'Well, it's just, *Nepal*...I've always thought it kind of sounds like "nipple", doesn't it?'

I give him a pitying look. 'Dan—how old are you?'

'Thirty. Same age as you. Why?'

'Well act it, for God's sake.'

He grins at me. 'Just trying to lighten the mood a bit.'

I glare back at him. 'Well, don't. My girlfriend's just dumped me. I'm allowed to feel depressed.'

As I heave myself awkwardly up onto a bar stool, Dan leaps nimbly onto the one next to me. He pulls Jane's note out from his jacket and starts to study it.

'Tibet. She certainly wanted to make herself scarce, didn't she?'

'Christ, Dan,' I say, snatching it from him and stuffing it into my back pocket before he can read any further. 'Don't mind my feelings, will you?'

'Sorry, mate. It's just that, well, you don't seem that upset.'

I stare forlornly at the bar in front of me. 'I'm too stunned to be upset, Dan. I'm surprised, shocked, confused...' I search for the right word.

'Bitter?' he asks.

'A little. It hasn't really sunk in yet.'

Dan shakes his head. 'No, a pint of bitter? Or something stronger? What do you want to drink?' He nods towards Wendy, the Admiral Jim's regular barmaid, who's just appeared in front of us. She's pretty, in a flat-chested Meg Ryan kind of way.

'Ah. Bitter, please. Sorry.'

Dan flashes a smile at Wendy. 'Pint of bitter please, gorgeous, and my usual.'

Wendy glowers at him, still not having forgiven Dan for doing his normal sleep-with-once-and-never-call-again routine with her flatmate the other week.

'Hi, Edward,' she says cheerily, giving me a big smile while still ignoring Dan. 'No Jane this evening? Left you has she?'

When I don't answer, she flicks her eyes across at Dan, who mimes cutting his throat. Her expression rapidly changes.

'Oh God, Edward. I'm so sorry,' she says, blushing. 'I had no idea. Really.'

I force a half-smile. 'That's okay.'

Wendy leans across the bar and rests a hand on my arm. 'How are you feeling?'

As she says those words, I have to stop and think. It's a very good question; how *am* I feeling? Numb, certainly, a bit like that soldier in the opening scene of *Saving Private Ryan* who's lost his arm but walks around looking for it as though nothing's wrong, as if he's refused to admit to himself what's just happened, and so doesn't feel any pain. Though the trouble with that is eventually, when the shock wears off, he will.

I settle for the obvious. 'Pretty rotten, actually.'

Wendy gives my arm a squeeze. 'Well, if you want to talk about it, you know where I am.'

Dan clears his throat impatiently, obviously a little put out at having been ignored earlier.

'I think you'll find that's what I'm here for, sweetheart. A bit of man-to-man talk over a conciliatory pint. Give Edward here the benefit of my experience. That's if we ever get served, of course.'

Wendy stares at him, open-mouthed. 'And what makes you think that you're such an expert on relationships?'

Dan looks at her as if she's stupid. 'Because I've had so many, obviously.'

Wendy shakes her head, pours my pint, then bangs a glass of wine down on the counter in front of Dan, causing it to nearly spill onto his trousers.

'Four pounds ninety.'

Dan reaches into his jacket pocket then looks across at me apologetically. 'Sorry, mate. Forgot the old wallet. Didn't think we'd be coming out.'

With a sigh I hand Wendy a fiver, and we take our drinks and find a corner table.

'So,' says Dan, once we've sat down, and he's made sure that his trousers are Chardonnay-free. 'Did you have any idea? That she was going to do something like this, I mean.'

'Of course not!'

'No surreptitious phone calls to Pickfords, anything like that?'

I think back over the last few weeks, trying to find any evidence of unhappiness. 'We'd had a few arguments recently, but nothing too serious. Just the usual stuff, really.'

'What sort of "usual" stuff?'

'You know'—I do an uncannily accurate, although very childish, impression of Jane's sometimes whining voice—"When are you going to get off your backside and do something about that beer belly of yours; smoking's a disgusting habit; don't you think it's time you thought about getting another job…" Like I say—just the usual.'

Dan rolls his eyes. 'Jesus, mate. How long has that been the usual?'

'Er…last six months, I guess.'

'Six months? Did you not think something might be wrong?'

I shake my head. 'I just thought it was part of that "Women, can't live with them…" stuff.'

'Any other signs? Everything all right with her job?'

I shrug. 'I guess. We didn't really talk about her work that much.'

'What about her emotional state?'

I take a sip of my beer. 'What do you mean?'

'Well, for example, I once went out with a girl who was so emotional she cried at the slightest of things. Kittens, soppy films, you name it. One whiff of anything sentimental and on came the waterworks. Even, a couple of times, after sex.' He grins at the memory. 'Was Jane ever like that?'

I think back to our recently all too infrequent below-duvet liaisons. 'She never cried after sex. Though the last time…'

'The last time?'

'She, er, cried during.'

Dan attempts unsuccessfully to smother a laugh, but to his credit tries a bit harder when he realizes I'm not joking.

I light a cigarette and blow smoke at the ceiling. 'Why didn't she say something? Rather than just upping and leaving me like this?'

'It sounds to me like she was trying to.' Dan waves my smoke away but for once decides not to comment on what he usually refers to as my 'filthy habit'. 'How long had the two of you been going out for again?'

'Jesus, Dan. Try not to talk about Jane and me in the past tense so quickly please. Ten years.'

'Bloody hell! Ten years? A whole decade?' Dan's longest ever relationship probably just about lasted a month, and that's only because he was ill for two weeks in the middle of it all.

'Yup.'

'And did you, I mean, *do* you, love her?'

I redden slightly. 'What do you think?'

'And you never thought about, you know,' he lowers his voice, 'the "m" word?'

I shake my head. 'I kind of just…assumed that we'd always be together.'

'Did you ever tell her that? In more romantic terms, obviously.'

I stare glumly into my beer. 'Obviously not.'

'Ah.'

Dan pretends to be interested in something floating in his wine glass until I break the awkward silence.

'I mean, it's not as if I've ever cheated on her.'

'Never? Not even once? In ten years?' says Dan, aghast.

I look back angrily at him. 'No. Of course not. We don't all have your…'

'Opportunities?'

'I was going to use the word "morals", but that would suggest that on some level you actually had a few.'

Dan shrugs. 'Harsh, but fair.'

'I mean, okay, so maybe I wasn't the most attentive of boyfriends. But I was faithful. And reliable. And…' I struggle to find something else, 'good at my job.'

Dan shakes his head. 'Doesn't matter a jot, mate. Funny creatures, women. Do you think Mrs. Einstein was impressed with all that stuff about Albert's relatives?'

'*Relativity*, Dan.'

'Exactly. Nope, she was more concerned whether he remembered her birthday, or forgot to put the toilet seat down.'

I sit there miserably for a while, until Dan leans across to me. 'Listen,' he says, 'would it make you feel any better if I told you that she tried it on with me once?'

I look up with a start. 'She didn't, did she?'

'Nope. But would it make it easier if I said she did?'

'Be serious, Dan. Did Jane ever say anything to you? About us?'

He shakes his head. 'Nothing.'

'You're sure?'

'Yup. Oh, apart from that she wished that you were more like me. And had a bigger…'

'Dan!'

'Relax!' He rolls his eyes. 'I'm just trying to cheer you up.'

'Dan, cheering someone up normally consists of trying to make them feel better about *themselves*, not harping on about how great you are.'

Dan looks surprised. 'Really?'

I take Jane's note out again and stare at it, searching for clues, until Dan reaches across, takes it from me, and wordlessly slips it back into his pocket. Suddenly, my despair turns to resentment at the way she's just dismissed ten years in less than ten sentences. I find the photo of her and me in my wallet, and throw it angrily onto the table.

'Bloody cheek! "*You've let yourself go*". Hardly. I mean, we're all a little heavier than we were at college.'

Dan pats his stomach proudly. 'I'm not.'

'You wouldn't be. I mean us normal people. I'm not that different to how I used to look, surely?'

Dan opens his mouth as if to mention something, then thinks better of it, and stands up.

'Hold on a sec.'

He walks over to the other side of the pub, removes a clip-framed photograph from the montage between the toilet doors, and puts it down on the table in front of me. It's of the three of us at a fancy-dress party here at the Admiral Jim last December. Jane, courtesy of a blonde wig, white charity-shop evening dress, and a not inconsiderable amount of padding, is dressed as Marilyn Monroe. She's pouting at the camera, flanked by Dan and me, him all teeth and daytime-TV tan in his no-effort-required James Bond dinner suit. I'm brandishing a plastic sword, and squeezed into the Roman legionnaire's outfit I'd bought from Woolworth's toy section in desperation late that afternoon.

Dan eventually stops admiring himself in the photo, and squints at my outfit.

'Who were you supposed to be again?'

'Russell Crowe. You know, in *Gladiator*!'

'Russell Crowe?' laughs Dan. 'You look more like Russell Grant. In a mini-skirt!'

I snatch the picture away from him and stare at it crossly. 'It was a child's outfit. Of course it didn't fit properly.'

Dan passes me the college photo and urges me to compare the two. 'Even so, mate. You've got to admit that you've put on a few pounds over the years.'

I stare at the two images in disbelief. It's like one of those 'before' and 'after' adverts you see in the Sunday supplements for the latest miracle exercise machine. Except the wrong way round.

'Well, I'm just a little more cuddly. In fact that's what she calls…I mean, used to call me. Cuddly Teddy.'

Dan grimaces. 'Pass the sick bucket. Too much information, mate.'

'It's true. In fact, she used to say that I was improving with age. Like a good wine,' I say, nodding towards Dan's glass.

'Well, trouble is, now she obviously thinks you're corked.'

'Ha bloody ha, Dan. Very funny.'

I sip my pint silently for a few moments, before Dan awkwardly clears his throat.

'Seriously, though. There could be a reason why you've "let yourself go".'

I nearly spit out my mouthful of beer. 'What do you mean?'

'You know, stopped making the effort. Put on all this weight. Started dressing like the airline's lost your luggage.'

'Dan, I know what you were getting at by the phrase "let yourself go". I meant "what was the reason?".'

Dan takes a deep breath. 'Well, here's me, and obviously I have to look as good as I do for my job…'

'Mind your head on the ceiling.'

'…but I also like to look like this because I want women to be attracted to me.'

'Yeah, but that's just vanity. Selfishness.'

Dan shakes his head. 'It's not a selfish thing. Quite the reverse, in fact.'

'I don't understand. How can that not be selfish?'

'Because, if you think about it, I don't actually do it for me. I do it for other people. Women. Whereas what you're doing is selfish.'

'Why?'

'Because I care about how other people see me, therefore I care about other people. You, on the other hand, are saying "I don't mind how I look. I'm just going to suit myself". And I'm afraid that that attitude has the opposite effect where women are concerned. It repels them.'

I'm not quite getting Dan's warped logic. 'So your point is?'

Dan looks at me patronizingly. 'My point is, mastermind, and it's just a thought, that maybe you didn't just "let yourself go" by accident. Maybe, subconsciously, you wanted to split up with Jane. And the easiest way for that to happen without you being the bad guy was for her to leave you. So how did you achieve that? By letting yourself get into a state where she didn't find you attractive any more.'

The pub has filled up a little, and I think that I must be struggling to hear Dan correctly above the noise of the assembled drinkers.

'So let me get this straight. You're saying that I've gradually come to realize over the last ten years that Jane and I aren't suited any more, and so recently I've been cunningly stuffing my face in an attempt to make her leave me, rather than me just do the easy thing which is turn round and say, "Jane, it's not working." And what's more, I've been doing this without knowing it?'

Dan shrugs. 'No, that's not what I'm saying. I'm just suggesting that it's a possibility. That's all.'

'That's bollocks.'

Dan holds up his hands. 'Hey—don't shoot the messenger. It's just an idea.'

'Well it's a stupid idea. Why on earth would I want Jane to leave me? Particularly when we've been together for so long.'

'All I'm saying is, where relationships are concerned, don't confuse length with strength. Jane was a very different person when you first met her, and as we've just seen, you were a very different person then too. What are the chances that over the last ten years you've both evolved in exactly the same direction? I mean, look at her now, quite the high-flying career woman, always chasing the next promotion, another challenge. You've been in the same job since you left college, and the biggest decision you have to make every day is what to have for lunch.'

I can't quite believe this. 'So we've grown apart? Is that what you think?'

'Possibly.'

'And therefore I've driven her away, so I can find someone more suitable?'

'Maybe.'

I shake my head. 'Well, have you considered that the problem with that approach is that it leaves me in pretty bad shape to go out and meet someone better, doesn't it?'

Dan folds his arms defensively. 'I don't make the rules, do I?'

'Thank goodness!'

Dan tries a different tack. 'So you think the two of you are still compatible?'

'Of course!'

'Well then, let me ask you this. What is it, sorry, *was* it, that made her so special, in your opinion?'

'Well, the way she…How she…Well, lots of things.'

'Okay. So tell me something. If you went out to a bar now and saw Jane across the room, would you fancy her? Would you think you and her could have a life together?'

I don't even have to consider my answer. 'Yes. Obviously.'

'And what do you think she'd do if she saw you for the first time now? Do you think she'd fancy you? Or would she break into a rousing chorus of "Who ate all the pies?"'

'Well, I think she'd…I mean, hope she would…' I stop myself, because Dan has picked up the two photographs and turned them round so I can see them or, more specifically, see myself in them. And suddenly, shockingly, sadly, whilst I don't like where he's going with this, I can see exactly where he's coming from.

As I sit there, struggling to come to terms with this revelation, Dan leans smugly back in his seat. Unfortunately he's forgotten that he's on a stool and nearly topples over, but even this admittedly amusing spectacle can't raise a smile from me. Embarrassed, he looks around to check that no one's seen, only to catch Wendy smirking at him from behind the bar.

Dan regains his composure and drains his glass, satisfied that he's fulfilled his counselling duties for the evening.

'So, what now?' he asks.

I sigh. 'Onwards and upwards, I guess. Back in the saddle.'

Dan clinks his empty glass against mine. 'That's the spirit.'

'Any spare numbers for me in your little black book? Actually, yours is probably a big black book, isn't it?'

Dan shakes his head. 'Don't have one.'

'What? Mister I've-shagged-more-women-than-you've-had-hot-dinners? I find that hard to believe.'

'I don't,' he insists. 'What would be the point of keeping their phone numbers?'

'So you could call them the next…Ah.' I've answered my own question. Dan does operate something of a scorched-earth policy when it comes to women.

'Exactly. Treat 'em mean, keep 'em keen, and all that. But not too keen. Don't want them getting the wrong idea.'

'Come on, Dan. Everyone wants someone special in their life, surely? Even you.'

'I've got someone special in my life.'

'Who?'

'Me.' He reaches across the table and pokes me in the stomach. 'And by the way, be careful when you make the "hot dinners" comparison, because by the looks of you, that number is pretty high.'

'Yeah, well, all those women only want to sleep with you because you're a TV personality.'

Dan looks confused. 'But I *am* a TV personality. I'm "TV's Dan Davis". The two things are inseparable.'

'Insufferable, more like,' says Wendy, depositing two more drinks onto our table and removing the empties. 'On the house, Edward,' she adds, giving Dan a disapproving glance.

'So, are you going to be okay?' asks Dan, once Wendy has moved out of earshot.

I put my head in my hands. 'I suppose so. I'm only thirty years old; much too young for a mid-life crisis.'

'And much too young for middle-age spread. According to Jane,' he adds, getting up and striding off towards the gents before I can think of a suitably rude reply.

As I sit self-consciously on my own at the table, a couple of attractive girls walk in and make their way towards the bar. Both bottle-blondes, they're dressed more for a Saturday night out in Ibiza rather than a chilly Sunday evening in Brighton, and I can't work out which are the larger strips of material—the ones they're using as skirts, or the glittering pieces which barely contain their breasts beneath the denim jackets they're obviously unable to fasten. They order what I'd guess are a couple of Malibu-and-Cokes from Wendy, then the taller of the two suddenly glances over in my direction. She points across to where I'm sitting and whispers something to her friend, and when they both turn to face me, I have to fight the impulse to look over my shoulder. As I sit up straighter in my chair, they pick their drinks up and walk over towards me.

This happens all the time when I'm out with Dan, and I brace myself for the usual small talk along the lines of 'what's your friend's name?' or 'has he got a girlfriend?', before Dan puts them out of their misery and asks for a number. I quickly hide the photographs, glance across at the toilet door for reinforcements, and then it hits me—they haven't seen him yet! He was in the gents when they came in, which means it's me they're coming over to talk to. Me! Not Dan. Ha! Let myself go, have I?

Taller blondie reaches my table first, and leans down towards me, affording me a clear view of her not inconsiderable cleavage. Her chest is obviously still feeling the effect of the chilly sea air, and I have to try hard not to stare as I remember Dan's 'Nepal' comment.

'Are these two free?'

I bite off the impulse to say 'almost'. 'Pardon?'

'Is anyone sitting here?' She points at the two spare stools round the table, one of which has just been vacated by the toilet-bound Dan, and exchanges a glance with her friend.

Yes! I can still pull! I've still got it! This isn't going to be so bad, this single life. In fact, I probably won't be single for all that long. I think of the kudos I'll get when Dan comes back and sees me sitting down with these two. I can't wait to see his face. He won't mind standing up.

I change my expression from astonishment to what I hope is my most charming smile.

'No, please, feel free. My name's—'

'Thanks, love,' says taller blondie, cutting me dead. She and her friend help themselves to a stool each and head back towards a vacant table by the bar.

'But…Excuse me.'

As they both stop and swivel round on their stilettos, taller blondie peers at me before raising a badly plucked, several-shades-darker-than-the-hair-on-her-head eyebrow.

'What?' she hisses.

'It's just that, well, I thought you wanted to sit here.' I point at my table pathetically. 'With me.'

Taller blondie looks me up and down as if inspecting a sack of potatoes. And rotten ones, at that.

'Why on earth would *you* think that?' she says, before turning to her friend and miming horror. And as they head off and sit down, giggling between themselves, I can't work out what I'm more embarrassed about—the rejection itself, or the emphasis she'd put on the word 'you'.

When Dan returns from the toilet, he stares in puzzlement at his missing stool.

'Drink up,' I tell him, leaping to my feet and quickly draining my glass. 'And don't ask.'

9.49 p.m.

As Dan walks back with me to my flat, he asks me for the millionth time if I'm going to be okay. I nod bravely, though in truth my earlier numbness is starting to wear off.

'Yup.'

'You want me to hang around?'

'Nah.' I remember that he's filming in the morning, and make some lame joke about how he needs his beauty sleep, which he doesn't contradict. When I thank him for listening, he shrugs it off.

'Don't mention it. You're my oldest friend.'

For once, he sounds like he's actually being sincere, and I get a lump in my throat.

'Thanks, mate. We do go back a long way, don't we?'

Dan grins. 'No, I do actually mean "oldest". All my other friends are a lot younger than you.'

'I appreciate you coming out. You know, missing *Antiques Roadshow* and everything.'

Dan shrugs. 'S'alright. I'm taping it.'

'Oh. Good.'

As I head up the steps and open my front door, Dan clears his throat behind me, and I turn to see him waiting on the pavement, holding Jane's letter out to me.

'I think you've forgotten something.'

I stare at him for a moment, before making a decision. 'Chuck it away for me, will you?'

'So, you're just going to forget about her? Move on?'

'What else can I do? Look at what she wrote. She's left me. End of story.'

'Well…' He gingerly unfolds the note and stands there, reading, for a second or two.

'Well what?'

'She doesn't exactly say that, does she?'

I walk back down the steps. 'What do you mean?'

'Well, now I read it again, it seems more like an ultimatum than a goodbye. Shape up. Sort yourself out. A wake-up call.'

Dan hands me back the somewhat creased piece of paper, and I hold it up to the street lamp, struggling to make out Jane's words, as if I've obviously missed something.

'How so?'

'Well, how she refers to the fact that you need to look at what's happened to you. And then there's the sentence: "Perhaps we'll talk…".'

'"Perhaps"? That doesn't sound very promising to me.'

Dan sighs, 'Edward, you have so much to learn. If I walked away every time a girl said "no" to me when I asked her out…'

'That happens, does it?'

Dan thinks about this. 'Well, rarely. But the point is, where a woman is concerned, "no" doesn't always mean "no". In fact, sometimes it's actually a "yes" in disguise. So, following on from that, "perhaps" certainly isn't a negative. It just means that she's not sure—yet. She needs convincing. And it's up to you to convince her.'

'Really?'

Dan shrugs. 'Perhaps.'

'Is that "perhaps" in the male or female sense of the word?'

'God knows. Just "perhaps".'

'So what was all that bollocks about in the pub? About us having grown apart? Me driving her away?'

Dan sticks his hands into his pockets. 'I dunno. I'm not a psychiatrist, am I? Just making conversation, I suppose.'

Not for the first time this evening, he's making very little sense to me. But in my depressed state, the idea that Jane might not be out of my life completely is a lifeline that I'm prepared to grab onto with both hands.

'So you're saying that if...' I swallow hard, 'I make some changes, maybe put a bit of effort in, Jane might be prepared to give me another chance?'

'Perhaps. I mean, maybe. Yes. Certainly reads like that to me.'

I remember how lousy the girls in the pub have just made me feel, and realize with a frightening clarity that I don't want to go through all that dating malarkey again. Besides, and possibly more importantly, I love Jane, don't I?

'Well in that case, I'm going to get her back.'

Dan claps me on the shoulder. 'Good for you.'

We stand there, grinning at each other like idiots, before reality kicks in, and my face falls.

'Ah. Only one problem with that decision.'

Dan frowns. 'Which is?'

'I don't quite know where to start.'

He looks at me earnestly. 'Well, you'd better begin by following her advice. Otherwise your chances of getting her back are, unlike you, very slim.'

Dan heads off down the street, and I wait until he disappears round the corner before letting myself back into my flat, where I walk through to the bathroom and splash my face with cold water. As I lean on the sink, staring disbelievingly at the empty space on the wall in front of me, Jane's words echo around my head.

Take a long hard look at yourself in the mirror. If only I could. She's even taken that.

Monday 17th January

8.00 a.m.

WHEN I WAKE UP, or rather, *get* up the next morning, given that I haven't actually been able to sleep that well, I know immediately that something's not right. Maybe it's the fact that I've managed to go a whole night without having to fight for possession of the duvet, but whatever, I'm acutely conscious of the space next to me where Jane should be.

As I smoke my first cigarette of the day, I realize with a shudder that it's possibly the first time in ten years that she hasn't been next to me for reasons other than occasional work trips away, or the odd family gathering. Even when we'd been arguing we'd still share the same bed, lying there back to back in stony silence, as far apart as possible, until that moment when one of us would extend a hand or a foot towards the other. Once that first physical contact had been made we'd cuddle up together and forget what had made us fall out in the first place. Ten years!

Jane and I met at college here in Brighton. Her nose was the first thing I noticed about her: cute, freckled, slightly turned up at the end, and often in other people's business. We were both on the same course, although she was in the year below, but kind of ignored each other until one night in the student union I'd accidentally spilt her pint of snakebite, and she'd insisted loudly in front of everyone that I buy her another. Not wanting to make a scene, I followed her to the bar and did what she wanted. I thought I'd been doing that ever since.

At the time I'd been renting a flat with Dan, who was on the media studies course, and by our third year, Jane had moved in too, although that was probably more for economic rather than romantic reasons. It took another six months before Dan got the hint, moved out, and rented a place of his own, and since then—up until yesterday —Jane and I have been living together.

I finished my course a year before she did, and bought this flat, using some money I'd been left by a mad aunt for the deposit, and waited around for her. I'd originally wanted to go back and study for my masters, but instead found a job, the same job I have now, and just kind of kept on with it. Jane, meanwhile, had worked her way up the marketing ladder, changing companies every few years, and until recently had been marketing manager for a large insurance company here in Brighton. We'd agreed that, seeing as I'd put down the deposit, she'd stump up for the furniture. It had seemed like a good idea at the time.

I drag myself through the shower, decide that I can't be bothered to iron my shirt, and select one of my half-dozen suits—a choice made easier because there are only two that still fit. As I shut the wardrobe door, the clanging of empty hangers on the rail serves as a stark reminder that Jane's clothes are all gone. At least the wardrobe is still there, although that's probably only because it's attached to the wall.

I get dressed, then trudge through to the kitchen and make myself a coffee, but have to have it black because no Jane also means no fresh milk in the fridge. There's half a packet of chocolate biscuits left in the cupboard, and I eat them all while debating whether to go into work today. I think about calling in sick, maybe just staying at home to watch crap daytime TV, but then I'll be seeing Dan later in the flesh anyway, and I'm already in my suit, so I decide that work's as good a place as any to sit and be miserable.

Besides, I don't have a TV any more either.

8.45 a.m.

My flat, in Lansdowne Place, is on the ground floor of a beautiful white Regency building just off Brighton seafront. I have what the estate agents call 'oblique sea views', which means if you stand on tiptoe by the window in the lounge, lean forward, and crane your neck to the right, just as you bang your forehead on the glass you should be able to catch sight of that grey heaving mass that passes for the English Channel. The building itself is grade two listed, which means you need to get planning permission if you want to do anything more complicated than put up a pair of curtains, so Jane and I hadn't bothered with anything other than a coat of paint when we first moved in. In truth, Jane's pictures, furniture, and growing collection of ornaments had made it home, and without them, I can see the place for what it really is: old, tired, and right now, quite empty.

As I head out to work, my upstairs neighbour, Mrs Barraclough, whose age I estimate to be somewhere between eighty and 150, catches me in the hallway. She's almost completely deaf, but despite this, seems to have an uncanny ability to hear about everything that goes on—Jane used to call her our building's equivalent of CCTV.

'Good morning, Mrs B,' I shout.

'You're still here then?' she asks, a surprised look on her face. 'I thought you'd moved out.'

Great. I've been up less than an hour and already the questions have started. I think about trying to explain, but don't know where to begin.

'No. I mean, yes. Jane...'

Mrs Barraclough fiddles with the volume control on her hearing aid. 'It's just that there was a removals van.'

'Removals van?' Of course. What was I expecting—that Jane had hired a transit and done it all herself?

'That's right,' says Mrs Barraclough. 'Men clumping in and out of the front door. Making a terrible racket, they were.'

'I'm sorry about that,' I say, thinking it must have been bad to disturb Mrs Barraclough, before wondering what on earth *I'm* apologizing for.

'She left you then, has she?'

'What? Oh no—she's just…gone away for a while.'

Mrs Barraclough looks confused. 'With all that furniture?'

Fortunately the postman chooses that moment to arrive, providing me with enough of a diversion to slip past Mrs Barraclough and out of the front door. As I reach the pavement, the sound of a car horn beeping loudly makes me jump, and I turn round angrily to see Dan's BMW speeding down the road towards me. As usual, he's got the roof down, despite the temperature probably being in single figures.

As he screeches to a stop by the kerb, I notice that—apart from the fact that Dan's a poser—there's another reason for his convertible appearance; there's a tall, thin cardboard box occupying the passenger seat.

Dan clicks off his stereo and removes his ever-present shades. 'Can't stay. Got something for you.'

'Oh. Right.'

I stand there stupidly until he nods impatiently at the box.

'Well go on then.'

When I lean over to lift it out of his passenger seat, I nearly pull a muscle in my back.

'What on earth's this?' I puff, leaning it against a parking meter.

Dan grins. 'Mirror. Full length. And with folding side panels, so hopefully full width as well. So you can get the whole picture, however grim that may be.'

'Thanks, mate.'

'Thought it might come in handy.'

'Don't you need it?'

Dan shakes his head. 'It's my spare.'

'Your spare? Why would anyone need a spare mirror? In case your main one goes wrong?'

'I've heard they can crack,' he says, slipping his sunglasses back on, 'in some cases. Anyway, must rush. My public awaits.'

With that, he floors the accelerator, roaring off before I can remind him that given the scheduling of *Where There's a Will*, his 'public' probably numbers little more than a handful of housewives, pensioners, and stoned students.

I pick the box up and struggle back inside, nearly knocking Mrs Barraclough over in the process, and dump it in the bedroom. Once I've got my breath back, I remove the packaging and set the mirror up next to the wardrobe, folding out the side panels as per Dan's instructions. Staring back at me, red-faced, is the person I've got to say goodbye to.

And I have to admit, he's seen better days.

9.05 a.m.

I leave my flat for the second time, checking that Mrs Barraclough is nowhere to be seen, and walk miserably down Western Road into town, quickening my pace past Norfolk Square, where the assorted winos and drug-users have already formed their usual discussion groups. After a further five minutes I pass Churchill Square shopping centre, making my way through the collection of truanting Burberry-hoodied youths hanging around the burger bars and discount mobile phone fascia booths, before finally crossing West Street.

My office is on Ship Street, in an area of Brighton known as the Lanes, an ancient network of streets packed with restaurants and pubs, and where every other shop seems to be a jeweller's. It's not to be confused with the North Laines, the other side of North Street, where Brighton's trendy set hang out. There, the shops sell everything from designer gear to skate wear, the pavements are lined with stalls stocking a range of strange incense-burning equipment and everything you could ever need to 'roll-your-own', and the traditional pubs have all been turned into bars with the word 'lounge' tacked onto their names. It's all a bit hip for me, and not somewhere I normally venture unless accompanied by Dan.

As I turn the corner, I hear a familiar voice.

'G'issue?'

Billy, Ship Street's resident homeless person, if that's not a contradiction in terms, leaps out of his doorway brandishing a copy of the *Big Issue*. I'd guess he's about forty, although it's hard to tell; some days he looks half that, other days he makes Mrs Barraclough look like a slip of a girl. Billy accosts me every day, sometimes more than once. In a bad week, or a good week, as far as Billy is concerned, I probably end up buying about half a dozen copies.

'Morning, Billy. How's life up Ship Street?'

'How do you think?' says Billy, blowing on his hands to emphasize how cold it is. 'Bleedin' marvellous.'

'Pleased to hear it,' I say, trying to walk on past him.

Billy flashes me a gap-toothed, stubbly grin and steps in front of me. I can already see an empty Special Brew can by his feet.

'What can I get you this morning?'

It's his favourite joke, given the fact that all he sells is the *Big Issue*. In fact it's his only joke, but today, I'm past the point where I can pretend to be amused.

'A return ticket to Tibet please.'

Billy stares at me for a moment. 'Do I look like a bleedin' travel agent?'

I look him up and down, but fail to spot any trace of a striped polyester blouse. 'No, Billy, you don't. Not dressed like that, anyway.'

Billy looks hurt, and I immediately feel guilty. 'What's wrong with how I'm dressed?' he asks, smoothing down his parka.

'Nothing, Billy. I'm sorry. You look very…' I can't in all honesty use the word 'smart', as Billy's coat has seen better days. As, I'm sure, has Billy. 'I was just trying to suggest that you weren't dressed like a travel agent. That's all.'

He peers at me suspiciously. 'Whassup with you this morning?'

Do I want to keep having this conversation today? No.

'Nothing. I'm fine.'

'Pull the other one.'

'Just women trouble.' I say, the prospect of pulling anything of Billy's not exactly filling me with pleasure. 'Nothing you can help me with.'

'Don't be so bleedin' cheeky,' growls Billy. 'I was married once, you know.'

This shocks me. For some reason I'd never even thought that Billy might have had a normal life before this.

'Really? What happened?'

Billy shakes his head. 'She didn't understand me.'

'What was it? The drinking?'

'No you deaf git. She didn't understand me. She was Polish. I just married her so she could get her visa. Paid me three hundred and fifty quid, they did. Only two words of English she knew were "I" and "do".'

Billy tilts his head back and roars with laughter, and as a waft of stale beer reaches me, I look at my watch, and realize that I am in fact quite late for work.

'Yes. Well. Very funny, Billy. Lovely talking with you, as ever.'

I make to walk towards my office, but Billy stops me. 'Do you want one or not?' he says, offering me the copy in his hand.

I catch sight of the cover. It's last week's edition. 'I've already got that one.'

Billy looks at me accusingly. 'You got yourself another bleedin' supplier? Whatever happened to bleedin' customer loyalty?'

'Billy, I bought it from you last week,' I reply, reflecting that 'bleeding' is obviously Billy's favourite adjective.

He peers at me suspiciously. 'I don't remember that.'

It occurs to me that given the amount of Special Brew Billy regularly consumes, he probably doesn't remember anything much—but then he probably has a lot of things that he'd rather forget. I find a couple of pound coins in my pocket and hold them out towards him.

'Here, just take the money.'

Billy stares at my outstretched hand. 'I can't do that,' he says. 'That's begging. I've got my pride.'

'Okay, okay. I'll take one. Happy now?'

I grab the copy he's thrusting into my face, and give him the two pound coins. As I hold my hand out for my change, Billy looks at me as if I'm simple.

'What are you waiting for?'

I redden slightly. 'My change?'

'Change? Do I look like bleedin' Barclay's Bank?'

'No, it's just that I…The magazine only costs one pound forty.'

'So? You didn't want one in the first place.'

'But…'

Billy shakes his head slowly. 'You're worried about your miserable sixty pence change and I don't know where my next meal is coming from.'

In truth we both know the answer to that question; from the off-licence across the street, but that thought makes me feel even more guilty. I give up, turn around, and walk down the street towards my office.

I work as a head-hunter for an IT recruitment consultancy: the imaginatively named Staff-IT. I say consultancy as if we're a big operation, but in reality there's only the two of us in the office: myself and my boss, Natasha, who owns the company. And when I say that there are two of us in the office, most mornings it's usually just me;

Natasha will still be in bed, or out seeing new clients, or sometimes combining the two activities.

Natasha has an interesting philosophy when it comes to new business development. She's quite 'glam'—all cleavage and blonde hair—and once she's targeted a new company or, more specifically, the man in charge, she'll go for him, both guns blazing. I like to joke that the more she goes down, the more our profits go up. But not to her face, obviously.

And although I'm more than a little scared of her moods, can't stand the way she's constantly rude to me, and hate the fact that she treats me like her dogsbody, in truth, we have the perfect business relationship: she gets the clients, I do the work, and that seems to suit us both fine.

I head in past the reception desk and take the lift up to my office where unusually, and unfortunately, Natasha is already there, talking animatedly on the phone. I walk through the door just in time to hear her shout, 'Well, just piss off back to your wife, then!' into the receiver, before she slams the phone down. Oh great. The start of another fabulous week.

When she sees me, Natasha glances theatrically at her Rolex, a present from our most recent 'satisfied' customer.

'Morning, Edward,' she says, sternly. 'Or should I say "afternoon"?'

'Morning,' I mumble, depositing my *Big Issue* in the bin beneath my desk just as I had done with Friday's identical copy. I'm hoping she doesn't do her usual Monday morning going off on one. Even though it might defuse her mood, I've decided not to tell her that Jane's left me. 'Sorry I'm late.'

Natasha peers across at me as I slump down into my chair. 'What on earth's the matter with you today?'

Don't tell her, don't tell her…

'Well?' she demands, her face darkening.

'Jane and I have split up.' Damn.

Natasha doesn't quite know how to process this piece of information. She's not good with personal small talk, unless it's of the 'pillow' variety, and certainly not with me.

'Oh, Edward. I am sorry,' she says, her expression softening a level or two from its normal 'turn you to stone' one. 'Do you want to talk about it?'

I shake my head miserably. 'Not really, thanks.'

Natasha looks visibly relieved, and picks her phone up to make a call, but when I just sit staring at my computer screen without bothering to switch it on, she puts the receiver back down.

'Come on, Edward. What happened?' she asks me. 'Are you sure you don't want to get a woman's perspective?'

'What good will that do?'

'Well for one thing, it might help you to work out why she left you.'

I look up sharply. 'Why does everyone assume that Jane left me? Why couldn't it have been the other way round?'

Natasha opens her mouth to answer and then thinks better of it. Instead, she stands up and walks towards the door.

'Come on,' she says, 'let's have a coffee and you can tell me all about it.'

Now I know that she's genuinely concerned. Normally it's only ever me who fetches the coffee from the deli across the street.

'Okay. Why not? Thanks.'

Natasha reaches into her handbag that's hanging on the back of the door, and produces a handful of loose change. 'Could you get me one too?' she says, sweetly. 'My shout.'

When I walk back into the office a couple of minutes later carrying two cups of cappuccino, Natasha's whispering into her mobile. 'Call you back,' I hear her say. 'Crisis at work.'

I hand her a coffee, and she comes over and perches on the edge of my desk.

'So,' she says, doing her best to look interested. 'What happened?'

'There's not that much to tell. She's left me. And left me a note telling me why.'

Natasha rolls her eyes. 'A note? I hope she didn't give you any of that "it's not you it's me" rubbish?'

'Er, no. Quite the opposite, in fact.'

I explain the events of the previous evening. Natasha, to her credit, actually seems to *listen*, raising one carefully plucked eyebrow when I mention where Jane's gone.

'And you really had no idea?'

I stir my cappuccino dejectedly. 'Nope.'

'Bloody hell, Edward. For someone who makes a living listening to what other people are looking for, you've been pretty oblivious to what's been happening in your own life, haven't you?'

I nearly drop my coffee in my lap in surprise. 'What do you mean?'

'How long were you together?'

'Ten years.'

Natasha takes a sip of her coffee. 'Well, it's obvious, isn't it?'

'Obvious? It's not obvious to me.'

'Obviously.'

I'm wondering how many more times we can say the word 'obvious' when Natasha looks at me and sighs. 'Two words. Status quo.'

I look at her blankly. Even though she's nearly forty, I'm fairly sure she doesn't mean the rock group. 'I don't understand.'

She thinks for a moment. 'Okay. Consider how your job works.'

'My job? What on earth does that have to do with it?'

'Well, think about what it is you do. You approach people who work at one company, and try to get them to go and work for someone else.'

'Thank you for explaining that to me. I always wondered what it was I did.'

Natasha ignores my sarcasm. 'So, how do you convince them to move?'

'Offer them more money, usually.'

Natasha sighs. 'Okay, more money, perhaps. But think beyond the money.'

'Beyond the money?' I'm finding this hard, because in my experience, most people in our industry are only interested in the money.

'Yes. Fundamentally you're trying to convince them that the benefits of a new position outweigh the benefits of their current one. Maybe it's more money, maybe it's a promotion. Maybe both.'

'And this has to do with me and Jane how?'

'Well, think about those people who come to us and tell us they're looking for a new job, but don't really want to leave their old one.'

'The tyre-kickers?'

'That's right. They go through the whole interview process and then, even though they've got no intention of actually leaving, resign from their current position and tell their existing company that they've got a job offer somewhere else.'

'Ye-es?'

'And how do their employers usually respond?'

I think about this for a second. 'Well, if they want to keep them, they'll usually offer them more money, or a promotion, or something.'

'You see,' says Natasha. 'So maybe Jane's tyre-kicking.'

I nod for a few moments, then stop nodding abruptly. 'I'm sorry. I'm just not getting you. Are you saying that I should have given her some money?'

'No. I'm saying that maybe she wanted to change the status quo.'

'Ah. Which means?'

Natasha sighs loudly. 'I'll spell it out for you. Maybe she wanted to get married. Ever think of that?'

'But she never said…'

Natasha smiles at me. 'Edward, they might not admit it, but most women find the idea of marriage attractive.'

Whereas you find the idea of married men attractive, I think. 'You're saying that she left me to get me to propose to her?'

'Not definitely, but I'm saying that it's a possibility. Maybe she felt she'd been there for long enough to deserve that promotion, and then when it didn't come…Well, you can't blame her for handing in her notice to see what you'd do.'

'So I should just propose to her when she gets back then?'

Natasha shakes her head vigorously. 'Oh no. It sounds like it's gone way past that point now.'

'How do you mean?'

'Okay. In language even you can understand. She's "resigned", right?'

'Isn't it more of a sabbatical?' I ask, hopefully.

'Not technically. People on sabbatical expect to come back to the same job. She's looking for something to change.'

'Something? Or someone?'

Natasha sighs. 'Whatever. The point is, she's gone, and you need to improve her working conditions before you even think about offering her a new contract. Assuming…'

'Assuming what?'

'That she wasn't doing some other part-time work on the side.'

Oh *no*. I haven't even considered the possibility that Jane might have left me for someone else. She can't have. Surely I'd have known? And I can't even afford to let myself think about it. Not if I'm going to have any prospect of winning her back.

'But surely she's bound to at least give me another chance when she gets back? Especially if she isn't seeing…hasn't got another job yet?'

'Edward, at the risk of keeping this metaphor going for too long, she emptied her desk before she left. I don't think that's a good sign.'

The phone rings, and I just stare glumly at it. Natasha picks up the receiver and asks the caller to hold.

'Edward, you're going to be no use here today. Go home. Take some time off. Think about what I've said. And come back when you're ready.'

I'm a little surprised by her compassion. 'Thanks, boss.'

'You're welcome. So I'll see you tomorrow?'

I do a double take, but Natasha's smiling as she says this.

I collect my things and walk slowly back home, thinking about what Natasha's said. And although I'm not so sure she's right, I am left with a nagging doubt.

People don't usually resign without another offer on the table.

12.06 p.m.

I'm standing outside a house near Hove Park, watching the filming of next week's *Where There's a Will*. In front of me, Dan is flirting with the make-up girl, who looks about twelve years old. As she fusses over his hair, he catches my eye and makes the 'what-can-you-do?' face.

I often like to kid Dan that he owes his entire television career to me. And it's true, almost. About three years ago, Natasha had given me a couple of tickets to some charity auction she'd been invited to but couldn't make. I'd of course asked Jane but she'd not been particularly keen—'Some drunken piss-up where you're supposed to pay fifty pounds for a pair of Robbie Williams' soiled underpants? No thanks!' had been her exact words. When I'd mentioned it to Dan, once he'd ascertained that there would be women there, he'd gone for it like a shot.

Anyway, we're in the bar afterwards, where I've accidentally (if you can call any actions induced by the imbibing of two bottles of champagne an accident) poured my drink down this girl's top.

She would have made a scene if Dan hadn't flashed his smile and rushed to her rescue, and they immediately hit it off, if you see what I mean. It turns out that she's a TV producer for the BBC, and the next thing you know, Dan's screen-testing for this new antiques programme she's working on. The rest, as he likes to say, is entertainment history.

With a couple of dabs of a sponge, the make-up girl reluctantly finishes whatever it was she was doing. Dan turns and grins at the camera.

'We're rolling,' shouts the director.

'Hello,' says Dan, smile on full-beam, 'and welcome to this week's edition of *Where There's a Will*. As the saying goes, "You don't know what you've got until it's gone." Well, this is the show where you don't know what you're going to get until your parents are gone. Today, we're in Hove at the home of John and Susan Walters, to help them sort through the estate of John's parents Ted and Renee.'

'Cut,' shouts the director. 'Perfect, Dan. Let's set up for the next shot.'

The camera equipment and lights are moved into position, and Dan is joined in front of the house by a nervous-looking middle-aged couple.

'And…cue Dan,' shouts the director.

Dan's expression changes from sycophantic to sympathetic. 'Hello John, hello Susan,' he says. 'Now, John, I believe your parents died in particularly tragic circumstances?'

'Yes,' replies John gravely, as Susan sniffs quietly behind him. 'They were killed when a tanker from the local dairy hit their car.'

'I am sorry,' says Dan, putting a consoling arm round Susan, which causes her to perk up somewhat. 'But still, there's no point crying over spilt milk, is there?'

'Cut,' shouts the director. 'Just stick to the script will you, please, Dan?'

'Okay. Sorry.'

The cameras move to close-up, and Dan readies himself for the show's catchphrase.

'So…' he announces, letting Susan go and rubbing his hands together. 'Let's see what you've been left.'

'Cut,' shouts the director, and the filming moves inside John and Susan's modest semi, where what looks like a load of junk from a car-boot sale is spread around the lounge.

'So, this is what they've left you?' asks Dan, once the cameras are rolling.

'That's right,' replies John.

'Well, as you know, we have our antiques expert Digby on hand to tell us if any of these, er, heirlooms are actually worth anything.'

At the mention of his name, an orange-skinned man wearing a pinstripe suit and a bow tie moves into shot. He shakes everyone's hands, then casts a knowledgeable eye over the assembled objects.

'What do you reckon, Diggers?' says Dan, as John and Susan gaze on expectantly.

Digby picks up a Charles and Diana commemorative wedding mug and holds it reverentially up to the light, as if he's just stumbled across the Holy Grail.

'Well, it's too early to tell, but these, for example, are very collectible.'

'Great,' says Dan, turning back to the unhappy couple. 'And what are you hoping to do with the money?'

John speaks up first. 'We want to buy a new car.'

'Or perhaps do up the house,' says Susan.

John doesn't miss a beat, and picks up a photo of his parents. As he gazes at it, the camera zooms in to catch the tears welling in his eye. 'It's what they would have wanted.'

Dan turns back to camera. 'Okay. But will it be a new Porsche or a new porch? We'll let Digby get on and do his stuff. Join us after the break, and remember, where there's a will...'

'There's a way!' shout the assembled crew, somewhat unenthusiastically.

'Cut,' shouts the director. 'Take five, everyone.'

Dan ambles over to where I'm standing, looking a little disgruntled.

'Bloody amateurs,' he says, shaking his head.

'Well, I liked your ad-lib,' I say. 'Very funny. New director, is it?'

'No, these people we work with every week. The "public". They sniff a few times in the right places but quick as you know it they're ready to bin the sentiment, flog the family jewels, and spend the cash. I sometimes think the only thing they really want is to be on TV.'

'Ah. Right.' I decide not to point out to Dan the irony of what he's just said. Apart from his constant pursuit of the opposite sex, his whole life is dedicated to increasing his screen time.

'Anyway,' he says. 'What are you doing here? You haven't got the sack as well?'

'I should be so lucky. No, Natasha's given me the day off. Thought I'd try and sort out a few things. You know, work out where to start.'

'Tell you what,' says Dan. 'Why not come round later, and I'll give you a hand? Two heads, and all that.'

'Sounds good. What time?'

Dan looks at his watch. 'Well, I should be finished here about fiveish, so lets say about six?'

'Six o'clock it is.'

Dan glances back towards the make-up girl, who's gazing adoringly in his direction.

'On second thought make that seven.'

7.00 p.m.

I've spent the best part of the afternoon getting the flat back into some sort of a liveable state, which really just meant spreading the remainder of the furniture around a bit, buying some batteries for the portable stereo I find in the cupboard under the stairs, and hiring a TV and video combination from the shop at the end of the road and resting them on a stand that I made from the cardboard box Dan's mirror came in.

By early evening I'm bored, and it's a relief when seven o'clock comes. When I press the buzzer for Dan's flat, and he answers the door wearing a pair of bright yellow rubber gloves, my first thought is that little miss make-up is still there.

'Dare I ask?' I say as he shows me in.

Dan looks at his Marigold-clad hands as if seeing them for the first time. 'Oh, *these*? Cleaning the flat, would you believe.'

Dan lives in what I guess is known as a loft development: a converted perfume factory that's now all stripped floorboards, chrome fittings, and exposed brickwork. It's very modern, very flashy, very trendy. Very Dan, in fact.

'Really?' I almost don't want to know why.

'I was just about to defrost the refrigerator but,' he nods towards the huge stainless-steel Smeg appliance in the corner, 'a fridge too far, and all that.'

'What happened to your cleaner?'

'Christina? Went the way of the others, I'm afraid.'

'You didn't…?'

Dan has a habit of employing stunningly attractive Eastern European cleaners, and then does his usual trick of trying to sleep with them. He feels so guilty about this afterwards that he invariably has to sack them.

Dan grins sheepishly. 'Afraid so.' He peels his rubber gloves off and dumps them in the pedal bin. 'How are you doing?'

'I've been better.'

But the truth is, I've been worse as well. I can't quite rationalize it; I feel lonely, I feel hurt, I feel cheated, even. But I also feel motivated to do something about it.

When I tell Dan about my conversation with Natasha, he just laughs it off.

'Typical female response. It's not all about marriage, you know.'

'No, Dan, I don't know. And that's the problem.'

Dan checks his watch. 'Come on. You can buy me a drink and we can go through some strategies. Set out some guidelines.'

'Such as?'

'Well, why don't you start by trying to remember what it was Jane fancied about you in the first place?'

'What good would that do?'

'She was attracted to you once, right? Well why not try and remember what it was about you she liked, and then see if you can't reproduce that?'

In the absence of any other ideas, this one seems as promising as any. 'Should we take a pen and paper?'

Dan walks over to his couch and picks up an expensive-looking silver laptop.

'No need, mate. Modern technology.'

7.10 p.m.

We're in the Admiral Jim, sitting down at a table by the window. I've bought us both a drink and ordered something to eat—my usual, fully loaded 'Admiral Burger', and a somewhat healthier chicken salad for Dan. As we wait for the food to arrive, Dan fires the laptop up and then sits there, fingers poised above the keyboard.

'Right. Here we go. Start, Programs, Excel…'

'Am I going to get a running commentary of every key you press?'

Dan ignores me. 'File, new, save as "Edward Middleton. Spreadsheet". Or should that be "Middle-Age Spreadsheet". Get it?'

'Yes, Dan. Hilarious. Can we just get on with it, please?'

'Suit yourself. Okay—cast your mind back. What was it Jane said first attracted her to you?'

'Er…'

'Come on, Edward. Don't be embarrassed. What was it?'

'She always used to say that I was a good listener.'

'Er…Okay. That's something, I suppose. But what else? I'm thinking physical characteristics, rather than rubbish like that.'

'She said I had lovely eyes.'

'Well, that's a good start. You've still got them, although they're a little bloodshot, and hidden behind those awful NHS reject pieces of plastic that you call glasses.'

'Bugger off. They're designer. Or they were when I bought them.'

Dan rolls his eyes. 'Mate. They, unlike you, have dated since then. What else?'

I think back to when Jane and I started going out, which seems like a long time ago, especially now. 'My smile. Jane always said I had a lovely smile.'

Dan peers at me closely. 'Let's have a look, then.'

'What do you mean?'

'Smile at me. Give us a grin.'

'This is ridiculous.'

'Edward, we're trying to conduct an objective assessment here. Come on—give it your best shot.'

I glance around the pub to check no one is looking in our direction. When I beam at Dan, he makes a face.

'Blimey, mate. What have you been trying to chew through? Apart from a lifetime of coffee and cigarettes.'

I can feel myself blushing. 'What do you mean?'

'Well, look at these,' says Dan, flashing me his perfect TV grin. 'What do you see?'

'I can't see much. I'm too dazzled. They're like piano keys.'

'Exactly. Whereas yours are more like the sharps and the flats. Have you never heard the word "dentist"?'

'Bloody cheek. Of course I have.'

'When was the last time you went for a check-up?'

I think about this for a moment. 'Just after we came back from holiday. Thailand, I think it was. I'd chipped a tooth trying to open a beer bottle to impress Jane.'

'Classy,' says Dan. 'And when was that, exactly?'

'I'm not sure. Thailand? Nineteen…'

Dan holds up a hand. 'Let me stop you there. What year is it now?'

I look at my watch for some reason. 'Two thousand and—'

'Exactly,' interrupts Dan. 'So nineteen-anything is bad. You, my friend, need some serious assistance in the dental department.'

'But I hate the dentist.'

'Why?'

'I'm scared of the injections.'

Dan laughs. 'Go and see mine. You won't feel a thing. Anyway, it's just a little prick.'

'So my flatmate tells me,' interrupts Wendy, depositing our food on the table in front of us.

'Right,' continues Dan. 'What else? She can't just have fallen for your personality. As winning as it is,' he adds, as an afterthought.

'Well…she said I was a good kisser.'

'Whoa,' he says, sitting bolt upright. 'That's as far as I'm prepared to advise you.'

'And she always used to say I was funny.'

'Funny ha ha or funny strange?'

'What do you think?'

Dan pretends to be confused for a second or two. 'So anyway,' he says. 'Let's recap. Eyes, smile; two things that fundamentally we should be able to get back to somewhere near their former glory. As for your sense of humour, well, I suppose that's still there. Just not much in evidence at the moment.'

I peer at the laptop screen—it seems like a very short list. 'Is there anything you want to add to that? After all, you've known me for as long as Jane has.'

Dan scratches his head. 'Er…Good point. Well, you…you're very, er…' He looks at me blankly.

'Thanks, mate.'

'Hold on,' he says. 'There's got to be something.'

'Which is?' I ask, after he's left a silence a little too long for my liking.

'Well…You've got me as a friend. How many people can say their best mate's a TV star?' He sits smugly back in his chair.

'Dan, try to remember. This is supposed to be about me.'

'Ah. Okay. Well, you've…got a good personality.'

'Thanks. Isn't that always what they say about ugly girls?'

'You're generous,' chimes in Wendy, who's obviously been earwigging from behind the bar. 'And you're kind. And reliable. Unlike a certain somebody.'

I manage a tight-lipped smile. 'You see,' I say to Dan. 'I have hidden depths.'

'And, unfortunately, not-so-hidden widths,' he replies.

As Dan sits there, tapping furiously at the keyboard, I cover my chips in ketchup and eat them hungrily. Eventually he stops typing, and looks up at the screen.

'Can we get on to your bad points now?' he asks, folding his arms. 'I've got a few for that one.'

I brace myself. 'Go on then.'

'"Appearance,"' he says, reading through his list. '"Body". "Car". "Diet". "Exercise". "Flat"…'

My jaw drops. 'You've done this *alphabetically?*'

Dan nods, without a trace of guilt. 'Well, I didn't know how else to rank them.' He turns the screen round to face me, and I scan down it with growing disbelief.

'Car? What's wrong with my car?'

'Edward. You drive a Volvo. And a Volvo estate at that.'

'So? What's that got to do with anything?'

Dan ignores my question. 'Anyway. The good news is that the physical things are all superficial. Easy to change. However...' His voice tails off.

'However?'

'It's just that, as we know, where relationships are concerned it's not just about the physical stuff, is it?'

'It is for you.'

'Yes, but we're talking about Jane. Look at what she wrote. It's obvious that there was other stuff too.' He spins the laptop back around. 'For example, "Job..."'

'Job?'

'Yes. You've been doing the same job since college. She hasn't.'

'Yes, well. Most relationships only have room for one career person. In ours it was Jane.'

Dan spears a piece of chicken and pops it into his mouth. 'Well, maybe she wanted it to be you.'

'Are you going to spend the whole evening picking holes in me?'

Dan puts his fork down and hits the 'save' key. 'Listen, Edward. You asked for my help.'

'I know. But I was hoping for more of a character assessment, not a character assassination. And besides, I'm just not sure your views are valid. After all, you're a man.'

'Well, if you won't take my word for it, we need to get a second opinion. And seeing as Jane's in Tibet...'

'Any suggestions?'

Dan considers this for a moment or two. 'Listen. Hard as it is for me to believe, there was a time that Jane found you attractive. Unless, of course, you got her drunk. Or pregnant. Or both. But she obviously fancied you once.'

'Back at college.'

'Exactly. So what we need is someone else who knew you then. Someone who maybe even fancied you. And someone who hasn't seen you since, if possible.'

I think back to my college days, working through my pre-Jane student love life. Sadly, only one name springs to mind.

'Sally Hall.'

Dan frowns. 'Sally Hall? Who's she?'

'You remember. Sally Hall. Accountancy student. Year above us. Dark hair. Huge…'

'Breasts?' asks Dan, hopefully.

'I was going to say "fan of the Cure". But now you mention it…'

Dan takes a mouthful of salad. 'Can't place her. Unfortunately.'

'She was the girl I went out with before I met Jane.'

He looks at me blankly. 'Still nope.'

'The one you "consoled" the night she and I split up. On the grass outside the student union. In full view of the hostel TV lounge, as it turned out.'

Dan smiles as he retrieves that particular memory from the archives. 'Ah. That was Sally Hall, was it?'

I nod. 'I wonder what ever happened to her.'

Dan shrugs, 'Probably still pining after me. Like the rest of them.'

'But how on earth do I get in touch with her? It was ten years ago.'

Dan puts a hand on my shoulder. 'Let me worry about that. Right now you've got more important things to think about.'

'Exactly. Getting Jane back.'

'Nope,' he motions towards his empty glass, 'getting the drinks in.'

I head off to the bar as instructed. When I get back to the table, Dan is staring intently at the screen, and seems to be typing in his credit-card number.

'What are you doing?'

'Shush. Tell you in a moment.'

'Can I…'

'Shut up for a second, will you?'

I do as I'm told, and chew my burger quietly. Eventually, Dan puts his wallet away and looks up from the keyboard. 'Yes, Edward?'

'I just wanted to ask how we find Sally Hall?'

'Already taken care of.'

'How…What…When?'

'Edward, Edward…' says Dan. 'Let me introduce you to a recent invention called "the internet".' He spins the screen round so I can see it. 'Ta-da!'

'I know what the internet is, Dan. How come you can get online here in the Jim? I didn't know it was a hot spot.'

Dan smiles, 'Anywhere around me is a hot spot. Especially my trouser area.'

'Please, Dan. I'm eating.'

He taps his laptop affectionately. 'The joys of wireless technology. The girl from PC World came round and set it up for me.'

I can sense a story coming on. 'Oh yes?'

Dan nods. 'Yup. I can now access the internet from my living room, bathroom,' he breaks into a grin, 'even in bed, as it turns out.'

I take the bait that he's dangled in front of me. 'In bed?'

'Well, we had to test it. But in fact it's got a range of about three hundred metres, which just happens to be the approximate distance from my flat to this pub.'

On the screen I recognize the 'Friends Reunited' logo. Beneath it is the heading 'University of Brighton, 1995', and a list of vaguely familiar names, including, of course, a recently updated entry for a 'Dan Davis'.

He clicks on the 'previous page' button, and reads off the screen. 'Here she is. Sally Hall, class of '94. No photo, unfortunately. Living in London, working in Pimlico as a finance director…blah blah blah. Quite the career girl, it seems. And she was interested in you?'

I nod. 'I was quite a catch.'

Dan looks at me pityingly. 'Note the word "was" in that sentence. Anyway,' he says, clicking the mouse button a few times, 'this is what you wrote.'

I stare at him, aghast. 'What do you mean "what I wrote"?'

Dan takes a sip of his wine, then reads his email back to me. 'Dear Sally. Hi, Edward Middleton here. Remember me? I certainly haven't forgotten you. Long time no see, but I need to ask you a favour.'

I go white. 'Please tell me you didn't click "send"?'

'I could tell you that, but it would be a lie. Anyway—what have you got to lose? Apart from the seven pounds fifty you owe me for the joining fee.'

I shake my head incredulously. 'My dignity?'

Dan puts his glass back down onto the table. 'Edward, Jane ran out on you yesterday, cleared out your flat, and went off to Tibet without telling you. I'd say your dignity is the last thing you should be worried about.'

As I reread the message, it doesn't take me very long to realize that Dan's probably right.

'What if she doesn't respond?'

'Oh, she'll respond,' he says. 'They always do.'

'So,' I say, through a mouthful of burger. 'While we're waiting to hear back from Sally, where do we start?'

Dan consults his spreadsheet. 'Well, the most obvious one.'

'Which is?'

'We need to do something about the amount you've got on your plate.'

'Are you saying that I've been neglecting Jane because I've been too busy?'

'No, I mean in front of you, you fat bastard. Look at your burger—cheese *and* bacon, chips, mayonnaise…It's no wonder you're overweight.'

I look down at my admittedly chunky waistline. 'It's just a bit of a beer belly.'

Dan pokes me in the stomach. 'Mate, you look like you've been living in the brewery.'

I push my plate away reluctantly. 'Well, I suppose I could cut down a little on the food front.'

He pings my beer glass with his finger. 'And the alcohol's got to go too. Especially the beer.'

'What?'

'It's very fattening.'

'Really?'

Dan rolls his eyes. 'I refer you to our conversation of a few moments ago. Why do you think it's called a "beer belly"?'

'Ah.'

Wendy walks past, and notices my half-eaten burger. 'Something wrong with your food?'

I shake my head, and stare longingly at my plate. 'I need to go on a diet. Apparently.'

Wendy looks me up and down. 'You don't need to lose any weight. I like you cuddly.'

'Yes he does,' smirks Dan. 'He's got bigger breasts than you have.'

Wendy reddens slightly, then picks up Dan's wine glass. 'Can I get you another drink?'

He looks confused. 'But I haven't finished this one yet.'

'Yes you have,' she replies, emptying it in his lap.

Dan jumps up, grabs a bar towel, and starts to mop his crotch, much to the amusement of the rest of the bar.

'What on earth did you do that for?'

'Why do you think?' says Wendy, glaring at him. 'You have a real gift, you know.'

'Not for you I don't, sweetheart,' replies Dan.

As he disappears into the gents to dry his trousers under the hand dryer, I follow Wendy back to the bar.

'So why this new healthy regime?' she asks.

'Dan's idea. He seems to think I've got a chance of winning Jane back.'

Wendy looks a little surprised. 'Really? Why? I mean, what did she say in her note?'

I recount Jane's letter, surprising myself that I seem to know it off by heart.

'What do you think?' I ask, hopefully.

Wendy smiles sympathetically at me. 'I think if you love her, it's got to be worth a try. Anyway, what can I get you? The usual?'

Sadly, it's time for me to try the unusual. I look back over to our table, where Dan, back from the gents, is typing away again.

'Another glass of wine for Bill Gates over there, and I'll have… What do you have that isn't beer?'

Wendy scratches her head. 'Well, there's wine, obviously, spirits, the usual array of soft drinks…Or how about a coffee?' She points to a gleaming contraption behind the bar. 'We've just got this brand new machine.'

'It doesn't have alcohol in it?'

'Not the way I make it.' Wendy walks over and presses a button, causing the front to light up. 'What sort would you like?'

I gaze at the impressive piece of machinery. 'What kind do you have?'

Wendy consults the laminated menu card. 'Espresso, latte, cappuccino, mochaccino, frappuccino, latteccino…' She looks up mischievously. 'Al Pacino…'

'Doesn't it just do normal coffee?'

Wendy stares at the array of buttons in puzzlement. 'Probably. But I couldn't guarantee it.'

'Okay. Forget it. I'll just have a glass of water, please.'

Wendy switches the machine off, not a little relieved. 'Ice? Slice of lemon?'

'Oh, go on then. Push the boat out.'

When I carry the drinks back to our table, Dan looks approvingly at my choice of beverage.

'Cheers,' he says, taking a sip of his wine. 'So. The diet is one thing. How about the exercise part?'

I light up a cigarette and inhale deeply. 'Exercise?'

Dan does a bad Michael Caine impression. '"You're a big man, but you're out of shape." Yes, exercise.'

'But I don't know the first thing about exercising.'

'Well, I'll help you.'

'You?'

'Why not?'

Unfortunately, I can't think of a reason quickly enough. 'What do you know about training someone?'

'I keep myself in pretty good shape, don't I?' says Dan, tensing a bicep.

Oh no. I can just imagine where Dan's going with this. He's probably already thinking of making his own workout video.

'S'pose.'

'So let's start tomorrow. I run most mornings. Why not come with me?'

I hurriedly try and think of an excuse, as the idea of trailing along the seafront behind Dan hardly appeals.

'Er, I've got to work,' I lie.

'Well, we'll go before work then. That is, unless you'd rather stay in bed with…Oh no, she left you, didn't she. Because you got too fat.'

'All right. No need to rub it in. Tomorrow morning it is.'

Dan grins at me. 'Shall we say eight o'clock?'

'Fine.'

'Good. I expect you to be ready to go, in your sports gear.'

'Right.'

'And you'll have to do something about the smoking as well.'

I take a long drag and stub my cigarette out. 'Okay.'

Dan shuts his laptop. 'That's that then.'

'Great. Only one slight problem regarding tomorrow morning.'

'What's that?'

'I don't have any sports gear.'

'You're kidding?'

'Why would I? I don't do any sport.'

Dan sighs, and looks at his watch. 'Come on,' he says. 'We should just about make it.'

'Just about make what?' I say, a little alarmed.

'Late-night closing,' he replies. 'We're going shopping.'

7.46 p.m.

We're in Brighton Marina, where the shops stay open later than in Churchill Square, heading for Sports Shack, one of those large chains that's always staffed by spotty adolescents, and frequented by people looking for the kind of running shoes that will only ever be used to run away from the police. We wander round for a few minutes, ignored by the assistants, until I accidentally knock over one of the trainer displays.

A spotty adolescent materializes instantly. 'How can I help you?'

'I need to buy some sports gear.'

'Well,' he says, disinterestedly, 'you've come to the right place. For what sport?'

'Er…I'm not actually sure.'

'Fitness training,' says Dan.

The assistant gives me a look that seems to say 'about time too'. 'Second aisle on the left.'

I follow Dan to the aforementioned section, where he walks up and down, passing me a selection of jogging pants and sweatshirts.

'How do you know my size?'

Dan doesn't say anything, but just points to the label, where I can quite clearly see the letters 'X' and 'L'.

I pick up a sweatshirt with a hood, slip it on, and turn to Dan. 'What do you think?'

He rolls his eyes. 'Are you planning to sell drugs on the street corner?'

'Of course not.'

'Well, take that off then.'

Dan finds a pair of shorts, holds them up, looks round at me, then seems to think better of it, quickly putting them back on the rack.

'Right,' he says. 'Trainers. Size?'

'Nine and a half.'

He selects a pair of brightly coloured Nikes and throws them at me.

'Catch!'

I, of course, drop them, and nearly do again when I see the price. 'Ninety pounds? For a pair of trainers?'

'If you're going running, it's important to have good shock absorption. That's what you're paying for.'

'So I don't damage my knees?'

Dan grins. 'Or the pavement.'

After I've staggered to the cash desk, and handed over the best part of two hundred pounds, Dan and I pile back into his car and head home.

'See you in the morning, then,' he says, as he drops me off. 'Eight o'clock?'

I grunt a reply, retrieve my bags from the boot of his car, and head inside, not relishing the prospect of the morning run, as even just carrying all my new gear is hard work. Once I'm sure Dan's gone, I head out to the video store and rent *Rocky III* for inspiration, then on the way back buy a packet of cigarettes, a six-pack of lager, a large bar of Dairy Milk, and order a large meat-feast pizza with extra cheese. This is my farewell meal to the old Edward, my goodbye to all my old vices; and as I watch Stallone do his stuff I relish every mouthful, savour every drop, and appreciate each unhealthy puff, and when I've finished, I pack the rubbish into a large black bin liner, head off to bed, and sleep like a baby.

Tuesday 18th January

8 a.m.

SUFFICE TO SAY, I'M not feeling my best after last night's indulgences, and I'm sitting on my bed, trying to work out how to lace up my new running shoes, when Dan rings the doorbell. In an attempt to be colour coordinated, I'm wearing my new red tracksuit on top of a red sweatshirt, which strains a little over my stomach.

Dan snorts with laughter when he sees me. 'Bloody hell, mate. All you'd need is a white beard and you'd pass as Santa.'

'Ha ha.'

'Don't you mean "ho ho ho"?'

'Dan, please, it's too early.'

'Sorry.'

While I pull my trainers on, Dan unzips his spotless Tommy Hilfiger top and does a couple of energetic stretches. Even though it's a chilly January morning, he's wearing shorts, no doubt to show off his muscular, hairless legs, which seem to be suspiciously tanned given the time of year.

'So, what's the plan then?' I ask him nervously.

'Like I said. We're going for a run.'

'Which involves?'

Dan sighs. 'Well, it's a bit like walking. Only faster.'

'No, Dan. I meant where are we going, how far, that kind of thing.'

'Need-to-know basis,' says Dan, leading me out of my front door and down the steps.

'Don't we need to warm up or something beforehand?'

'Nah. Best warm-up for running is running. Come on.'

Dan hits the pavement and takes off at a light jog in the direction of the seafront, me following about five yards behind. By the time we reach the end of my road, I'm already starting to feel the pace, and it's with some relief we have to stop at the crossing.

'So…how…far…?'

'See the cafe over there?' says Dan, jogging on the spot as we wait for the lights to change.

I look across at where he's pointing, about four hundred yards away. That doesn't look so bad.

'Yeah?'

'Well, my usual run is past that, along to the marina, and then back.'

'What?' I say, horrified. 'That took us ten minutes last night. Driving.'

'So?'

'In the car,' I add, just in case he hasn't got me.

Dan looks at me with disgust. 'Don't be such a wuss. I thought you wanted to get fit?'

'Fit, yes. Not train for the London Marathon.'

As the green man beeps at us, Dan sprints across the road, followed by me at a somewhat more leisurely pace. My new trainers are already beginning to hurt.

8.05 a.m.

Brighton's West Pier is a shadow of its former glory—a hulking, sagging wreck that's losing the battle against the relentless tide and the passage of time. In many ways, it's just like me this morning.

For the next few minutes our 'run' consists of Dan alternately jogging forwards, then turning and sprinting back to where I'm hobbling slowly along. We get as far as the Angel statue that delineates the Brighton/Hove border before Dan turns around to see me in a state of near collapse. He jogs back over to where I'm fighting for breath by the side of the road.

'How are you doing?' he asks, still hardly breathing himself.

'Badly,' I pant.

'Come on. You're bound to get your second wind soon.'

'Second wind? I'm not sure I've even had my first one.'

'Just try to keep it going.'

'I can't,' I puff, my face the same shade as the rest of my outfit. 'I'm flagging—'

'I can see that,' interrupts Dan, 'but if you just keep moving…'

'No. Flagging down a cab. To take me home. This is ridiculous. We've only been at it five minutes, and already every part of me aches.'

Dan punches me playfully on the shoulder. 'Come on, Edward. You know what they say: "No pain, no Jane".'

I shake my head, partly to keep me from further humiliation, but mostly to avoid any more of Dan's awful puns on my girl-friend's name.

'I'm sorry, mate,' I say, in between gasps for breath. 'I appreciate you coming out with me this morning, but this just isn't going to work.'

Dan shrugs, starts to say something, and then is distracted by two attractive girls jogging past in the opposite direction. He looks at me, then at them, then back to me, a pleading expression on his face.

'Go on then,' I say. 'Fetch.'

As Dan sprints effortlessly off in pursuit, I wait by the road for a taxi. The first two drive straight past, obviously reluctant to pick up someone who looks like they might expire on their back seat, but eventually one takes pity on me, and I climb awkwardly in, mumbling some excuse about having twisted my ankle while out jogging.

It's only a short distance back to my flat, but ironically I find myself realizing something. I'm actually at the beginning of a very long road.

9.51 a.m.

When I eventually limp into work, having decided that I can't sit at home and mope around all day, unbelievably there's an email in my inbox from Sally Hall. She's still using the same surname, which suggests to me she's not married, and when I nervously click 'open' there's a phone number—her work number, I guess—and just one word: 'Intrigued'. I call Dan for advice.

'Well, phone her, dummy.'

'And say what?'

'That you'd like to meet up. And that it's important, but you can't tell her why over the phone.'

'But what if she says no?'

'She won't. Trust me.'

I put the phone down, and after I've steadied my nerves with a guilty cigarette, pick it up again and dial Sally's number. Her secretary—she has a *secretary*—puts me through, and although I nearly bottle out when she asks, 'Will Ms Hall know what it's concerning?' after a few seconds, Sally comes on the line.

'Well, well. Edward Middleton. To what do I owe this honour?'

I've not spoken to her for ten years, but recognize her voice immediately, even though it's heavy with sarcasm.

'Hi, Sally. How are you?'

'As I said in my email. Intrigued,' she replies. 'Nothing for ten years and then, out of the blue…' She leaves the sentence hanging.

We chat a bit, about people we knew at college mostly, and then I remind her that I need a favour.

'So you mentioned. What kind of favour?'

I clear my throat. 'I can't really tell you over the phone. But something's happened to me, and I need your help. Can we meet?'

Sally leaves a suspicious pause. 'Okay. Just let me check my diary.' There's the sound of tapping on a keyboard, then, 'How does Thursday next week sound to you?'

'Can't you do any sooner?' I ask, conscious that my three-month clock is ticking.

'I don't think I can,' says Sally. 'I'm away tomorrow on business. I don't get back for a week.'

So, not only does Sally have a secretary, she also has a job where she's away on business. And for a week at a time. The closest I get to being away on business is walking to the end of Ship Street to post a letter.

'Well, how about today? Lunchtime? It won't take long.'

Sally sounds hesitant, 'I don't think I can…'

'Please,' I say, putting as much urgency into my voice as I can muster. 'It's really important.'

There's an even longer pause, and then, 'Fine. Somewhere public, though.'

I have to think fast. She works in Pimlico, so… 'How about Victoria Station? One-thirty? In front of WH Smiths?'

Sally laughs. 'Ooh. How romantic. And how will I recognize you?' she asks, playfully. 'Do you still look the same?'

I'm about to laugh myself, and nearly tell her that that's the point. Thinking about it, Jane doesn't seem to recognize me any more, so why should Sally? My eyes flick to my waste bin, where yesterday's *Big Issue* is still sitting, and I have an idea.

'I'll be carrying a magazine,' I say. 'Just in case.'

'Well, I'll see you at one-thirty, then,' says Sally.

As I put the phone down, it suddenly occurs to me that there'll probably be rather a lot of people carrying magazines in the vicinity of Victoria Station's biggest newsagent, and I'm wondering whether to call Sally back when a voice from the doorway makes me jump.

'Making a date already?' asks Natasha, who's come in at the tail end of my phone conversation.

'Not a date, exactly. More of a second opinion,' I say, explaining Dan's theory to Natasha. When I've finished, she shakes her head.

'What on earth are you doing that for?'

'I thought it might help me find out where I've gone wrong. And what I should be aiming for.'

'But you're assuming that Jane is still looking for the old Edward. The one she met at college. Maybe her tastes have changed since then?'

And while I worry that Natasha might be right, I don't have anything else to go on.

1.07 p.m.

I'm sitting on the 12.19 to London, reading through the second copy of the *Big Issue* that I've had to buy from Billy in as many days, as, unfortunately, while I'd been nervously primping myself in the toilet, the cleaners had come and emptied my bin of the one I'd been planning to take with me. I've already had a dilemma about what to wear, but realized I'd left it too late to go home and change, so the jeans and jumper I wore into work today have had to do.

I get to Victoria a little early for our rendezvous, so lean on the window outside WH Smiths and scan the crowd, trying to spot her. The station's pretty busy, Smiths turns out to have two 'fronts' and, as I feared, there seem to be lots of people carrying magazines, so I'm wishing my choice of a meeting place had been a little bit more specific. Never mind how *I've* changed, will I still recognize *her*, I wonder? What does ten years do to any of us, unless you're Dan and you dedicate your life towards the pursuit of youth? Female youth, that is.

I'm a little nervous, I must admit, not to mention cold, and I'm cursing the fact that my leather jacket has seen better days, so I'm hopping about, trying to keep myself from shivering, while simultaneously trying to display my magazine as prominently as possible. All of a sudden, I hear a female voice.

'I'll take one of those. Your last one, is it?'

I look up, startled, to find a pretty young girl standing in front of me. She's dressed smartly, and holding a Starbucks cup in one hand. For a second, I think it might be Sally, but if so, she's been spending even more time on her appearance than Dan.

'Pardon?'

'It's one pound forty, isn't it?' she says, reaching into to her purse.

'What is?'

She points to the magazine I'm holding. 'The *Big Issue*. One pound forty.'

'Yes,' I answer without hesitating—after all, I've bought enough copies to know—before even wondering why on earth she's asking. But just as it occurs to me to say something, the girl smiles at me sympathetically, and presses a couple of coins into my palm.

'Here's one pound fifty. Keep the change.'

I unthinkingly take the money she's offered me before my brain finally clicks into gear, and I try to give it back to her. 'No, I'm not…'

She clasps my outstretched hand. 'You poor thing. You're freezing. Here—a nice hot cup of coffee for you too.'

As she grabs hold of my *Big Issue* and tries to exchange it for her cup, I suddenly realize what's happening.

'What are you doing? Let go.'

I pull the magazine out of her grasp with a sharp tug, nearly spilling coffee on her shoes in the process.

'I've just paid you for it,' she protests, starting to look a little alarmed.

'But it's not for sale. Here.'

I try and hand her money back, but it's too late, and she just backs away from me. As the words die in my throat, I feel a tap on my shoulder, and turn round to see Sally standing next to me. She looks good—a little older, sure, plus she wears glasses now, although I'm pleased to see that her figure's still the same. But it's her expression I can't seem to work out, as it's hardly the friendly recognition I was expecting.

'My God, Edward. Has it come to this? I know you said on the phone that you'd been through something, but…'

'No, you don't understand. I'm not homeless.'

Sally frowns at me. 'Well, what are you doing selling the *Big Issue*, then?'

'I'm not selling it.'

'You just sold one to that girl. And then snatched it straight back off her.'

'No, I didn't *sell* it to her.'

'Yes you did. I saw you.'

'No. She…tried to buy it from me. But it's not the same thing.'

Sally shakes her head slowly. 'And she tried to give you a nice cup of coffee too. Which you practically threw back in her face.'

'No. You've got it all wrong. I'm not homeless. I have a flat. In Brighton. And I've got plenty of money. Look.'

I reach into my jacket and get out my wallet to show Sally, much to the disgust of a middle-aged couple and their teenage son standing nearby, who have witnessed the whole incident.

'How could you?' says the woman. 'Taking money from those who really need it.'

'Shame on you,' adds her husband.

'Wanker,' says the son, followed by 'Ouch!' as his mother gives him a clip round the ear.

A small crowd is beginning to form. 'What's wrong?' asks a large donkey-jacketed man, walking up to the couple.

The woman points at me scornfully. 'He's pretending to be homeless so he can sell the *Big Issue*!'

'Disgraceful.'

'Shouldn't be allowed.'

'You need help, you sad git.'

'I—I'm not…' I look around in vain for the young girl so I can give her money back and clear this whole mess up, but she's disappeared somewhere into the throng of commuters. To be honest, I'm wishing I could do the same, before the crowd light torches and chase me along the platform. Fortunately, Sally takes control and leads me away.

We walk quickly out of the station and find sanctuary in a nearby pub, where I explain my dilemma with Jane. But once I've finished, instead of the sympathy I was hoping for, Sally starts to laugh.

'So, let me get this straight. The girl you dumped me for ten years ago has suddenly dumped you?'

'That's right.'

'And so you want the girl you dumped's advice, on how you've "lost your way", so you can try and win back the girl you dumped me for?'

When I nod hopefully, Sally stops laughing abruptly. 'I don't know whether to be angry or feel sorry for you.'

'Please, Sally. I need your help.'

'And just why should I help you, Edward? After all, I'm the injured party here. And besides, I never liked that Jane Scott. She stole my boyfriend, don't forget.'

'Sally, that was a long time ago. And we'd been going out for, what, three weeks? We hadn't even…'

Sally folds her arms defiantly. 'That's not the point.'

'Well, if it makes any difference, I apologize for treating you so badly. I did feel guilty about it at the time.'

'Well,' sniffs Sally, 'that's something, I suppose.'

'Even though…'

'Even though what?'

'From what I remember, you got over me pretty quickly.'

Sally gets all defensive. 'What do you mean? How exactly did I get over you "pretty quickly"?'

'By getting under Dan Davis. That night. On the lawn.'

It's Sally's turn to look guilty. 'You knew about that?' she says, blushing.

'Sally, we all knew about that. Quite a few of us saw it. Some even took photos. I think Dan still has the negatives.'

For a moment, a dreamy look passes across her face. 'Dan Davis. Whatever happened to him?'

'I don't know,' I say, fed up with constantly having to answer that question. 'Prison, I think.'

'Prison?'

I nod, and offer Sally a cigarette, but she waves the pack away disapprovingly. I light one for myself, and take a long drag. 'Anyway, back to me. Please. Just tell me—how am I different?'

Sally leans forward in her chair, puts her elbows on the table, and studies me over the top of her glasses.

'You want me to be honest?'

I swallow hard. 'Brutally.'

'Well, there's the cigarettes, for a start.' She waves my smoke away from her face. 'Disgusting habit.'

I get the hint, and stub my Marlboro out reluctantly. 'Sorry.'

'Much better,' says Sally, taking a deep breath. 'Now, are you sitting comfortably?'

1.51 p.m.

I'm wishing I'd brought a pen and paper, so comprehensive is Sally's dismantling of my present self. Fortunately, though, from memory it's not too dissimilar to Dan's list, and while the details may be a little blurry, what is clear to me is that Jane is right. I have 'let myself go' in the fullest sense of the words.

Eventually, thankfully, Sally announces that she has to get back to work, so I walk her back to Victoria and flag her down a cab, pecking her on the cheek before she climbs in. I take the tiniest bit of comfort when she doesn't flinch.

As I close the taxi door behind her, she's possibly feeling a little guilty, because she tells the driver to wait, and winds the window down.

'Listen, Edward, I hope I wasn't too hard on you. At college you were, I mean, you were never...like this. Girls fancied you. *I* fancied you. But now...' Her voice tails off, but she doesn't need to finish the sentence. 'What's happened to you since then?'

I shrug dejectedly. 'I don't know. Life, I guess.'

'Or Jane's influence, maybe?' suggests Sally, archly. 'Anyway,' she adds, 'it was nice seeing you again. Despite the circumstances.'

'You too, Sally. And thanks.'

'Has it been any use?'

I nod, gratefully. 'I'll let you know how it goes.'

She smiles. 'Do that. How long have you got until she comes back?'

I look at my watch. 'Two months and twenty-seven days.'

Sally stares at me for a moment, then starts to whistle something and it's only as the cab pulls away that I recognize the tune.

It's the theme from *Mission Impossible*.

2.15 p.m.

I'm sitting on the train back to Brighton, flicking through the selection of glossy magazines I've just bought at the station. I've got *GQ, FHM, Arena, Esquire*, and even a couple that seem to be soft-porn publications, judging by the number of barely clad women adorning their covers. I've also raided the women's section, hoping that by the time we get to Brighton I'll be able to put together a profile of my age group's ideal man. But even before we've pulled into East Croydon, I've managed to confirm what I've been starting to believe: I'm so not him.

As I stare miserably out of the window at the Sussex countryside, a young couple get on and sit down opposite me. They've obviously spent their lunchtime in the pub, and can't seem to keep their hands off each other. After a few nauseating minutes, they head off towards the toilets, and I don't see them again until we're disembarking at Brighton, by which time they're red-faced and giggling furiously. I can't wait to get off the train, and push my way past the other passengers. Ah, young love. It's enough to make you sick.

And how do I cope with this blow I've been dealt? This pit of despair I find myself wallowing in? I go back home, unplug the phone, and chain-smoke a packet of cigarettes while listening to my Queen albums at such a high volume on my portable stereo that even Mrs Barraclough has to bang on the ceiling to complain.

I turn the music up even further to drown her out, but when I remember that the next track is in fact 'Somebody To Love', which will only add to my depression, turn it back down again, only to realize that the banging has got even louder, and is now coming from my front door. I sheepishly open it, expecting to have to apologize to Mrs B, but instead I find Dan standing there, mid knock.

'What the hell are you playing at, not answering your phone or the door?' says Dan, pushing past me and into the flat. 'And why is that crappy music on so loud?'

'It's not crappy music.'

Dan ejects the disk from the machine and looks at it scornfully. 'Haven't you got any music from this century?'

'Not any more,' I say, nodding towards the still-empty CD rack.

'Remind me to add "music" to the spreadsheet.'

'What are you talking about? Queen are one of the foremost…'

'Well, I don't see them releasing many new albums.'

'Perhaps because their lead singer is dead? That usually stops musical flow.'

'Oh really? When did he die?'

'I don't know. Some time in the early nineties, I think.'

'Ah,' says Dan, wrinkling his nose at the overflowing ashtray before opening a window. 'About the same time as the air in here. Come on. Let's get you out and about.'

'Well, what's "hip" nowadays, then?' I ask him, picking up my jacket.

Dan looks at me and sighs. 'Well you quite patently aren't if you're using language like that.'

'Hip's a current word.' I think for a moment. 'Hip Hop. There you go. I've heard you play that in your car.'

'It's not quite the same thing. But in language you can understand, yes, my musical tastes are "hip". Yours, on the other hand, are more hip replacement.'

I fold my arms defiantly. 'I've got two words for you. "Bohemian Rhapsody".'

Dan just shakes his head. 'How did you become so middle-aged? It's like you just leapt from your twenties into your forties.'

'Dan, you don't understand. When you're part of a couple, all this stuff becomes less important. Why do you need to listen to the latest bands if you already know what you like? In my day, a DJ was someone who stood behind a bank of flashing lights and played other people's records. Not someone who made his own.'

Dan grabs me by the shoulders and shakes me. Hard.

'Edward. You don't get it, do you? It's still your day.'

6.52 p.m.

Not surprisingly, Dan's choice of venue for me being 'out and about' is the Admiral Jim. On the way there, I give him a run down of Sally's appraisal, which makes me feel even more depressed.

'You see,' says Dan. 'That's your problem. You always focus on the negatives.'

'Dan, my girlfriend's left me, I'm overweight, gone to pot, and my career is going nowhere fast. I'd say the only things I've got to focus on are negatives.'

'All I'm saying is, look on the bright side.'

'Your cheerful optimism is going to get you killed. There isn't a bright side.'

'There's always a bright side. You just need to look for it. Then concentrate on the positives.'

'Jesus, Dan. You're not about to break into song, are you? What positives?'

'Well, for one thing, because your girlfriend's left you, it means you've got your flat to yourself.'

'Brilliant. Just me rattling around at home, all the time thinking that something's wrong because Jane's not there. Next?'

'Well, you can eat what you want. No having to think about Jane's strange foodie requests.'

'Except that I can't because I'm on a diet. Next?'

'Well…' Dan scratches his head. 'You're free to date other women.'

'Except they don't give me the time of day. And besides, it's Jane I want to date.'

'Okay, how about this. You can fart in bed.'

'Always used to. Don't think Jane noticed.'

'Yeah, right,' calls Wendy, from behind the bar.

'You can stay up as late as you like.'

'Which would be exciting if I was five years old.'

'You're not making this easy for me, are you?'

'Dan, some people's lives aren't all roses and please themselves. I've gone through a traumatic experience—one that I'm going to have to work extremely hard to remedy. It's an ordeal that I'm going to have to suffer in the hope of a payoff at the end, which therefore doesn't mean that I'm likely to enjoy it. Any of it, in fact.'

Dan sighs. 'All right, have it your own way. I'm just trying to cheer you up.'

'Yes, well, sometimes people don't want to be cheered up. They want to feel miserable. In some ways it's easier if I do. At least then I've got something to keep me motivated.'

Dan shrugs. 'Fair enough. Only trying to help.'

'And you are helping, mate. And I do appreciate it. Just try not to be so bloody cheerful all the time.'

'Sorry,' says Dan, putting on a miserable face. And for the first time today I manage to crack a smile.

Wednesday 19th January

8.55 a.m.

I DON'T FEEL MUCH better this morning, despite Dan's valiant attempt to lighten my mood, and I'm still in a pretty lousy frame of mind by the time I leave for work. As I turn into Ship Street, I spot Billy asleep in his doorway—despite the fact that he's snoring loudly, he's still managing to hold onto his can of Special Brew. By his feet, he's fashioned a blanket into a receptacle for change, so I drop the one pound fifty I'd 'made' at Victoria into it.

Billy starts awake, and spots the money immediately. He puts down his beer and, still a little groggy, tries to hand me another copy of the *Issue*. When I wave him away, he looks up at me suspiciously.

'Well, whassat for, then?'

I peer back at him, noting how relatively smartly he's dressed, the fact that he's obviously managed to shave some time in the last couple of days, and how he's still taking as much pride as he can in his appearance, despite his situation. Given what happened to me yesterday, and his and my respective circumstances, I feel more than a little ashamed of myself.

'Inspiration.'

Billy circles his index finger next to his temple. 'You need help,' he says, taking a long swig from his can. 'Professional help.'

And it's at that moment that I realize Billy's a genius.

7.03 p.m.

We're in the Admiral Jim, where Dan is staring curiously at me across the table. 'What on earth are you looking so pleased about?'

'I know what I need to do to get Jane back.'

Dan raises one eyebrow. 'Oh yes?'

'I've seen an advert. In the local paper.'

'Steady on, mate,' Dan cautions. 'Those penis-lengthening pills don't work.'

'And you know that how, exactly?'

Dan shifts uncomfortably in his seat. 'Never mind. I thought it was you we were talking about. What advert?'

I remove the *Argus* from my briefcase and open it to where I've marked the appropriate page. 'Here.'

Dan snatches it from me. '"Life Coach." What on earth is a life coach?'

I grab the paper back from him. 'You know, someone to talk things over with. Discuss my goals, my motivation. My focus. Help me find my path.'

'Bollocks,' snorts Dan. 'Life coaches are for losers with no mates who don't live near a pub. How much is he charging?'

I scan quickly through the advert. 'Fifty pounds an hour.'

Dan nearly drops his wine glass. 'Fifty quid? Do you know how many drinks that is?'

Dan's brow furrows as he tries to work out the relatively simple sum of fifty divided by two point five. I put him out of his misery.

'Twenty, Dan.'

'Exactly. Twenty. We could sit here, sort out your little problem, get absolutely pissed, and have enough left over for a doner kebab with extra chilli sauce from Abra-kebabra on the way home.' He nods approvingly towards my glass of water and salad sandwich. 'Well, I could, anyway.'

'Yeah, but this guy's a professional.'

Dan looks indignant. 'Professional con-artist, more like. What can he possibly tell you that I can't?'

When I don't answer him immediately, Dan takes my silence as agreement. In actual fact, I'm just trying to work out where to start.

'Well…'

'Exactly. Lose weight, smarten yourself up, before you know it Jane will be back in your flat and flat on her back.' He holds out his hand. 'Fifty quid please.'

'I'm not sure it's quite as simple as that.'

Dan laughs. 'What could be more simple? Jane left you because you'd let yourself go. Well, get a grip. It's not rocket science.'

'But how?'

'I'll help you.'

'What. Like with the exercise?'

'Yes, well, I've been thinking about that. I'm afraid you're too far gone down that road for me to be of any use. You need to get yourself a trainer.'

'I've got two. You were there when I bought them.'

'A personal trainer, dummy. But the rest of the stuff—how to act, how to dress, how to talk to women—they're my specialist subjects.'

'You think?'

Dan nods. 'You don't need to be wasting your hard-earned on some touchy-feely sandal-wearing vegan tree-hugger when in reality there're lots of better things you could be spending it on.' He downs the remainder of his Chardonnay. 'Another drink for your best friend, for example.'

7.22 p.m.

We're sitting at the bar, where Wendy is showing us an article she's read in the *Daily Mail*'s 'Femail' section.

'"Health-check your relationship"?' scoffs Dan. 'I can already tell you that Edward's is so ill that it's in need of major surgery. Liposuction, for example.'

'Shut up, Dan. Go on, Wendy.'

'Well, apparently, you've got to ask yourself a few simple questions,' she says. 'Firstly, are you happy in the relationship? Secondly, how does your partner enhance your life? Thirdly, if this person suddenly vanished from your life, how would you feel? Fourthly, where in your relationship league does this person sit? And lastly, how balanced is the relationship?'

'Okay,' I say. 'Fire away.'

'Right. So let's look at these from Jane's point of view. Was she happy?'

'Obviously not.'

'If you could let me answer them please, Dan?'

'Sorry. Go on.'

'Well, Edward?'

'Um…obviously not.'

'How do you think she felt you enhanced her life?'

'Er…Well, can I come back to that one?'

'If you suddenly vanished from…'

'Well, I have, haven't I, and she's the one who instigated the vanishing, so I guess not so bad.'

'Where in her relationship league table would you be?'

'At the top, I guess. Based on length.'

'And how balanced would you say the relationship was?'

'Fairly. We split everything down the middle.'

'Everything?' asks Wendy. 'Like the cooking? Cleaning? Driving? Sex?'

'Well, apart from those things. Financially, I mean.'

'Okay. Right, let's turn those questions around. Were you happy?'

'Yes!'

'How did she enhance your life?'

'Just by being there.'

'If she suddenly…'

'I think we all know the answer to that one.'

'Where in your relationship league table would she be?'

'That's a league with very few teams in it,' interrupts Dan.

'Shut up, Dan. Wendy, I appreciate your input, but how is this helping, exactly?'

Wendy puts the newspaper down. 'I just thought if we could work out what it was in the relationship she was unhappy with, then perhaps that would give you something more to go on.'

'Thanks, but I think I know what it was she was unhappy with. Me. And I don't need a quiz from the *Daily Mail* to tell me that.'

'You're sure about that, are you?' asks Wendy.

'Er…Why?'

'Well, if we ignore for one moment the possibility that she has, indeed, gone off you, and was trying to let you down gently…'

'Let me down gently? By moving her stuff out without telling me and buggering off to the other side of the world?'

'…it could also be that she's simply trying to work out some stuff, and seeing where, if anywhere, you fit in.'

'What sort of stuff?'

Wendy shrugs. 'Perhaps it's everything: the flat, her job, Brighton, even. Maybe she's going through one of those "what's-it-all-about?" phases. I mean, she's thirty, right?'

I have to think for a minute. 'Er, nearly. But what's that got to do with anything?'

'Because just as forty is an important age for men, thirty is for women. Did the two of you ever talk about getting married? Having kids?'

'Don't you start. No, we didn't talk about it.'

Wendy looks surprised. 'Not once in ten years?'

'No. Besides, she always seemed pretty independent.'

'It's true,' says Dan. 'Jane's the one who wore the trousers. Just as well, with her legs.'

As I punch Dan on the shoulder, which hurts me more than him, Wendy looks at me sympathetically. 'Edward, sometimes the strongest woman in the world just wants a guy to seize control. To take over. She gets tired of having to make all the decisions, and of organizing every single thing that you do.'

'But Jane seemed quite happy to do all that.'

'Happy? Or was it just that if she didn't, nothing would get done?'

'Er…' Not surprisingly, I don't have an answer to that.

'Okay,' she says. 'This is how some relationships work, and I know it's not particularly PC, but the guy goes out to work, and the woman's job is to look after the guy. Keep the home clean, raise the kids, cook dinner, that sort of thing. Now, as I say, that may not be a particularly modern view, but it suits a lot of people. The problem you two had was that Jane loved her job, she was very much the career woman and earned a lot of money. It takes a lot to give that up. Particularly if you're not sure you can rely on the man in the relationship to support you.'

'But I've got a good job…'

'That you're always moaning about and threatening to leave. Hardly the best security from Jane's point of view. And what about the "kids" thing?'

'What "kids" thing?'

'You and Jane. Having them. Neither of you were getting any younger. What were your plans in that department?'

I scratch my head thoughtfully, 'I dunno really. I guess we just thought we'd have them one day. Or not.'

Wendy sighs exasperatedly 'We thought? Or you thought? Did you and Jane ever discuss it?'

'Not really.'

'Why?'

'Just because it never kind of came up, I suppose.'

'Never came up, or because you avoided it?'

'Well, not in so many words.'

Wendy tries another tack. 'Did she want children?'

'I don't know. She loves kids, though. Other people's, I mean.'

'And what about you? How do you feel about it?'

I shrug. 'Fine either way, really. If she wanted them that would be okay, and if she didn't…Same, really.'

'So, fundamentally, you're not bothered about one of the major decisions every couple has to make?'

'Well, I wouldn't put it that way.'

'What way would you put it?'

I give this a bit of thought. 'Well, it's more a case of if Jane decided she wanted kids, then…'

'Let me just stop you there. So having children would be a decision she'd have to make. Another thing that she'd have to instigate?'

'I suppose. But I'd be happy to support her, both financially and, you know, emotionally, and all that.'

Wendy rolls her eyes. 'Edward, for every woman who reaches the age of thirty, having children is the biggest issue they've got to deal with. We know that unless we make a decision about it soon then we may be leaving it too late. Firstly, we've got to decide whether we actually want them at all. Next, we have to work out whether the person we're with would make a good father. And then we've got to decide whether we can bear to stay with them for at least the next eighteen to twenty years while we're stuck at home bringing up the kids.'

'Kids?'

'Oh yes, as in the plural, because you can't really stop at just the one.'

'Can't you?'

'My parents did,' interrupts Dan, who's been pretty quiet throughout most of this discussion.

'I'm not surprised,' says Wendy. 'But, Edward, that's why we have to take drastic action sometimes. It's not like in our twenties, where relationships are just about us, and if things aren't right we can simply end it and move on. There are time factors that come in to play here. The older we get, the more pressure we put on our partner to be the right one, particularly where our decision regarding kids is concerned. Let's face it, if we do decide you're not the right one, we can't just go away and instantaneously have a child with someone else. We've got to go through the same relationship process, then actually *get* pregnant, and then carry the little sod around for nine months. So the longer we leave it, the older a mother we're going to be, and the more chances there are of complications or that we can only have one child. You guys can keep fathering until you're old and grey. We've only got so many eggs.'

'So…' Dan frowns. 'Jane's deciding whether she's going to put all her eggs in Edward's basket, so to speak.'

'Kind of,' says Wendy. 'She's coming up to a crucial time in her life—I as a woman can sympathize with that—and maybe she just wants to be sure. I think if she'd just left him, moved out, stayed here in Brighton, and maybe started looking for another boyfriend, then Edward should be worried. But instead, she's gone off to Tibet on this "finding herself" mission, because she needs to find herself before she can decide whether she wants to find someone else.'

This is great—the idea that the reason Jane left might not all be down to me, but rather down to some other issues she needs to get straight in her own mind is something I'm more than happy to entertain. But on the other hand, if it is partly because she might have been thinking about starting a family, then that's something else I've got to sort out before she gets back.

I shake my head. 'I can't believe this is all because of bloody children. But maybe she doesn't want kids.'

'Maybe,' agrees Wendy. 'But the fact that you're sitting well and truly on the fence probably doesn't help her one bit. See it from her point of view—she's coming up to that age where she's got to start thinking about making a decision, and you're doing the old "whatever you decide dear…" It's not like choosing a new duvet cover—this is the most important issue she's ever going to face, the biggest decision anyone ever has to make; it will affect both of you for the rest of your lives in the biggest possible way and you *don't have an opinion on it?*'

'Ah.' I'm starting to see Wendy's point. And I'm also starting to feel pretty stupid.

'If we're going to spend nine months feeling sick, suffering back ache, watching our bodies change—sometimes irreversibly— needing to pee every five minutes, culminating in a day or two's intense effort, pain, and stress when we have to try and squeeze something through a part of our body that's only used to much, and in Dan's case, much much smaller things going in and out, then spend several years not sleeping, stressed, with sore nipples, changing crappy nappies, breathing a sigh of relief when he or she finally goes off to school but at the same time crying our eyes out when they do, then spending the next thirty or forty years worrying about every little thing…Well, we need to be sure that the person we're doing it with is at least a little bit interested, not to mention committed.'

Dan nudges me, 'You'd need to be committed if you want to have kids.' He nudges me again. 'Like in a mental institution…'

'I got it, Dan.'

'Yeah, but you didn't laugh.'

'Because it wasn't funny. Go on, Wendy.'

Wendy smiles, and goes back to reading the *Mail*. 'I've finished, really.'

'Thank goodness,' whispers Dan, sticking his tongue out and miming hanging himself.

And as Wendy chases him round the bar with her rolled-up newspaper, for the first time I realize that this isn't just about me sorting myself out. It's about Jane as well.

And more importantly, it's about us.

Thursday 20th January

11.21 a.m.

I'M AT MY DESK, scanning through the 'Health and Fitness' section of the *Argus*, until an ad catches my eye. '*New You*. We can transform you. Call Sam Smith', followed by a mobile number. Sam Smith. He sounds like an upright kind of bloke. I take a deep breath, pick up the phone, and dial.

Sam answers after three rings, but turns out to have a very girly voice.

'New You, personal trainers.'

'Oh. Yes. Hi. Can I speak to Sam Smith, please?'

'This is she.'

This wasn't what I was expecting, and I'm considering putting the phone down, when Sam's voice comes back on the line.

'Hello?'

'You're a girl?'

'Last time I looked.'

'But you're…I was expecting…I mean, Sam, that's usually short for Samuel, isn't it?' I'm aware that I'm blushing down the phone.

'Or Samantha.' Her voice hardens a little, 'But if that's a problem for you, I can recommend someone with a little more hair on their chest.'

I think about this for a second or two, and realize that it's probably not a problem at all. Who better to knock me into the kind of shape that Jane will find attractive than another woman.

'No. No, that's fine. My name's Edward, and I need to get fit, you see. My, I mean—'

Sam interrupts me, 'Edward, let me stop you there. I'm with a client at the moment, but why don't we get together later today?'

I swallow hard. 'Today?'

'Just for an initial chat,' says Sam, noting the alarm in my voice. 'Shall we say six o'clock? Then you can tell me exactly what it is you're trying to accomplish, and we can work out how we're going to achieve it.'

We arrange a place to meet, and I put the phone down, feeling slightly nervous about what I'm getting myself in to. Telling Sam what I'm trying to accomplish will be fairly straightforward. It's the 'achieving it' part that I'm worried about.

6 p.m.

I'm in a cafe on the seafront, drinking the worst cup of coffee I've ever tasted, while waiting for Sam to arrive. I've already been sitting nervously at the table for ten minutes, and I'm trying to hide an ashtray full of my discarded cigarette butts when she walks in through the cafe door.

The moment I spot her, I suddenly feel rather fat, extremely unfit, and very, very self-conscious. Compared to me, Sam positively glows with health. With short dark hair framing a pretty face, a cute, slightly upturned nose, and the most beautiful brown eyes, stick her in a black cocktail dress and she'd be Audrey Hepburn circa *Breakfast at Tiffany's*. Without the cigarette holder, of course.

She's not that tall; perhaps a shade over five feet in her Nikes, and wearing a bright blue tracksuit that hugs her athletic, almost ballet-dancer figure. I smile at her, conscious that I'm holding my stomach in, which, when I catch sight of my reflection in the window, gives me a bit of a pained expression.

She walks over towards my table. 'You must be Edward.'

'Sam?' I say, before realizing that I've just asked possibly the most unnecessary question in the whole universe.

'Nice to meet you.'

'You too,' I say, trying hard not to wince when she shakes me firmly by the hand.

As Sam sits down opposite me and orders a decaf coffee from the waitress, I wonder why I 'must' be Edward—am I the fattest, most unfit person in the whole cafe? I look around quickly and then realize that actually, apart from the waitress and Sam, I'm the only other person in the whole cafe. But even including the waitress, who's perhaps nudging fifty, I'm probably still the most unfit person here.

'So,' says Sam, pulling a clipboard out of her rucksack and uncapping a biro with her teeth, 'as I said on the phone, I thought we ought to sit down and have a chat first, so you could tell me what your goals are.'

'That's easy,' I say, reaching into my pocket to retrieve Jane's photo. 'This.'

Sam takes it from me and studies the picture closely, a puzzled expression on her face.

'Blimey. That's a bit drastic. I mean, exercise can work wonders, and I know my ad says we can transform you, but...'

'But what?'

'I think you may need the help of a good plastic surgeon. And maybe some hormone treatment?'

I find myself blushing furiously as I blurt out my reply. 'No. You don't understand. This is Jane. My girlfriend. Ex-girlfriend. She's left me. And I need to get her back.'

'Oh,' says Sam, looking more than a little relieved. 'Right. Sorry.'

'I've got three months to...To make her fancy me again.'

It's not the first time I've said it out loud, and although it still sounds a little strange to me, Sam doesn't seem to think so. She hands the photo back to me, looks me up and down, then lets out a small whistle.

'Three months? That's going to be tough.'

'Whatever it takes.'

'Well,' says Sam, writing my name down on the clipboard, 'in that case, all I can say is that Jane's a lucky girl.'

Sam runs through some personal details, general health questions, and family medical history, noting my answers down, before looking me directly in the eye.

'So tell me a little bit about your lifestyle, and be honest. Do you smoke?'

As the waitress brings Sam's coffee over, my eyes flick guiltily towards the pile of cigarette butts in the ashtray. 'No. I mean, yes. Trying to give it up though.'

Sam follows my line of vision. 'Well, you should think about trying a little harder. What do you like to do in your spare time?'

I shrug. 'Most evenings I go to the Jim.'

Sam raises her eyebrows before realization kicks in. 'That would be "Jim" as in "Admiral", rather than g-y-m?'

'Afraid so.'

'Are you into any sports?'

'Darts. And I'm quite good at pool.'

Sam shakes her head. 'Try and think of something that's not pub-based, please.'

'Football.'

Sam looks pleasantly surprised. 'Five-a-side, or Sunday in the park? Where do you play?'

'Sorry,' I say, guiltily. 'I thought you meant watching.'

Sam sips her coffee, makes a face, and pushes the cup away. 'Can you swim?'

I glance through the cafe window at the churning grey sea, and decide to lie.

'Nope.'

'Do you own a bike?'

'Same answer. Sorry.'

Sam sighs thoughtfully, and when she puts her clipboard down on the table, it seems to have an alarming number of crosses on it.

'Right. Could you stand up, please? Let me get a proper look at you.'

I do as ordered, thankful that the waitress has disappeared, and that we still seem to be the only customers. Sam looks me up and down, and I find myself blushing again, especially when she pokes a finger into my lardy stomach.

'Take your shirt off, please.'

'What?'

'Your shirt. Take it off.'

'Why?' I look around, somewhat self-consciously.

'I need to be able to assess the base point. Get an idea of your current physique, fitness levels, that sort of thing.'

I've read about this in the copy of *Men's Fitness* I flicked through in the office this afternoon. Body-fat percentage, skin-fold callipers, working out my ideal weight and all that.

'Here?' I can hear the gurgle of my self-respect disappearing down the drain.

Sam nods. 'Don't be shy. No one's looking.'

As she rummages in her sports bag, presumably for the callipers, I slip off my jacket and tie, and pull my shirt off over my head. Unfortunately I haven't undone enough of the buttons, and it gets stuck around my neck. When I eventually manage to get it off, I notice Sam's holding a Polaroid camera, and before I can stop her or put my shirt back on, she's taken my picture.

'What are you doing?' I say, blinking from the flash.

'I'll tell you in a minute,' she replies, putting the photo down on the table to develop. 'Now, let me show you how we can work out how overweight you are.'

'Don't you need to take some measurements?'

But Sam's testing procedures are less sophisticated than that. She turns me to face my half-naked reflection in the cafe window, grabs me by the shoulders, and shakes me from side to side, producing a rather unpleasant ripple effect, particularly for an old couple walking their dog outside.

'Watch closely,' says Sam. 'It's quite simple really. If it jiggles, it's fat.'

As I look at my reflection, I jiggle. Everywhere. In fact it reminds me of one of those fairground mirrors that distort your normal appearance. Only trouble is, this *is* my normal appearance.

'Right,' says Sam, making another note on the clipboard. 'You can put your shirt back on now.'

'And what was the photo for? Blackmail?'

Sam smiles, and hands it to me. 'Motivation. This is for you to stick on the front of your fridge. Every time you feel like snacking and you go to open the door, I want you to look at it and remind yourself why you shouldn't.'

'Point taken,' I say, slipping on my tie and buttoning my collar up. 'So, have you ever trained anyone with the same goals as me?'

'To get women?'

'A woman,' I correct her. 'Singular.'

'Oh yes,' says Sam. 'Almost all of them. Except the gay guys, of course.'

I'm a little surprised at this. 'You mean there's been other people this has happened to?'

'What—been dumped, want to get back in shape? Yes, a few. But in general, you men are only after one thing, if you'll excuse the phrase.'

'You're kidding?'

Sam shakes her head. 'People come to me for a variety of reasons—to lose weight, tone up, get fit, improve in a particular sport—but really, it all boils down to the same motivation.'

'Which is?'

'They just want to look good naked.'

As I do my tie back up, Sam puts her clipboard down, and meets my gaze.

'What?' I look back at her, nervously.

'You're sure you want to put yourself through all of this? For a woman?'

I swallow hard. 'Can it be done?'

Sam folds her arms. 'Well, I've seen worse. Not much worse, mind. And while I won't be able to turn you into Brad Pitt, you might at least get to see your toes again. You may even be able to touch them. But you'll definitely be a better shape. And you'll certainly be *in* better shape.'

'Great. So, how often do we need to, you know, do it?' I ask, nervously. 'I was thinking maybe twice a week?'

'Edward, by the looks of things, twice a day would be more appropriate. But I don't want to kill you.'

I laugh at this, but then I realize Sam's not making a joke.

'So, when can we start?'

'Well, we've only got three months, right?'

I nod. 'And counting.'

'So it had better be tomorrow. We'll go for an introductory session and see how we get on. How does seven o'clock sound?'

I look at my watch. 'I should be home from work by then.'

'No. Seven a.m. You know, in the morning,' she adds, just in case I haven't understood.

'Isn't there another time we can do?' I say, conscious of the whining in my voice. 'A little, er, later?'

Sam pulls her diary out of her bag and consults it. 'Well, I'm pretty booked up at the moment. Unless you can spare an hour during the day?'

I can just see me getting that past Natasha. 'Er…my boss doesn't normally approve of me taking a lunch hour.'

'Right. Well, seven a.m. it will have to be.'

'Okay. Seven it is, then.'

'And then there's the small matter of my fee. It's forty pounds an hour.'

I swallow even harder. 'Fine. And I'd like to pay you up front every month, if that's okay?'

Sam looks a little surprised. 'That's more than okay. But why?'

'Because I've got a feeling that I'm not really going to enjoy this. Any of it. If I'm paying you on a daily basis, I might be tempted to stop, and at least if I've already paid you for the whole month I'm more likely to keep going.'

Sam shrugs. 'Whatever works for you. Oh yes, and you'll need to give me a key to your front door.'

I frown. 'On top of the money? What for?'

Sam smiles back at me. 'Because you're going to find this hard, and there will be mornings when you won't want to let me in. If this is going to work, you can't afford to miss any sessions. And I mean, any.'

While she packs her things away into her rucksack, I settle up with the waitress, then walk Sam to the door.

'So,' I say, 'see you tomorrow, then.'

'See you tomorrow,' she calls, as she jogs off into the cold night air. 'Seven o'clock, don't forget. On the dot.'

7.04 p.m.

When I get back home after my chat with Sam, I bump into Mrs Barraclough in the hallway.

'Sorry Mrs B,' I say, picking up her shopping bag, which she's dropped in the encounter.

'Pardon?' She peers up at me through her thick bifocals.

'I said "sorry". For bumping into you. Can I help you upstairs with your shopping?'

Mrs Barraclough only lives one flight of stairs above me, but at her age, it seems to take her the best part of an hour to negotiate them, particularly when she's laden with her weekly shop.

She smiles sweetly at me, revealing that she's forgotten to put in her false teeth.

'You wouldn't be a dear and help me with my shopping, would you?'

'That's what I just said.'

'Pardon?'

I suddenly worry that I'm in danger of having this conversation for the rest of my life. 'Your shopping,' I say, pointing to the carrier bag I'm holding. 'I'll help you.'

Realization dawns on Mrs Barraclough's face. 'Oh, silly me,' she says, fiddling with her hearing aid. 'I like to turn it down when I go out. Because of all the noise.'

'That's okay,' I shout, which makes Mrs Barraclough jump, because she's obviously turned the volume up too high.

While she adjusts it back down to a less eardrum-shattering level, I start up the stairs, but when I get to the first-floor landing, I look behind me, and she's only managed to get about a third of the way up. I'm faced with the awkward dilemma of waiting for her to reach the top, which by my quick calculation might take about fifteen minutes, or leaving her bag outside her flat and then trying to get past her on the stairway, thus running the risk of knocking her all the way back down again. I decide on the former.

'I've left your bag outside your front door,' I say, once she's finally made it to the top.

'Thank you, Edward,' she replies, leaning gratefully on the banister. 'I'm sorry to keep you. I'm not as young as I used to be. And this cold weather…'

'You should let me do your shopping for you. When it's as cold as this, I mean.'

She thinks about this for a minute, still blocking my escape route. 'You're a good lad, Edward. That Jane's a lucky girl. Will you stay for a cup of tea?'

Ah. She obviously hasn't worked out that Jane has, in fact, left me. Possibly because I told her otherwise, of course.

'Well…'

Mrs Barraclough's face lights up at the idea. 'Only I don't have much company nowadays. Not since my Arthur died.'

Oh God. I'd forgotten that Mrs Barraclough must have had a husband once, but then I suppose she is called *Mrs* Barraclough. Now I think about it, she's been living on her own since Jane and I first moved in, which means she must have been without him for nearly a decade. As she shuffles towards me along the landing, I realize that I can't possibly refuse.

It takes Mrs Barraclough a further five minutes to find her keys in her handbag, another two minutes to actually open the door, and by the time I'm sitting in her lounge waiting for her to make the tea, I'm starting to worry I'll miss tomorrow's appointment with Sam. I've never been inside Mrs Barraclough's flat before; it's a similar layout to mine, but where my flat is currently empty, there's not a single space on Mrs Barraclough's shelves, mantelpiece, or inside her glass-fronted cabinets that isn't covered or filled with ornaments, photographs, or souvenirs. Digby from *Where There's a Will* would have a field day in here.

Eventually, Mrs Barraclough appears in slow motion through the multicoloured plastic ribbons that hang down over her kitchen doorway, and deposits a tray bearing two cups of tea onto the table in front of me. The tea is slightly orange in colour, reminding me a bit of Dan's skin tone, and thick enough to stand a spoon up in—again, a phrase that I could use to describe Dan. Not wanting to hang around, I drink it quickly, a task made not that difficult given the fact that it isn't particularly hot, although as I swallow, I prefer not to think about what the lumps are.

As we sit there, Mrs Barraclough tells me all about Arthur; how lucky she was to have found him, how close they were, and how she misses him every day.

'You know,' she says, resting a wrinkled hand on my arm. 'The day he died, I held him in my arms, and told him I'd see him again soon. And I'm just waiting for that day, now.'

As I swallow the last mouthful of tea, there's a lump in my throat for a different reason. Maybe she does know about me and Jane splitting up after all, and perhaps this is her way of trying to tell me something? That time together is precious, possibly, and you have to make the most of it, because who knows how long you'll have? I resolve to remember this, particularly if things get tough over the next few months.

Finally, there's a long enough pause in the conversation for me to make my escape. As I stand up to leave, Mrs Barraclough retrieves a photograph from the mantelpiece, and hands it to me.

'Who's this?' I say, blowing the dust off the glass-fronted frame to reveal a picture of a younger Mrs Barraclough, holding a large tortoiseshell cat in her arms.

Mrs Barraclough looks up at me, a confused expression on her face.

'Why, that's me and Arthur, of course.'

Friday 21st January

7 a.m. On the dot.

I'VE SET MY ALARM for 6.30 this morning, giving myself just enough time to shower, dress, and force down a bowl of cereal, and I'm ready when Sam rings the doorbell, zipping up my workout top as I let her in. She's wearing a green version of the tracksuit I saw her in yesterday, matching green gloves, and carrying the same small rucksack on her shoulders.

'So, what are we doing this morning?' I say, showing her through into the lounge. 'I've cleared a space in the front room.' In reality, of course, I haven't had to clear any space in the front room. Jane took care of that for me.

Sam takes me through a few basic stretches, then throws open the curtains and peers out into the blackness. 'I thought we'd start with a little jog. Along the seafront.'

'Outside? But it's freezing this morning.' As soon as I've said this I realize how whiny and pathetic my voice sounds.

'That's fine,' replies Sam. 'It'll stop you passing out from heat exhaustion.'

'But…'

'Come on, Usain Bolt. Follow me.' And with that she's off, along my hallway, through the front door, and jogging down my street towards the seafront. I trail along after her, enjoying, briefly, the sight of her taut buttocks bouncing up and down in front of me, until I remember just how out of shape I am, and concentrate instead on putting one foot in front of the other.

We head across the road, down onto the promenade, and along past the angel statue. I'm a little surprised that I've made it this far without stopping, but that's probably because Sam seems to be a little bit more sensitive to my fitness levels than Dan was. As I struggle to see where I'm going through the fog my breath is making, Sam jogs easily alongside me, urging me to pick up the pace a little as we near the pier. And maybe it's the fact that Sam's a professional, or more likely it's because I didn't stuff my face with pizza and beer last night, but funnily enough, this doesn't actually feel so bad.

7.10 a.m.

Even in my relatively inexperienced state, I understand that there are ways to make a good impression where women are concerned. Being sick in a bin on the seafront in front of Sam isn't one of them. And what's worse, it's one of those bins with only a side opening, so I have to try and aim horizontally through the relatively small and not particularly clean gap. I fail miserably, managing to splash the tops of my new trainers with this morning's regurgitated cereal.

Sam jogs back over to where I'm using the bin for support, removes a packet of wet wipes from her rucksack, and passes me one.

'Do you want to rest for a bit?'

I stop heaving and shake my head. 'No. Let's keep going. I don't think I've got anything left to sick up.'

Sam grimaces. 'That's comforting to know.'

I'm mortified. 'I'm so sorry,' I say, wiping my face.

'Don't worry.' Sam puts a supportive hand on my shoulder. 'It happens to everyone their first time.'

'Really?'

'Well, not quite everyone.'

'I thought I could do a bit better than this.'

'You will. It's all about setting yourself goals and monitoring your improvements. For example,' she points a few hundred yards further along the promenade, 'by the end of next week, I want you to be able to get to that bin over there before you feel like throwing up.'

We start off again, Sam maintaining more of a leisurely pace as I struggle to keep up. By the time we get level with the end of the pier, I'm moving so slowly that an old couple out on their motorized wheelchairs seem to zoom past me.

We follow them along the seafront, then, as they disappear into the morning gloom, turn up Preston Street, finally stopping outside a doorway between a pizza restaurant and a kebab house. Ominously, the sign above the entrance reads 'Swetz'.

'Come on,' says Sam, as she shows me inside. 'Surprise for you.'

I already have a feeling that I'm not going to like Sam's surprises. Problem is, I'm breathing so hard I can't actually ask what it might be.

We make our way up the stairs, Sam taking them two at a time, whereas I need to pull myself up by the banisters. By the time we get to the top, my worst fears are confirmed—it's a gym—and what's worse is that manning the reception is Arnold Schwarzenegger's larger, younger, better-looking brother. He's tall, tanned, wearing a pair of those baggy multi-coloured trousers that only bodybuilders and Rastafarians can get away with, and displaying a ridiculously muscular pair of arms from his cut-off-sleeve sweatshirt.

As we walk in, he looks up, ignoring me at first, and flashing a set of perfect teeth in Sam's direction.

'Well, if it isn't the lovely Samantha.'

'Morning, Simon.'

'And who's this?' says Simon, flicking his eyes across at me. 'Another lamb for the slaughter?'

I hate him instantly. 'Edward,' I say, holding out my hand.

This is a mistake, because when Simon shakes it, I suddenly feel like my fingers are trapped in a Black and Decker Workmate. And a clammy one at that.

'Call me Sy,' says Simon.

'Can't stand around and chat,' interrupts Sam, leading me through an archway and into the exercise studio. 'Mustn't let Edward cool down.'

Cool down? I'm sweating like a pig, and feel like I'm running a temperature. Once we're out of earshot, I turn to Sam. 'Who on earth was that?'

Sam shakes her head. 'My ex-boyfriend, would you believe,' she says. 'Simon owns this place. He still lets me bring the occasional client here.'

'Ex-boyfriend? Why did the two of you split up?' I've resolved nowadays to always ask questions like this when I get the chance. Plus, it means I might get a slightly longer rest. 'If you don't mind me asking?'

Sam looks back at Sy, who's standing at reception tensing his scarily big biceps in front of the full-length mirror.

'Isn't it obvious?'

'Er…'

Sam rolls her eyes. 'Why do you think he calls himself "Sy"?'

'Because it's short for "Simon"?'

She nods. 'Yes. But also because that's what he thinks the girls all do when they see him.'

'But he's…Huge.'

'And so is his ego,' laughs Sam. 'Anyway, like I said, enough chat. This, Edward,' she says, leading me into the centre of the room, 'is a gym. And that's spelt g-y-m.'

I stare in horror at the heavy machinery lining the walls.

'What are we doing here? I mean, now. So soon.'

'Well, I'd normally start a new client off with some bodyweight exercises, but by the looks of you, that might be a little tough. And seeing as we don't have a lot of time…'

We head over to what appears to be some torture equipment in the corner, labelled 'chest press'. On it there's a little picture of a man who seems to be made purely out of muscle, with arrows helpfully pointing to where his chest actually is.

Sam gets on first, selects a weight from the stack, and demonstrates the exercise a few times. When it's my turn, I'm surprised to find that I can't even shift the weight she's been using once.

'I think it's stuck,' I say, my face an attractive shade of purple.

Sam leans across and removes the pin completely from the stack, so all I'm lifting is the mechanism itself. It's still a struggle, but I'm pleased when I manage the twenty rep target she's set me.

We move on to the 'leg extension', where I'm just about to ask whether it will make me taller until the burning in my thigh muscles makes speech impossible. Then it's a jelly-legged walk across to the 'pec deck'; a machine whose sole purpose seems to be to dislocate my arms from their sockets.

We spend the next half an hour doing a circuit of the gym, Sam encouraging and helping where necessary. The high point is when I manage two sets on the 'abdominal crunch'—which strikes me as a great name for a low-fat breakfast cereal—without too much discomfort. The low point comes soon after, when I'm straining at a particularly heavy weight on the leg press and I fart loudly, provoking barely disguised sniggers from some of the other gym users. Sam, to her credit, pretends not to notice.

By the time I feel like I've worked muscles in places where I didn't even know I had muscles, we retire to the exercise mats, where Sam takes me through some further stretches. I'm pleased when I can at least touch my shin, although touching my toes seems like the North Face of Everest at the moment.

Eventually, and after what seems like an eternity, we're finished.

'Well done,' says Sam, as she leads me towards the exit.

I'm almost too knackered to reply, just managing to get out a wheezy, 'And I'm paying you for this?'

As we walk out past Sy, he looks up from his copy of *Steroid Monthly*. 'Call me,' he says to Sam.

'There are a number of things I could call him,' she whispers, as we head down the stairs, before jogging slowly back down to the seafront.

'Is it okay if I leave you to get home on your own, Edward?' she asks, looking anxiously at her watch. 'I'm meeting another client shortly, and we've overrun a bit.'

'Sure.' I nod, relieved that the session is over. 'No problem.'

'So, a light jog back to your flat, and you're finished for the day.'

She's not kidding. 'Great.'

'You did well. So I'll see you Monday?'

'Not tomorrow?'

Sam smiles. 'No. I've already got a regular Saturday morning, and I don't do Sundays. Besides,' she adds, ominously, 'you might need to recover a little.'

I watch Sam's departing figure as she jogs off towards her next appointment, then, when she's safely out of sight, I limp back up to the main road and lean against the bus stop until the number 7 arrives. It's only two stops to the end of my street, and I don't dare sit down in case I can't get up again.

Once I'm home, I take the phone with me into the bathroom, just in case I have to call the cardiac team, and stand in the shower for a long, long time, until my heart rate eventually returns to normal. And yet, despite my exertions, I feel strangely elated. Whether it's the fact that I've started on my journey to get Jane back, or the exercise releasing some endorphins into my bloodstream, I can't tell. But I feel good. Or, rather, I feel bad.

But in a good way.

Saturday 22nd January

9.30 a.m.

WHEN I WAKE UP this morning, for the first time since Jane left I can't feel the pain in my heart. That's because I hurt everywhere else. Everywhere. It takes me five minutes to get out of bed, my stomach muscles screaming at me when I try to sit up, and then my leg muscles joining in as soon as I try to stand. When I eventually manage to shuffle into the bathroom to use the toilet, even my peeing muscles hurt.

I consider putting in a call to Sam to complain, but that would mean having to pick up the phone, so instead I go back to bed, but even there I can't find a position that's comfortable to lie in. I'm so sore that when I hobble painfully into the kitchen to find a couple of aspirin, I decide that the effort of reaching up to the top shelf in the cupboard to get them is potentially more painful than the relief I might get from taking the tablets in the first place, so I give it a miss.

By midday, I've managed to shower and dress, a task made even longer because I've had to wait for my hair to drip dry—I haven't been able to raise my hands above my head to dry it with a towel. As I get ready for my lunchtime rendezvous with Dan at the pub, I have to leave my shoes undone, because I can't bend down to tie my laces. Even blinking hurts.

Cursing both Sam and Jane for putting me through this, I inch my way down the steps, seriously considering taking a taxi the four hundred yards to the Admiral Jim. By the time I make my way painfully in through the doorway, I'm half an hour late, and Dan's waiting impatiently at the bar, flicking through a copy of *Heat*.

'Incredible!' he exclaims, throwing the magazine down in disgust. 'It says here that that Darren Day has got himself a stalker. Darren Day! What's wrong with these people?'

'I know.'

'Yeah,' continues Dan. 'Stalking the likes of him when they could be after me. Unbelievable!'

'Oh. Right.'

I think about heaving myself onto a bar stool but decide that it's probably less uncomfortable to stand.

'Look at the state of you,' Dan says, noticing my pained expression. 'Heavy night?'

'Heavy morning, actually.'

Dan raises one eyebrow. 'Oh yes?'

I don't dare shake my head. 'It was my new trainer.'

He looks down at my feet. 'What's wrong with it?'

'No. My new personal trainer.'

Dan rolls his eyes. 'Jesus. I leave you to do something on your own and you go and pick the wrong one.'

'But…'

'Some sergeant-major type yelling at you to drop and give him twenty, I bet. No wonder you're in such a state. These people usually just want to show off how fit they are, which means you injure yourself attempting to keep up.'

'Yes, well, Sam's not like that. She's actually very…'

Dan's jaw drops. 'A girl? A girl did this to you?'

'No. Well, yes.'

'Ha! Now I've heard everything.' He puts on a stupid sing-song voice. 'Edward's trainer's a girl.'

'Dan, can we just drop it, please. You're the one who suggested I needed to start exercising.'

'Yeah, but…A girl!'

'Dan!'

Dan holds his hands up. 'Fine. Drink?'

I gaze longingly at the bottles of beer in the fridge behind the bar. 'Mineral water please. Sparkling.'

Dan waves Wendy over. 'Another glass of wine please, Wenders. And a mineral water for my fragile friend here.'

'Sparkling,' I add.

'Ooh,' says Wendy, 'sparkling! Are you celebrating something?'

Dan smirks. 'Edward's got himself a personal trainer.'

'Good for you, Edward,' she says, pouring me a glass of Perrier and placing it on the bar in front of me. Given how sore my arms are, I'm reluctant to pick it up, and seriously consider asking Wendy for a straw to minimize the need for physical movement.

'Okay,' says Dan. 'Joking aside. That's phase one. Exercise. Now, onto phase two, and my particular area of expertise: women.'

'Women?'

'Yes. You need to meet more.'

'How on earth will that help me?'

Dan sighs. 'What's the best and fastest way to learn a new language, do you think?'

'Er…one of those tapes?'

'No, you idiot. If you want to learn French, move to France. You'll be speaking it in no time.'

'So…I should move into a house full of girls?'

Dan savours the idea for a moment. 'In an ideal world, that would be an option. However, you just need to speak to more women. Immerse yourself in their worlds. Familiarize yourself with their routines. Maybe even sleep with a couple of them.'

'Don't be ridiculous.'

Dan makes a face. 'You're never going to get a new girlfriend if you think like that.'

'I don't want a new girlfriend. I want my old one back.'

'Which is why you've got to start engaging with other women. Learn how they tick. Try a little harmless flirting. That way you'll be better prepared for Jane's return.'

Strangely, for an idea that's come out of Dan's mouth, this actually seems to make sense. 'Okay. Point taken.'

'So. How many women do you encounter on a regular basis?'

I stare thirstily at my glass of water, which is gradually going flat on the bar in front of me. 'Well, there's Wendy. And Mrs Barraclough. And Natasha, of course.'

'Well, for a start, Wendy doesn't count.'

'Why not?' says Wendy suspiciously, expecting some insult to come flying her way.

'Because she's too involved in this process. And Mrs B is about, what, a hundred? Mind you, she's probably had sex more recently than you.'

'Dan, please! What about Natasha?'

'Hmm. From what you've told me about her, she makes *me* look like a monk. So I'm afraid you need to go out and meet some new ones.'

'Do I really have to?'

Dan sighs. 'Yes. Because looking at the situation with you and Jane, you've obviously lost the ability to relate to them.'

'Rubbish. I speak to women all the time at work.'

'Really?' Dan thinks for a moment. 'So what do you do when you're interviewing a candidate and they're attractive?'

'Dan, I work in the IT industry. I don't get attractive candidates.'

'Sandra Bullock was good-looking in that film about computers.'

'Let me explain something to you. That's because she's what's known as an "actress". She's not a real computer person.'

'Surely there must be some attractive ones?'

'Dan, picture a girl who, between the ages of sixteen and eighteen, has decided that she's more interested in computers than boys or going out, so then dedicates three years of her life to studying the things so she can spend the rest of her life staring at a screen and typing nonsense into the keyboard.'

'You mean they're all geeks?' says Wendy, before heading off to collect some glasses.

'No. Not exactly.'

'There must be the odd geek goddess?' says Dan, smiling at his own joke.

'Dan, in—' I look at my watch, and I don't know why; it must be automatic—'nearly ten years of working for an IT recruitment consultancy, I can probably think of half a dozen women who you'd charitably describe as good-looking.'

'Okay,' says Dan, still not convinced. 'So what did you do when you interviewed them?'

'I asked them some work-related questions, they answered, I wrote their answers down.'

'And none of them ever tried it on with you to get the job?'

'Dan, you don't get it, do you? I don't decide who gets the jobs we head-hunt for. I interview candidates, decide on their suitability, and then recommend to the client whether they see them or not. If they like them, and then take them on, we get paid. If not, we have to try and find someone else. So sleeping with me would be like'—I think of an example—'you sleeping with the tea girl on *Richard and Judy* to try and get a presenter's job.'

Dan blushes. 'We all learn by our mistakes. She was attractive though. And made a great cuppa.'

I finally pluck up the courage to pick up my glass. 'Anyway, what's your point?'

'Well, fundamentally you spend most of your working week

stuck in an office, right? So the only real contact you get with women is on the telephone, and on the odd occasion you do actually meet a woman in the flesh, from what you say, chances are she's not that attractive.'

'Not that that means anything.'

Dan makes the 'yeah, right' face. 'Of course not.'

'So your conclusion is?'

'My conclusion is, firstly, that whenever you meet a woman professionally, you need to start probing them. Getting a bit more personal. Trying to find out a bit more about how they work, rather than where they work.'

'Fine. And secondly?'

'Secondly, that you need to get out more. Much more. And where's the best place to go to meet girls?'

'Er…'

Dan smiles, as if he's letting me into a trade secret. 'Hen nights.'

'Hen nights?'

Dan nods. 'We live in Brighton. The hen-night capital of the western world. Go out on any Saturday night around here and the pubs and clubs are full of them.'

'And how does that help me, exactly?'

'Because where there's a bride-to-be?'

I sip my water gingerly. 'Are you really expecting me to get any of these questions right?'

'Try.'

'There's a fiancé?'

Dan leers back at me. 'Nope. Bridesmaids.'

'Dan, I haven't been to a nightclub since, I don't know, college? And besides, at the moment, I can hardly walk, let alone dance.'

'We won't be doing any dancing, dummy.'

'But isn't that what you do at a club? Dance?'

'Oh no,' says Dan, ominously. 'Wait and see.'

11.30 p.m.

'I don't know why I let you talk me into coming.'

Dan puts an arm around my shoulders. 'Think of it as an experiment. Why do you think women and men go out to nightclubs?'

I shrug him off painfully. 'Like I said earlier. To dance?'

'To pull, stupid. So all you're doing is putting yourself in a situation where there are lots of women out to meet guys. And you're a guy…'

'But, there'll be lots of other men there.'

'Yes, but as the saying goes, worry about the customer, not the competition. What's your biggest strength?'

'I'm a good listener.'

'Exactly. And women love a good listener. You'll be fine. You just need to loosen up a little.'

'That's a little hard when I'm so stiff from this bloody training.'

'Relax. You never know—you may just enjoy yourself. We might even turn it into an all-nighter.'

'Dan, as far as I'm concerned, at my age an all-nighter means not having to wake up at three a.m. to go to the toilet.'

Dan looks at me in disgust. 'I sometimes wonder how Jane could have torn herself away from the whirlwind of excitement that was your relationship. Now shut up and follow me.'

We head down West Street and past a long queue of people, who give us evil looks as we pass. Dan walks straight to the front of the line and nods to the bouncers on the door, who give him that strange secret handshake thingy and show him in. As I try to follow, still limping a little from yesterday's exercise, one of them puts a hand the size of a shovel on my chest.

'Where do you think you're going, sonny?'

Sonny? I'm just about to reply 'home' when Dan intervenes, and although I fear it pains him to say 'he's with me', we're both let inside. As we push our way through the two sets of swing doors, the wall of sound nearly knocks me off my feet.

The inside of the club is one massive, strobe-lit, cavernous space, with a ridiculously busy bar at one end, and a few private booths at the other. In the middle there's a huge dance floor where at least a thousand people seem to be crammed together, and unless I'm very much mistaken, they seem to be dancing.

Dan leans over and shouts in my ear, telling me to get the drinks in, while he heads off to 'scout the area'. I push my way through to the bar as instructed, and I'm still standing there ten minutes later when he comes back to join me.

'What are you playing at?'

'I can't seem to get served,' I shout, still trying to catch the eye of the barman, who's much more interested in staring down the tops of any girls pressed close to the bar than noticing me.

Dan shakes his head. 'Give me some money.'

Obediently, I take out my wallet. When I produce a five pound note, Dan looks at me in disbelief.

'It has been a while since you've been out clubbing, hasn't it?'

He helps himself to a twenty, folds it in half lengthways, then holds it up over the bar. Almost immediately, the barman heads across to where we're standing, and Dan orders a couple of drinks—a bottle of beer for him, and my now usual sparkling water—waving the change away when they arrive.

'That was generous of you. With my money.'

Dan shrugs. 'Ensures we get served first next time. Otherwise picture the scenario—you're chatting up a girl, you offer to buy her a drink, then head off to the bar…If you're not back in two minutes tops, chances are someone else is already in there.'

'I bow to your superior knowledge. So what next? Do we, you know, hit the dance floor?'

'What, you and me together? Yeah, right. Mate, unless you're John Travolta, trying to pull a girl through your dancing skills is a big mistake. What happens at nightclubs is this: girls dance, men watch.'

Sure enough, as I look at the dance floor, it does seem to be mainly women, dancing in twos, threes, and in several cases, in large fancy-dressed groups. There's the odd brave or drunk guy up there with them, but in general, all the other men in the club seem to be looking on from around the outside.

'Okay. I'm watching.'

'Right. Think of it like one of those wildlife programmes you've seen about the Serengeti. These are the prey, and we, or rather I, am the hunter. We watch the prey for a while, selecting the one we want, and then, when the time is right…'

'We pounce?'

'Nope. We let them come to us. Well, to me. And then you step in and grab a piece of the action.'

'And how do we, sorry, you, lure them, exactly?'

Dan taps the side of his nose conspiratorially. 'Watch and learn, Eddy-boy. Watch and learn.'

We take our drinks and stand by the edge of the dance floor, where we can get a good view, or more likely, where Dan can make certain he gets spotted. Sure enough, within minutes, a couple of girls have stopped dancing and are heading over in our direction. They're both dressed in the standard uniform of Brighton clubbers—as little as possible—and clutching bottles of brightly coloured mixers. By the looks of them, they're about sixteen.

The taller of the two pokes Dan unsteadily on the shoulder. 'You're that Dan Davis, aren't you?' she shouts, ignoring me completely. 'From the telly.'

Dan beams back at her. 'That's right.'

'My mum loves you.'

Dan blanches slightly at this remark, but doesn't miss a beat. 'And I love your mum. What are your names?'

'I'm Donna,' she replies. 'And this is Tracy.'

Dan shakes them both by the hand. 'Hi Donna. Hi Tracy. And this…' he says, nodding in my direction, 'is Edward.'

I sense that this is my 'in'. My big moment. An opportunity to learn from these girls, to refine my chatting-up skills, so that when Jane comes back, I can wow her, just like I'm about to wow these two with my sparkling wit, while coolly sipping my sparkling water. Hey—maybe I can use that line…

As I open my mouth to speak, Donna and Tracy look round, size me up, decide that I'm not worth talking to, and turn their attention back to Dan. What's worse is that all this takes approximately one tenth of a second, and as the night progresses, this is about as much 'action' as I get. For example:

11.49 p.m.

I'm stood there as Dan talks to Tiffany and Sharon. I get a shouted 'hello' out of Sharon, but that's it.

12.08 a.m.

I'm stood there as Dan talks to Claire, Debbie, and Angela, who are out on a hen night. Only Angela is getting married, but all three of them seem to think I'm invisible.

12.24 a.m.

I'm stood there as Dan talks to Philippa and Annabel. I have a brief conversation with Philippa, although the word 'conversation' is stretching it, as she almost instantaneously decides she'll break off from our 'chat' to ask Dan to dance. Annabel doesn't ask me, and I'm certainly not going to ask her.

12.26 a.m.

I'm stood there as Dan dances with Philippa. Annabel has gone to the toilet.

12.33 a.m.

I'm stood there as Dan dances with Philippa and Annabel.

It's about now that I realize the fundamental flaw in this night-club approach. I may be a good listener, good at conversation even, but not when I can't hear a word the person I'm talking to is saying. Equally, having to shout back to them at the top of my voice doesn't help, and especially not when the person I'm trying to talk to has all her attention focused on Dan.

After several more repeats of this, I give up. When a sweaty Dan finally arrives back from the dance floor, I tap him on the shoulder.

'I'm going home,' I shout in his ear.

'What for?' He glances at his watch. 'The night is still young.'

'Yes,' I shout back. 'But I'm not. Will you be okay here on your own?'

Dan looks at me like I'm stupid, flicking his eyes across to a group of women dressed as schoolgirls, who are giggling and pointing at him.

'I think I'll get through it.'

I push my way back through the swing doors, past the bouncers, and out into the Brighton night air. The queue, like me, doesn't seem to have moved the slightest bit forward.

Sunday 23rd January

11.45 a.m.

I'M NOT QUITE SO sore this morning, but I'm still glad that I don't have to do any exercise again until tomorrow, as the thought of doing anything more energetic than my usual lazy Sunday certainly doesn't appeal.

I think about trying to reach Dan on his mobile, but given the situation I left him in last night, that's probably not such a good idea. I'm also feeling a little guilty that he might feel obliged to spend time with me now that Jane's gone, and besides, Sunday was always Jane's and my day.

By mid afternoon, I've finished the papers, and I'm bored. It's too cold to go out for a walk, but I don't really want to spend the rest of the day in an empty flat on my own, so instead, I decide to try and do what people apparently do in these situations: find out who my friends are.

I don't really have many other 'mates', so to speak. What with Jane, and work, and going to the Admiral Jim with Dan, I've never really had much spare time. Of course, Jane and I have, sorry, *had*, a couple of friends who we'd meet up with occasionally, usually at their places—Jane didn't like to cook, she said, or was it because she was embarrassed about the flat, I now wonder—where we'd take along a bottle of cheap Australian plonk and sit and talk about boring stuff into the small hours, me joining in where required, but really just wondering when I was going to be able to have another cigarette.

But when I think about them now, the idea of going to see them without Jane in tow seems, well, redundant, really. I'd feel like a spare part, a gooseberry, and of course I'd have to tell them all that Jane has left me—and how would I even begin to try and explain that away?

So instead, I hit upon a solution. I'll just call up the male halves of these couples we know. Do I consider them friends? I suppose so. Do I consider them *my* friends? Tricky one, given that usually our relationships have consisted of just sitting there, nodding sagely and exchanging the odd knowing glance while our better halves moaned about us over a glass of Chablis.

Now I come to think about it, I can't remember a single conversation of substance I've had with any of them. Rebecca and Richard—she's Jane's friend from work, and Richard? What does Richard do? Something in the city, I think. Or there's Julia and Mark, from Ealing. Mark's an accountant, I think, and even fatter than me, but they've got kids now anyway. And then there's, oh God, the most boring couple on earth, Dawn and Alan. Surely they'll be a safe bet. They live fairly nearby. And I have their number.

Alan picks up the phone after the eighth ring, as if he's finally worked out where the strange noise is coming from.

'Hello?'

'Hi, Alan. It's Edward.'

'Edward?'

The pause as he tries to place me grows longer and longer, and eventually gets so embarrassingly long that I have to step in and put him out of his misery.

'You know, of Jane and Edward?'

'Ah, yes. Edward,' he says, grateful for the lifeline I've thrown him. 'How are you?'

'Great. You?'

'Good thanks. And Jane?'

That stops me a bit in my tracks. I decide to go for honesty. 'She's…in Tibet, actually.'

'Tibet?' says Alan. 'What on earth is she…Hold on a second. Dawn's trying to tell me something.'

I hear the unmistakable sound of a hand being placed over the mouthpiece, followed by a few seconds of muffled conversation, which I'm guessing is Dawn explaining to Alan what's happened between Jane and me.

'Women, eh?' I say, once I hear the hand being removed, before realizing that it's actually Dawn I'm now talking to.

'Hello, Edward. How are you?' she asks.

It's an innocent enough question, but something about the matter of fact way she poses it makes me realize that she's not really interested in my answer.

'I'm fine, actually.'

'We were so sorry to hear about you and Jane,' she continues. 'Still, it's probably for the best.'

We? Alan didn't seem to know about it until approximately thirty seconds ago. And probably for the best? For whose best? I'm so indignant at this that I can't even answer, which is a silence that Dawn feels she needs to fill with other platitudes.

I want to ask her to put Alan back on, and why she felt the need to take over the conversation. I'm uncomfortable talking to her—that 'probably for the best' has left me in no doubt as to where her loyalties lie. I endure a minute's worth of 'people grow apart' and 'want different things', which I'm tempted to counter with 'no one asked me what I wanted', when Dawn finally pauses for breath.

'Anyway,' she says, 'what can we do for you?'

We? It's quite patently obvious that you can do nothing for me. It's Alan I want. Alan that I'm reaching out to in my hour of need. Alan who's deserted me already, the rat. But then that would imply that I'm a sinking ship, and I'm definitely not sinking.

'I wanted to…Is Alan there again please?'

There's the briefest of pauses this time, and then, 'He's busy right now. Can I take a message?'

Busy? What on earth can he suddenly have started that he wasn't doing two minutes ago when he was free enough to answer the phone? Brain surgery? Servicing the car? Constructing a model of the Eiffel Tower from matchsticks?

And then, with a frightening clarity, it occurs to me what Dawn is doing. She's keeping me away from him. She's decided that it would be wrong for me to have anything to do with her husband, so she's shielding him, screening him, protecting him, in case some of my aura, my bad luck, my undesirability rubs off. Dawn plainly doesn't think our friendship exists outside coupledom, so if one of her friends has decided that I'm chuckable, then there's obviously no place for me in their cosy little world. She can't imagine there might possibly be something I want to share or discuss with Alan that I couldn't possibly want to say to her. And what's more, I know she can't believe that I would have the nerve to think they might want to be friends with me, now that Jane's out of the picture.

'Er…Well, can he call me back?'

This takes her by surprise. So much so that she blurts out what she's probably been trying not to say for the last couple of minutes.

'I don't think that would be such a good idea.'

Don't you? I want to ask. Why? Why couldn't you just have done the decent thing, and just have said 'yes'? That way you'd know he wasn't going to call, I'd know he wasn't going to call, and then when he didn't call it would be over. Done with.

Finally, and about time too, dignity gets the better of me, and it is dignity, because although I'm tempted to say something rude, or smart (although partly because I can't think of anything smart to say), I just hang up. It's the mercy-killing approach. Fuck them, and their cosy little suburban lifestyle, and their taking bloody sides. They deserve each other, Alan and Dawn.

But while their small-minded pettiness makes me sick, I envy their solidarity. Their coupleness. The fact that they're a unit. Did Jane and I ever used to be like this? Together against the world, shielding each other from life's unpleasantness, from what it can throw at you, protecting each other from, well, from the likes of me.

Within thirty seconds of putting the phone down, I make a decision. I'm done with the Alan and Dawns of this world. Dawn the Yawn and Anal Alan. They always were Jane's friends, not mine, and now, they've proved it. We never had anything in common anyway, he and I, and as for her...

No, when Jane and I are back together, I'll make sure we get a new bunch of friends. It'll be a whole new Dawn for us, if you like.

But perhaps not a new Alan.

Wednesday 26th January

7.21 a.m.

MONDAY'S AND TUESDAY'S WORKOUTS follow the same cycle of
stretching and retching, but today's session is, to use a technical
exercise term, a bugger. Sam starts me off with a light jog along
the promenade, past the ruined West Pier, and then along towards
the Palace Pier, picking our way through the cans, bottles, chip
wrappers, and occasional piles of sick from the night before. It's a
cold, blustery morning, the overnight rain has frozen in puddles
on the pavement, and there's half the usual morning crowd of
joggers around.

As we pass the donut stand at the end of the Palace Pier, I start
to make the loop that takes us back up onto the promenade and
towards the gym, but Sam keeps on going, and I have to turn round
and sprint to catch her up.

'What?' I pant. 'Where?' Whole sentences still being beyond me
this early in my training programme.

Sam grins across at me, still hardly breathing compared to my
fish out of water impression.

'Something a little different today,' she replies, enigmatically.
'No gym.'

I have to stop myself from punching the air in delight. No gym!
No muscles screaming at me to stop. No agony tomorrow morning.
And more importantly, no Sy sneering at me from behind his over-
developed pecs.

My delight is short-lived as we jog a further two hundred yards along the promenade, beneath where the road slopes up towards the marina, and stop at the bottom of the longest, not to mention steepest, flight of stairs I've ever seen.

'OK,' instructs Sam, 'follow me.'

With that, she bounds up the stairs, taking them in pairs. I follow like a dutiful dog, managing the first twenty or so steps two at a time, and I'm even able enjoy the sight of Sam's pert, red-tracksuited posterior pumping away at my eye level as I do my best to keep up. But all too soon I feel the muscles in my legs start to burn, my lungs tighten, and even the lure of Sam's bouncing buttocks can't keep me going. As they fade into the distance, I cut my stride from two steps to one step, and even have to start tugging on the handrail to get me up the final few.

When I reach the top, gasping for air and looking desperately for a place to sit down, Sam grins at me.

'Good,' she says. 'But let's keep moving. It'll help get the lactic acid out of your legs faster.'

Mercifully she heads back in the direction of the pier, and as I shuffle after her, the pain in my legs and lungs starts to lessen slightly, and I even begin to feel chuffed that I've managed the stairs without stopping or, more impressively, throwing up. We follow the pavement back down the hill, and then to my horror, Sam turns back towards the bottom of the steps.

'You can't…You're joking?'

Sam shakes her head. 'Nope. Three times. Great exercise for the heart, legs, and stomach. All top athletes do this kind of thing.'

She runs off back towards the start of my torture circuit, and I jog reluctantly after her, reasoning that as I've managed it once, if I take the first few stairs more easily rather than chasing off behind Sam's behind, then the rest shouldn't be so difficult.

How wrong I am. While Sam leaps up them without pausing for breath, the minute I hit the first one I know I'm in trouble. I just about manage to get halfway up before collapsing against the rusty handrail.

Sam reaches the top, turns round to see me, and then, annoyingly, runs back down to where I'm heaving for breath.

'You know,' I say, in between gasps for air, 'if there's ever a vacancy for a guard at Guantanamo Bay, I'll be sure to put you forward.'

She shrugs. 'Get used to this. We'll be doing it once a week. Only I won't tell you which day.'

After a moment or two's rest, I set off again, and manage to make it up the rest of the way, but only by pushing down on my knees with my hands in the way that those mountaineers you see making a final assault on the summit of Everest do, although even at 28,000 feet they can probably still climb faster than me this morning. By the time I eventually get to the top, my legs feel like jelly, and I'm not sure I'll make it home, let alone manage another go.

Sam yawns theatrically, and looks at her watch.

'Are you ready? One more time?'

My look obviously conveys my answer, but she just turns round and starts to jog back down the slope again. I stare at her retreating back, wondering whether she'd mind if I just waited for her here, and then reluctantly begin a weary shuffle after her.

When I get to where she's waiting at the corner, she stops her jogging on the spot.

'Okay,' she says, 'on second thoughts, that's enough of those for today. We don't want to overdo it. You did well.'

'Well?' I'm sure my face must be the same colour as her tracksuit. 'What was "well" about that?'

'You didn't throw up. Or fall down the stairs. Or do both at the same time. Come on, home.'

It takes another five minutes of slow jogging before I can get back to anything like a regular breathing rate. My heart is hammering in my ears, and when we eventually reach the bench on the promenade that's become our stretching point, I collapse onto it, a relieved expression on my face.

'So what was that all about?' I ask, once I can eventually talk again.

'Variety.' Sam grins, as she leads me through our warm-down. 'Keep the body guessing by pushing it with different things.'

'I thought the whole point of this training was to do the same routine every day, and after a while it'd get easier?'

Sam shakes her head. 'I find that my clients don't respond if we just keep on doing the same things, day in, day out. Eventually people get bored, and leave…' Sam's voice tails off as she realizes what she's said.

And later, as I limp back to my empty flat, I appreciate that she may have a point.

7.02 p.m.

I get back from work just in time to catch Mrs Barraclough in the street outside the flat. Literally, as she slips over on a patch of ice by the steps. Fortunately she's not that tall, which means she doesn't have particularly far to fall.

'Careful, Mrs B,' I say, helping her to her feet. 'Where on earth are you off to on a night like this? It's freezing.'

'I need a couple of things from the shops.'

I can't bear the thought of her heading out on her own. 'I've told you,' I say, 'I'll go for you when the weather's like this.'

'But…Are you sure?' says Mrs Barraclough, fumbling in her handbag for what seems like an eternity before producing a shopping list.

'No buts,' I order her good-naturedly. 'Hand it over.' Which gets me a funny look from a couple of passers by, who quite possibly think I'm trying to mug an old lady.

'That's very sweet of you, Edward.'

With a smile, I take the list, stuff it into my pocket, and head out to Tesco's. Normally I'd take the car, but Sam's told me to walk wherever possible, and so despite the fact that I can still feel this morning's stair session, I decide to go by foot. *Any chance to burn those excess calories,* as she constantly reminds me.

It's the first time I've been in Tesco's without Jane, which strangely makes me both sad and excited at the same time. I'm sad because even though our weekly shopping trips were sullen affairs, me reluctantly pushing a wonky-wheeled trolley behind her up and down the aisles while she consulted her list, or spent ages deciding which of two identical bumper-sized packets of toilet rolls were actually the best value, it was one of the few things we used to do together. As a couple. And that realization in itself makes me sadder still. But I'm excited too, because with Jane not here, I can, theoretically, buy anything I want without her tutting over the calorie content, or more likely the alcohol content. Except that of course I can't, and ironically the reason I can't, is because Jane's not here.

But on balance, I feel pretty okay being here on my own, and the reason I feel okay is because I'm doing someone else a favour. A good deed. And this feeling lasts approximately thirty seconds, until I take Mrs Barraclough's list out of my pocket.

Though I don't need any shopping myself, I realize that before I can even contemplate braving the checkout with these things in my basket I'm going to have to buy a few additional items, just to disguise the slightly sinister nature of my purchases. A pair of tights. A jar of Vaseline. A packet of batteries. A tin of boiled sweets. A box of tissues. As the shopping list of an old lady, this isn't so bad. As the shopping list of a thirty-year-old male, however, it smacks of something akin to perversion. And the worst part is that just as I'm looking in horror at them all, and frantically deciding what else to get, Wendy taps me on the shoulder.

'Gosh, Edward,' she says, peering mischievously into my basket. 'You do miss Jane, don't you?'

Thursday 27th January

3.09 p.m.

AFTER MY NIGHTCLUB NIGHTMARE, I'm mindful of any other opportunities I can find to talk to women. Fortunately, today we're interviewing for a marketing manager for a local software company, and, again fortunately, this means that most of the candidates will be female.

I pass on the first two, partly because they've both, to borrow one of Dan's phrases, 'fallen out of the ugly tree and hit every branch on the way down', but mainly because my nerves get the better of me. The third interviewee, however, looks promising. Her name is Emma, she's about my age, relatively attractive, and, it says on her CV, single. Once I've finished the interview proper, I try to keep my voice as neutral as possible.

'So, Emma. Can I just ask you a couple of personal questions?'

She smiles. 'Fire away.'

'Age?'

'Twenty-nine.'

'Marital status?'

'Single.'

I keep staring at my note pad, as if I'm checking her answers off against a list.

'Any children?'

'No. Not yet.'

'Not yet? Does that mean you want them?'

Emma frowns at me. 'Are you allowed to ask me that?'

'It's just for our records, you understand.'

'Well, I haven't decided yet. Possibly.'

'Interesting.' I pretend to make some notes. 'And you say you're single?'

'Yes.'

'And why is that?'

Emma shifts uncomfortably in her chair. 'What's any of this got to do with the job?'

'I'm just trying to build up a more rounded picture of you. It helps us to present you as a candidate.'

She seems to just about buy this, and settles back down. 'Well, I've just come out of a relationship.'

Perfect. 'And did you end it, or did he?'

'That's really none of your business.'

'Okay. Not to worry. What would you say is the most important factor you look for in a man?'

'I beg your pardon? Do you mean as a boss?'

'No.' I start to appreciate that I haven't really thought this through. 'As a, um, boyfriend.'

Emma stands up angrily, and starts to gather her things together. 'This is the weirdest interview I've ever had.'

'But we've nearly finished,' I say, trying to calm her down. 'Just one last question…'

'Is it about the job?'

'Er…no.'

As Emma storms out of the office, slamming the door behind her, I can't help feeling that this approach isn't going to work either.

Saturday 29th January

6.15 p.m.

I'M LEANING ON THE bar at the Admiral Jim, filling Dan and Wendy in on my week. Although I've graduated to having my mineral water in a pint glass, it still feels funny to be stood in a pub and drinking something that isn't beer-flavoured.

'I still think you should have given my nightclub idea more of a go,' says Dan, munching cruelly through a packet of mixed nuts in front of me.

'You don't get it, do you? Look at you, Dan. You're the male equivalent of Bo Derek in the film *Ten*. Women chat you up. The sad fact is, however nice I am, however considerately I behave, however good a listener I am, the first thing they'll notice in an environment like that is how good-looking I am. Or, how good-looking I'm not, to be correct.'

'That's not true,' says Wendy, loyally.

'Yes it is. I'm the sort of person who has to grow on people.'

Dan laughs. 'What—like a fungus?'

'You know what I mean.'

'But that's assuming people are really fickle,' says Wendy. 'And that they'd only be interested in someone of their "level", looks wise.'

Dan nearly chokes on a cashew. 'Dur.'

'What do you mean, "dur"?'

'Basic laws of dating, isn't it?' he replies.

'Have you ever gone out with anyone who's not been a "ten", then?'

Dan doesn't even have to think about this. 'Nope.'

As Wendy rolls her eyes at me and heads off to serve someone at the other end of the bar, I turn back to Dan.

'So the only thing that makes you fancy someone is how they look?'

'Is this your first day here?' he says, giving me a look which suggests I've just asked the stupidest question in the world.

'You're saying that if you met someone who you thought was funny, charming, intelligent, successful, and yet didn't quite match up to your expectation in terms of physical perfection, you wouldn't even think about going out with them?'

Dan throws a pistachio into the ashtray, not wanting to risk splitting a nail trying to get it out of its shell. 'Nope.'

'But wouldn't you want to marry someone like that?'

'Well, that's pretty academic, isn't it?'

'How so?'

'Well, to marry them, I'd probably have to have gone out with them beforehand, and if I didn't fancy them, I wouldn't go out with them. Whereas…'

'Whereas what?'

'Well, someone like you, you're more likely to go out with someone for, shall we say, less than aesthetic reasons.'

'What do you mean by that?'

'Well, you know. Got to play in your division and all that.'

'What are you going on about?'

'Well, I'm Champions League material. Manchester United, if you like, so I'm looking to meet Real Madrid, or similar. You, on the other hand, well, you're currently Vauxhall Conference division two, or whatever it's called. Down in the lower leagues, anyway. But challenging for promotion, of course.'

I ignore Dan's insult, aware that he doesn't see it as one. 'So what you're saying is that like can only be interested in like?'

Dan nods. 'Yup. No point otherwise.'

'But that infers that if you're, shall we say, a less than good-looking guy, then you can only realistically set your sights on a girl of the same "ilk", even though you might fancy the Claudia Schiffers of this world, because that's just being realistic.'

'Pretty much sums it up.'

'And the only reason that those people can be happy with their less-than-perfect-looking partners is because they've had to bite the bullet and learn to focus on other stuff apart from the aesthetic?'

'Now you're getting it.'

I look at him in disbelief. 'Well here's a theory for you. Your approach is so shallow, that eventually, after the looks fade, you might just find yourself on the scrapheap because you've left it too late to meet a woman with substance.'

Dan looks confused. 'A woman with "substance"?'

'Yes. Other than silicone. Someone you can talk to long after the fires of passion have burned out. Someone with whom you have more in common than just what brand of moisturizer you prefer.'

Dan holds his hands up. 'Don't shoot the messenger. It's just basic Darwinism, isn't it? Survival of the fittest.'

'Dan, Darwin didn't mean "fit" in the "cor, she's fit" sense. And anyway, women in general aren't as fickle as you, thank goodness. They want to see good providers. Home makers. Guys who are good with their hands…'

'Hur hur.'

'Not in that sense.'

Dan shakes his head. 'Who told you that bollocks? Women may admire someone who's handy around the house, but they'll drop him like a shot if someone better-looking comes along.'

'Dan, you're talking about yourself again. Fortunately, not all women share your views.'

'Mores the pity. And anyway, it's more of a philosophy.'

'Well, it's a rubbish philosophy.'

Dan examines a pecan before popping it into his mouth and chewing it thoughtfully. 'Okay. Think how the process works. Boy meets girl, there's an attraction, they get chatting, start dating, move in together, and if they don't completely piss each other off, they stay together and have kids. Blah blah blah.'

'Except in your case. Dan meets girl, they sleep together, Dan never calls girl again,' chimes in Wendy.

'We're not talking about me here. We're talking about how things generally happen.'

'But what about the other way?'

Dan looks confused. 'There's another way?'

'Yeah, you know. Perhaps two people meet, maybe they work together, or live nearby, and they get to know each other over the years, and then one day something happens, or one of them asks the other one out. It's not all about instant attraction. You can grow to love someone.'

'I'm sorry, Edward. You've just described dating for ugly people. People who manage to convince themselves that looks aren't important, because they've realized that they're not good-looking themselves. In my world, it's always down to attraction.'

'Isn't that rather fickle?'

Dan shrugs. 'I don't make the rules up,' he says, repeating his favourite phrase.

'So you're saying that if you were talking to a less-than-model-looks girl, you'd never find her the slightest bit attractive, even if she was witty, intelligent, made you laugh…'

'Let me just stop you there. Why would I be talking to an ugly girl in the first place?'

'Dan, that's an awful thing to say.'

'I'm just being honest. You and I have different needs. At the moment, my life revolves around two things: my TV career and my sex life, and not necessarily in that order. I'm not interested in great conversation—I can get that from you. If I want good cooking, I'll go to a restaurant. If I want my flat cleaned, I'll pay a cleaner. You? You're looking for someone to make a life with. Me? I just want someone to make out with. End of story.'

We stand there in silence for a while, as Dan finishes off his nuts.

'But anyway,' I say, watching him hold the packet up to his mouth and shake out the last few remaining bits, 'accepting that your idea of meeting other women does have some merit.'

'Ye-es?'

'Purely for research purposes, of course.'

'Of course.'

'What's next? I mean, where else can I find a group of women who'll talk to me?'

'No joy with the work angle?'

'Nope. Natasha's told me I can't harass any more of the female candidates.'

'What about the Lonely Hearts ads?' chimes in Wendy.

'No way,' says Dan. 'Listing of cat-owning spinsters, if you ask me.'

'What are you talking about?'

'Lonely Hearts? They're lonely for a reason, I tell you.'

'I'm sorry—what have cats got to do with it?'

'Everything,' says Dan, picking up a copy of the *Argus* from the bar and turning to the 'Personal' section. 'Look at most of the ads: "Must have GSOH and like cats." "Animal lover preferred." "Likes sunsets, fine dining, and cats." Show me a woman who owns a cat and I'll show you a woman with issues.'

Not for the first time, Dan isn't making any sense. 'What kind of issues?'

Dan pulls up a stool. 'Women have cats not because they're alone, but because they're lonely. Lonely is different from being alone. Alone suggests more of a temporary situation—"my boyfriend's just left me, and I'm currently alone", whereas "lonely"? That's a long-term state.'

'I still don't understand. Why should owning a cat be an indication of social leprosy?'

Dan sighs. 'Okay. At the moment, Jane's been gone what. A fortnight?'

I fight the urge to look at my watch, and lose. 'One week, six days, and twenty-three hours,' I say. 'Approximately.'

He looks at me pityingly. 'And have you felt the need to rush out and buy a pet to replace her?'

'Of course not.'

'So, at what point do you think you'd need to go out and get one?'

'I don't understand.'

'How long do you think you'd have to be without someone in order to feel so lonely and desperate that you decide to go out and get yourself a substitute in the shape of some four-legged flea-ridden feline?'

'I don't know.'

'Nor do I, but it would have to be a long time, right? And if a girl's been lonely for a long time, long enough to want to get a cat, then you can guarantee it's not through choice.'

'Maybe…maybe she got the cat with her boyfriend, who then left her, and she got custody of it?'

'Mate, how many men do you know who, when asked by their other halves whether they'd like to go out and get a cat, agree?'

'Good point.'

'So, if she's got a cat, steer clear. If she's got a child…Whoa!'

'Dan!'

Dan seems lost in thought. 'If she's got a hot-tub, however…'

I pick up the paper and scan down the page. 'Well, what if I just read through some of the ads then? I might learn something there.'

Dan shakes his head. 'No chance. They'll all say stuff like "must enjoy romantic walks on the beach" when in reality what they really want is something completely different.'

'Such as?'

'Damned if I know. But I'll tell you this—next time a woman asks you to put up a shelf or repaint the spare room, you try suggesting a romantic walk on the beach instead and see how far you get.'

I throw the paper back down exasperatedly. 'So, we've established no Lonely Hearts ads then. Well…what about this internet-dating lark? Maybe log on, have a chat, do it that way?'

At the mention of the phrase 'internet dating', Wendy heads back over from the other side of the bar.

'Steer clear,' she warns. 'Definitely not something you want to get involved in.'

'Why on earth not?'

'Well, why do you think most people sign up for internet dating?' she says, before answering her own question. 'It's for one of two reasons. Well, three reasons, if you include the fact that a lot of them are looking for an affair. But the main two are either that they're too unattractive or socially inept to find a partner in everyday life, so their only chance is to go online and hope that they can build up a relationship with someone who will fall so head over heels with them without actually seeing their picture that they won't be put off by the actual physical revulsion they'll feel when they actually meet up with them face to face. Or, they're using internet dating because during the natural course of their lives they don't have the time, or the inclination to make the time, to go out and find a girlfriend or a boyfriend through the usual channels. The downside of this approach is, of course, that once they meet someone, unless they make a fundamental effort to rejig their priorities then they won't actually have the time to have a proper relationship, and it'll fizzle out because of perceived lack of interest, when in reality, they never had the time to put in the effort required to develop that interest in the first place. In fact, that's the main reason why internet dating doesn't work; people are too busy working to meet other people, so when they do, unless they give up their jobs, they're too busy to do anything about it.'

I think Wendy's stopped, and I'm about to ask her something, but she's actually just paused for breath.

'Plus, the women you usually find on these sites are tired of going out to the usual pubs and clubs and being leered at by all sorts of men who think that the combination of five pints of lager and a similar amount of Old Spice suddenly makes them irresistible to the opposite sex. They hold out the hope that by some miracle Brad Pitt's younger, better-looking cousin is going to say "To hell with all these people I meet through the course of my normal life, I'm going to sign up to one of these internet sites where I might just meet the girl of my dreams." Trust me, Edward, you don't want to even go down that line. You might meet someone, exchange a few emails, and before you know it they're swearing their undying love for you while saying corny things like "Am I allowed to say how much I want you?". Unfortunately, what they really mean is "my wife doesn't understand me", and you realize they've just been stringing you along the whole time. When you tell them that you're not interested in having an affair, all of a sudden there are no more mails in your inbox.'

'But…'

'Besides, you're trying to duck out of the real issue here. You've got to meet them face to face. Otherwise they're not going to give you the truth.'

'Much as I hate to agree with anything Wendy says,' says Dan, 'she's right. You've got to meet them the normal way.'

'Ah,' says Wendy. 'But therein lies Edward's dilemma. What is the normal way? Go out to a pub or a bar, get drunk, then lurch up to someone equally drunk who you wouldn't dare talk to sober and end up snogging them? Surely it's much better to meet someone in a safe environment, where you can take time to get to know each other and then decide whether you want to meet up or not?'

'So it's only drunk guys who approach you, is it?' says Dan. 'I wonder why that is?'

'I'd need to be drunk to go out with you,' replies Wendy. 'Or drugged.'

'And you wonder why you haven't had a male in your inbox for a while,' says Dan.

'Yes, well, that's because I want to meet someone who makes my stomach flip when I see them,' she replies, staring menacingly back at him. 'Not turn.'

I step in between the two of them. 'Children, please. Wendy, you were saying?'

'Yes,' she says. 'Your problem is that you need to meet them face to face. In person. And as many as possible. Which is why you're going speed dating.'

Saturday 5th February

6.44 p.m.

I'M RINGING DAN'S DOORBELL, on the way to tonight's speed-dating event. I'm a little late, as I've been wondering what, from my limited wardrobe, to wear this evening, and in the end, I've gone for what I believe is known as the 'smart casual' look: my best pair of jeans, although I've struggled a little to do the top button up, and a fairly new baggy jumper, on the basis that it should both conceal and flatter.

When Dan opens his door dressed like he's off to a movie premiere, I begin to doubt the wisdom of asking him along to hold my hand this evening, but I can't bottle out now. And besides, it'll be good to have a second opinion. Even from him.

He stares at me for a moment before showing me inside.

'Aren't you getting changed first?'

'I am changed.'

'Jesus. What were you wearing before?'

I can feel myself start to blush. 'I wanted to look like I'm not trying too hard.'

'You've succeeded.' Dan laughs. 'In fact you look like you're not trying at all. Let me remind you—we're going out to meet women. You're dressed like a scarecrow. And what do scarecrows do?'

Unfortunately, I know the answer to this one. 'Frighten the birds away?'

'Exactly.'

Dan disappears into his bedroom, rooting through his wardrobe until he finds something suitable.

'Here,' he says, beckoning me over. 'Your jeans look just about faded enough to be trendy, but that jumper looks like it was knitted by your mother. Put this shirt on. And don't tuck it in.'

I stand there for a moment, staring at Dan, until he rolls his eyes and turns his back. Self-consciously, I slip off my jumper and try the shirt on. Luckily, Dan's much wider in the shoulder than I am in the waist, so it doesn't fit too badly.

'Much better,' says Dan, looking me up and down. 'But something's missing…'

He looks through his wardrobe again before closing the door in disgust, then slips off his own jacket and holds it out to me. 'Here. Try this on. But don't try and fasten it—with that gut, I fear for the tensile strength of those buttons.'

I put the jacket on and examine my reflection in the mirror. It looks pretty good, I have to concede. 'Cheers, mate.'

'And if you do see any nice women tonight, try not to get too excited. I don't want your drool down the front of my shirt.'

'Cool jacket, Dan. How will they ever resist me?' I say, strutting up and down in front of the mirror.

Dan shakes his head. 'Edward, it's a nice jacket. Not a magic jacket.'

I ignore his insult and tap my watch. 'Can we go now?'

'Hold on,' he says. 'Final touch required.'

Dan leads me through into his chrome-and-marble en-suite, where he opens the rather large bathroom cabinet. It's stocked almost to overflowing with moisturizers, exfoliators, and bottle after bottle of aftershave.

'What do you fancy?' he asks.

I look at the selection of brightly coloured bottles. Worryingly, Dan seems to have arranged them alphabetically.

'What have you got?'

'What haven't I got?'

I read through the names. '"Contradiction", "Envy", "Eternity", "Escape", "Intuition", "Obsession"…What do you recommend?'

'Why not try "Desperation"?' he suggests. 'Oh, hang on, you smell of that already.'

After careful consideration, Dan hands me a bottle with some unpronounceable name, and supervises me as I splash some onto my face.

'Not too much now,' he cautions. 'We've got to get you through the streets safely.'

7.15 p.m.

We've stopped off at the Admiral Jim, so I can partake of some Dutch courage beforehand. As a special treat, Dan's allowed me a beer, and I drink it slowly, savouring every mouthful.

'So,' he says, rubbing his hands together expectantly. 'What's the deal again?'

I pull out the flyer Wendy gave me from my pocket and read it out to him. '"Brighton's women are out on the hunt for men—could you be one of them?"'

'I know I'm not "one of them,"' says Dan. 'Are you sure you've got the right kind of event?'

I nod. 'All we have to do is turn up, and we'll get to meet twenty-odd women—that's twenty, plus or minus, rather than strange, I mean.'

Dan shakes his head in disbelief. 'And all of them gagging for it?'

'Well, "looking for love",' I say, reading from the back of the leaflet.

'Same thing,' laughs Dan. 'And I don't even have to buy them a drink?'

'Nope. In fact, we get a free glass of wine. And then get to spend three minutes with each girl.'

'Result!'

'Be serious, Dan. It's the best chance I've got to actually go and talk to a number of women face to face. Don't mess it up for me.'

'As if,' he says.

'So listen,' I ask, as I sip my half pint anxiously, 'once I'm sat in front of all these girls, what on earth do I say to them?'

Dan leans forward on his stool and lowers his voice. 'It's easy,' he says. 'The key to success with women is sincerity.'

'Sincerity?'

Dan nods. 'Yup. If you can fake that, you're sorted. So even though they may not deserve one, start with a compliment. Tell them you like their hair, or that they're pretty, or even that they look a bit like someone famous.'

'Someone famous?'

'Yup. But, obviously, someone good-looking and famous. Ask what they do, have they been to one of these things before, that sort of thing. Keep it all nonchalant, and the time will fly by.'

'But what if I run out of things to ask?'

'Don't worry,' says Dan, 'just get them started. They're women, don't forget, so they'll be quite happy to do all the talking.'

'Right.'

'But,' he adds, 'if the conversation does dry up for any reason, talk about anything that comes into your head. Something you're interested in, for example.'

'Such as…films?'

Dan nods. 'Films will do. But ask them about themselves. What they like, not what you like.'

'Got it.'

'And remember, it's not what you say, but how you say it.'

'But I thought you just said they'd do all the talking?'

'Okay. Then remember, it's not what you don't say, but how you don't say it.'

'Huh?'

Just then, Wendy walks over to our table, wearing a rather tight T-shirt.

'Blimey,' says Dan. 'Is it cold in here, or are you trying to smuggle a couple of peanuts out from behind the bar?'

Wendy ignores him, and turns to face me. 'So, tonight's the night?' she asks, looking me up and down appreciatively. 'Out on the pull?'

'Just for research purposes, you understand,' I stammer awkwardly.

'I'm just teasing you, Edward. You'll enjoy yourself.'

'And you've been to this particular one before, right?'

Wendy laughs. 'We go quite a lot, me and the girls. It's a fun night out.'

'Ever, you know, met anyone?'

'It's only saddos who go to this kind of thing,' interrupts Dan. 'No offence, Edward.'

'None taken.' I turn back to Wendy. 'But seriously, what do you mean by a fun night out? Don't you go there to, er, meet boys and stuff?'

Wendy smiles and shakes her head. 'Maybe the first time. But then you realize that most of the guys who are there are there for one reason and one reason only.'

'Which is?'

'Because they can't get a girlfriend any other way,' says Dan.

I look to Wendy to contradict him. Sadly, she doesn't.

'Well, at least the women there tonight will get a good indication of what Dan's like in bed,' she says, mischievously.

Dan frowns. 'What do you mean by that?'

'Three minutes and you're done,' she says, before scampering back behind the bar.

'Which reminds me,' says Dan. 'Have you brought any protection?'

'Why? In case one of them attacks me?'

'No—"protection",' he says, tapping his wallet, 'Just in case you get lucky.'

'Dan, my idea of getting lucky this evening is if I get any clues as to how to get Jane back. And besides, why would I want to sleep with any of them?'

'Why wouldn't you?'

'Because of Jane, dummy. I don't want to cheat on her.'

'But now's your big chance. While she's away.'

'Dan, you don't get it, do you? I'm not looking for a "chance". Big or otherwise.'

Dan looks at me in disbelief. 'I'm still amazed that in the ten years the two of you have been together, you've never been unfaithful.'

'Nope.'

'You've never slept with another woman?'

'Never.'

'You're sure?'

'I think I'd remember.'

'Not even a prostitute?' He lowers his voice an octave or two, 'A "lady of the night"?'

'No.'

'Come on, you can tell your Uncle Dan…'

'No! And the thought of you as an uncle is pretty creepy, I can tell you.'

'Well, you must have thought about it?'

'No. Why would I have?'

Dan looks at me with an expression that conveys 'Why wouldn't you have?'

'Not even an illicit snog with Natasha at the office Christmas party?'

'God no. There's a woman that you could kiss and when you stop you find that she's stolen your tonsils.'

'Well, you can't expect me to believe that in the ten years— I'm sorry mate, I just have to keep repeating that to make sure it's true—that you've been together you've never even looked at another woman.'

'Of course not. I mean I've *looked*, of course, but I've never wanted to do anything about it.'

Dan looks at me incredulously. 'So what happens when you're out on the street, or in the supermarket, and you see an absolutely drop-dead gorgeous woman?'

'Am I out with Jane at the time or not with Jane?'

'With Jane.'

'In that case, nothing. I may notice her, but I'm certainly not going to do anything so rude as stare.'

'Worried about getting caught? Sensible.'

'No. Some of us just don't do that sort of thing.'

'Okay. So what if you weren't with Jane. Imagine you're at the vegetable aisle, for example, and you see this stunning woman, perhaps picking up a cucumber, inspecting it for size and firmness...'

'Dan, please.'

'Sorry, mate. So what would you do?'

'I'm not with Jane?'

'Nope.'

'Well then...Same thing. Nothing.'

'Nothing?'

'Because, what on earth would I have to gain by "doing" anything? I might allow myself to enjoy the sight for a few moments, but I'm hardly going to go and talk to her, am I?'

'Why ever not?'

'Because I've got a girlfriend I don't want to be unfaithful to, and besides, what on earth is she going to see in the likes of me anyway?'

'Aha,' says Dan. 'Now we're getting to the bottom of it.'

'What do you mean?'

'The reason you don't do anything isn't because you want to be faithful to Jane. It's because you don't think you'll get anywhere with Miss Cucumber.'

'Hang on. So what you're basically saying is that not-so-good-looking guys are only faithful because they don't get the opportunity to be unfaithful?'

Dan nods. 'Pretty much.'

'Not because they're actually decent human beings?'

'It's in the male programming, mate. We're genetically designed to sow our seeds. Look at cave paintings.'

'Cave paintings?'

'Yup. They're all "hunt the mammoth" and fighting and stuff. No pictures of weddings, or happy couples holding hands. You'd hardly find the word "monogamy" in any Neanderthal's vocabulary.'

'You don't find it in yours, either. What does that say about you, I wonder?'

'Ah, but you at least admit that you've looked?'

'Yes, but…I look at Porsches on the street every now and again. It doesn't mean that I want to buy one.'

'But you wouldn't mind a quick test drive?'

'Okay, bad example. But I'd feel guilty next time I tried to drive the Volvo.'

Dan raises one eyebrow archly. 'So you *are* worried about being caught?'

I shake my head. 'It's not about that.'

'Ha,' scoffs Dan. 'So you're telling me that if Claudia Schiffer turned up here one day…'

'Claudia Schiffer? In the Admiral Jim?'

Dan puts on a very bad effeminate German accent, managing to sound more like a camp Arnold Schwarzenegger '…and said "Come on Ed, fancy a kvickie? Jane vill never find out", you'd turn her down?'

'Yes.'

'Even if Jane would never know?'

'You're completely missing the point. I'd know.'

'And you'd tell your best friend what it was like, yes?'

'Dan, we're not all built like you.'

'Thanks very much.'

'I didn't mean it as a compliment. I meant having a gap in our DNA where the morals are supposed to be. Some of us enjoy fidelity, constancy, security. These things are benefits, not penalties. A good relationship can be like, well, a comfy pair of slippers.'

Dan makes a face. 'And you and Jane had a good relationship, did you?'

'Yes. Of course.'

'So why did she take off her slippers and change into running shoes?'

'Dan, the point I'm making is that some of us believe in loyalty. If I was ever unfaithful to Jane then I don't know that I'd be able to look her in the face again.'

'You don't have to stare at the fireplace when you're poking the hearth.'

'Christ, Dan. Where women are concerned you don't have a decent bone in your body, do you?'

Dan grins. 'It's my bone in their body I'm more concerned about. But seriously, how would you feel if the slipper, sorry, shoe, was on the other foot?'

'How do you mean?'

'What if Jane was unfaithful?'

I look at him suspiciously. 'Can we change the subject, please?'

'No, I'm curious. Supposing she was. Could you forgive her? Say she comes back from Tibet and falls head-over-heels with you again, but she tells you that while away she got drunk on fermented yak milk one night and joined the...how high is Everest again?'

'Five miles.'

'Five-mile-high club by shagging one of the Sherpas. How would you feel then?'

'I'd...' I swallow hard, 'forgive her.'

'You sure? Even if you knew that someone else had roamed all over her Himalayas?'

'Well, she'd…obviously have had her reasons.'

'Aha. But you've just said to me that you could never do it to her. Why should you accept it if she does the same thing to you?'

He's got me there. And the reason he's got me, and it's something I haven't ever told Dan about, is that just before Christmas, Jane was unfaithful to me. Well, it was more just a snog with another guy really, but as far as I'm concerned that's still being unfaithful. Okay, so maybe she didn't actually sleep with anyone, but when lips meet lips, that line has most definitely been crossed.

We all look at members of the opposite sex from time to time, perhaps fantasizing about what we might like to do with them, or even to them, or have them do to us. But as long as that's where it stays, as a fantasy, I guess that's about okay. I mean, where my diet's concerned, I might dream about eating pizza, for example, but until I actually take a bite, it doesn't count as cheating, does it?

And that's what Jane did. Took a bite. And with a guy from work, apparently. I say apparently because I wasn't there, so I'd had to take her word for it. *Trust me*, she'd said, unaware of the irony in her words. *That's all that happened. A kiss.*

Jane had been away at a work conference in Birmingham, of all places, hardly the most romantic of cities. A two-day event at the NEC, and they'd all been staying over in the Hilton Hotel. Anyway, as she tells it, they'd been out to dinner, her and her marketing team, and then headed to the bar, and then to the hotel's nightclub, and then back to raid one of their mini-bars—I can't remember whose room she said they were in now. But she and this Martin got chatting, and as everyone else drifted off to bed they were the only two left.

Martin had a girlfriend, she'd explained, *so nothing was ever going to happen.* And what about you? I'd wanted to ask. You had a boyfriend. Was that not relevant? Besides, she said, she couldn't remember who'd kissed who. And that made it all right?

It was the drink, she'd said. It wasn't that she fancied him or anything, apparently, it's just that alcohol makes her feel horny—which was news to me—and he was there, and I wasn't…Anyway, they kissed, she felt guilty, they stopped. End of story. That's how she portrayed it, although she didn't really admit anything to me. Didn't give me a chance to feel angry with her. Just sort of told me in a matter-of-fact 'it happened, let's just move on' kind of way. In fact, she even made me feel guilty about getting angry about it. *Jesus, Edward. It was only a drunken snog. Get over it. It's not as if it meant anything.* And then she'd stormed out, and waited for me to go and apologize to her for getting angry because she'd been unfaithful to me. Women.

We'd never mentioned it again. But for weeks I couldn't look at her without thinking about it. How did they kiss? Where did they kiss? And with tongues? Did he touch her? Let's face it, you don't kiss someone in a drunken snog and not touch them anywhere else, do you? It would be like trying to drive a car without putting your hands on the steering wheel.

And do you know how I found out? Did she come straight home and tell me, clasping my hand as she tearfully confessed all? Did she bollocks. I found out by email. From her. Although not directly, and certainly not on purpose. She'd forwarded me an email that Martin had sent her regarding the Christmas party, not thinking that I'd scroll down and read the part about him looking forward to catching her underneath the mistletoe. *Especially since Birmingham*, he'd added.

I knew Martin. I'd even bought him a pint, the ungrateful git. And for a while, every time I kissed her, I kept thinking of his face, which isn't a good thing if you're a heterosexual man.

Oh yes, and here's the best bit: *It'll make us stronger*, she'd said, as if what she'd done was a good thing. But tell me something—how do these things ever make a relationship stronger? It's not like a broken leg, where the bone actually grows back thicker, is it? If your car breaks down, you may get it fixed, but it doesn't suddenly become faster or safer as a result of the breakdown, does it? Quite the opposite; you're always slightly nervous that whenever you drive it, it'll let you down again. Or to take a more extreme example, if you'd had cancer, and beaten it once, you'd still always be worried that the cancer might come back, and worse than before.

Because that's what unfaithfulness is, isn't it? A cancer that's always there in the back of your mind, eating away at the foundations of the relationship. It's happened once, it could happen again, so you're always looking for telltale signs or symptoms to show that it's reappeared. Say you live in Tokyo, and your house gets demolished by an earthquake. Would you rebuild it, knowing that you were in an earthquake zone, confident it'd never happen again? I don't think so. And at the time, that's how I felt. Like our relationship had been rocked by an earthquake. And maybe I hadn't realized just how much damage had been done.

For a while I wondered whether I should try and get even; go out and snog someone to get my own back, but why stoop to her level? The truth is, I hadn't wanted to. And besides, I'm not the cheating kind. No—I'd just wanted things to go back to how they were between me and my beautiful girlfriend. Though as I think about it, sitting here on the moral high ground, I'm a little troubled by what Dan's implying: that it wasn't Jane's looks that kept me from straying.

It was mine.

7.55 p.m.

We're standing in the foyer at the Metropole Hotel, where tonight's speed-dating event is taking place. The organizer, Emily, a pretty brunette, barely glances at me as she hands me a little sticky label with my name written on it, but makes a great show of personally ensuring that Dan's is stuck on properly. Dan, of course, tenses his pectoral muscle as she does so.

We're ushered into a side room to join the other hopefuls: a rag-tag collection of last-ones-to-be-picked-at-games who make even me look relatively attractive. They're all trying to size each other up without making eye contact, and when they spot Dan, I'm sure one or two of them think about leaving.

Dan wrinkles his nose. 'God, will you look at this shower,' he says, a little too loudly. 'And a couple of them could do with taking one.'

'Keep your voice down.'

'Why? In case one of them bursts a pimple in my direction? I'm glad I'm not in the same boat as any of them.'

Same boat? Dan looks like he doesn't belong in the same gene pool.

We help ourselves to our 'free' glass of wine, generously included in our £25 entry price, which I down in one; probably not a good idea given my lack of food and the beer I've just drunk.

At eight o'clock precisely, Emily claps her hands to get our attention. 'Now, you bunch of hunks,' she begins.

'Bunch of what?' whispers Dan, looking around incredulously. 'Is she in the same room as me?'

'Waiting next door,' continues Emily, 'are twenty women, who are all *very* eager to meet you.'

Dan nudges me. 'Cue massive disappointment.'

One nervous chap in the corner clears his throat. 'So, how does this work, exactly?' He must be about my age, but has the acned skin of a teenager, and speaks like his voice has just broken.

'Well,' says Emily, 'basically, once you get inside, the girls stay still while you move around.'

'No change there then!' interjects Dan, provoking a ripple of nervous laughter. Emily looks up sharply, angry at being interrupted, but when she sees who made the comment, her expression changes to a smile.

'And don't forget,' Emily adds, 'you've only got three minutes with each lady, so make every second count.'

She hands us all a clipboard and a pen, telling us we're to put a tick next to the names of any of the girls we like, and we're shown through into what I guess is the hotel's ballroom. True to Emily's word, there are twenty tables, at each of which sits a girl clutching an identical clipboard. They look up hopefully as we shuffle in, and it's all I can do not to turn back around as I see their faces fall.

I try and position myself away from Dan, so as not to suffer unfairly in the immediate comparison stakes, but instead he sidles up next to me.

'Happy hunting,' he whispers.

I walk towards the nearest vacant chair, the phrase 'Christians and lions' running through my mind, as Emily's shrill voice brings the proceedings to order.

'Okay, love-hunters. Time starts…now!' She rings a bell, then moves to stand guard by the door, more, I imagine, to keep us from escaping than in case any hotel guests walk in accidentally.

My allotted table is occupied by a not unattractive redhead whose name, her badge tells me, is Melanie. I'm a little bit nervous, not to mention a little bit drunk, and as I sit down in front of her, I don't know what the correct greeting procedure should be. When I look up from my clipboard, Melanie is pointedly holding her hand out towards me.

'Hello, Edward,' she says, without a trace of a smile.

'Sorry,' I say, giving her a slightly sweaty handshake. 'I didn't know whether there was a "no touching" rule. Like in prison?'

Great. My opening line suggests I have some knowledge of jail procedures. As Melanie picks up her clipboard, locates my name, and uncaps her biro purposefully, I try and remember Dan's advice. *Start with a compliment. Start with a compliment…*

'Wow. You're gorgeous, Melanie. How come you're single?'

Melanie looks at me with disdain. 'I've just broken up with my boyfriend,' she says, flatly. 'My friends thought this would cheer me up.'

Ah. Big mistake. Change the subject? No—go for the jugular. 'Oh no. Why was that? The break up, I mean.'

'We wanted different things.'

'Such as?'

'Well, I wanted to settle down and have kids, whereas he wanted to shag that little tart from accounts. All men are bastards.' Melanie stares daggers at me, daring me to challenge her.

'Oh. So, er, have you ever been to one of these things before?'

'No.'

'Me neither.'

'Really? That surprises me.'

Ah. So far Dan's 'get them talking' strategy doesn't seem to be working.

'Er…'

After a further thirty seconds of silence, Melanie folds her arms. 'Well, do you want to ask me anything else, or are you just going to sit there and look stupid?'

To be honest, just sitting here and looking stupid seems actually to be the most appealing option. I consult my clipboard for help, but it doesn't provide any. Instead I try to keep to Dan's advice, even though by the amount of talking he seems to be doing at the next-door table, he's obviously ignoring it himself.

I take a deep breath. 'So…'

'Yes?'

'What's your favourite film?'

Melanie stifles a yawn. '*Fatal Attraction*.'

'Ah. Right.'

Unlike Dan's sexual partners, I'm beginning to think that three minutes is actually quite a long time. I look around for Emily, willing her to ring the bell, but when I manage to catch her eye she just smiles back at me in what I guess is supposed to be encouragement.

By now, Melanie is drumming her fingers on the table in front of me, and I'm wondering, given her recent experience, whether there's any point in me trying to canvass her opinion on the current dating dilemma facing the modern women, when finally, thankfully, I hear a ringing sound. There's a simultaneous scraping of chairs, and we all move around one place.

As a smug-looking Dan sits down in front of Melanie, at least I take some consolation that he'll suffer the same treatment. Ha! This'll show him. But something's happened to Melanie in the ten or so seconds it's taken us all to change places. In fact, it seems to be a totally different Melanie from the one who's just given me the cold shoulder. She beams at Dan across the table, and within a moment or two, I actually hear her *laugh*.

Oh well. As I sit down at the adjoining table, my new partner— a blonde for whom the term 'buxom' was probably invented—gives me a cursory glance before staring across at Dan next door. After a minute or so, I have to clear my throat to get her attention.

'Sorry,' she says, still gazing at Dan. 'But isn't he that guy from the TV?'

'Yes. Dan Davis. He's my friend.'

The girl looks at me strangely. '*Your* friend?'

She's wearing a very low-cut top and her name is, well, I can't quite seem to make it out, given the curve that her cleavage is imparting on the sticky label.

'So. Hello, er…' I'm still struggling to work out what it says on her name tag.

'Are you staring at my breasts?'

I blush almost instantly. 'No I was trying to read your name tag. Honest.' But of course, now that she's mentioned her breasts, I can't help staring.

'Yes you are. You're staring at my breasts.' She raises her voice so the whole room can hear her. 'He's staring at my breasts.'

The women look round in collective sympathy, and I can feel their icy glares. The men, of course, all stare at whatever-her-name-is's breasts.

'I can't help it. I mean, I'm not.' I point towards her chest area. 'It's your name tag. It's in the same...vicinity.'

'You're doing it again, you pervert.'

At the next-door table, Dan breaks off from telling Melanie how great he is.

'And you obviously didn't want them stared at, love,' he says. 'That's why you've worn that top.'

My partner, whose name I still don't know, can't work out whether to be annoyed at Dan, or flattered that he seems to be paying her some attention before it's his turn. Equally, Melanie seems to be angry that 'my' girl is muscling in on her precious three minutes with Dan, and so gets menacingly to her feet. It's in danger of getting ugly, until Emily rings the bell furiously.

I move on, thankfully, and sit down opposite a sweet-looking girl, who holds out her hand to me. I shake it nervously.

'So, hello, er, Rose,' I say, glancing as briefly as I can at her name badge.

'Hello, Edward,' she replies, in the most beautiful Irish accent. 'Can I just ask you a few questions?'

This wasn't in my plan. 'Sure, I suppose...'

Rose fastens a fresh piece of paper which seems to be laid out like a checklist into her clipboard, and writes my name at the top. 'Okay. Question One. Any history of cancer in your family?'

Huh? 'No, I don't...'

'Heart disease?'

'No.'

'Are you a drug user?'

'Apart from Neurofen? No.'

Rose ignores my admittedly poor attempt at humour.

'Ever had a homosexual experience?'

I think about this one carefully. 'Well, there was one time when this guy I'd never met before tried to buy me a drink. Does that count?'

'Do you smoke?'

'Yes, but I'm trying to give it…'

Rose's face falls. 'Ah. Bad for the sperm count. What underwear do you favour? Boxers or briefs?'

I'm just about to answer when I get an uneasy feeling. 'What's this all about?'

Rose puts her clipboard down and cups her hand to her ear. 'That ticking sound? Can you hear it?'

I listen carefully, but can't detect a thing. 'Nope.'

'It's my biological clock.'

'Ding!'

That's me—not Emily's bell, and I leap to my feet in shock.

And this is the high point of my evening, as the rest of the 'dates' pass by in a blur of enquiries about my financial status to what car I drive. I'm supposed to be a professional interviewer but these girls knock spots off me. One of them talks so much and so quickly I fear she's taken the 'speed' aspect of the night literally, and I zone out, listening in instead to Dan's 'enough about you, let's talk about me' approach at the next-door table. Amazingly, and yet not surprisingly given the competition, he seems to get away with it.

When finally, after what seems like a lot more than twenty times three minutes, we finish, Emily herds us back into the side room. She collects our tick sheets as she does so, telling us to call her on Monday to find out who our 'matches' are. I've ticked three, just to be polite, but can't say I hold out much hope of any reciprocal interest, although that's probably for the best given my motivation for being here in the first place. As eye-opening as the evening's been, it fundamentally tells me nothing that I really want to know.

All the glasses of free wine seem to have disappeared, so Dan and I do likewise and head back to the Admiral Jim.

'Thought there were a couple of nice ones there,' he says.

'You think?'

Dan nods. 'Especially that one who thought you were a perv. She had a real couple of nice ones.'

'How many did you tick?'

'None.'

'None?'

He shrugs. 'Didn't need to.'

'But if you haven't ticked them, then Emily can't put them in touch with you.'

Dan puts his hand into his pocket and removes a number of scraps of paper, on which are scribbled various names and phone numbers.

'Beat the system, you see.'

'And are you going to call any of them?'

He shrugs again. 'Shouldn't think so. Although...' he says, picking out one and screwing up the rest. 'That Emily was quite cute.'

I look at him disbelievingly. 'You go speed dating and end up getting the number of the organizer?'

Dan puts an arm around my shoulders. 'Well, you've either got it, or you don't.'

And sadly, he's right. Based on tonight's performance, I don't got it.

Monday 7th February

11.15 a.m.

ON DAN'S INSISTENCE, AND although I'm pretty sure what the outcome will be, I call Emily to find out how many 'ticks' I got. When she starts off by saying 'Well, it's not all about the number of ticks,' my suspicions are confirmed, but just as I'm expecting her to give me a big fat zero, she actually says 'one', and although I apparently didn't tick her, she's given one of the girls—Caroline—my email address.

I search through my slightly alcohol-muddled memory of the evening, trying to recall which one she was, before remembering I'd made notes on them all, so I anxiously scan my list, skimming over the words 'psycho' and 'bunny-boiler' until I come to her name. Caroline: seemed a little distracted, works in admin, drives a silver Ford Fiesta, likes country pubs.

It's not much to go on, and while I seem to remember that she was actually quite pretty, in truth I forget about it for the rest of the morning. Natasha has already phoned to say she's not coming in, and by mid-afternoon, just as I'm contemplating snoozing on my desk, I'm surprised by the 'ping' of an email appearing in my inbox.

I'm even more astonished to see that its from Caroline, saying how much she enjoyed meeting me, and wondering whether I'd like to meet up some time. So astonished, in fact, that I go to see Dan for advice.

Dan sighs exasperatedly. 'Go out with her, of course.'

'But I'm not looking to—' I make the speech marks sign with my fingers—'"go out" with anyone.'

'Of course you're not. Just think of it as a dry run for when Jane gets back. You want to be able to win her over, don't you? Well what better way than to be able to chat her up from scratch? And this is a chance for some practice.'

'Great idea. So how do I do that, then?'

Dan leans back in his chair, finally pleased that we're touching on his one area of expertise.

'Are you sitting comfortably?'

'Should I be taking notes?'

'That might be an idea,' says Dan, in all seriousness. He sits there, no doubt waiting for me to produce a pen and paper.

'Just get on with it.'

'Okay. So what do you know about this woman?'

'Well, not very much. In fact, I'm not sure I can remember what she looks like. But I'm sure I'll know her when I see her.'

'That's encouraging. What did you write down?'

When I tell him, his face lights up. 'Brilliant. She likes country pubs. Perfect opportunity for you to mail her back, and tell her you know this fantastic little place just outside Brighton and perhaps she'd like to meet you there for a drink one night this week.'

'Great. What fantastic little place?'

Dan sighs. 'You and Jane really didn't get out much, did you?'

'So, what next?'

'Right. You arrange to meet her fairly early in the evening. Say seven o'clock.'

'Why's that?'

'Because that way she probably hasn't had time to eat anything in between work and meeting you. And,' he adds, testing me, 'that's good why?'

'Because if she hasn't eaten…I can get her drunk quicker?'

Dan considers my answer for a moment. 'It's good, but it's not right. The reason you try and get her to miss dinner is because she'll then be hungry.'

'You're not being disgusting again, are you?'

'No. Not at all. If she's hungry, and things seem to be going well, then all you need to do is suggest that the two of you get something to eat, thus turning a casual drink into a dinner date.'

'Brilliant. And how do I know if things are going well?'

'In your case, if she hasn't left.'

As usual, I ignore Dan's insult. 'So, after the pub, where would you take them?'

'Me? Heaven and back, obviously. But you? I'd settle for a restaurant. Italian, probably. Shows just about the right level of sophistication.'

'Italian?'

'Yup. And a couple of pointers. Firstly, garlic. Good if she orders it, bad if it's only you. And always tell them that the spaghetti is very good, even if you've never been there before.'

'Spaghetti? Why?'

'You can tell a lot about a girl from the way she eats spaghetti. Lip suction, tongue control…'

He makes a noise with his mouth that I guess is supposed to be sexy but reminds me more of Hannibal Lecter in *Silence of the Lambs*.

'And then, if the meal goes well?'

He grins at me. 'If the meal goes well? Bingo!'

'What—on the pier?'

Dan stares at me for a second, then puts his head in his hands.

Wednesday 9th February

6.51 p.m.

THE INAPPROPRIATELY NAMED RAM Inn is our 'safe' venue—Emily advised we always met for the first time at a 'safe' venue—a picture-postcard thatched pub built several hundred years ago, and just off the main road between Brighton and Eastbourne.

I park the Volvo and walk nervously over towards the pub, peering in through the window just in case Caroline's early. I can't see her, so, mindful of Dan's advice not to wait inside on my own and risk being stood up in full view, decide to sit in the car until she appears.

I watch the passing traffic until, a few minutes later, Caroline arrives, her silver Ford Fiesta sweeping in off the road with a crunch of gravel, although in truth I might not have recognized her but for the fact that I'd noted down what car she drove.

She parks a space away from the Volvo, possibly worried that something may fall off it and damage her car, but when I get out to meet her, instead of returning what I hope is my best welcoming smile, Caroline looks rather confused.

'What are you doing here?'

I laugh nervously, thinking she's making some kind of first-date joke, and decide to play along.

'Oh, just passing. Thought the pub looked nice. How about you?'

'I'm meeting someone, actually.'

'Oh really?' I say. 'Me too.'

'At seven o'clock,' she adds, glancing at her watch.

'What a coincidence. Me too.'

'Oh,' says Caroline.

We stand there for a few uncomfortable moments as I try to work out what to do next. Is our date not officially allowed to start until the pre-arranged time? Are we supposed to wait until seven o'clock to go into the pub? Or is she just waiting for me to take the lead? This is obviously some sort of game, but I don't seem to know the rules.

As Caroline looks at her watch for a second time, I give up.

'Shall we just go inside?'

'Well,' she says, hesitantly. 'We're supposed to meet outside.'

I stamp my feet against the cold. 'Yes, but not stay outside, surely?'

Caroline glances over towards the pub, which does look rather warm and inviting. 'You think he might be in there already?'

'It's me,' I say, a little confused myself now.

'Yes,' says Caroline, looking anxiously around the car park. 'From speed dating. You're the one who was staring at that woman's chest.'

Ah. So far this really isn't going as well as I'd hoped. 'Yes. Well, no, I wasn't staring, exactly.'

'What's your name again?'

'Edward,' I reply. 'We've got a date, remember?'

There's a moment or two of stunned silence, and then a look of horror flashes across her face.

'*You're* Edward?'

'That's right.'

'Oh my God.'

'What?'

'I must have ticked your box by mistake.'

'Ah.' Judging by her face, I obviously don't tick any of her boxes.

'I'm so sorry,' she says. 'I thought you were someone else. I mean, that someone else was you…'

Great. And three guesses who that must have been.

Caroline still hasn't locked her car, and I can tell she's seriously considering getting back into it and driving straight home. I realize that, if I don't want this evening to be a complete blow out, I have to think on my feet.

'Well, at least stay for a drink. It'd be a shame to have come out all this way…'

Looking at her expression, I can tell immediately that Caroline wouldn't think it was a shame at all. More likely, she'd think it'd be more of a shame to waste even an hour of her life with me. But something, maybe even compassion, clicks inside her brain, and she half-smiles.

'Okay,' she says, blipping her car shut and walking with me towards the pub. 'But just the one.'

I open the door for her, and we walk inside, dodging the standard-issue horse-brasses and bunches of dried hops that hang from the low wooden beams.

'You go and sit down,' I tell her, 'I'll get the drinks.'

Caroline thinks about protesting for a moment, but then I guess reckons that at least she won't have to waste any money on this evening.

'Okay.'

'What would you like?'

'Just a tomato juice. Please.'

'Sensible girl.'

'Pardon?'

'Because you're driving? A tomato juice?'

Caroline frowns at me. 'What's that got to do with anything?'

I shrug, and head to the bar, aware that I've made a rod for my own back now. If I've told her that she's sensible for not drinking alcohol because she's driven here, and I've obviously driven here too, then does that mean I can't have any either? I know I'm not supposed to, given my training regime, but at the moment I need something to calm my nerves. I decide to compromise, and order a half of shandy, which gets me a funny look from the landlord, especially when I hurriedly change it to a pint of shandy, reasoning that the bigger my drink, the more time it'll take me to drink it, and therefore the longer Caroline will have to stay.

As I pull my stomach in, draw myself up to my full height, and carry the drinks over towards where Caroline's sitting, she looks up from where she's been staring glumly at her watch and starts to mouth something. I lean forward and quicken my pace in an attempt to hear what she's trying to say but instead the only thing I manage to catch is the top of my head on the low beam that straddles the ceiling.

I don't know how long I'm lying, dazed, on the floor, but when I open my eyes I'm met with an upside-down view of the landlord, who's leaning over me, his expression somewhere between concern and amusement.

'People are always doing that,' he says.

'I'm not surprised,' I reply, still a little woozy. 'There should be a sign.'

Wordlessly he nods towards the beam, the centre of which is worn smooth from what can only be generations of unwary patrons smacking their heads. The word 'duck' is clearly inscribed on the front.

He helps me up into a sitting position, and I gingerly put my hand up to my skull, where I can already feel a bruise as large as a walnut. There's something dripping down my face, and when I pull my hand away, it's soaked red. My first thought is that I've cut myself, and it's bad.

'Call me an ambulance,' I say, panicking at the bright ruby stain spreading down my white shirt.

The landlord hands me a bar towel. 'It's tomato juice. You'll live.'

By now, there's a circle of people stood around where I'm sat, in a puddle of shandy and tomato juice, their looks of concern fading when they realize what's happened. As the landlord extends a hand to help me up, I wave him away and climb unsteadily to my feet, dabbing myself down with the towel before suddenly remembering why I'm here, or rather, who I'm here with. But when I look over in Caroline's direction, she's nowhere to be seen.

As the landlord pours me a conciliatory pint, I peer miserably out through the window, just in time to see a silver Ford Fiesta disappearing at speed from the pub car park.

Thursday 10th February

7.21 a.m.

'WHAT A BITCH,' SAYS Sam when I recount the story in the gym the following morning, and show her the bump on my head.

'Well,' I wheeze, halfway through a set of sit-ups. 'You can't blame her really. After all, she was doing me a favour.'

Sam lets go of my feet suddenly, causing me to roll over backwards and knee myself painfully on the exact spot where I hit my head.

'Edward, don't talk like that. You're hardly a charity case. What she did was downright rude, leaving you like that. You might have been seriously hurt.'

'Well, fortunately, only my feelings were. But she didn't find me attractive, full stop. At the moment, I just have to accept that, and be grateful for any scraps I get thrown.'

'Edward, you're a decent guy. That counts for a lot, you know.'

'Yeah, maybe. But not when I go clubbing, apparently.'

'You went clubbing?'

I nod. 'The other weekend. Dan thought it would do me good to maybe chat up some other women.'

'Dan?'

'My best friend. Unfortunately. He makes Sy over there look like Mother Teresa.'

Sam laughs at the image. 'What happened?'

'Well, he's so good-looking that all the girls we met just ignored me—I think the longest conversation I had was when one of them said to me "your friend's nice"—while they gathered round him like flies on you know what.'

'A shit? Edward, do you really think chatting up a girl in a nightclub is going to help you get Jane back? Or even going out for the evening with someone you've only known for three minutes?'

'I just thought, well, *Dan* thought, that it might give me a bit of insight into what women want.'

Sam pulls me to my feet, leads me across to the stepper, and I climb on reluctantly.

'Well, maybe you need to stop trying to work out what it is they want,' she says, 'and think a little more about what it is you want.'

'So what about you?' I ask, as Sam presses the 'level up' key. 'Anyone special in your life?'

'No. Not at the moment. Well, not for a while, since my brief period of mental illness when I went out with Sy. It hardly fits in with my lifestyle.'

'But you must meet loads of people. Men, I mean.'

'Why's that? What are you inferring?'

'You know, because you're…'

'An attractive woman?' teases Sam.

'I was going to say "personal trainer". But, yes, now you mention it.'

'Thanks, I think. And yes, I do meet a few through work, but I make it a rule never to date a man I can beat in a sprint. And besides, I could never date a client.'

'Why ever not?'

'Imagine if I was to get a reputation for going out with my male clients. Brighton's a small city, and as soon as that happened? I can't see any woman letting her husband use me as a trainer.'

'But don't you miss, you know, not having…'

'Sex?'

'I was going to say "a boyfriend". But again, now you mention it.'

Sam smiles. 'To tell the truth, Edward, I'm so knackered by about ten p.m. after all these early mornings that the only thing I want in bed nowadays is an extra hour. I'm trying to make it in this business, maybe I'll even save up enough to buy my own gym one day, and sometimes you have to make sacrifices if you want something badly.'

'I know what you mean,' I say. It's about now I'd be lighting up my first cigarette of the day.

'Besides, in my experience, men don't like it if you care about your career, and certainly not if your work means you're out of the house so early every morning that they have to make their own breakfast. And then, when you tell them you fancy an early night, but that means you actually want to go to sleep...'

'In your experience?'

Sam nods. 'The guy I went out with before Sy. We'd been seeing each other for about a year before we decided to move in together. And that's where the problems started.'

'What happened?'

'Let's just say that someone who I enjoyed seeing once or twice a week wasn't so much fun every day. He just seemed to have no ambition. No drive.'

'And?'

'I'll tell you something, Edward. When someone loves you, there's nothing they won't do for you. When they stop loving you, there's nothing they will. And so, eventually, I just got fed up. I got tired of clearing up after him, of always being the one who had to do everything. Trust me, once you've picked up the hundredth pair of dirty socks from the floor on his side of the bed, the romance soon goes out of the window. And get this—his idea of an evening's entertainment was to watch Sky Sports with a takeaway for company. Whether I was there or not.'

Gulp. Sam's just described my old every-Wednesday-night routine.

'He wasn't into exercise?'

'Nope. The only six-pack he was interested in getting had "Budweiser" written on the side.' Sam goes quiet for a moment. 'But yes, in answer to your earlier question, in an ideal world, I'd love to have a boyfriend. And,' she says, nodding curtly, 'everything that goes with that. But the guys I meet nowadays are usually married and only after a bit on the side, or they're the type that come into Sy's gym and therefore they're all like Sy himself, so at the moment I've prioritized, just like you're doing. What is it you miss about your old lifestyle the most, for example?'

I stop climbing and let the foot pedals sink me back down towards Sam's eye level. 'Pizza, probably.'

Sam laughs. 'And there's me thinking you were going to say "companionship" or something like that. At least you're honest.'

'Sorry I didn't think you were asking about me and Jane. I thought you meant…never mind. Of course I miss her. I miss talking to her; telling her about my day, and her laughing when I tell her the latest about what Natasha's been up to. I miss the comfortable silences; the arguments about what we'd watch on TV; refereeing the arguments she'd have with Dan; the brave face she'd put on whenever I'd offer to cook her dinner. I miss holding hands with her when we'd walk along the seafront. I miss her falling asleep on me during whatever DVD we'd rented, and then having to explain the plot when she woke up just before the end. I miss her smile, the smell of her perfume, the look of her in her business suit, the look of her out of her business suit…Most of all, I miss her just being there.'

Sam looks at me strangely. 'Blimey, Edward. You really do, don't you?'

I stare at her for a second or two, then snap back, a little too aggressively, 'Why the hell do you think I'm putting myself through all this. It's not just for the pleasure of your company, you know.'

When I slump against the machine, catching my breath for a different reason, Sam walks round next to me and puts an arm round my shoulders, a task that can't be too pleasant given the amount I'm sweating.

'I'm sorry,' she says, when I've regained my composure. 'I forgot that it was still so, you know, raw.'

'I'm sorry too. For snapping at you. I just get a little angry sometimes when I think about how Jane just upped and left me. The... the life that she just left behind.'

Sam gives me a squeeze, and puts on an American accent. 'Well, I want you to focus on that anger, that strength of feeling, get back on that stepper, and you work it, buddy. Or something like that.'

That gets a smile out of me. 'You betcha!'

I leap back on the machine and start pumping away, much harder than before.

'Steady on,' says Sam. 'You don't want to pull something.'

But, ironically, that's exactly what I do want to do.

7.43 p.m.

When I walk into the Admiral Jim, Dan's sat opposite Wendy at the bar, staring intently at his mobile phone.

'They do have ring tones, apparently,' she says to him. 'You know—to let you know when someone's calling?'

'Huh?'

'Just so you don't have to stare at it the whole time.'

Dan shushes her. 'I'm waiting for an important call.'

'Results from the paternity clinic?' I suggest.

'Shut your face. It's to see if I'm in panto next year.'

Wendy winks at me. 'Panto? You? Don't you have to be famous to be in panto?'

Dan takes the bait. 'I *am* famous. Well, famous enough for panto, at least.'

Wendy counts me in. 'Oh no you're not,' we chorus.

'How would you two losers know?'

I shake my head. 'Very disappointing, mate. You won't get very far if you don't know the basics.'

Dan looks annoyed. 'What basics?'

'You know. "Look behind you".'

Dan swivels to look over his shoulder. 'What are you talking about?'

'There's a tiny house…' sings Wendy. Dan just looks at her strangely.

'Why do you suppose he wants to be in panto anyway?' she says to me. 'Aren't you supposed to wait until your career is on the slide?'

'Yes, well, Dan fancies himself as a bit of an actor.'

'Dan just fancies himself, full stop.'

'No, seriously. Ever since he got a bit part as "Corpse Number Two" in *Casualty*.'

'That's not acting. All he had to do was lie there and pretend to be dead,' says Wendy, pouring me a drink before heading off to serve some customers.

'Which pretty much describes his sexual technique,' I call after her. 'Apparently.'

I pick what's evidently the latest in the long line of Dan's mobile phones up off the bar and examine it. It looks like something out of *Star Trek*.

'I still can't believe you don't own a mobile,' says Dan, taking it back from me, as if he's afraid I might break it.

'What's the point? I'm either at home, where I've got a phone, or in the office, where I've got a phone, or at the pub, where I don't want to be disturbed.'

Dan looks at me in disbelief. 'Edward. Everyone has a mobile nowadays. And not having one…it's like…well, some kind of social stigma. Like not being able to drive, or having an ugly girlfriend. Which, coincidentally…'

'But why would I need one?' I say, cutting him off.

'Because the whole dating scene revolves around mobiles

nowadays. You meet a girl, you get talking, what's the first thing you do?'

'Er…I know this one. Ask her what her favourite film is?'

'No, dummy. You get her phone number.'

'That would have been my second answer. Phone number. Right.'

'And how do you remember it?'

'Write it down?'

'Sure. Because you've come out to the bar equipped with a pencil and paper.'

'Well, I go and borrow them from the barman.'

'Great idea. Only to find when you get back, she's gone, or is being chatted up by someone else. You snooze, you lose, remember.'

'So what do I do?'

'You punch her number into your mobile phone.'

'But I haven't got one.'

'Exactly. Which is why, if you're going to follow this thing through properly, you need to get one.' Dan flips his open and presses a few of the keys, causing the display to light up. 'And you need to get the smallest, latest, most expensive and flashiest model you can afford.'

'Why? It's just a phone.'

'Yeah. And that's what she'll be thinking, especially when she sees that the huge bulge in your trousers is actually caused by nothing more than your prehistoric brick of a mobile. Your phone should be what you aspire to be yourself—slim and sophisticated.'

'Very funny.'

'And then the next day, seeing as you've got her phone number now, what do you do?'

'Call her?'

'Nope. Not first time round.'

'Why ever not?'

'Because what you don't want is a reaction. You phone her, she either doesn't remember who you are, or she reacts with such indifference that you'll never want to see her again.'

'So?'

'So instead you send her a text. Which you can't do if you don't have?'

'A mobile phone.'

Dan breathes a sigh of relief. 'By Jove, I think he's got it.'

8.03 p.m.

I'm savouring only my second nicotine fix of the day, as Dan regards me from across the table. Suddenly, he reaches over and pinches my cheek.

'Ow. Get off. What are you doing?'

Dan lets me go. 'I was just thinking…'

'What?'

'Have you thought about plastic surgery?'

I nearly drop my cigarette in surprise. 'I don't need plastic surgery.'

'Yes you do. Look at your eyes. You've got bigger bags than Louis Vuitton.'

'That's just because I'm tired. From all these early starts.'

'But what about those wrinkles?'

'What wrinkles? I don't have any wrinkles.'

'Well, maybe not now,' concedes Dan. 'But that's because you've got a fat face. Fat people always look younger than thin people, because the fat fills out the wrinkles. But when they lose that weight…'

'What are you going on about now?'

'It's true. Just look at that Nigel Lawson. As a fat chancellor he looked in pretty good nick. Then he lost all that weight, and suddenly he looks like he's ready for his pension. Or what's left of it, after what his lot did to the economy.'

'I'm not having plastic surgery. Just drop it.'

'Fine.'

'Thank you.'

Dan continues to stare at me. 'Or…'

'What?'

'Have you thought about Botox?'

'Botox?'

'Yeah. Basically, they inject you with this stuff that removes all your wrinkles. Makes you look ten years younger almost overnight.'

'What sort of stuff?'

'I dunno. Its some kind of poison, I think. Paralyses the muscles that cause wrinkles. *Voila!* Face as tight as a baby's arse.'

'Poison? What sort of poison?'

'That food poisoning one. Bot-something.'

'Botulism?'

Dan nods. 'Yeah. That's the fella.'

I stare at Dan's remarkably line-free face. 'How come you know so much about it?'

He shrugs. 'Got to think about the future. Protect the assets.'

'So let me get this straight. You want me to get food poisoning injected into my face on purpose, just so I can look a few years younger?'

'If you like.'

'And this'll be really cheap, I suppose?'

'About two hundred and fifty quid a pop,' he says. 'I imagine.'

'I can't just come round to your flat for dinner, *get* food poisoning, and achieve the same effect?'

'Cheeky bugger. But you'll think about it?'

'Dan, number one, I hate injections. Number two, I don't want poison injected into my face, or anywhere, now I come to think of it. And number three, I don't want to walk around looking like I've got a bloody mask on for the rest of the year. So no, I won't think about it.'

Dan sits back in his chair and holds his hands up. 'Fair enough. Only trying to help. But…'

'But what?'

'In that case, you really ought to give up the smoking. Completely. Very bad for the skin. Not to mention the teeth. Or the wallet.'

I stare fondly at the Marlboro in my hand. 'I'm trying. But on top of everything else I've had to give up—the beer, the chocolate, the pizza—it's hard.'

'Rubbish,' says Dan. 'Giving up smoking? Piece of piss.'

'How would you know? You've never given up anything in your life.'

'I'm serious. It's easy.'

'Yeah, right. How does the joke go? "So easy I've done it hundreds of times".'

'Listen. Do any of your friends smoke?'

'Er…nope.'

'Does anyone at work smoke?'

'Seeing as there's only Natasha and me in the office, and she doesn't, then no.'

'So is there anyone you know, anyone at all, who you could possibly bum a cigarette off if you get desperate?'

I think about this for a moment. There's only Billy, who I know smokes roll-ups, but that would be just too low.

'No.'

'Well, do you want to know the easiest way to give up?'

'Go on…'

Dan reaches across, takes my last Marlboro from me, and grinds it out distastefully in the ashtray. 'Stop buying cigarettes.'

Monday 14th February

7.27 p.m.

IT'S VALENTINE'S NIGHT, AND I'm waiting for Dan in the Admiral Jim. That's not as sad as it sounds for either of us; my 'girlfriend' if you can still call her that, is several thousand miles away, and Dan never ever has a date on Valentine's evening, thinking it too much of a commitment thing.

I haven't received a card from Jane this morning, but I've just put that down to the fact that she probably wasn't able to find a post box, or even a card shop, come to think of it. Besides, I haven't sent her one either, although that's mainly because I don't know where exactly she is.

Dan's almost half an hour late, and I'm just about to call him on my new mobile, courtesy of 'Fone Home' (which I can't say unless it's in E.T.'s voice) in the high street, when he appears, grinning sheepishly. 'Sorry, mate. Had a job getting out of my front door.'

I don't take the bait. 'What are you talking about?'

'You know. With all the Valentine's cards blocking it.'

I sigh. 'Have you purposefully been hanging around outside for half an hour in the cold just so you can make that pathetic joke?'

Dan's face falls. 'Well, not quite half an hour.'

The Jim is having some kind of Valentine's theme night, with heart-shaped balloons flying above the tables, and the bar staff all dressed in pink. Not surprisingly it's pretty quiet, although I'm sure the same can't be said for thousands of tables-for-two at Brighton's various restaurants this evening.

As Dan pulls up a stool, Wendy appears behind the bar. She's wearing a pair of red heart-shaped, battery-operated, deeley-boppers, which flash on and off alternately. They're somewhat out of tune with her miserable expression.

'Evening you two lovebirds,' she says. 'What'll it be?'

'My usual,' says Dan, 'and another half for Edward.'

'What do you mean "another half"? I haven't had a beer.'

'Sorry mate. I meant to say "an other half".'

'Very funny.'

Wendy shakes her head. 'So what have you two got planned tonight? Something romantic?'

Dan stick his tongue out at her. 'It's my only night off in the year. I want to do something fun. Any suggestions, Eddy boy?'

'Dan, it's bloody Valentine's night. We can either go and sit in a restaurant surrounded by loved-up couples trying to inject some romance into their meaningless relationships, go home and watch the umpteenth rerun of *When Harry Met Sally* or some other romantic rubbish, or sit here. Which would you prefer?'

'Good point.' Dan turns his attention back to Wendy, who's flashing away opposite us. 'So, no date tonight?'

'Only with a large glass of wine when I get home.'

'What's your boyfriend doing this evening?' asks Dan.

Wendy reddens slightly. 'I don't have a boyfriend.'

'Why not?' I've asked this in the spirit of sympathy, and then suddenly realize that it's not the cleverest of questions. Particularly on Valentine s Day.

Wendy pulls up a stool. 'Well, number one, I work in a pub, so even though I meet a lot of men, they're usually drunk when they ask me out. Number two, because I work in a pub I'm busy most evenings and weekends, so don't have a lot of social life anyway, and number three, on the odd occasion I do go out with anyone I meet here, they're only after one thing. Besides,' she says, nodding at Dan, 'most of the single guys who come in here turn out to be losers anyway.'

'No offence taken,' says Dan.

'That's a shame,' replies Wendy.

'Ah,' I say. 'Hence the reason you're working this evening.'

'Exactly. I selflessly volunteered, so the other barmaids could spend the night with their nearest and dearest.'

'Nothing to do with the fact that they're paying you triple time, then?' suggests Dan.

'Maybe,' says Wendy. 'But at least I've got the pleasure of your company on this, the most loved-up of evenings,' she adds, dryly.

'Jane adored Valentine's Day,' I sigh. 'I used to cook her dinner, do flowers, chocolates, the works.'

'Romance the pants off her, you mean,' says Dan. 'It's just one big marketing con to sell truckloads of naff cards and vastly over-priced chocolates, all so suckers like Edward here can get his yearly shag. I'm surprised you women don't just ask for the money instead.'

'So why didn't you keep it up for the rest of the year?' asks Wendy.

'Hur hur,' laughs Dan.

She ignores him. 'The romance, and stuff, I mean.'

I shrug. 'I didn't know I had to. I thought it was a bit like hunting, you know, once I'd snared her…Well, all the hard work had been done, apart from birthdays and Valentine's…'

Wendy shakes her head. 'Edward, a relationship needs constant attention. It's a living thing, not just a habit. You've got to keep on top of it.'

'Hur hur,' laughs Dan again, until I dig him in the ribs.

'It's like owning a car,' continues Wendy. 'You can't expect it to keep going on its own. It's bound to need a few minor repairs down the years.'

'And, of course, regular servicing,' chimes in Dan, smuttily.

'And not just once a year,' says Wendy.

I look across at Dan, daring him to make a comment.

'What?' he says.

I'm starting to feel a bit guilty now, and try to explain myself. 'Valentine's Day was different. Kind of a tradition. Besides, we didn't go in for any of that romance stuff in the early days.'

'Why not?'

'Because we were students. Back then, romance was remembering someone's name in bed the next morning.'

'Sounds like my life today,' muses Dan.

Wendy rolls her eyes. 'Well, when was the last time you bought Jane flowers, for example? And please don't say "February the fourteenth last year".'

I have to think about this one. 'Er...I can't remember. Oh, hold on, yes I can. We were driving back from London one afternoon last summer and we'd stopped to fill up with petrol. The garage was selling off bouquets of roses that had reached their sell-by date, so I surprised her with some.'

Wendy shakes her head, sending her deeley-boppers into spasm. 'I'll bet you did. And you haven't "surprised" her with any since?'

'Nope. "Don't waste your money on things like this," she'd said.'

'So you just didn't buy her any. Ever again?'

I give Wendy a puzzled look. 'Well, she'd told me not to.'

Wendy sighs. 'You really haven't been listening to her, have you? When she said not to waste your money on things like that, you assumed she meant flowers in general, right?'

I nod, unaware of any other possible interpretation.

'Right.'

'Get real, Edward. She meant those particular flowers. Petrol-station flowers. And certainly not "special offer" petrol-station flowers. No girl in her right mind wants her boyfriend to stop buying her flowers. Ever.'

I'm still a little confused. 'I don't get it.'

Wendy folds her arms. 'Let me tell you how romance works. Both of you. All a woman actually wants is to feel special. It really is as simple as that. And special-offer petrol-station flowers certainly don't make us feel special. When we stop feeling that way, well…'

Wendy reaches up and presses a button on the side of her headband, causing the lights to go out in the two red flashing hearts.

I get it.

Wednesday 16th February

7.44 a.m.

THIS MORNING IS A turning point for me in my training programme. Not only am I not sick, but I don't even feel sick. I manage the stairs three times without stopping, and even though (of course) I'm knackered by the time I've finished, I actually believe that, given the right amount of rest— perhaps a day or two, I tell Sam jokingly—I could even do it once more. Sam's pleased with my progress, and to celebrate she puts me through the kind of stretching routine that would have had the Spanish inquisitors wincing and saying things like 'steady on'—in Spanish, of course.

We head back and Sam puts me through another kind of torture, this time a Swedish interval training technique called 'Fartlek'—a word I'd find funny if the training weren't so exhausting—where I have to sprint then jog alternately between the lampposts that all too frequently for my liking line the promenade. By the end, Sam's hard pressed to tell the difference between my sprinting and my jogging, and 'Fartlek' has joined 'IKEA' on my list of Swedish things I hate, but all in all I'm quite chuffed with myself. Sam is pleased with me too, although the glint in her eye seems to promise more severe exertions in the days to come.

'What was "interval" about that?' I ask her, once I've got my breath back.

'The jogging parts,' says Sam. 'Obviously.'

'When you go to the theatre, the interval is the bit where you stop and have a break. Not keep watching a slightly slower play.'

'Stop complaining,' orders Sam, 'or I'll make you do it again.'

I salute her. 'Yes, boss. Sorry, boss.'

'So, are you starting to enjoy the training yet?' she asks me, as we jog back home.

'Well, "enjoy" is pushing it a bit, but I can see that I'm making progress. And that's the important thing.'

And funnily enough, as well as feeling fitter, I feel more alert too. I'm sleeping better, though possibly because I'm so tired from a combination of the training and my early starts, not drinking, and not smoking—strangely, Dan's 'don't buy cigarettes' seems to be working. And while I really miss the cigarettes, and the beer, and of course the pizza, I still miss Jane more.

And that's what makes the difference.

Friday 18th February

8.54 a.m.

ALTHOUGH I CAN JUST about manage the training sessions, the walk to work afterwards is the thing that kills me. What's more, I'm so stiff from the workouts that I'm not nimble enough to avoid Billy any more. As a result I end up almost doubling my usual purchase of *Big Issues*.

'You'll be able to retire soon,' I tell him, as he tries to sell me my fifth copy of the week.

'Very funny,' sniffs Billy. 'Besides, why would I want to give all this up?' He gestures across the road, where a pair of seagulls are ripping a dustbin bag to shreds on the pavement.

'Come on, Billy. You must dream about the time when you can finally get off the city streets.'

He laughs. 'What, a nice little doorway in the country somewhere?'

Billy has got himself the homeless person's *de rigueur* accessory—a dog. True to form, it's one of those canines whose breed defies classification, and for whom the word 'scraggy' seems to have been coined. To cap it all, Billy's tied one of those standard issue red bandanas round its neck.

'Who's this then?' I ask.

''S'Eddie,' mumbles Billy, reaching down to give the dog a protective scratch, as if he's afraid I might suddenly try and take him.

'Eddie? I'm touched.'

'Whaddya mean?'

'Well, you know. His name.'

'What are you on about?'

'Eddie. Your dog. You've named him after me.'

Billy grins up at me mischievously. 'That's your name, is it? Edward? Big Ed?'

'Where did you get him?' I say reaching down to stroke Eddie, which provokes a growl. From Billy.

'Found him, didn't I? Scavenging in those bins over there.'

I snatch my hand away quickly, then wonder whether it was Eddie or Billy who'd been doing the scavenging.

'Well, I'm sure he'll be good company for you.'

'Yeah, but I dunno if I can afford to keep him,' says Billy, waving a *Big Issue* under my nose. 'Two mouths to feed, and all that.'

As Eddie gazes up at me with his big brown eyes, and Billy looks down at me with his bloodshot ones, I reach into my pocket for a couple of pound coins.

11.15 a.m.

Billy s not the only person to get someone new in his life. When Natasha comes bounding in mid-morning, she's got a spring in her step, and a smile on her face, two factors that make me reach the only possible conclusion: she's just had sex.

'We've got a new client,' she announces, triumphantly flinging a copy of *Computer Business* on my desk. 'Page forty-two.'

I pick the magazine up and find page forty-two as instructed. There's a feature about the latest hot-to-trot UK dot-com company, Go-Soft Technologies, complete with a picture of their chairman—the fat, balding, forty-something multimillionaire Terry Woodward.

I look at Natasha and raise one eyebrow. 'Go-Soft? Unfortunate name.'

'They make software for the travel industry, Edward,' she tuts. 'And anyway, he wasn't last night. Or this morning, come to think of it.'

I can't help but shudder. 'So, is it a big one? The campaign, I mean.'

'Oh yes.' She smiles. 'Advertising in the *Sunday Times*, no less.'

'Blimey. You must have been good.'

'What do you mean?'

'If he wants to brag about it in the *Times!*'

Over the years I've realized that, although admittedly rare, there are occasions when I can actually take the micky out of Natasha without her having a fit. The day after the signing up of a new client, i.e., the day after she's had sex, is usually one of them.

Natasha sits herself down at her desk, and I think I can detect the slightest tinge of embarrassment on her face.

'Yes, well, he's coming in later to take me out to lunch, so I'd keep those comments to yourself if I were you.'

I grin across at her, grateful for the upswing in her mood. 'Yes boss.'

12.45 p.m.

An hour or so later, the aforementioned Terry arrives. In truth, I hear him before I see him, or rather hear the roar of his Porsche's engine as he blips the throttle before double-parking it outside, leaving the hazards on in the hope Brighton's Parking Nazis won't get him. Some chance.

I peer down into the street below, getting a perfect view of the sun glinting off the top of his bald head. He's dressed expensively, in that dot-com new-money kind of way, as if he's been told to go out and buy some style. It nearly works, too, apart from the bright red tie that I'm guessing someone else has picked out for him. And I can imagine who that someone else is, especially when I catch sight of the wedding ring he's wearing.

I'm bending over by the filing cabinet when he breezes in, so he doesn't see me. Instead, he walks over to Natasha, and kisses her full on the lips.

'Last night…' he starts to say, before Natasha can stop him. 'You were…it was…I've never…'

Natasha clears her throat. 'Terry, I'd like you to meet Edward. Edward works for me,' she adds, although possibly more for my benefit than Terry's.

Terry wheels round, catches sight of me, and turns the same colour as his tie.

'Nice to meet you,' I say, walking over and shaking his hand. 'You were saying?'

'I was?'

'About last night?'

Terry turns a shade or two redder. 'Oh yes,' he says. 'Natasha's… sales pitch, I mean. She made a very firm case as to why I should use her, or rather, Staff-IT's services.'

'Really?' I say, thinking *I bet she did. And more than once, probably.*

Natasha glares at me. 'We better hurry,' she says, picking up her handbag and leading Terry towards the door. 'I've booked us a table for one o'clock.'

'Lovely,' replies Terry. 'I'll be able to brief you fully on my requirements.'

As I look at the two of them, thinking that there'll probably be more in the way of de-briefing going on, Natasha smiles sweetly at me.

'Edward. You're welcome to join us,' she says, but her tone tells me that actually, I'm not.

5.30 p.m.

I'm just packing up and getting ready to leave when I hear the Porsche again. It roars off after a few seconds, and a flushed Natasha arrives back in the office.

I look at my watch. 'Must have been a good restaurant.'

'More of a liquid lunch, actually.'

I grimace. 'Too much information. And in a Porsche? You have my admiration.'

Natasha shrugs. 'Convertible. More head room, so to speak.'

I pick up my briefcase, trying hard to get rid of the image Natasha's just conjured up in my mind.

'And will you be seeing him again? After the campaign's finished, I mean?'

'I hope so,' she says, perching on the corner of her desk. 'I like this one.'

You like them all, I think, *until the business dries up. Or you scare them back to their wives.*

'And he's married, I take it?'

Natasha sighs, and for once seems to drop her guard. 'Edward, they always are. Maybe that's why I'm attracted to them. You know, wanting something that I'm not supposed to have. Or can't have.'

'Have you tried, you know, going out with someone who isn't? Married, I mean.'

'It's not as straightforward as that. Look at me—I'm attractive, successful, financially independent, no "baggage". You'd think that men would be queuing up to go out with me. But oh no—it's me who has to do all the chasing. The younger, good-looking guys who I might fancy physically can't deal with the fact that I earn more money than them and want to enjoy it—it makes them feel insecure, apparently. The older guys who earn more money than me and are divorced, I don't fancy, because they think that their money makes them attractive, which it might do, but only to someone who doesn't have any. The other guys my age, my level, my status, if you like, are usually married, and can't, or won't, leave their wives either because of the children, or they're scared it'll cost them too much money in the divorce courts. So who does that leave for me? Very few options, I can tell you. And of those few that are available, of course every other single woman out there is competing with me for them.'

'So why do you think the Terry of this world have these affairs?'

'That's easy,' says Natasha. 'These are men who've been married to the same women for twenty years. They probably met when neither of them had much money, and he drove a boring car, and their life was pretty dull. Now he's made all this money and had all this success, he thinks he can afford a flashier model, but the truth is, he can't, because the actual costs in getting it far outweigh the benefits. The kids have left home and the guy, who's been out moving and shaking with the movers and shakers, suddenly comes home to find his wife, who's perhaps dedicated the last twenty years to bringing up the family while he's been out bringing in the big bucks, suddenly saying, right—now this is our time. Trouble is, he finds out that now that the kids have gone they've got very little in common any more.'

For a moment, despite the fact that Natasha's made my working life hell for the past decade, I almost feel sorry for her. Because the truth is that she does like them all. And they all like her. It's just that, on balance, they seem to prefer their wives.

'So what are you hoping? That you'll suddenly meet one of these software bosses who isn't married, and the two of you will be able to live happily ever after?'

Natasha shakes her head. 'No. Because chances are if they get to my age and they're not married already then either there's something wrong with them that no amount of money can compensate for, or they decide that they want a trophy wife. And sadly, trophies only look good when they're shiny and new.'

'But, at the risk of playing pot to Terry's kettle, he's not exactly the best-looking of guys.'

'Edward, are you learning nothing? It's not all about looks. He may be a bit overweight, and not have much hair, but he's funny, successful, confident, and that's what makes him attractive.'

I point to the copy of *Computer Business* on my desk, still open at page forty-two. 'And the fact that he's worth eleven million pounds doesn't make a difference?'

Natasha doesn't answer, but walks across to my desk and rests a hand on the side of my face.

'Oh, Edward. If only you were loaded,' she says, mischievously.

'What?'

'I'm kidding,' she says, noting the look of alarm on my face. 'Of course it doesn't make a difference. Well, not to me, anyway.'

'Well, in that case, is now a good time to talk about my pay rise?'

7.47 p.m.

'Why ever not?' says Dan when we get to the Jim later, the concept of turning down sex with anybody so alien to him.

'Because a) she was joking, b) she's my boss, and c) I don't think I'd get out alive.'

'I'd shag her,' says Dan. 'She sounds like a fox. And she's loaded.'

I point to the empty bar stool next to me. 'You'd shag that if you could find a hole.'

Dan shrugs. 'Fair cop. And speaking of which…'

I look over my shoulder where a blonde policewoman has just walked into the bar. She heads over towards a group of businessmen sat in the corner, asks for one of them by name, then proceeds to remove her uniform, much to the delight of his colleagues.

As she gets down to her underwear, Wendy walks over and, amid cries of derision from the party, and even louder cries from Dan, asks her to leave. The stripper shrugs, plants a kiss on the bemused birthday boy, and heads for the door, slipping her jacket back on as she does so.

Dan stares longingly at her departing backside. 'Won't be a minute,' he says, heading off in pursuit.

True to his word, he isn't even sixty seconds. 'Result!' he says, hitting 'save number' on his mobile phone.

I look at him incredulously. 'You're going to go out with a stripper?'

Dan thinks about this for a second or two. '"Go out with", no. "Stay in with" however…And speaking about staying in, it's time to do something about your flat.'

'My flat? What's wrong with my flat?'

'What, apart from the lack of furniture? You may have taken a vow of chastity, but you don't have to live like a monk.'

'But what happens when Jane comes back? What is she going to do with all her stuff?'

'That load of old junk?' Dan makes a face. 'Take it to the dump.'

'This is going to be expensive, isn't it?' I say, resignedly.

Dan attempts a bad American accent. 'You want Jane? Well, Jane costs. And right here's where you start paying.'

Saturday 19th February

11.14 a.m.

BRIGHTON TOWN CENTRE ON a Saturday morning is not my favourite place, jammed full of groups of scary teenage lads, and even scarier teenage girls. As I make my way through the melee that is Churchill Square Shopping Centre, mothers not much older than the screaming kids they push around in oversized pushchairs block my way. A couple of times they bang painfully into my ankle; when I turn around to remonstrate, their scowl suggests physical violence, and it's an encounter from which I might just come off worse. I eventually reach the peaceful sanctuary of Sofa So Good, the huge furniture store on the ground floor of the centre, where Dan is locked in conversation with one of the gorgeous female assistants.

'About time too,' he says, when he sees me.

'Sorry. Traffic was bad.'

'Never mind. Edward, this is Susie. Susie, this is Edward. He's the one I told you about. No girlfriend, no style, and more importantly, no furniture.'

Susie scrutinizes me for a moment or two. 'So this is Mr MFI?'

Dan nods. 'That's right. And he needs your professional help.'

She whistles. 'It'll be tough, but I'll see what I can do.'

I look disbelievingly at the two of them. 'I am standing within earshot, you know. Besides, what's wrong with cheap self-assembled furniture from MFI?'

'Made For Idiots,' she says, leading us through to the middle of the store. 'Where would you like to begin?'

Dan smiles at her, though to me it looks more like a leer. 'I thought we could maybe start on the sofa, and then move into the bedroom?'

As Susie blushes and giggles, I stare incredulously at Dan. 'Don't you ever switch off?'

Susie shows us various pieces of furniture, Dan nodding or shaking his head where appropriate. Whenever I try and make a comment, he shushes me quickly.

'Aren't I allowed an opinion? It is my flat, and more importantly my money, don't forget.'

Dan takes me to one side, and tells me to sit down. I settle into a calf-skin sofa so luxurious that almost immediately my leather jacket tries to mate with it.

'Think of it this way,' he says. 'If you were ill, you'd go to the doctor, right?'

'I guess.'

'And if he prescribed you some tablets, would you question him, or suggest a different type of medicine?'

'No, I suppose not.'

'Well, this is just like that. So shut your face and listen to the experts.'

Susie shows us funky tables with unpronounceable Scandinavian names, beds that look like sleeping is the last thing you'd want to do in them, and lamps that seem to be more like pieces of sculpture. After an hour or so, we've been through the whole store, and a good part of my bank balance. But to his credit, Dan has picked out some particularly nice pieces, and we arrange delivery for the following month.

'You,' Dan tells me, 'owe me lunch. And you,' he adds, turning to Susie, 'owe me dinner.'

I stand there mutely as Dan and Susie swap numbers, before we head out of the store and down into the Lanes in search of food.

'What do you fancy?' I ask Dan.

'Apart from Susie? Dunno.'

I shake my head. 'I've seen it all now. You don't even bother to ask them out any more. You just *tell* them they're going out with you. "You owe me dinner." Amazing!'

Dan doesn't hear me, as he's suddenly distracted by an attractive girl walking past in a sari.

'How about Indian?'

I shake my head. 'Is everything you do influenced by women?'

Dan doesn't even have to think about this. 'Pretty much,' he says, sheepishly.

We head back along the seafront then cut up Preston Street, Brighton's Asian-restaurant-heavy road, but can't decide between the all-you-can-eat buffet at Bombay Mick's or a more traditional curry at Aloo, Aloo. In the end, we do what we always do, and head off to the Admiral Jim.

'Afternoon, boys,' Wendy greets us with a smile, or rather, me with a smile and Dan with a scowl. 'You're later than usual today. What have you been up to?'

'Shopping. For furniture.'

'Oh,' says Wendy, as Dan orders a plate of penne carbonara, and I settle for the relatively healthier chicken salad. 'That sounds…exciting?'

As she takes our food order through to the kitchen, Dan and I go and find a table.

'Thanks for your help earlier,' I say, once we're sat down.

'Don't mention it,' replies Dan. 'That was a nicely upholstered bit of stuff back there, I thought.'

I nod. 'Yes. I particularly liked that sofa.'

Dan looks at me as if I'm daft in the head. 'No. *Susie.*'

'Ah. Of course. Are you going to go out with her?'

Dan sips his beer. 'Probably. I like shop girls. Always keen to please. "The customer is always right", and all that.'

I nod in the direction of the bar. 'Doesn't seem to apply where you and Wendy are concerned.'

'Yeah. A tougher nut to crack entirely, that one. I think she might even, you know, play for the other team.'

'Dan can't you conceive that there are actually women on this planet who don't fancy you?'

Dan looks at me strangely. 'Are you serious?'

When Wendy comes over to deposit our cutlery, I stop her.

'Wendy. Question for you.'

She eyes me suspiciously. 'Yes?'

'Well, we were talking about attraction, and Danny-boy here was telling me that most women he met fancied him.'

Wendy makes a face. 'I don't.'

'That's what I told him.'

Dan coughs. 'Yes, but that's probably because you bat for the other side.'

Wendy eyes the knife in her hand. 'Oh, I see, you're saying that because I don't fancy you, I must be a lesbian.'

'That's about the size of it,' replies Dan, nervously.

I brace myself for the violence, or Dan's wine ending up over his head, but instead, Wendy just calmly lays out Dan's knife and fork in front of him.

'You know,' she says. 'I've never had a lesbian experience. Never even so much as considered it, to be honest, and I can't say that I find other women in the slightest bit attractive. But thinking about it now, I can honestly say that yes, if it was a choice between sleeping with Dan and a spot of…'

'Carpet munching?' suggests Dan, helpfully.

'I'd probably choose the second option, in favour of the unpleasantness of Dan's sweaty, short-lived thrusting.'

'See,' says Dan, a little less sure of himself now.

'In fact,' continues Wendy, a little too loud for his liking. 'I can probably imagine what you're like in bed. No, hang on. I don't have to imagine, because my flatmate told me. Every little thing, actually. And when I say "little thing", I mean "little thing".'

As she pats him on the head before walking nonchalantly back to the bar, Dan's face falls even further.

'Uh-oh.'

'What?'

'Enemy at three o'clock.'

I look at my watch. 'What are you talking about? What's happening at three o'clock?'

'No, dummy. Don't look, but three o'clock as in over there.'

'Where?'

He nods over my shoulder, and I instinctively look round at the corner table, where two girls have just sat down. The one on the left is looking over in our direction, and making what even from a distance I can tell are unfavourable comments about one, or perhaps both, of us. Although if I had to guess, I'd say they'd probably be about Dan.

'Jesus, Edward. 'What part of "don't look" didn't you understand?'

'Who's that? Or is it both of them?'

Dan ducks down and tries to hide behind me, despite the fact that he's obviously already been spotted. 'Bloody hell, Edward. I don't think it's such a good idea, you trying to lose all this weight. There's not so much of you to hide behind now.'

'What have you done this time? Or rather, who have you done?'

'On the left. The one with the cigarette. Lynne. Met her last month at some party or other.'

'And don't tell me, you slept with her the once, and then just happened to "lose" her number?'

Dan stares at me for a second. 'Brilliant. Why didn't I think of that?' He sits up straight, smiles over towards the two girls, then makes a face of surprised recognition.

'Where are you going?' I ask, as he gets up and starts to walk over towards their table.

'Salvage operation,' he replies. 'Watch and learn.'

There's a brief, heated exchange. Thirty seconds later, he's back with his tail between his legs.

'Got any other great ideas?'

'But…'

'Well, keep them to yourself,' he hisses, before heading off to the gents.

Once Wendy brings our food across, Lynne stands up and walks slowly over from her table. She takes a long drag on her cigarette, then taps the ash all over Dan's lunch. I look at her in amazement as she repeats the process, smiles pleasantly at me, then goes back to her seat without a word.

When Dan comes bounding back from the toilet, he stares at the steaming plate of pasta in front of him.

'What's all this?'

'Er…' I look over to where Lynne is sitting, staring back at our table, daring me to tell. 'I thought you might like some black pepper.'

Dan nods, tucking his serviette into his collar. 'Good call. I'm starving.'

I watch, fascinated, as he jabs his fork into the food and mixes it round, the little black flecks of ash coating the pasta quills as he does so. He sticks a huge forkful into his mouth and chews it thoughtfully.

'Mmm. This is great. You should try some. The bacon tastes really…'

'Smoky?'

Dan nods appreciatively. 'That's the word. Help yourself.'

I shake my head, and take a mouthful of salad. 'I'll pass, thanks. Diet, and all that.'

As Dan munches away, much to Lynne's consternation, the penne doesn't drop. But I'm starting to realize something—that where women are concerned, perhaps the most important lesson I can learn from Dan is how *not* to be like him.

Tuesday 22nd February

8.19 p.m.

'WHAT'RE YOU WRITING?'

'Sam's suggested I keep a diary.'

'What—how often you masturbate? Is that part of her exercise programme too?'

'Don't be disgusting, Dan. A food diary. It'll help me keep track of my eating habits. Make sure I'm following a healthy diet. Not snacking. That sort of thing.'

On Sam's advice, I've done a sweep of my kitchen and thrown away everything 'unhealthy', or in my language, 'tasty'. Also gone is all the bread, pasta, and even my favourite chocolate Hob-Nobs, which I've replaced with some rice cakes that have all the flavour and consistency of a beer mat. I'd probably get more nourishment from biting my lip, but drastic measures are called for, particularly given what the bathroom scales are telling me.

'Oh. Right.' Dan sits there silently for a few seconds, then peers at what I'm writing. 'There's two zeds in "pizza".'

'Can't you take anything seriously?'

'Not usually, nope.'

'This all may be a big joke to you, Mister Genetically Modified, but it's serious stuff for me.'

'Sorry, mate. How is the old diet lark going?'

'Well, I'm giving Atkins a try at the moment.'

'Atkins?'

'Yup. Which means I can have bacon and eggs for breakfast.

Every day. This is a good thing, because I like bacon and eggs, and coincidentally, it's about the only thing I know how to cook.'

'And is it working?' asks Dan.

'Not yet,' I reply. 'But it's still early days. Although I'm a little worried about the potential side effects.'

'Side effects?'

'Flatulence and bad breath, apparently.'

Dan makes a face, and moves his chair away from mine. 'Mate, some days your breath is like a chemical weapon anyway. But I wouldn't worry if I were you.'

'Why ever not?'

'Well, it's not as if you're going to be getting close enough to anyone for them to notice, is it?'

Monday 28th February

6.56 a.m.

I'M LYING IN MY bed with the light off, watching the digital display on my clock radio slowly advance. When it reaches 7.00, I hit the 'snooze' button in an attempt to stop the ringing, before realizing that the noise is actually Sam at the front door.

I lie there, hoping she'll go away, but after a further thirty seconds of determined ringing I hear my front door opening—I'd forgotten she had a key—followed by the sound of footsteps walking along the hallway towards my bedroom. When she knocks on my door, I pull the duvet cover over my head in an attempt to hide. Unfortunately, despite this professional camouflage attempt, Sam still manages to find me.

'Come on, sleeping beauty,' she says, trying to tug the duvet cover from my grasp. 'Those inches won't just lose themselves, you know.'

'I'm tired. I thought we could give it a miss this morning.'

'Oh no you don't. It's for your own good.'

I hang on for dear life, but unfortunately Sam has a better grip than I do, plus, of course, she's a lot stronger. She whips the duvet cover off me, just at the very same moment that I remember I couldn't find any clean boxer shorts yesterday so decided to sleep naked. I grab the nearest thing I can find to cover my predicament, which turns out to be a bad move, as it's my clock radio, which is of course plugged into the wall, meaning I can't move.

Sam looks at me mischievously. 'Now you're stuck.'

'Go away. I'm not getting up.'

Sam reaches into her bag, and produces her Polaroid camera. 'I'll give you ten seconds.'

'You wouldn't dare!'

She pops the flash up. 'Nine, eight…'

'Okay, okay.'

'Seven, six…'

'Well at least have the decency to turn around, then.'

As Sam walks out of my bedroom, I drag myself out of bed, and pull on my workout gear. Two minutes later, I'm ready for her.

'Good boy,' she says, as I walk into the lounge. 'These are the important days—where you really don't want to do it. These are the ones that prove that you're…'

'All right, all right. Enough of the pop psychology. I'm up, aren't I?'

'Ooh! Get you! What side of the bed did you get out of this morning?'

'Well, you should bloody well know,' I reply, grumpily.

'Edward, is something the matter?'

I slump against the wall. 'It's just…What's it all for? I'm getting fitter, sure, and I can run further without feeling sick, but…'

'But what?'

'I don't seem to be losing any weight.'

Sam adopts the tone of a schoolmistress. 'Have you been getting on those scales again?'

I stare guiltily at my feet. 'Might have been.'

'How many times do I have to tell you? It's not how much you weigh. It's how you look. And more importantly, how you feel about yourself.'

'But I…'

'Come here and take your sweatshirt off.'

'What?'

'Take your sweatshirt off. I want to prove something to you.'

I reluctantly pull my top off and drop it onto the sofa. 'What?'

Sam pulls her camera out again, and snaps a quick photo.

'Now, fetch me the one we took at the start,' she orders.

I walk into the kitchen and remove it from the front of the fridge. 'Here you go.'

Sam scrutinizes the two photos, and hands them to me with a smile. 'Now, look at the two of them together.'

I hold the pictures up and peer at them, and then have to do a double take. The one of me today is starting at least to look like a shadow of my former self. They're not quite before and after—more sort of a before and halfway through—but at least they're the right way round this time.

'But, the scales…I don't understand.'

Sam smiles patiently. 'What did I tell you when we started? Ignore what the scales say. The reason you haven't lost much weight isn't because you haven't lost any fat. It's because you've put on muscle at the same time. And muscle is heavier than fat. The important thing is your body shape. And looking at these…' She takes another look at the photos. 'It looks like old cuddly Teddy is on his way out for sure.'

'But, even when I look in the mirror…'

'That's because all you see is the same thing, albeit slightly slimmer every day. You won't notice a difference until you stop and look at it like this. And imagine what someone who hasn't seen you for a while—say, for three months—will think…' Sam leaves the sentence hanging, but the implication is crystal clear.

I take the photos back from her and stare at them in disbelief. While I still have a spare tyre, at least it's more low-profile compared to the over-inflated one in the original picture. And when I look closely at my arms and shoulders, is that a bit of definition I see?

Sam leads me through to my kitchen and sticks the two photos back on the fridge door, side by side.

'There,' she says. 'Something to keep you motivated. And are your clothes *feeling* any looser?'

I peer down at the waistband of my jogging pants. There does seem to be slightly less straining going on.

'A little. But I just put that down to them having stretched.'

Sam grabs me gently by the arm, and starts to lead me outside. 'So, Edward,' she says. 'Shall we begin?'

I smile sheepishly back at her. 'Let's.'

And finally, as I follow Sam out into the morning air and down to the seafront, I feel like we're really getting started.

7.45 a.m.

I don't know if it's what I've seen, or the effect of Sam's motivational chat, but this morning is the best workout we've ever had. I manage to get further down the promenade than ever before until I feel like dying, and then even set a few personal bests in the gym. Sam starts humming the *Rocky* theme tune as I get a level up on the cross-trainer, and it's all I can do not to high-five her as I step triumphantly off the machine. She leads me over to the stretch mats, and when she tells me what we're doing next, I suddenly regret the fact that she saw me naked this morning.

'I beg your pardon?'

'I said we're going to do some ball work.'

'Ah. Ball. Singular. I thought you said…never mind.'

Sam walks over to a cupboard in the gym and produces what looks like a space-hopper, minus the horns and inane face, which she bounces back over to me like an oversized basketball.

'What on earth are we going to do with this?'

'Sit on it.'

'I only asked.'

'No, I mean, sit on top of it, and I'll show you.'

I perch on the ball and wobble unsteadily, nearly falling over backwards.

'What's the idea of this?'

'Core stability,' says Sam.

'I didn't know my core was unstable.'

Sam smiles patiently. 'Get up and I'll demonstrate.'

As I stand in front of her, she puts both hands on my shoulders and gives me a little shove. I nearly fall back onto the exercise mats.

'Ouch. What was that for?'

'Now you do the same to me. See if you can move me. In the physical sense, of course.'

This will be easy. I'm probably at least twice Sam's weight. I put my hands on her shoulders and push, at first lightly, and then I put a little more beef behind it. But when it comes to it, despite pushing as hard as I can, I can't even budge her.

Sam grins triumphantly. 'Core stability. Like anything in life, you need a solid foundation.'

'Is this another one of your training philosophies, or are you trying to lecture me about relationships again?'

'I'll let you work that one out.'

Sam directs me to sit back on the ball, and I just about manage to get my balance when she hands me a couple of five kilogram dumbbells. 'Now, shoulder press. Twenty. If you can manage them.'

'No problem.' I've been lifting nearly twice as much recently, but when I first try and press the weight, I almost topple over again. 'What the…'

Sam catches me. 'Steady, Eddie. Take it slowly.'

What I thought would be easy turns out to be exactly the opposite. I just about manage the twenty, before Sam flips me over and tells me to rest my feet on the ball in the press-up position. If the previous set was difficult, then this is nearly impossible, and I complete about five before I slump on my face on the floor.

We progress through a series of sit-ups, squats against the wall, and back raises, until I collapse on the mat from exhaustion. And yet, it feels good. I feel like I can take what Sam throws at me, and give it a proper go. What's more, I'm building a solid foundation.

And I'm starting to appreciate just how important that is.

Tuesday 1st March

7.54 p.m.

'UNIVERSAL LASER CORRECTION?'

I'm round at Dan's, leafing through a brochure he's given me on a new laser eye surgery clinic that's just opened up in Hove.

'Don't worry,' he assures me. 'It's just like going to the dentist, really.'

'Except the dentist can't blind you. Doesn't it hurt?'

'What?' says Dan. 'You've got the chance to be free of those ridiculous glasses for ever and you're worried about a little discomfort?'

'And you've had it done yourself, have you?'

'Not exactly.'

'So why should I?'

'Have you never heard the phrase "Men who wear glasses get women with fat arses"?'

'I'm not sure that's quite how it goes.'

'Anyway, what's a few days' mild discomfort compared to a life-time's freedom from being called speccy four-eyes.'

'You're the only one who calls me that. You could just stop.'

'And your vision's only going to get worse, particularly now your girlfriend's gone.'

'What do you mean?'

'You know. It makes you go blind…'

'Don't be disgusting.'

'Well, at least go for a check-up. It doesn't cost anything.'

I point to a paragraph in the brochure. 'What about the fifty-pound consultation fee?'

'Oh, yeah,' says Dan. 'Apart from that.'

Wednesday 2nd March

11.14 a.m.

I'm in the office, dialing the number for Universal Laser Correction. After one ring, a girl's voice answers.

'Hello, ULC.'

I suddenly wonder if they chose that acronym on purpose. 'Yeah, hi, I'd like to make an appointment for a consultation please.'

There's a pause while she checks in the diary. 'How about Friday?'

'Friday? As in the day after tomorrow?'

'That's right. How does ten a.m. suit you?'

With Natasha currently going through one of her nearly human phases, I think I should be able to get the morning off work. 'Sounds fine.'

'And do you wear glasses or contact lenses?'

'Glasses. Does that make a difference?'

'Yes,' she says. 'It means that if you want to go ahead with the procedure, we can do it on the same day.'

I swallow hard. 'The same day?'

'That's right. And just to let you know, we're doing our special opening offer this week. One hundred pounds off if you have both eyes done.'

I wonder for a moment who'd bother only getting one eye treated. It doesn't occur to me until later that it might be because some people go in and have one done first, and find it so painful that they can't bring themselves to go back in for the other.

'Er…Great.'

'All I'll need is your credit-card number. For the consultation fee.'

'I need to pay now? I can't pay on Friday?'

'We find it's better if patients pay up front,' she says. 'Stops them getting cold feet and not showing up.'

'That happens, does it?'

There's a pause, and then a very implausible, 'No.'

Friday 4th March

7.21 a.m.

WHEN I TELL SAM what I'm up to, she looks horrified.

'Whew. I'm not sure I could go through with that. What if it goes wrong?'

'Thanks a lot. Anyway—that's easy for you to say. Your eyes are perfect.'

'Pardon?'

'Vision. You've got perfect vision.'

'How long are you in for?'

'Out on the same day, apparently. And they say I should be OK to train on Monday.'

'Well, we'll work you extra hard today anyway,' she says, a glint in her eye. 'Just in case.'

Ten minutes later, I'm starting to regret telling her.

'So tell me, Sam,' I puff, in a vain bid to get more rest time. 'How did you get into this personal training lark?'

Sam effortlessly hoists a couple of weights up off the floor and hands them to me. I nearly drop them, they're so heavy.

'Well, I was a dancer as a kid, but then I got…'

'Too old? Too fat?'

Sam pokes me in the stomach. 'No, injured. I broke my ankle, and after that I couldn't really dance the same again. So I did an aerobics training course, worked in a gym for a while, and then this. Plus I'm a real sadist, and this seemed the only legal way to get money and torture people at the same time.'

Sam moves me on to a set of what she tells me are called 'lunges', which basically means that I hold a heavy weight in each hand, step forward onto alternate legs, and bend at the knee. After ten, I'm struggling with even holding on to the weights, let alone the fact that the burning in my thighs is almost unbearable.

'Sam, I don't quite get the theory behind this. You get me to exercise so I can hardly walk, and then you make me go on a run?'

'Ah, but that's what you're paying me for, you see. My expertise. I've spent years studying this so you don't have to. And anyway, I've got a surprise for you this morning.'

Oh *no*. Not another of Sam's surprises. 'An early finish, a taxi home, followed by a continental breakfast?'

'No, we're going to do a new kind of stretching. Passive stretching, to give it its full name.'

'Whoopee,' I say, deadpan. 'That sounds really fun. Though I do like the word "passive". That's the opposite of "active", right?'

'Sit down, and try and touch your toes.'

I do as instructed, and flop down onto the mat. Keeping my legs straight I reach forward and try and touch my toes, but only get about halfway down my shin before the pain in the back of my leg becomes too much.

'Ouch.'

'When was the last time you could do that, do you think?'

'I dunno. It's not the kind of thing I'd usually write in my diary.'

Sam kneels down behind me. 'Okay, well let me show you this. Try again, but this time, relax.'

I lean forward again, wondering how I can possibly relax given how much it hurts. But suddenly, I feel the not unpleasant sensation of Sam's chest pressed against my back, easing my torso forwards, and while it's still sore, somehow it also seems easier. What's more, I actually manage to touch my toes.

Sam holds me in that position for a few delicious seconds, then lets me up again. We move through various positions, Sam taking the time to push me carefully to greater extremes of flexibility, and by the time we've finished, I'm feeling so loose that I could probably get out of the gym by doing the limbo under the door rather than walking through it.

'There,' she says, 'that wasn't so bad, was it?'

Wasn't so bad? It's probably the first thing I've done in these sessions that I've actually enjoyed, although perhaps not for the most virtuous of reasons. I have to stop myself from asking whether we can do it again.

9.45 a.m.

I've only just got dressed when Dan arrives, ready to take me down to the laser clinic.

'Bloody hell, mate,' he says. 'You look awful.'

'Good morning to you, too.'

'Ready?'

'I'm not so sure. Maybe I've been a bit hasty…'

Dan picks up my glasses and puts them on. 'You really want to look like this for the rest of your life?' he says, pretending to bump into things around the flat. 'Fat arses, don't forget.'

I snatch them back off his face. 'All right, all right. Point taken. Let's go.'

We get into Dan's car and drive down Church Road towards the clinic; Dan presses 'play' on his stereo.

'Got some special music to get you in the mood,' he says, grinning as some old rock and roll that I don't recognize fills the car.

'Who on earth is this?'

'Ray Charles.'

'That's not funny.' I hit the 'CD Change' button, and the opening bars of Stevie Wonder's 'Superstition' boom out of the speakers. 'Don't you have any music that hasn't been recorded by blind people?'

'Just trying to make you feel better about this morning. You know, that there can be life after losing your sight.'

'Thanks, mate. Very considerate of you.'

When we get to the clinic, Dan's out of the car and marching through the front door before I've even got my seatbelt off.

'Come on,' he says. 'Chop chop. Or should that be "zap zap"?'

'What are you in such a rush for?'

Dan sticks his tongue under his lower lip. 'Duh. A clinic? Nurses?'

I follow him inside and give my name to the receptionist. She's obviously having problems with her eyes, as she can't seem to tear them away from Dan.

We sit down to wait, and after a few minutes, I watch in horror as a woman comes walking out, led by someone who I guess is her anxious husband. She's wearing bandages over both eyes, and looks even paler than me.

The nurse calls my name, and I look anxiously across at Dan, who's engrossed in a copy of *Hello!*.

'See you later, mate,' he says. 'Not that you'll be able to say the same thing.'

Monday 7th March

7.02 a.m.

WHEN I OPEN MY door to Sam this morning, she seems more than a little relieved that I can actually recognize her.

'It went okay then?'

I nod. 'What do you think?'

Sam studies me quizzically for a moment. 'You look less…'

'Nerdy?'

'Yes. Well, not that you did before. You just look a bit…fresher. And you've actually got nice eyes. If a bit bloodshot.'

'Thanks. I think.'

'So, did it hurt?'

I have to come clean. 'Only my pride. I couldn't go through with it.'

'But…Your glasses?'

'I went for contact lenses instead. When it came down to it, the thought of someone firing a laser into my eyes…'

Sam grimaces. 'Good point.'

'And then, when I met the optician who was going to do the operation, something about her wasn't quite right.'

'Which was?'

'She was wearing glasses.'

'Ah,' says Sam. 'So, how do you find the contacts?'

'Well, I normally just have to look in the little pot where I put them the previous night.'

'No, silly. I mean compared to your glasses? The convenience?'

'Well, I'll probably have to set my alarm a little earlier every morning, because now I have to retrieve each lens from where it's been bathing for the night, then pick it up and balance it precariously on the end of one finger, check it for fluff, fingerprints, and anything else likely to reduce me to a squinting, eye-watering wreck, before leaning as close into the mirror as I can, which because I don't have my glasses on, usually means I bump my forehead on it. Then it takes a supreme effort of will to try and keep my eye open while I insert the lens, all the while making sure it doesn't fall off my finger into the sink, which hopefully I've remembered to put the plug in to stop my lens falling down the plughole, and then making sure I don't blink just as I'm putting it in, therefore knocking it off my finger and either into the sink or onto the bathroom floor, from where I have to retrieve it and rinse it again before starting the whole procedure once more. If, by some miracle, I do manage to get it into my eye first time, I then have to spend the next five minutes blinking frantically, praying that I manage to get the thing centered on my eyeball. And then I have to repeat the whole procedure for the other eye. So no, to answer your question, it's not quite as simple as just picking up my glasses and putting them on.'

'Well, it's certainly an improvement,' says Sam. 'Jane's sure to notice the difference.'

'Thanks.'

And I must admit, whenever I look at myself in the mirror, I do look younger. And better. And while this is probably due to the fact that I'm not sporting a large pair of untrendy glasses any more, it could equally be due to the fact that as my eyes are watering so much, this produces the 'soft focus' effect that you used to get on old films whenever the female lead had her close-ups. Whatever, but it seems to do the trick.

Sam waves a hand in front of my face. 'Now, if you could just see your way to coming out for a run?'

We head off for our usual circuit, and I have to stop myself from continually reaching up to push my glasses back into place. When we get to the gym, Sy stares at me for a few seconds, before asking me whether I've had my hair cut differently, and that evening, it even takes Wendy a couple of minutes to work out what's changed.

Natasha, on the other hand, doesn't even notice.

Wednesday 9th March

7.56 p.m.

WE'RE SITTING AT THE bar in the Admiral Jim, and I'm reading through a leaflet that Dan has just passed me on dance classes.

'I'm not going to win her back if I can suddenly dance, am I? And what if *she* can't? I'll look a right idiot if I whisk her on to the dance floor and start to salsa on my own in front of a bemused Jane, won't I?'

Dan laughs at the image. 'All women can dance. It's genetic, like cooking and nagging and ow!' He rubs his ear where Wendy's flicked him with a beer towel. 'And besides, the men are supposed to lead the women.'

'As opposed to lead them on,' says Wendy.

I shake my head. 'You're missing the point, Dan. Jane didn't leave me because I had two left feet. She left me because she'd got tired of us, and me making like Patrick Swayze in front of her isn't going to make any difference.'

'Looking like Patrick Swayze might,' suggests Wendy, rather unhelpfully.

'And it's not really about how I look.'

Dan frowns. 'It isn't?'

'Of course not. And that's what I'm starting to realize. It's about how she feels, whether she thinks I care. And if she thinks I don't care about myself, then she certainly won't think I care about her.'

Dan whistles 'Blimey, Sigmund. You've really thought about this, haven't you?'

I nod. 'Well, what's the alternative? I teach myself ten new skills and expect to wow her with my newfound abilities? It's not what I do—it's that I think about doing it that counts.'

Dan leans in towards me. 'Speaking about learning new skills, what are you going to do about, you know, the other?'

'The other what?' asks Wendy. 'Other man?'

'Nah. The *other*. Sex.'

I sit up, flustered. 'What do you mean, "what am I going to do about it"?'

'Well, you know, you've obviously got…' He lowers his voice, though only to a stage whisper, 'a problem.'

'No, Dan, I don't have a problem. We had a problem. Me and Jane, that is.'

Wendy nods. 'Sex is all about compatibility. Not performance.'

Dan does a double-take. 'It isn't?'

'No,' she says. 'In fact, as far as women are concerned, when it comes down to it, there are only two things a man has to be in bed.'

'Really?' says Dan, fascinated.

'Enthusiastic,' says Wendy, before heading off towards the other end of the bar, 'and grateful.'

'Or deaf and blind, in your case,' Dan calls after her.

'She's right,' I say. 'The compatibility part, I mean. Whether you click in bed.'

Dan smirks. 'I would have thought "clicking" was a bad thing. Squelching, yes, but clicking, no.' He squeezes his palms together to produce a series of rather disgusting noises.

'Dan, be serious,' I say, when I'm sure Wendy's out of earshot. 'Jane stopped fancying me. That means she didn't find me sexually attractive any more. That's why she didn't want to sleep with me.'

'Or cried when she did.'

I find myself reddening at the memory. 'How many times do I have to tell you? That was just the once. And anyway, that was probably hormonal, or some other emotional thing.'

'What, like disappointment?'

'Dan, please.'

He grins. 'Tell you what. All you need to do is get a woman who you know to sleep with you. Perhaps someone you're friends with, who'll be able to give you an honest assessment of your strengths and weaknesses in the bedroom department.'

'Don't be ridiculous.'

'Let's ask Wendy.'

'Dan, steady on…'

'No, dummy. Ask her what she thinks of the idea. Not whether she'll be the one. Though come to think of it…'

'Dan. Don't you dare…' I start to say, but it's too late; Dan's already beckoning her over.

'Question for you, Wenders,' he says.

'The answer's no,' says Wendy.

'Not that question' says Dan. 'Eddie-boy and I were discussing sexy women, and I said you…'

Wendy blushes slightly at the unexpected compliment from Dan. 'That's very, er, nice of you.'

'No—I said you might know someone who might be prepared to sleep with him. From a purely objective point of view, of course. Unless you'd be interested in the, ahem, position yourself?'

'Shut up, Dan,' I tell him. 'Wendy, don't feel you have to answer that. In fact, either of those.'

'Why not?' says Dan. 'She'd be doing you a favour. Give you some pointers on your technique, and all that. And she'd only have to do it the once.'

Wendy leans against the bar. 'Dan, something you quite evidently fail to understand is that it's not all about technique.

Anyone can press the right buttons. It's pressing them in the right order that's difficult. And especially with a new partner.'

'You've been going out with the wrong men, sweetheart.'

'I'm serious,' says Wendy. 'For women, it's never that good the first time, mainly because we're too anxious to really let ourselves go. Sure, the excitement of the initial meeting can be a good thing sometimes, but it's only further along in the relationship that you start to refine your skills together, and get really good at it.'

Dan puts his drink down on the bar. 'Bollocks. Whenever I get a woman into bed, she's great. Really enthusiastic. Will do anything for me—and I mean anything. And do you know why I think that is?'

Wendy rolls her eyes. 'Please do educate us, O master.'

'Because she's trying to impress me. It's her one big chance to show me what she can do.'

'Kind of like an audition?' I suggest. 'To see if she can get the part, so to speak?'

Dan sniggers. 'Oh, she gets the part all right. And it's a repeat performance.'

Wendy nudges me. 'For one night only.'

Dan shrugs. 'So? Why do you have such a problem with that?'

'Because real women have feelings. And they're easily hurt.'

Dan shakes his head. 'So what? That's not my fault. I mean, it's not as if I'm promising them anything, is it? I don't say to them "let's go out for a drink some time" intending it to mean we're now an item. If it came up in a court of law, I think you'd find it implied only the once. Anything more is just a bonus.'

Wendy sighs with exasperation. 'Dan, women don't think like that. Quite the opposite, in fact. You treat them as if it's a test drive, one quick go round the block, and then if you don't like it, you can just walk away. But by that time they've already got their hopes up.'

'How so?'

'Because most women don't see dates as one-nighters, unless you're paying them. If a woman agrees to go out with you, it's usually because she's decided that you might be boyfriend material, and because of that, she's watching you carefully for the whole night to decide if you can fulfill that role. Whereas because you're only going out with them for the one night, you spend the whole evening trying to get them into bed.'

'So why do they all sleep with me then?'

'God knows. Perhaps they're drunk. Or desperate. Or more likely, perhaps the impression you give is that you'll only consent to seeing them again if they go to bed with you.'

'Or,' says Dan, 'perhaps they fancy me, and want sex as much as I do?'

I laugh. 'Dan, rabbits who've been fed oysters laced with Viagra don't like sex as much as you do.'

Dan folds his arms. 'All I'm saying is, it's not the Victorian times any more. Women are just as sexual as us blokes, and if they're up for it, well, who am I to deny them a basic human urge?'

'"Up for it"?' says Wendy. 'You silver-tongued devil. Tell me exactly how it is you manage to talk them into bed again?'

'I don't talk them into bed. At least not straight away. I talk them onto the sofa. Or the kitchen table.'

I grimace. I've sat on Dan's sofa. And eaten at his kitchen table, come to think of it.

Wendy sighs. 'Sorry Dan, but you're wrong. Assuming that at least some of these women are the type who only want to sleep with you because you're on television…'

'And that's a bad thing?'

'…the majority of them sleep with you because they think it's the only way to move the relationship forward.'

Dan waves a finger at Wendy. 'But who wants to go out with a woman who'll sleep with you on the first date? Ea-sy!'

I shake my head. 'Dan, have you ever heard the phrase "double standards"?'

'Tell me something,' continues Wendy. 'How do you feel the next morning, when you've got rid of them?'

Dan pretends to ponder this one. 'Well, let me see. I've had a good night out, and then I've had sex. How do I feel? Hmm. That's a tricky one.'

'Let me turn this around then. Do you know how my flatmate felt the morning after?'

Dan shrugs again. 'Tired but happy, hopefully.'

'I mean, when you didn't call her? Like you promised you would.'

Dan shifts uncomfortably on his stool. 'Part of a growing number?'

'And what are you going to do when you've slept with all the women in Brighton?'

'Move, probably,' he says, nudging me, and I can't help but smile. Wendy, however, fails to see the funny side.

'Don't you care about their feelings at all?' she asks, indignantly.

'Jesus, Wendy. If ever there was someone in need of a damn good shag it's you. Lighten up a little, please. It's only sex.'

'It's only sex to you. It's something more to us women. And it's obviously something more to Edward. Have you got no other goals in life apart from sleeping with as many women as possible?'

Dan thinks about this for a moment. 'Well, there's world peace, obviously. And I'd like to cure poverty. My own, that is.'

Wendy stares at Dan in disbelief. 'I'm wasting my time here, aren't I? You just don't realize the damage you're doing.'

'Wendy,' he says, picking up his wine glass and taking a sip, 'all I am doing, if you'll excuse my language, is fucking them.'

'No, Dan,' she replies, before heading off in disgust to collect some glasses. 'You're fucking with them. There's a big difference.'

Dan watches her go, then turns and peers accusingly at me,

even though I've been staring quietly into my glass for the last few exchanges.

'Don't tell me you agree with her?'

I look up, awkwardly. 'Well, she maybe has the tiniest of points. I mean, you do seem to have rather a one-track mind.'

Dan puts his drink down on the bar, and switches into master-and-pupil mode. 'Tell me something, Edward. What is the fundamental difference between men and women?'

I look at him strangely. 'Well, there's the—' I make the international breasts sign with my hands—'physical characteristics, obviously.'

'Nope.'

'The fact that only women can bear children?'

'Wrong again.'

'Opposable thumbs? No, hang on, that's monkeys. Er...'

Dan sighs loudly. 'You have so much to learn, my child. I'm talking about the mating ritual. When they go out for the evening, for example.'

'They spend hours getting ready and then end up wearing the first outfit they tried on?'

'Nope. Although that is true. The fundamental difference between men and women is when women go out for the evening, they absolutely know they're guaranteed sex if they want it. Most men, however, are totally reliant on the good grace and agreement of the female of the species for that particular outlet of pleasure.'

'Most men?'

'That's what I'm trying to tell you. I'm not most men,' he says, without a trace of arrogance. 'And if you'd been given a gift like this, you wouldn't want to chuck it away without utilizing it as much as possible.'

'So you're saying that the reason you behave like a tart...'

'...is the same reason that dogs lick their balls. Because they...?'

I know this one. 'Can.'

'Exactly.' Dan looks at me mournfully. 'Do you think I *enjoy* this bachelor lifestyle? A new woman every weekend? Trawling the bars and clubs to find someone to keep me warm at night?'

I don't even need to think about my answer. 'Yes. I think you do, actually.'

Dan grins at me. 'True. But then, who wouldn't?'

'I wouldn't, Dan. I like being in a relationship. I like the companionship, the sameness of it all. I thought I was done with all this "battle of the sexes" stuff, which, incidentally, I'm beginning to realize isn't a fair fight.'

'It's not even a fight for me,' says Dan. 'Just a standoff, until the other side lets down their guard. But I'm a realist,' he says, pointing to his face. 'This isn't going to last for ever. I'm like an athlete. I've only got a few years in my prime before I'm going to have to hang up my boots, and until that day comes, I'm going to bloody well have some fun.'

'Even if it's at the expense of other people's feelings?' I say. 'According to Wendy.'

Dan puts his head in his hands. 'How on earth did we get from flipping dance classes to pick on Dan time?'

'But don't you worry that you'll be leaving it all too late. What if once you've found out that you've lost this "gift" you're not able to attract the sort of woman that you fancy?'

'Well, I suppose I'll just have to find a rich older woman who'll be so grateful to have me that she'll happily compensate me for my having to drive down the wrinkly highway. And anyway, this isn't about me, remember. It's about you. And your "problem".'

'Dan, for the last time. I don't have a problem.'

'You're sure? Don't want to get it independently verified?' he says, nodding at Wendy, who's slamming glasses noisily into the glass washer behind the bar. 'Maybe learn a few new tricks?'

'No!'

Dan sips his drink thoughtfully for a few moments. 'You could always go to, you know, a "professional".'

I can't believe what I'm hearing. 'Dan, forgetting for a moment the fact that it is in fact illegal, and I don't actually want to go to prison, are you seriously suggesting that I pay to sleep with a prostitute so she can give me a few pointers on my between-the-sheets technique?'

He shrugs. 'Why not? You're paying that Sam girl to get you fit—why is this any different? All you're doing is shelling out for a professional service, so to speak.'

'Dan, how many times do I have to tell you, I'm not going to be unfaithful to Jane.'

'Going to a prostitute isn't being unfaithful.'

'How on earth do you work that out?'

'Like I say, because you're paying for a service. There's no emotion involved.'

'Rubbish.'

Dan sighs. 'Okay. Say, for example, that Jane makes really nice cakes. Then one day, you find that a friend of hers makes cakes too. Unbeknown to Jane, her friend gives you one of her cakes and you eat it. And you like it. And you start wanting her cakes more than Jane's, despite Jane's cakes still being available, maybe sneaking off and eating them without Jane knowing.'

'That's being unfaithful.'

'Exactly. But, say Jane's gone away for a while, and you haven't had a cake for ages, so you go to the supermarket and buy a cake to eat. It's just a cake, someone else you don't know has made it, and you don't plan to go back and keep buying cakes from the super-market. In fact, once Jane comes back, you'll be quite happy to eat Jane's cakes again. Is that still being unfaithful?'

I stare at him. 'Where do you get this stuff from?'

Dan grins. 'I make most of it up.'

'And it shows.'

'But seriously,' he continues, 'it wouldn't hurt for you to think of a way to liven things up a bit in the bedroom. You know, introduce something new. Before she introduces someone new.'

'Such as?'

'Well, did the two of you ever talk about your fantasies? Dressing up, and the like?'

'I'm a bit straighter than that. I like normal sex. And I think Jane's the same.'

'Did you ever ask her?'

'Not in so many words. But she never intimated that she might like to do anything slightly…'

'Risqué?'

'Exactly. Unlike you, it doesn't have to be pervy for most people to enjoy it.'

Dan looks a little offended. 'I'm not being pervy. It's just that I like a bit of variety.'

'Dan, you sleep with a different woman every time. You can't get much more varied than that.'

'Exactly my point. You don't. So I can't believe that after ten years there's nothing you'd like to try.'

'Well there isn't.'

'No?'

'No.'

'You're sure?'

'Positive.'

'Honestly?'

'Yes, honestly.'

Dan takes a mouthful of Chardonnay, then looks at me over the top of his glass.

'Nothing at all?'

'Okay. There is maybe one thing.'

He raises one eyebrow. 'Which is?'

'Something I saw in a porn film once. One of your porn films, actually.'

'Oh yes?'

I check again that Wendy's not within earshot, but lower my voice anyway.

'I'd like to have sex with two women.'

Dan looks confused. 'Do you mean, ever? Or at the same time?'

'At the same time, of course.'

'Well, in that case, you better think about what I've said.'

'What on earth for?'

Dan looks at me earnestly. 'Because if you do manage to win Jane back, and it's for keeps, then you may not get to achieve either of those things.'

Thursday 10th March

6.41 p.m.

A WEEK OR SO before I'm due to receive all my new furniture, there's a ring on my doorbell. It's Dan, and he's not alone.

'Present for you,' he says, leading a woman in through my front door. She must be about forty, although she's dressed like one of the teenagers that hang around Churchill Square. 'Thought you could benefit from her experience.'

'Dan,' I whisper, leaping to the wrong conclusion as usual. 'I've already told you I'm not interested in, you know, paying for it.'

'No, dummy. This is Alexis. She's a designer. From *House Tricks.*'

'*House Tricks?*'

'Fine, thanks for asking.'

As Dan dissolves into fits of laughter, Alexis wears the expression of someone who's heard that particular joke a thousand times. And didn't find it funny the first time.

'Ah. Sorry Alexis.'

Dan puts an arm round Alexis' shoulders and gives her a squeeze. 'She's here to give your flat the once over. As a favour to me.'

As I show them through to the front room, and Alexis starts to look around, I can just imagine what Dan's promised her in return.

'When did you last decorate this place?' she asks me, obviously struggling to hide her distaste.

'Er, it was like this when I bought it.'

Alexis looks horrified. 'Gosh. How some people live. When was that? Recently?'

'Fairly,' I lie.

Dan smirks to himself. 'If you can call nine years ago "recently",' he whispers.

Alexis rolls her eyes. 'Incredible. Just look at the colour scheme. And those *curtains*.' She shudders, as if she's just discovered a rotting corpse beneath the window.

As I dig Dan in the ribs, Alexis walks around the flat, simultaneously making notes in a green leather Filofax and tutting as she goes. When she comes back to us, she's obviously not happy.

'Are you sure we can't use this?'

Dan shakes his head. 'Best not.'

'Not even for the Christmas out-takes reel?'

I clear my throat. 'What's the verdict?'

Alexis takes a deep breath. 'Well, structurally, it looks fine. And the layout's not bad. But the carpets? Very seventies. The colour scheme? Very eighties. The curtains? Very nineties. You need to make it more…'

'Noughtie?' suggests Dan.

'And now's the time to do it,' continues Alexis. 'When you've got no furniture.'

'So, what's the quick fix?' I ask, meaning 'What's the cheap fix?'

Alexis consults her Filofax. 'Bin the carpets, sand and seal the floorboards. Strip the walls and repaint neutrally. Chuck the curtains, replace with blinds and, as the kids say, sorted.'

'And how long will that take?'

'You? Ages. The *House Tricks* team? One weekend. We can rush it through and pretend it's a rehearsal. But it'll cost you.'

Fortunately she's addressed this last comment to Dan, who puts his arm back around her shoulders, and walks her out through the door.

Friday 11th March

7.07 a.m.

I'M IN MY FLAT, waiting for Sam, who's uncharacteristically late this morning, when my phone rings.

'Hello?'

I hardly recognize the gruff voice on the other end of the line.

'It's me,' croaks Sam. 'I'm ill.'

I don't know what to make of this news. On the one hand, it's great, because I might get the morning off. On the other hand, with just over a month to go, I can't afford to miss any sessions.

'So…you're not coming?'

'No, Edward. Not this morning,' she says, hoarsely.

'But…I'm all dressed and ready.' Sometimes I sound like a five year old.

'Well, you'll just have to go on your own.'

On my *own*? This wasn't part of the deal. 'Well, what should I do?'

Sam clears her throat, which does sound rather sore. 'Just the usual. Twenty minutes warm-up jog along the seafront, followed by two circuits round the gym. Sy will help you if you get stuck.'

Oh no. Sy? I think briefly about going back to bed, but reason that as long as I'm up I might as well train.

'Okay. I'll give it a go. Will you be all right?'

'I'll be fine,' she says, sounding anything but.

7.31 a.m.

It feels funny, being out running on my own. I miss having Sam there to encourage and cajole me, I miss the way she knows just how to keep me working hard, and what's more, I miss the sight of her in her tight tracksuit bottoms.

I manage the usual run to the pier and back fairly easily, but can't say I enjoy it in the slightest. It occurs to me to bypass the gym and head straight home, mainly because I'm scared of Sy, but I'm worried that Sam will find out if I do, and I'm more scared of that.

When I walk in through reception, Sy smiles up at me from the desk; a smile which quickly fades when he sees that Sam's not there.

'On your own today, Big Ed?'

God I hate him. 'Afraid so. Sam's not well today. She said you'd help me if I got stuck.'

Almost immediately, I regret saying those words, as a mischievous grin crosses Sy's face.

'Come on then,' he says, stripping off his sweatshirt to reveal the smallest of vest tops over a perfectly toned, immaculately tanned, but somewhat acned physique. 'We'll train together.'

And so begins my worst training session ever. Sy spends the next half an hour systematically trying to humiliate me, intent on showing me just how fabulously strong and fit he is, rather than helping me through my own personal programme. Where Sam would normally be motivating, Sy's whole approach seems to be one of belittlement. I find myself called a 'wuss' when I can't lift the weights that Sy seems to throw effortlessly around; I'm a 'big girl's blouse' when I can't match his total on the stepper; and even a 'fat poof' when I have to sit down after an unusually heavy set of squats.

By the time I get home, I feel like crap, not just because Sy's managed to completely knacker me out, but also because he's managed to make me think that I'm a complete failure. There's only one thing for it if I don't want to go through this again. A quick trip to the supermarket, and then the chemists, and I'm ready.

9.15 a.m.

When I ring her front doorbell, I'm greeted by the sound of barking, before Sam comes to the door, wrapped in her duvet.

'Edward?' She looks a little surprised, especially when I push past her and make my way into her kitchen. 'What are you doing here?'

I hold up my carrier bag. 'Lemsip. Fresh orange juice. Vitamin C tablets. Soup. I thought you might need some looking after.'

She stares at me in amazement. 'I didn't know you cared.'

'Well, the quicker you're back on your feet, the quicker we're back on track.' Sam obviously thinks I'm joking, but I don't have the heart to tell her I'm serious.

I lean down awkwardly to put the juice in the fridge, still tender after my morning session.

Sam looks at me strangely. 'Has Sy been saying something?'

I wince again as I stand up straight. 'It's not so much what he said…'

Sam shakes her head. 'He really is a complete git. I don't know what I ever saw in him.'

'Why *did* you go out with him?'

Sam thinks about this for a moment. 'I suppose he just wore me down, really. Every time I saw him he'd ask, and eventually I decided the easiest way to stop him from asking would be to actually go out with him. Little did I know how in love he was.'

'With you?'

'With himself.'

'I should introduce him to Dan.'

I make Sam a Lemsip, and sit with her while she drinks it. By now, the barking has become a little more frenzied, accompanied by a scratching from the door to the back garden. I look questioningly at where the noise is coming from.

'That's just the dog,' says Sam.

'Really? A dog? That barking sound?'

'No need to be sarcastic.' She nods towards the back door. 'You can let him in if you like. He doesn't bite. Well, he's never bitten me, anyway.'

I open the kitchen door, and a whirling ball of black and white fur comes barrelling in, leaping up on Sam before jumping up on me, catching me rather painfully in the testicles.

'Oliver,' orders Sam. 'Down.'

'Oliver? I didn't know you were a fan of Laurel and Hardy?'

Sam shakes her head. 'No—it's just that he's a collie.'

'So—Ollie the collie?' At the mention of his name, Ollie jumps up on me again, but I manage to fend him off before he can do any more damage.

'Sorry,' says Sam. 'He's just a bit excitable.'

'That's okay,' I say, scratching Ollie behind one ear. 'I love dogs. Jane would never let me have one in the flat.'

Sam looks at me strangely. 'I thought it was *your* flat?'

Ollie picks that moment to bolt back into the garden, returning a second or two later chased by a smaller black and white ball of fur.

'And that's my cat,' says Sam. 'Obviously.'

'Strange name for a cat?'

Sam looks puzzled for a moment. 'What—Felix?'

'Never mind.'

'Sorry,' says Sam, again. 'I'm not quite with it this morning.'

'They could be related,' I say, looking at the two animals, who are currently chasing each other round the furniture.

'How do you mean?'

'Both black and white.'

'I know,' says Sam. 'But at least their licences were cheaper.'

'Than what?'

'Colour.'

Tuesday 15th March

11.31 a.m.

THE OFFICE PHONE GOES only once this morning. It's Natasha.

'Hi, Edward. Any messages?'

'Hold on.' I go through the usual pretence of searching my desk for yellow Post-its. 'Nope.'

'Okay,' she says, sounding a little tetchy. 'I'm on my way in.'

Natasha lives in one of those ostentatious mansions on the main approach road to Hove. It's less than two miles from the office, but it normally takes her a good hour between the 'I'm on my way in' call and actually walking in through the door. That's not because of the distance, or even the traffic, but mainly because I've learned over the years that Natasha's 'I'm on my way in' actually means 'I've just got up and got rid of whoever was spending the night,' or even 'I've just got home.' I therefore know that I've got at least sixty minutes while she has some breakfast, puts on whatever designer creation shows off her breasts to the maximum effect, and shouts at her cleaner/gardener/pool man, before pointing her Mercedes in the direction of the office.

When Natasha eventually arrives, it's clear she's in a bad mood again. She seems to think the fact that she hasn't got any messages is actually my fault, rather than simply that no one wants to speak to her, and decides to take this out on me. If she was a boy she'd have been the class bully and, thinking about it, I'm not sure that she wasn't anyway. Today, her line of attack is the Go-Soft campaign, and she's on at me before she's even got her coat off.

'Have you spoken to them yet about the CVs we sent through?'

'No, I—'

'Why not?'

'I was just about to explain. Because on Friday you said to hold on until—'

'And what about going through the database to find some back-up candidates just in case?'

'But normally we wouldn't do that until they've interviewed our first pass—'

'Well, they're not going to be doing that unless you call them, are they?'

This typically goes on for at least five minutes, each of Natasha's questions rising in volume and pitch until she's practically screaming at me. As usual, I try and ride out the onslaught until something distracts her, usually I hope it will be a coronary. This time, mercifully, and just before she gets to full volume, the phone rings. When I pick it up with more than a little relief, a man's voice asks to speak to Natasha.

'Who's calling please?'

'Terry.'

Ah. This could mean a complete change in Natasha's mood. Either she'll switch into sweetness and light mode or, more likely if Terry is calling to cancel an assignation, she'll go completely nuclear and things will be thrown around the office, and possibly at me.

I press 'hold', and announce this welcome diversion to Natasha, who gestures angrily towards her desk, then transfer the call to her phone. As she turns her back to me, I hear her spit the words 'This had better be good' into the receiver.

Now, more than ever, I could murder a cigarette—otherwise I might just murder Natasha. I pick up my jacket and hurriedly make my escape, annoyed that she treats me like this, but even more angry that I let her. Jane used to tell me I should tell Natasha where to stick her job, and go and work for someone else, or even set up on my own. And you know, after some of Natasha's more unreasonable onslaughts, I'd threaten to leave, and even get as far as writing my resignation letter. But then the next day it would be a completely different Natasha in the office, all friendly, buying me coffee, telling me how she couldn't run the company without me, and I'd tear it up. *I'm a bigger person that this*, I'd think. *I can handle her outbursts every now and again.*

I'd say that it's because of professional pride that I stay, and that I don't want to give up on a job I love, but really, it's the money. That's why I put up with the shouting—because Natasha pays me so well. I'd like to think she does it to reward me for my selfless dedication to the company, but in reality, I think it's the only way she feels she can stop me from leaving. And so far, it's worked.

I take the stairs down and walk out into the street, at a bit of a loss. I haven't yet figured out what my alternative to the cigarette break should be now that I've stopped smoking, and I feel silly just standing in the street outside, so instead I go and peer longingly through the window of the Cookie Shop round the corner, until the staff give me funny looks from inside. It's still too early to go back into the office—Natasha normally takes about fifteen minutes to defuse herself—so instead I take a walk around the block where, of course, I bump into Billy, Eddie sitting devotedly by his feet, gnawing on a bone. It's a cold day, and Eddie's wrapped in a blanket, well insulated against the chilly sea breeze. So is Billy, judging by the pile of empty Special Brew cans by his feet.

As I stand there, waiting for Billy to make the usual big show of rooting around in his pockets for my change, a question suddenly occurs to me.

'Billy, can I ask you something?'

He eyes me suspiciously. 'S'pose.'

'Where did it all go wrong?'

Billy thinks for a moment. 'Well, if you ask me, probably when you stopped caring about how you looked...'

'No, not with me and Jane. With you, I mean.'

Billy looks at me strangely. 'Whaddya mean by "wrong"?'

I indicate his bags, and the cardboard sheeting behind him in the doorway. 'All this. The homelessness. The drinking.'

For a minute, I think he's going to get angry. Instead, he reaches down and pats Eddie affectionately.

'Edward, you've failed to realize something. For a lot of us, this isn't because it went "wrong". There's the odd day when I want what you've got—well, not what *you've* got, exactly—but when I think it might be nice to have a home, a family, money, a proper job. But then I think about the life you lot all follow. Cooped up in a bleedin' office, doing the same thing all day every day, going home to your boring existences where all you do is collapse in front of the telly every night because you're too knackered to talk to each other, or stuck in a crap relationship, always arguing, worried about the future. Well, I wouldn't swap this for that, I can tell you. I've got my freedom, I'm out in the fresh air,' he clears his throat noisily. 'I've got my 'ealth. And, quite frankly, from where I'm standing, there's a lot of people worse off than me.'

When I get back to the office ten minutes later, Natasha is sitting at her desk, smiling to herself. I'm guessing either that the phone call has gone well, or she's dreaming up new ways to cause Terry pain.

And as I sit and stare at my computer screen, I can't stop thinking about what Billy's said. I'd always thought that he'd been forced into what he's doing—a cycle of drink and despair finally pushing him into a life on the streets. But the fact that he's *chosen* to live this way...

From my point of view, I can't work out what on earth he must have been running away from to live like he does now, but one thing I can respect. It's his decision.

6.04 p.m.

By early evening I've had enough, and pack up ready to leave. Natasha has been calmer all afternoon since the Terry call, and seems fairly ensconced at her desk. She tells me she's doing a late interview, so I might as well leave her to lock up.

I get most of the way home before I realize that I've forgotten my keys. Normally Jane would be there to let me in, but of course this isn't 'normally' any more. I think about calling Natasha to check that she's still there, but if she's doing a late interview then she won't appreciate the interruption. Muttering obscenities under my breath, I turn round and walk briskly back to the office.

I get there by half past, and breathe a sigh of relief; the lights are all still on. The real reason for Natasha's continued presence in the office also becomes clear—Terry's Porsche is double parked outside, a parking ticket flapping underneath the windscreen wiper. Late interview? Yeah, right.

I bypass the lift; again, ever mindful of my instructions from Sam, and jog up the stairs to the third floor. By the time I reach my office, I'm a little out of breath, but it's nothing compared to the panting sounds I can hear coming from inside. *Oh no*. Terry and Natasha are *shagging*. I just hope it's not on my desk.

At least I think they're shagging, but after a few moments I begin to wonder whether he's murdering her, such are the screams that are coming out of Natasha's mouth.

I don't know what to do. I can't go home without my keys, and I obviously can't walk in and get them right now. Equally, I can't go and wait in the pub round the corner, because if I mistime it and come back later after Natasha's gone, I won't be able to get back into the office to get them. There's nothing for it—I'll just have to wait until they've finished. As unpleasant as the prospect is, I sit myself down quietly a few yards along the corridor, just far enough to be able to detect when the coast is clear.

6.44 p.m.

I'm marvelling at both Terry's stamina and Natasha's vocal ability, although I pity her poor neighbours, when finally, miraculously, the proceedings seem to come to an end, and the office falls silent. Silent, that is, until my mobile rings, loudly, from where it's sitting in my jacket pocket, from where I'm sitting near the office door. It's my new ring tone—Queen's 'Don't Stop Me Now'—that I'd downloaded the other day, and had proudly demonstrated to Natasha this afternoon.

I leap up and fumble for it, hitting the 'off' button just as I notice it's Dan calling. There's a pause, and then:

'Edward?'

Natasha calls my name out from inside the office, though admittedly in a different way to how she'd been calling Terry's name a few moments earlier.

I clear my throat loudly and knock on the door. 'Er, yes. Hi. I forgot my keys. I've just come back, *this second*, to get them.'

As soon as I say this, I realize how lame my excuse sounds. If I had just come back this second, then I wouldn't obviously have heard what was going on, and certainly wouldn't have felt the need to knock on my own office door.

'Just a minute,' calls Natasha. There's a rustling of clothing, some frantic whispered discussion, and much scraping of chairs, before I hear her voice again.

'Come in.'

When I push the door open slowly, dreading what I'm going to see, Natasha is, to her credit, fully dressed and standing by the window, albeit slightly flushed. I nod hello to Terry, who's sitting at Natasha's desk—fortunately he makes no movement to stand up when I walk in, especially since I can see his trousers draped over the photocopier.

'Edward,' says Natasha. 'We were…'

'Yes,' agrees Terry. 'I was…'

'Fine,' I say. 'I'll just…'

I head over to my desk and pick up my keys, which are sitting in my in-tray, then get out of there as fast as I can.

8.03 p.m.

I'm round at Dan's, telling him the story over a cup of tea.

'I like a noisy woman,' he says, appreciatively.

'Hmm. Not that noisy, surely? I thought she was dying.'

Dan licks his lips. 'Louder the better, as far as I'm concerned. I once went out with a girl who screamed the place down. Took her to my parents for the weekend and was worried she'd wake the whole household. You should have seen the look on her face the next morning when my mum asked her if she'd "got off all right" the previous night.'

'But it's not just about the volume, surely? I mean, Jane wasn't particularly, you know, vocal, in bed.'

'What, apart from the sobbing?'

'If you mention that once more…'

'Sorry. You were saying?'

'Just that she wasn't, you know…'

'A screamer?'

'But I know she always enjoyed it.'

Dan arches one eyebrow. 'You're sure about that, are you?'

'Yes. Of course. And can we please not go down this line of questioning again.'

Dan ignores me. 'And it was good for you too? Despite her lack of appreciation, so to speak?'

'What are you going on about?'

Dan stands up, and opens the cupboard beneath his enormous flat-screen television to reveal his DVD collection.

'Let me show you what I mean.'

'Hold on. You haven't been filming your conquests, have you?' The thought of watching Dan having sex, especially on wide-screen and with surround sound, doesn't strike me as my preferred choice of Tuesday evening viewing. Or any evening viewing, come to think of it.

'Nah.' He produces a selection of DVDs. 'Pick one.'

They're all action movies: *Heat*, *The Matrix*, *Terminator 3*. I choose *Heat* and Dan sticks it into the DVD player.

'Watch this.'

He skips through to the shoot-out scene, presses 'play', then cranks the volume up. As Robert De Niro and Val Kilmer get shot at by half of the Los Angeles Police Department, I have to cover my ears.

We watch for a minute or two, until Dan presses 'pause'.

'Now, what you've just seen is widely regarded as one of the best action sequences in movie history, yes?'

I have to agree. 'Yup.'

'Okay, let's try it again.'

Dan hits 'back' followed by 'play', and the shooting starts again, but after a few seconds, he hits the 'mute' button. As bullets smash silently through car doors, and windscreens shatter without a sound, he turns to face me.

'What do you think now?'

'Well, it's…I mean, it's not the same, is it?'

'Not as good?'

'What are you trying to prove?'

Dan switches the TV off with the remote, and ejects the film. 'Face it, Edward, however good the action is, if the soundtrack isn't there, it's just not quite as enjoyable.'

Saturday 19th March

12.10 p.m.

WE'RE OUTSIDE MY FLAT, where Dan is staring disparagingly at my car.

'Picture the scene,' he says. 'Imagine you've just met Jane, and by some miracle, you get her to agree to go out with you. You arrange to pick her up from her house the evening of the date, and then you turn up in this old piece of junk.' He kicks one of the Volvo's tyres, then leans down to wipe the dirt off his shoe. 'Shame she didn't do you a favour and take the car as well.'

It is a bit of a wreck; the aerial's mangled from where I took it for its yearly car wash and forgot to retract it beforehand, there's a large scratch along the passenger side where one of Brighton's youth decided to run a key down it, two of the wheel trims are missing, and there's a bollard-shaped dent in the rear bumper thanks to Jane's parking 'skills'. She'd done well to dent a Volvo.

'So what if it's a bit old?' I put an affectionate hand on the Volvo's wing, dislodging a few more rust flakes in the process. 'Classic cars are cool.'

'You're right' says Dan. 'Classic cars are. Clapped out ones aren't. Tell me again, what on earth made you buy a Volvo?'

'I didn't buy it, if you remember. It was my mother's. She gave it to me when she bought her new Micra.'

'Aargh. Even worse. You're driving your mother's old car.'

'What's wrong with that?'

Dan looks at me incredulously. 'Well, apart from the obvious, you're driving a car that a sixty-year-old woman rejected. In favour of a Nissan Micra.'

We walk in silence to the pub, where I'm still reluctant to concede defeat.

'Stop sulking,' says Dan, as we head in through the door. 'It's true. Women notice this kind of thing. They're impressed, even.'

'Rubbish.'

'Okay. Let's get an independent opinion.' Dan beckons Wendy across. 'Wendy, you're a woman. You'll do.'

Wendy makes a face. 'Is that the best chat-up line you can come up with?'

'In your dreams, sweetheart.'

'My nightmares, you mean.'

I hold up my hand to stop this escalating. 'Wendy, we were just talking about cars.'

Wendy pretends to nod off. 'Sorry, what was that?'

'No, seriously. About the kind of car I drive, and what it says about me.'

Wendy leans on the bar next to me. 'Go on then. What sort of car do you drive, Edward?'

'It's a Volvo.'

'A Volvo? What sort of Volvo?' she asks.

'It's an estate.'

Dan laughs. 'You're telling me. Rusty piece of junk.'

'Shut up, Dan. A Volvo estate, Wendy. What does that say to you?'

'Ah,' says Wendy, pouring our drinks. 'Safe, practical...'

'Boring?' suggests Dan.

Wendy frowns. 'No, not boring, exactly. Just not very...'

'Exciting?' interrupts Dan.

'Will you stop trying to put words into her mouth?'

Wendy turns back to me. 'Sorry, Edward. But he's right. It doesn't sound like the most exciting of cars.'

Dan clears his throat. 'I drive a BMW, by the way.'

Wendy considers this for a moment. 'Wanker.'

Dan looks hurt. 'Just because I drive a BMW?'

'No, just generally.'

'It's a Z4. Sports.'

'Oh,' says Wendy, pretending to be impressed for a moment. 'You have got a small willy, then.'

I laugh. 'It's quite nice, actually.'

Wendy frowns. 'Dan's willy?'

I blush. 'His car. It's a convertible.'

Wendy smirks. 'Oh, sorry. Small *and* circumcised.'

Dan bristles. 'Okay smartarse. What kind of car do you drive?'

Wendy puts on a girly voice and sticks her finger in the corner of her mouth. 'A white one,' she answers, before scampering off to serve another customer.

As we take our drinks and go and sit by the window, Dan seems determined not to let it drop.

'Anyway,' he says. 'What on earth do you need an estate car for? When do you ever need to carry anything large?'

'Apart from your ego? Well, now, for example. New furniture.'

'Which you're getting delivered,' says Dan. 'And even if that were the case, that's just like one occasion every few years. Whenever you get dumped. Which, thinking about it, might be fairly often. But what about the rest of the time, when it's just you in the car?'

'And Jane.'

'Sorry,' replies Dan, patronizingly. 'Just you and Jane. But you still don't need an estate car. Volvo or not.'

'Well what should I get then? I can hardly afford one like yours.'

Dan ponders this for a moment while he stares out of the window. 'You want something a bit classy. A car that says: "I could have bought any car I wanted, but I chose this." Not too ostentatious, or over the top. A city car. Something that suggests you're a man of the moment. Trendy. A man about town. Something…' Dan *points* out into the road, as a new Mini Cooper flashes past, 'like that!'

'But aren't they expensive?'

'What are you saving up for?' asks Dan. 'Your wedding?'

'Ouch. But…A Mini?'

Dan sighs, and lowers his voice. 'Okay. To use Wendy's example, what would a Ferrari say about you?'

'Small, you know, thingy.'

'Precisely. So if you're working on reverse psychology?'

'Aha.'

'Exactly.'

I sip my water thoughtfully. 'How much are they?'

'New? Around sixteen grand, give or take an accessory or two.'

'Sixteen thousand pounds? But that seems rather expensive.'

'Expense is a relative term, Edward. Compared to your old banger, yes they are. Compared to my car, no they aren't. And the question isn't really "can you afford it?" Its more a case of "can you afford not to?"'

'It just seems like rather a lot of money to waste on a car. And besides, I've got better things to spend it on.'

'Like what? You've hardly got a huge mortgage, your idea of a holiday is to not go in to work, you've not, as far as I know, got an expensive drug habit…Now I think of it, you must be loaded.'

'Well, not loaded, exactly.'

'Come on,' says Dan. 'How much cash have you got?'

I do a quick tot up in my head. 'About fifty, give or take a few thousand.'

Dan's eyes widen. 'Fifty? Grand? As in "pounds"?'

'No, drachma, Dan. Of course pounds.'

'Where on earth did you get all that?'

'Dan, there's a concept you probably haven't heard of before. It's called "saving". That's when you put any extra money you earn into the bank and don't spend it on'—I wave my hand at him—'expensive cars, for example. Or designer watches. Or naff clothes with Italian men's names embroidered on the front.'

Dan whistles. 'Fifty grand. Did Jane know about this?'

I shrug. 'I don't know. We always kept separate bank accounts. I paid for my stuff, she paid for hers. There's no reason that she would have.'

'She might not have left so quickly if she did.'

'Bloody cheek. Women aren't attracted by money.'

'Sure,' he mumbles. 'And mice don't like cheese either.'

'What?'

'Mate, there's no such thing as a rich single guy. And I'm not saying women are attracted to money per se. It's more that the fact you *have* money generally means you're successful. And success is attractive to women.'

'So what am I supposed to do? Carry a copy of my bank statement around with me?'

Dan sighs. 'No. But if you've got it, flaunt it. And one way to do that is to trade in your crappy old motor for something a little bit flashier.'

'But, sixteen thousand pounds…'

'What are you saving it for, again?'

'I dunno. A rainy day, I suppose.'

'Well, get out your umbrella. Because when Jane left you, it started pissing down.'

2.23 p.m.

Dan and I are at the Mini dealership in Kemp Town, in the heart of Brighton's gay community, walking around the forecourt. We're there for ten minutes without anyone coming out to see us, Dan poring over the assembled cars on offer, me following him round reluctantly while trying not to recoil at the prices. Eventually, Dan pretends to look shifty, and starts trying a few of the car doors. Straightaway a salesman strolls out of the showroom.

'Can I help you, gents?'

'My friend needs a new car,' says Dan, pointing to a gleaming black Mini parked rakishly in front of the window. 'And I think this might be it.'

When I peer in through the window, it does look rather nice inside: black, leather seats, the dashboard all funky dials and chrome switches, gear knob glinting in the afternoon sun. What's more, it's second hand, and therefore 'only' eleven thousand, two hundred and fifty pounds, as Dan takes great pains to point out to me.

We manage to convince the salesman that we're bona fide customers, due largely to the fact that the middle-aged receptionist recognizes Dan from *Where There's a Will*, and he agrees to a test drive, squeezing into the back seat while Dan and I jump into the front. With a squeal of tyres we shoot out of the garage, and head off down Marine Parade. As we speed along towards the pier, weaving in and out of the traffic, I must admit that I'm certainly impressed with the little car's handling.

'What do you think?' asks Dan. 'Nice, eh?'

'Not bad,' I grudgingly admit, admiring the trendy interior, which Dan informs me is 'retro' styling, and therefore a good thing. 'But do you think I could have a drive now? Seeing as it's me who's supposed to be buying it?'

'Ah. Yes. Good point. Sorry.'

Dan pulls over so we can change places, and I slot myself into the body-hugging sports seat, stick it into first gear, and cautiously release the clutch. It's certainly a lot more frisky than the Volvo, and I manage to stall it twice as I pull away.

'Come on, Grandma,' he says, tutting as a Day-Glo-clad cyclist manages to overtake us. 'Give it a proper go.'

'How do you mean?'

He leans over towards me. 'Drive it like you've stolen it.'

I put my foot down, and the Mini leaps forward, the steering wheel alive in my hands. I make a fast right turn into Brunswick Square, the Mini sticking to the road like a go-kart, then cut left down a side street and back onto the seafront. When I stop to let some people cross at the zebra, they stare, and unlike when I'm driving the Volvo, it's in admiration. By the time I reluctantly pull bade into the dealership, I'm in love, all thoughts of expense and rationality having gone out of the tinted electric window.

'What do you think?' asks the salesman, unfolding himself stiffly from the back seat.

The look on my face gives my answer away. 'We'll take it,' announces Dan.

'So, what's your best price?' I say, walking once more around the car.

The salesman points to the price tag. 'Eleven thousand, two hundred and fifty pounds.'

I swallow hard. 'Do you take part exchange?'

'Of course. What do you have?'

I leave Dan signing an autograph for the receptionist, and lead the salesman off the forecourt to where I've parked the Volvo, out of sight round the corner. His face falls as he sees it.

'So what will the new price be? Including the part exchange?'

He takes a cursory look round my car, before leading me back inside the dealership. As Dan and I sit down at his desk, the salesman picks up his calculator, and taps away for a couple of minutes.

'Eleven thousand, two hundred and fifty pounds.'

'But that's the same.'

'I know, sir. Because I'm afraid it might actually cost us money to scrap your old car.'

'You can't go any lower?' I plead.

He taps away at his calculator again, then looks up at me. 'No.'

Dan folds his arms. 'Call it eleven grand and you've got yourself a deal.'

The salesman thinks for a micro-second, then shakes Dan's hand. 'Done,' he says, and five minutes later, we're filling out the necessary paperwork.

'So,' says the salesman, 'which one of you two would like to go on the registration document?'

'What?' says Dan, as he realizes the implication. 'We're not…I mean, I'm certainly not…'

I put an arm round Dan's shoulders, enjoying his discomfort. 'Come on, sweetheart. No need to be ashamed.'

'Bugger off,' he says, shrugging me away. 'I mean, for one thing, if I was, I could do a lot better.'

The salesman winks at me. 'Oh, I don't know,' he says.

And I take it as a compliment. Because God knows it's the first one of those I've had for a long time.

Tuesday 22nd March

7.34 a.m.

I'm struggling in the gym this morning, and have to cut my stepper session early. It's not that I don't want to do it—quite the opposite. It's that I really can't seem to find the energy.

'You do seem a bit listless,' says Sam. 'Are you sure you've been eating properly?'

'I think so. I was getting a bit fed up with this Atkins lark, so I bought some of those "lean cuisine" meals yesterday but was so hungry I had to eat two of them. They're tiny.'

Sam puts her hand over her mouth and I can tell she's trying to stifle a laugh.

'Edward, you're missing the point of them somewhat. They're supposed to be smaller than normal. That's how you lose weight—by not eating as much. And Atkins? Well, it's perhaps not the best basis for an exercise programme.'

'Yeah, but I'm starving all the time. And I mean, all the time.'

'Well, that's because you're exercising so much nowadays. We're creating a demand in your metabolism, and where do you think we want it to go looking for calories?'

'Burger King?' I'm still new to this exercise physiology lark.

Sam punches me playfully on the shoulder. 'No, you idiot. Those reserves of fat built up around your stomach.'

'But what can I do?' I ask her. 'It's getting so bad that I can't sleep.'

This, in fact, isn't strictly true; after all these early morning starts and heavy exercise sessions I'm usually asleep as soon as, no, make that before my head hits the pillow. But I do feel hungry pretty much every night.

'Have you tried drinking a large glass of water before each meal? That usually works as a pretty good appetite suppressant.'

'Yes, well, that's another problem. I'm drinking so much water now that my boss thinks I've got a bladder problem.'

Sam decides to cut the session early and we jog back to my flat, so she can take a look at my food diary.

'Edward,' she says, after skimming through a few pages, 'I think I see the problem. You're actually eating too little.'

'Too little? I thought I was supposed to be dieting.'

'No. You're supposed to be watching your diet. There's a difference. If you just eat sensibly and keep to your training programme, then you'll lose weight gradually but safely. What you're doing is not eating enough to give you energy for your workouts. And all this processed, pre-packaged stuff isn't really that good for you.'

'So what should I do?'

'Try cooking some healthy, low-fat food.'

I frown. 'Come again? I'm not sure what that means.'

'Which—"healthy" or "low fat"?'

'No. Cooking. Heating up I can do. Cooking, however, is a bit of a mystery to me.'

Sam looks at me pityingly. 'Tell you what,' she says. 'I'm free this evening. Why don't I come round and show you how? Shall we say seven o'clock?'

I'm a little stunned by this, not in the least because I'll probably have to spend a good hour or two cleaning the kitchen. But I still manage to answer almost immediately.

'Seven o'clock will be fine.'

3.24 p.m.

I'm in the office, speaking to Dan on the phone.

'It's not a date,' I protest. 'She's just offered to show me how to cook a healthy dinner, that's all.'

'Ah, the old "show you how to cook something healthy" ruse. These women will stop at nothing.'

'Listen, as far as I'm concerned, anything to get me off this lousy Atkins diet.'

'I thought you liked bacon and eggs?'

'Not any more.'

7.00 p.m.

Sam arrives, prompt as ever, carrying an Asda shopping bag containing some suspiciously healthy-looking contents. When she shrugs off her coat and hands it to me I have to try hard not to stare; it's the first time I've seen her out of a tracksuit, and her tight-fitting jeans and polo-neck jumper show off her figure perfectly.

I follow her into the kitchen, where she dumps her bag onto the work surface that I've spent the last half hour scrubbing clean, then heads over to the fridge to check my fat photo is still pinned to the door.

'Good boy,' she says, before starting to unpack the contents of her shopping, which includes a rather large bag of green stuff. 'Right, watch and learn.'

I lean on the counter next to her. 'Okay, Delia. What're you making?'

'What are we making, you mean,' she says, correcting me.

'But I don't know how to…'

Sam smiles, and rolls up her sleeves. 'The secret of healthy eating isn't rocket science,' she announces, opening up the bag of strangely shaped leaves. 'It's rocket salad.'

11.35 p.m.

'Omigosh,' says Sam, catching sight of her watch for the first time this evening. 'And we've both got an early start tomorrow.'

'You should have just brought an overnight bag,' I quip, before blushing furiously. 'I didn't mean…'

Sam puts a hand on my arm. 'I know you didn't, Edward.'

I walk her into the hallway and help her on with her coat. 'It's late,' I say. 'I better walk you home.'

Sam frowns up at me. 'What on earth for?'

'In case you, you know, get attacked or something.'

She grins. 'Edward, that's really sweet of you, but to be quite honest I'd probably have more success beating them off than you would.'

'Supposing there's two of them?'

'I'll outrun them. Benefits of being a personal trainer, you see.'

'Well, at least let me call you a cab.'

'That's okay. I'll walk.'

'Sam, it's nearly midnight, the pubs will have emptied out, and there's no way I'm going to let you walk home on your own. So either I come with you or I get you a taxi.'

'But…'

I hold up my hand to stop her protestations. 'No buts. That's the deal. You're on my time now.'

We stroll to the taxi rank at the end of Lansdowne Place, and fortunately there's a cab already waiting there, its 'For Hire' light shining brightly through the darkness.

'Thanks for dinner,' I say, getting out my wallet to pay the driver.

'Thank you. It was fun.' She smiles, and holds out her hand. 'And that was five hours. At forty pounds an hour, I think I can pay for the taxi.'

I'm still trying to process this information when Sam grins, and jumps into the back.

'Sucker. See you in the morning.'

As I wave the taxi off, and a group of drunk lads walk round the corner, I find myself wondering who's going to walk me home.

Wednesday 30th March

9.31 a.m.

WITH LITTLE MORE THAN two weeks to go before Jane gets back, I can put it off no longer. My hands are shaking a little as I pick up the phone and dial the number Dan's given me.

'Good morning. The Tooth Hurts.'

I almost put the phone down again when I hear the cheerful receptionist on the other end. 'Er. Hi. I was recommended to you by Dan Davis. I'd like to make an appointment for some,' I read off Dan's bit of paper, '"cosmetic dentistry", please.'

I can almost hear her simpering at the mention of Dan's name. 'How is Dan? Such a lovely smile.'

'He's fine. Especially since he came out of the closet.'

There's an astonished pause. 'Dan? Came out?'

'I know. Hard to believe, isn't it? But anyway, back to *my* appointment?'

'Oh, yes, right. When would you like to come in?'

I'm not sure that 'like' is the right word. 'As soon as possible, I suppose.'

I hear a rustling of paper. 'We've just had a cancellation for eleven o'clock this morning, if you can make it.'

This morning? Gulp! I nervously agree, and then walk round to the local chemists to buy a toothbrush, toothpaste and some dental floss, before heading back into the office washrooms and spending the next twenty minutes carefully brushing and flossing my teeth in preparation.

10.55 a.m.

The surgery is above a bank in one of the trendy shopping streets in the North Laines. I walk into the expensively furnished waiting room, and give my name to the stunning receptionist, who smiles as she takes my details, revealing the whitest teeth I've ever seen.

After a few minutes nervously flicking through the glossy magazines scattered around the waiting room, a door opens in front of me and a chap my age walks out, wearing the kind of teeth braces that wouldn't look out of place on a James Bond villain. He's accompanied by a gorgeous Chinese girl in a white coat, who shows him to the door, then walks over to reception, and picks up the clipboard with my details on.

'Good morning, Mr Middleton,' she says, as I'm ushered into the treatment room. 'I'm Amanda.'

'Edward,' I say.

'No, Amanda,' she replies, smiling at her own joke. If it's meant to put me at ease, it doesn't.

As I sit apprehensively in the chair, distracted a little by the extremely pretty nurse, I'm amazed at how attractive all the staff here are. And it's then that I suddenly realize that the reason Dan comes here is nothing to do with the fact that they're good dentists. I clamp my mouth shut, and wonder whether it's too late to get up and leave.

'Now, there's no need to be nervous,' says Amanda, as she electronically reclines my chair, thus making all thoughts of escape impossible. 'I haven't had a patient die on me. Yet. Now open wide...'

Gripping hard onto the armrests, I open my mouth. Amanda picks up a small silver instrument and starts probing.

'When was the last time you went to the dentist?' she asks, pressing my tongue down with a wooden spatula.

'Gaa gaa agga,' I say.

'Five years ago?'

'Ga.'

'And do you smoke?'

'Ag ga gaga a ug.'

'Good for you,' she says, removing the spatula and handing me a beaker of pink liquid. 'Smoking's very bad for the teeth. Could you just rinse for me and then spit?'

I do as instructed.

'Into the bowl, please.'

'Sorry.'

Amanda probes and pokes a bit more, making copious notes as she does so. Eventually, she returns my chair to the upright position.

I clear my throat anxiously. 'So, what's the verdict?'

Amanda consults her clipboard. 'Well, you've got a couple of fillings that need attention,' she says. 'But we'll need to start with a thorough clean to get rid of the build up of tartar and plaque. And then there's that chip on your front tooth—anyone would think you'd been trying to open beer bottles, or something. And then we can get started on the colour.'

I swallow hard, trying to get rid of the unpleasant fluoride taste in my mouth.

'And will it be expensive?'

Amanda's teeth, I notice, are perfect too. 'Well, we can fit veneers. That will work out to about three hundred pounds.'

'That doesn't seem too bad.'

'That's per tooth, Edward. And we'd have to do at least twelve of them if you want to get a decent smile back. Alternatively...'

I do a quick sum in my head. 'I'd like alternatively, please.'

'Alternatively, we can just file down that rough front tooth and then do laser gel whitening. It's quite a new technique, but the results aren't too different from veneers.'

'How much?'

'Five hundred pounds. And we can do it today.'

'You mean I won't have to come back?'

Amanda rests a comforting hand on my arm. 'Not if you don't want to.'

'Do it,' I say.

Amanda presses a buzzer and speaks into the intercom. 'Jules,' she says, smiling at me. 'Can you rearrange my next two appointments, please?'

'Fine,' says a metallic voice.

When I smile back at Amanda, she presses the buzzer a second time. 'Jules—on second thoughts, make that my next three.'

Amanda picks up the clipboard, fills in a few more details, then hands the pen to me.

'If you could just sign here, please.'

'What's this? A consent form?'

She shakes her head. 'No. A credit-card slip.'

1.00 p.m.

I've been injected, drilled, filled, sanded, rinsed, water-blasted, gel-coated, and shot at by a laser; my mouth feels like someone's been working on each tooth with a chisel and they've not been too careful around the gums, and I've paid nearly six hundred pounds for the privilege, but I'm smiling. And the reason I'm smiling is because I've got something to smile with! Not quite Dan's sunglasses at fifty paces variety, but a million smiles away from the uneven, nicotine-stained one of old.

I'm so tempted to try it out that when a girl walks towards me on the pavement, I wait until I get directly in front of her, then give her the full beam, only to be a little surprised when she makes a face at me and crosses the street. Surprised, that is, until I catch sight of my reflection in a shop window; half of my face is still paralysed, which makes me look like something out of an asylum, plus I've been drooling down the front of my shirt.

I shut my mouth and hurry home.

Thursday 31st March

7.21 a.m.

WE'RE IN THE GYM, and I can't quite believe what Sam's suggested.

'Boxing?'

'That's right.'

'Boxing?'

Sam nods. 'How many fat boxers do you know?'

I want to tell Sam that I don't know any boxers. I'm not the kind of person who has boxers as friends. I don't even like the dogs.

'But isn't it a little…'

'Dangerous?'

'No, unfair. I mean, I'm twice your size. Besides, I've just had my teeth done.'

'We're not actually going to be boxing each other, Edward. Just doing the training.'

Sam leads me downstairs and through a door labelled, ominously, 'Dance Studio'. Against one wall, next to a large pile of mats, there's a punch bag hanging from the ceiling. She walks over to the cupboard in the corner and retrieves a pair of boxing gloves and a skipping rope.

'Come on, Rocky. Lets get going. Five minutes of skipping to start with.'

'Skipping. Isn't that something little girls do?'

'Well, it should cause you no problems then,' she says, handing me the rope. 'Off you go.'

Now, I've seen all of the *Rocky* films. Recently, in fact, in the case of *Rocky III*. I've sat and watched the training scenes as Sylvester Stallone manages to lift trees, do impossible things on the sit-up bench, catch chickens, and even skip at a hundred miles an hour, and he's an *actor*, so how hard can it be? I grin confidently at Sam and take a handle in each hand.

Two seconds later, Sam is helping me to my feet.

'Right. Let's try again, shall we?' she says. 'But this time the idea is to *jump* over the rope. Not trip over it.'

After five minutes, during which I've probably managed no more than three continuous skips, I hand the rope back to Sam. I'm well and truly red in the face now, although this could be due more to shame than my exertions with the rope. She passes me the gloves and I slip them on.

'Ok, bag work.'

I saunter over to the punch bag and give it a push. It's surprisingly heavy, and I'm unable to make it swing more than a few inches. I give it a tentative punch, which hurts me more than the bag.

Sam looks at me pityingly. 'Like this,' she says, planting her feet firmly and unleashing a jab into the bag, followed by two left hooks. I wince as the bag rattles on its chain.

'Remind me never to get on your bad side.'

Sam stands behind the bag to steady it, and gets me to work a few combinations: right, right, left, right, right, left, and after a few minutes, I start to get into a rhythm. It's surprisingly enjoyable, not to mention unexpectedly tiring, but when I start to slow down, Sam has an idea.

'Picture the face of someone you're angry with on the bag,' she says. 'What about that boss of yours?'

As I concentrate, imagining Natasha staring at me, I unleash another combination, a little faster this time. I pick up the pace, and follow a series of jabs with a huge roundhouse right hand that even has Sam looking surprised. I'm dancing around now; rocking the bag from side to side as Sam struggles to hold it steady, and I'm dripping with sweat, but still keeping up the onslaught. Finally, it's Sam who's had enough, and she lets go of the punch bag.

When I jog round the studio, gloved hands raised in celebration. Sam just looks at me pityingly.

'Okay. Let's call it a day,' she says. 'Impressive work. You must really have it in for her.'

But the funny thing is, by the end of the session, it hadn't been Natasha's face I was picturing in front of me.

It was Jane's.

Friday 1st April

3.22 p.m.

I'M IN THE OFFICE, in the middle of one of Natasha's outbursts. I can't even remember what started her off, but what I do know is that I've been working hard all week trying to put the Go-Soft campaign to bed whilst she's been doing the same to their managing director.

So when she tells me that I'm lazy, I don't know what it is, but for some reason it gets to me. Really gets to me. I sit there as she rants on, clenching and unclenching my fists for a few moments, before wordlessly standing up and packing my briefcase. When I walk towards the door, Natasha looks up sharply.

'Where do you think you're going? I haven't finished.'

'Yes you have,' I say quietly.

'What did you say?' she snaps.

'I've had enough. That's it.'

'What are you talking about?'

I stand in the doorway, and keep my voice level. 'For nearly ten years I've put up with your complaining, never-happy attitude, knowing that the complexion of my day was going to depend on what side of the bed you got out of that morning, or rather, what side of whoever's bed you got out of, whenever you finally deigned to grace the office with your presence. And now, just when things couldn't be going any better business-wise, you have to come in and pick on me just because your latest married "boyfriend" doesn't want to leave his wife and take a chance on your psycho bunny-boiling behaviour.'

'Hold on a minute. That's…'

'Be quiet. *I* haven't finished. For the last few years it's been me who's kept this company afloat. Me. And what acknowledgement do I get? Nothing. Just, "Any messages, Edward?" or "Get me a coffee, Edward." Well, you can get your own coffee from now on.'

Natasha sits, open-mouthed, at her desk. 'What are you saying?'

'I quit. Goodbye. Have a nice life.'

'Is this some kind of April Fool's joke?'

'It's no joke,' I say. 'And the only fool here is me, for putting up with you for so long.' And with that, I turn around, and walk right out of the office.

'Edward. *Edward.* I didn't mean it. I'm sorry. Come back.'

As I stride along the corridor, I can hear Natasha calling after me. But I don't come back. I just keep on walking.

And it feels good.

Saturday 2nd April

11.15 a.m.

IN TWO DAYS' TIME I'm due to pick up the Mini. I think about taking the Volvo through the carwash before I trade it in but I'm worried I'll dislodge some more of the paintwork, or even a door, and that the garage will decide to charge me for taking it off my hands. I'm slightly concerned about the amount of money it's going to be costing me, particularly since I'm now unemployed, but despite this, I'm still quite excited when I call my insurance company to arrange a cover note. The chap on the phone goes through some preliminary questions with me, and then the next question he asks stops me in my tracks.

'So that's for you and the same named driver, is it? Miss Jane Scott?'

Blimey. I hadn't thought about that. 'Er...Can I add her on later?' I can sense confusion at the end of the phone and feel a sudden need to explain. 'She's gone away for a while, you see.'

'Well, when is she coming back?'

'I'm not sure. I mean, in about two weeks. Saturday April sixteenth, to be precise.'

'And will you want her to be driving your new car when she gets back?'

This, of course, is a metaphor, as well as a jolly good question, so I decide to tackle Dan about it. He doesn't answer his mobile, so I go round to see if he's in.

When Dan opens the door, he's holding a large plastic spatula and sporting a white smudge on the end of his nose. More worryingly, he's only wearing a pair of shorts.

'I hope that I haven't interrupted some cocaine-fuelled, pervy S&M session?'

Dan grins. 'Chance would be a fine thing. I'm baking.'

'Hence the lack of clothes?'

'No, "baking", as in "a cake", not hot. Although most of Brighton's female population may disagree with me on that one.'

He beckons me inside, and I follow him through to his kitchen, which resembles something of a disaster area.

'At the risk of asking an impertinent question, why on earth are you baking a cake? Has the supermarket run out?'

'Nope. Career enhancement. Today, *Ready Steady Cook*, tomorrow, the world.'

'What are you talking about?'

He looks at me as if I'm just off the boat. 'Celebrity chefs. They're the latest thing.'

'Just like antiques presenters were last year?'

Dan ignores me. 'You can't walk around television centre nowadays without bumping into some garlic-smelling twat in a tall white hat with a packet of sun-dried tomatoes sticking out of his pocket.'

'So, let me get this straight.' I survey the mess in front of me, including what looks like a cowpat on a plate. 'You've decided to teach yourself how to cook so you can become a celebrity chef?'

Dan nods. 'That's about the size of it. Before you know it, I'll be moving to rural France, feeding up the locals, shagging their daughters, all with a film crew up my arse.'

'Dan, without wishing to sink your soufflé, don't most celebrity chefs actually start out as chefs? You know, cook for people for a living, before becoming famous?'

Dan's face falls as flat as his Victoria sponge. 'You're kidding?'

'Nope. Most of them even own restaurants.'

'What about that one who swears all the time?'

'Yup. Several, I think.'

'The one with the hair like a toilet brush?'

'At least a couple.'

Dan throws his spatula into the sink in disgust, picks up a knife, and attempts to cut a couple of slices of cake, but can't seem to make much of an impression. He ends up having to chisel some off the edge.

'Just as well, really. It's harder than you'd think.'

'What? Your sponge?'

'Try some?'

'Can't. Diet. Sorry…'

Dan picks up a piece, sniffs it, then stamps open the pedal bin and deposits his culinary efforts, plate and all, inside. 'Anyway, what are you doing here?'

I repeat my dilemma about putting Jane on the Mini's insurance. Dan just laughs it off.

'Nah. You can always add her on later. If you want to let her drive it, that is. And speaking of driving, I'm off to hit some golf balls.'

'Dan, is all your conversation like a television link?'

'Want to come?'

I pick a ladle up out of Dan's unused utensil jar and attempt to swing it, nearly denting the stainless-steel fridge door in the process. 'I don't know the first thing about golf.'

Dan snatches the ladle back. 'Easy, Tiger. Well come along and watch me, then. You might learn a thing or two.'

I sit flicking through a couple of magazines in the lounge while Dan gets ready. When he eventually appears, he's dressed as if he's about to contest the Open.

'Look at you, mister all-the-gear-but-no-idea. I thought you were only going to the driving range?'

He shrugs. 'Got to look the part, Eddy-boy. That's half the battle. As you'll find out in a couple of weeks.'

Dan removes his clubs from the cupboard under the stairs and we head outside and into his car. I jump into the passenger seat, only to have Dan dump the bag on my lap.

'What's wrong with the boot?'

'Don't fit, I'm afraid. They'll have to ride up front with you.'

'Practical, these cars, then?'

As it's not raining, Dan lowers the roof, and we head off towards the range. On the way, we pass Wendy, who's heading in to work.

'Oh look,' she calls, as we slow down and beep her. 'It's Thelma and Louise.'

When we get to the range, Dan buys a bucket of balls, and I sit there as he thwacks them effortlessly into the distance.

'So, what am I learning here, exactly?' I ask, stifling a yawn.

'Well, here's how I see it,' says Dan, fishing a ball out of his bucket and placing it on the mat in front of him. 'Women are like golf balls, really.'

'How so?'

'Well, you tee them up, address them carefully, and then, if you make a good enough connection…'

I can hardly wait. 'Ye-es?'

Dan grins. 'In the hole!' he shouts.

Wednesday 6th April

9.33 a.m.

I'M BACK IN THE office. This isn't as wimpy as it may seem, even though I had started to panic a little that my not having a job might not sit too favourably with Jane's request for me to 'sort some things out'. But for the last few days Natasha's been leaving me messages everywhere, telling me how sorry she is, that she's been doing a lot of thinking, how what I said was right, and that things would definitely change.

And although I've heard this all before from her, something *has* changed. I can sense it. She's in the office more, there's a new respect in the way she speaks to me, and she's invited me to her fortieth birthday party next week, dropping hints about some announcement that she's going to make. She's even been bringing me coffee.

And yet I find it more than a little ironic that for all these years, every time I've threatened to leave, not much has actually come of it. It's only now that I've actually walked out of the door that it's made a difference.

Thursday 7th April

7.35 a.m.

I'M IN THE GYM with Sam, surprising myself that I'm managing to work out and talk at the same time, and telling her about the amazing difference in Natasha.

'She's even invited me to a party next Thursday,' I say, in between repetitions on the leg press. 'At her house.'

'Are you going to go?'

'I'm not sure,' I say. 'It's one of those posh affairs: marquee, champagne, band, and all that. Not really my scene.'

'What?' says Sam. 'That sounds lovely.'

'Maybe. But…'

'But?'

'Well, I'd feel a bit silly going on my own.'

'Ah.'

Sam suddenly looks awkwardly at her feet, and it takes me a good few seconds to realize why.

'Oh no, I didn't mean…I wasn't suggesting…I mean, if you want to…But don't feel…' I shut my mouth, feeling rather uncomfortable myself now.

'Edward, that's very sweet of you, if you're saying what I think you're saying. But I'd better not, don't you think?'

'Yes. I mean, no. Of course,' I stammer, not sure quite what line I've crossed, but pretty sure that I've crossed one.

We work out in silence for a few moments, before Sam regains her composure.

'So tell me. What made you finally stand up to Natasha?' she asks.

'I was just fed up of being told what to do all the time. And by a woman.'

'Well, good for you,' says Sam. 'Now ten more. And then on to the bench press.'

6.05 p.m.

We're due a progress meeting, so I head round to find Dan at his flat, munching through a pizza while watching a recording of *You've Been Framed*. He's laughing so much I fear he's going to have a seizure, and for some reason, he's still wearing his sunglasses.

'Aren't you taking this celebrity thing a bit far? Why not just park your stretch limo outside and be done with it?'

Dan makes a face. 'I wish.'

'Well take those ridiculous glasses off then.'

Reluctantly, Dan reaches up to remove his shades, revealing a corker of a black eye.

'Blimey. What happened to you?'

'We were filming this new idea for a pilot this lunchtime.'

'New show? You didn't mention any new show. What was it called, "Punch me in the face"?'

'Yeah, well, it's right up your street actually. You know all these makeover shows?'

'Thanks. Yeah?'

'Well, this is a new one for men. It's called *You Look Ridiculous!* I've based it on an idea I've had recently.'

'Oh yes?'

'Well, what we do is go to a town centre and find badly dressed men on the street. You know—either those total slobs like you used to be, or people who are complete fashion victims.'

'And?'

Dan takes a bite of pizza. 'And so I march up to them, microphone in hand, and ask them three basic questions on fashion and styling. If they fail to get any of them right, they win a free makeover.'

'So, what happened? And why the black eye?'

'Well, it seems we hadn't quite thought it through.'

'How do you mean?'

'It's lunchtime, and me and Mike, my cameraman…'

'Are you sure he wasn't your sound man, with a name like that?'

'Are hanging around Churchill Square, and we spot this bloke. Big fella, dressed like an arse.'

'What a wonderful mental picture that is.'

'And so we decide to try it out. Mike starts filming, I walk up to the guy, and say the programme's catch phrase…'

'Which wouldn't be "You Look Ridiculous" by any chance?'

'Exactly. Well, too late I smell the alcohol on his breath. He's obviously spent the best part of the morning in the pub, and doesn't take too kindly to my observation, and before I can explain what the show's all about…'

'Ah.'

Dan grimaces. 'Yeah, but you should see poor old Mike. He won't want to look through that lens again in a hurry.'

I'm about to ask him for more details, but he's suddenly distracted by a video clip of someone tripping over while carrying a birthday cake. They, of course, land with their face in it, which Dan finds hilarious.

'What's so funny about this?' I ask him, once the adverts thankfully come on. 'The fact that they film things like painting the fence, or climbing into the loft. How sad are they?'

'Don't be so snooty,' says Dan, fast-forwarding through the ad break. 'We're doing ours on Monday.'

'What?'

'We're spending the day filming out-takes.'

'On purpose?'

'Oh yeah. Got to have something to submit to the "bloopers" programmes.'

'Am I missing something? Aren't they supposed to be "mistakes".'

Dan looks at me as if I'm stupid. 'Yeah, like Trevor Whatsisname doesn't know the camera's still rolling when he says "fuck" on the news.'

'But why would they…?'

'Repeat fees. People only watch *Richard and Judy* once, but they'll watch Judy "accidentally" getting her baps out on that awards show time and time again. Oldest trick in the book. Anyway, we're not here to discuss the intricacies of the broadcasting world.' Dan hits 'stop' on the remote control, switches the TV off, and fires up his laptop. 'Where are we at now?'

'Well, I'm supposed to be going speed dating again this Saturday.'

'What do you mean, "supposed to be"?'

'It's just that…'

'Edward. What better way to find out whether all this work has paid off than to put yourself through that again. A random sample of twenty women, don't forget.'

'Okay,' I sigh. 'So is there anything else we need to do before then?'

As the spreadsheet appears on screen, Dan scrolls through the list, which miraculously seems to be getting shorter, crossing items off as he goes.

'Hold on,' he says. 'Something just occurred to me that we've forgotten.' He pages up to the middle and adds one word under 'H'.

'Hair? What's wrong with it?' I run my hand nervously through my shaggy brown mop.

'Well, have you ever thought about having it in a style?'

'Bugger off.'

'I'm serious. Who cuts it for you?'

I name a semi-trendy place on Western Road, and Dan frowns slightly. 'But I know the head stylist there. He's normally pretty good.'

'Ah.'

'What?'

'He's also normally pretty expensive.'

'So?'

'So I normally don't get him to do it. It's much cheaper when you have it done by one of the students.'

Dan inspects my head. 'What are they students of? Philosophy?'

'Very funny.'

'But, joking aside,' he says, 'it's almost unkempt enough to be trendy, but I think you ought to go for something a little more...' he searches for the right word, 'modern.'

I sigh. 'And I bet you know just the place?'

Dan nods and takes a last bite of pepperoni. 'Oh yes,' he says, reaching for his mobile phone.

Friday 8th April

5.25 p.m.

My appointment is at five-thirty, so I nip out of work a few minutes early and make my way to the salon, which is ominously next to a hat shop. 'Just ask for Michelle,' Dan had advised.

Michelle turns out to be the best-looking transsexual I've ever seen. A tall, willowy blonde, her huge breasts barely restrained by her T-shirt, she's quite breathtaking. Literally, when I see how much she charges for a haircut.

'Trust me, honey,' she says, in a voice several octaves lower than mine. 'I'm worth it.'

I'm shepherded through into the consultation room, where a large plasma-screen television on the wall in front of me is showing some sort of fashion TV, and offered a glass of wine, which I gulp down quickly.

Michelle sidles up behind me, studies my reflection in the mirror, then lays a hand on my shoulder; her fingernails would put a velociraptor to shame.

'How can I do you?'

I swallow hard. 'Dan sent me. He said…'

'Dan? How is that sweetheart? Such lovely hair.'

Great. Yet another member of the Dan Davis fan club. 'He's fine. Still battling with the drugs, though.'

'Dan? Drugs? Surely not.'

I nod. 'I'm afraid so. But I can't really say any more than that. Anyway, he told me I should ask you to, er…'

Michelle raises one carefully plucked eyebrow. 'Ye-es?'

'To make me a "babe magnet".'

Michelle lets out a deep belly-laugh. 'I can only work with what I'm given, you understand. But I think you have potential.'

The next hour is a blur of washing, shampooing, cutting, shaving, and drying. All the while I try not to flinch when Michelle presses her surgically produced breasts against me, which seems to be more often than strictly necessary, and I watch with alarm as a worrying amount of hair seems to be falling on my shoulders and the floor around me. Finally, when it seems that there's almost no more left to cut, Michelle produces a pot of something that seems to be called 'Fudge', and scoops out a handful.

She spins me round with one firmly biceped arm so I'm not facing the mirror, straddles me, and after a bit of teasing and shaping, spins me back again so I can see my reflection.

'*Voila!*' announces Michelle. 'You like?'

I'm a bit speechless. I hardly recognize the person staring back at me. 'I like,' I say, eventually. And I do like. She's worked a miracle, and it's of the Moses/Red Sea magnitude. Gone is the lank, shapeless side parting that I once had, to be replaced by a short, spiky, messy, dare I even say, trendy cut. It might not be babe magnet, but at least it won't repel them any more.

I spend the whole walk home admiring myself in shop windows, so much so that at one point I walk into a bollard, banging my right knee painfully. But it's worth it, despite the fifty-pound price tag, the five-pound tip and the further ten pounds I spent on that magic Fudge stuff.

The next morning, although I can't quite achieve the effect with the Fudge that Michelle's fingers did, I'd still get a decent score if this were a *Generation Game* test. And that's what all this whole thing is all about, as I'm beginning to understand.

Getting a decent score.

Saturday 9th April

10.02 a.m.

I'M IN MY BEDROOM with Dan, going through the entire contents of my wardrobe. There's a pile of clothes in front of me made up of stuff that I'm keeping, and next to it, a pile of items that I'm throwing away because they either don't fit me any more or, to borrow Dan's latest catchphrase, 'look ridiculous'. Suffice to say, the second pile is somewhat larger than the first, and not, apparently, because they don't fit me any more. After nearly an hour of this, I'm getting extremely bored.

'Dan—this just isn't me. I don't want to spend my day agonizing over whether it's all right to wear navy with green, for example.'

He looks at me earnestly. 'Edward, it's no good working on the chassis if the paintwork lets you down. You've got three minutes to make a good impression, and turning up tonight like some reject from the Oxfam shop is hardly going to help. Come on.'

'Where are we going now?'

'I need to take you shopping.'

11.15 a.m.

On the way into town, Dan calls into his flat, and emerges holding his digital camera.

'What on earth is that for?'

He slips it into his pocket. 'You'll see.'

'So, what's the plan?'

'We've got to get you the basics. Mix and match. So even you can't make a mistake. Try and put together a wardrobe where whatever top you choose will go with whichever pair of trousers you put your hands on. Kind of trendy dressing for idiots.'

We head on into the North Laines, and soon the surroundings start to make me feel a little uncomfortable, not because they're particularly threatening or dangerous, but because everyone's so damn trendy. People I'm guessing must be my age look years younger than me, and I realize it's because of the way they dress. But as we walk, I gaze through the various shop windows in bewilderment—from what I can tell, most of them seem to be selling fancy dress.

On a road where all the shops are named 'Street' this or 'Urban' that, we eventually find the place Dan's looking for. It's called 'Kred', and as we enter, we're greeted by someone who could be Dan's twin brother. They've got the same trendily unkempt hairstyle, the scruffy bagginess about their clothing that strangely seems to be so smart, and when they shake hands, it's more like a game of scissors-paper-stone than any handshake I've ever seen.

Dan puts his hands on my shoulders and ushers me forward, as if he's presenting me for inspection. 'Milo, I'd like you to meet Edward.'

Milo holds out his hand and, not knowing the correct routine, I just give him the 'thumbs up' sign, as Dan cringes with shame beside me.

'Milo,' continues Dan, 'Edward needs your help.'

'I can see that,' says Milo, looking me up and down. 'What's the occasion?'

'Life,' says Dan. 'He needs to make a good impression.'

'Better to not turn up,' laughs Milo. 'Or to send you in his place.'

I clear my throat loudly. 'Don't mind me.'

Dan and Milo continue to talk about me as if I'm not there and, quite frankly, I'd rather not be. I consider just heading for the door, but then catch sight of my reflection in the full-length mirror—the comparison between my jeans-and-sweatshirt combination and how Dan and Milo look keeps me rooted firmly to the spot.

After another few minutes of discussion, Milo sizes me up expertly, and produces a pair of jeans and a shirt from the rack.

'Try these,' he says, showing me into the changing rooms at the back of the shop. I do as instructed, and walk out of the cubicle to find Dan sitting in an armchair, enjoying a glass of wine.

'Much better,' says Milo, un-tucking my shirt for me. 'The clothes make the man.'

Dan looks up at me and swallows his mouthful of Chardonnay. 'In the absence of anything else, lets hope so,' he says.

Milo selects a range of trousers, T-shirts, and jumpers, and I try them all on dutifully. Eventually, I get a little tired of being a clothes horse.

'Can't I try and pick something?'

Milo and Dan look at each other conspiratorially. 'Give it a go,' says Dan, trying hard not to smirk.

I try on a pair of three-quarter-length trousers, the type that Dan normally wears, but on me they look like a normal pair that have just shrunk in the wash. Next, I pick up a pair of Levi's, assuming that I can't go wrong with them. It says 'Anti-fit' on the label, and I'm sure I've read about these in *GQ*.

'What about these?'

Dan scrutinizes the label. '"Anti-fit"? Well, they should suit you, then.'

I snatch them off him and disappear into the changing room, emerging red-faced a few seconds later to look for a larger size.

When I eventually manage to squeeze into a pair, I parade up and down in front of the mirror. 'What do you think?'

Dan looks at me critically. 'Honest answer?'

Uh-oh. 'Please.'

'They make you look deformed.'

'Bugger off!'

'No, honestly. Look.' He pulls out his digital camera, walks behind me, snaps a photo and then shows me the picture on the screen. From behind, I look like my legs are distended, with my knees and crotch approximately two-thirds lower than where they should be. I take them off quickly.

By the time Dan's on his third glass, we've settled for a couple of pairs of trousers, one pair of combats, one pair of trendy jeans, two jackets, and a selection of interchangeable shirts and tops that should give me the combination of outfits we'd been aiming for. And then lastly, as I rifle through the rail at the back of the store, a Paul Smith suit catches my eye.

From the moment I put it on, I can sense something's different. It's a million miles away from my traditional, shapeless Marks and Spencer work suits. The jacket, with its brightly coloured lining, hugs my new, slimmer physique, making me look even broader at the shoulders. The trousers seem to fit and flatter, and there's not even the slightest bit of straining at the waistband. And even though it costs more than all my other suits combined, I love it. Even Dan seems impressed when I emerge, grinning, from the changing room.

As I carry my bags out of the shop, I've parted with the best part of seven hundred pounds, but I don't care. Because judging by what I've just seen in the mirror, I think I'm finally starting to get it.

We walk back into the centre of town, and I turn to face Dan. 'What's next?'

He thinks for a minute. 'Boots.'

'Cowboy? Chelsea? Desert?'

Dan shakes his head. 'Nope. The Chemist's.'

12.21 p.m.

We're in Boots, standing in the aisle ominously marked 'Men's Grooming', where Dan is holding up a tube of something expensive.

'What kind of skin have you got?'

'What kinds are there?'

'Greasy? Dry? Sensitive? What d'you reckon?'

'Thick, I'd think, from years of putting up with your insults. And anyway, how on earth do I know if I've got sensitive skin?'

Dan gives me the tube to hold and then slaps both my cheeks.

'Ow. What was that for?'

'Did it hurt?'

'Yes, it hurt!'

'Then you've got sensitive skin.'

He snatches the tube back from me and throws it into my basket. I take it out again, and study the label.

'What do I need moisturizer for, anyway?'

Dan looks at me as if I've asked the stupidest question ever. 'To moisturize, dummy.'

'But why do I need to moisturize?'

'Otherwise you'll be too dry after exfoliating.'

'So why don't I just not exfoliate? Then I won't need to moisturize.'

'Ah,' says Dan. 'But if you don't exfoliate then you won't get rid of that build up of...'

'Of moisturizer from the day before?'

'Now you're just being awkward.'

'But this stuff's just for women, surely. Why on earth do men have to moisturize?'

Dan rolls his eyes, not for the first time today. 'Because men have skin too.'

We make our way further along the skin-care section, before Dan stops and studies the shelves.

'Okay,' he says. 'I'm going to let you into a little secret here. How do you think I maintain my healthy colour?'

I look at Dan's slightly orange-tinted skin. 'Eat a lot of carrots?'

He shakes his head, picks up a brown-coloured bottle, and studies it reverentially.

'Two words: fake tan.'

'Fake tan? What on earth do I need fake tan for?'

'Think about it. Jane's been away for three months, basking in the mountain sunshine, whilst you've been stuck under the grey English skies. You'll look comparatively blue next to her unless you do something about it.'

'Well, why don't I just go and have a sunbed or something?'

'You could, assuming you want to add skin cancer to the lung cancer you're already in danger of. Trust me, fake tan is the way to go. And we'd better get a couple of bottles.'

'What on earth for?'

'Because where you're concerned, there's an awful lot more surface area to cover.'

Dan throws another pot of something into the basket and heads off towards the adjacent aisle. I trail along obediently behind him, and by the time we get to the checkout, I'm struggling to carry my basket.

'Are you sure I need all this stuff? Isn't there just like the one product I could buy?'

'What?' says Dan. 'One product. To make you look good to women?'

'Well, yes.'

Dan thinks about this for a moment. 'Why, now you come to mention it, yes there is.'

'Oh. Right,' I say, pleasantly surprised. 'And where do we get that from?'

'The Ferrari garage.'

As he heads off to make sure 'we' haven't forgotten anything, I wait in the queue, and given the nature of my purchases it's not the best time, perhaps, to bump into Sam. She's looking as good as usual, dressed in a short leather jacket, and a rather tight pair of jeans.

'Is this all for Jane when she gets back?' she asks, peering into my shopping basket.

'Er, no. It's for…I mean, yes. I thought I'd stock up. You know. So she can feel right at home.'

Sam picks up a tube of something from my basket and examines it. 'And she uses "Nivea for Men", does she?'

'Oh yes. It's her favourite.'

Just then, Dan sidles up behind her, staring at Sam's backside before catching my eye and making an appreciative face. He clears his throat, and she turns around.

'Hi there,' he says. 'What's your name?'

Sam looks at Dan suspiciously, not realizing he's with me.

'Why do you want to know?'

Dan flashes his TV grin. 'I thought I might get a tattoo. Wanted to make sure I got the spelling right.'

Sam turns to me and makes a face, then smiles pleasantly back at Dan. 'And that line usually works, does it?'

Dan raises one eyebrow. 'You tell me.'

She regards him quizzically for a moment, before cutting him dead. 'Actually, no.'

'Sam,' I laugh. 'Let me introduce my friend Dan to you. Dan, this is Sam. My trainer.'

Dan does a double take. In fact, it's more of a triple take. 'You're Sam? Edward never said…I mean…Hello!' This last word comes out of his mouth as if he's suddenly become Leslie Phillips.

Sam holds out her hand. 'Nice to meet you, Dan.'

It's my turn to cringe as Dan grabs her fingers and plants a kiss firmly on the back of her hand.

'And you're Ed's trainer?'

Sam pulls her hand back and wipes it surreptitiously on her jeans. 'That's right.'

'So, do you think you could help me?' he says. 'You know—build up the old stamina?'

Sam looks at him levelly for a moment. 'Oh, I've got a feeling you don't need my help in that department.'

Dan leers back at her. 'Edward's told you all about me, has he?'

She thinks for a few seconds. 'No, actually. He's only mentioned you in passing. Why?'

'Well, because, er…' I rarely see Dan lost for words where a woman is concerned, and I'm enjoying his discomfort.

Sam peers at him closely. 'You do look familiar, though.'

Dan recovers his composure slightly, switching his TV persona back on. 'Well, I do get recognized on the street all the time.'

I nod. 'Usually by angry husbands.'

'You might have seen me on television,' he continues. 'I'm Dan Davis.'

Sam frowns. 'No, I don't think that's it.'

Dan's newly found confidence falters slightly. 'Have you ever seen *Where There's a Will?*'

Sam shrugs. 'I don't think so. What night's it on?'

'It's a daytime programme,' I say. 'Eleven o'clock on a Tuesday morning.'

'Oh,' says Sam. 'No, I don't watch daytime TV.'

'Because of your job?' asks Dan.

'No, because I have a life,' she replies. 'But I'm sure I've seen you somewhere before. What else have you been on?'

As Dan reels off his admittedly short television résumé, Sam shakes her head, before realization dawns.

'I've got it,' she exclaims. 'You go to my waxer, don't you?'

Dan starts to go very red. 'You must be mistaken.'

'I don't think so. I never forget a face. Or a hairless pair of legs. Wax Worx. On Middle Street? I'm sure I've seen you there.'

As Dan stands there, open-mouthed, Sam winks at me. Mercifully for Dan, it's our turn at the checkout, and so I tell her I'll see her on Monday.

'Yes. See you on Monday, Edward. And nice to meet you, *Don*.' She grins at me, and strolls away before Dan can correct her.

As Dan watches her go, he nudges me. 'You didn't tell me how fit she was.'

'I know,' I say. 'And really strong too, for her size. She can lift—'

'No, dummy. Fit as in "wa-hey" fit. Not in the cardiovascular sense. Although she does have a great pair of lungs on her.'

'Please, Dan. She's my trainer.'

'So you're not interested in her?'

'She's helping me get Jane back. You remember Jane?'

'Well then, you won't mind if I have a crack?'

I think rapidly, trying to formulate my answer. How to say no, without making Dan feel I'd rather not see Sam suffer the usual Davis treatment. Fortunately, the cashier is asking me for my card, which gives me a few extra seconds to work out an answer. By the time I've punched in my PIN, I have it.

'Well, you're welcome to try, but I'd rather you didn't, just yet.'

Dan looks at me suspiciously. 'Why?'

'Because I'd like to finish my training first. Last thing I want is for her to desert me in my final week because she's fallen head over heels for you.'

Dan nods slowly, as if he's doing me a favour. 'Fair enough. After you've finished.'

'Oh yes. And one more thing.'

'Yes?'

'You go to a *waxer*?'

'Keep your voice down,' says Dan. 'And anyway, it's more of a beauty therapy place really. Manicures, facials…'

'And hair removal?'

'All right,' admits Dan. 'Hair removal. Don't forget, my job relies on me looking good, even in close up. These little touches are important. And while we're on about it…'

'What?'

'That's something else that *you* might want to think about.'

'What are you talking about?'

'Your eyebrows.'

'My eyebrows?'

'Or should I say "eyebrow".'

'What's wrong with it…I mean, them?'

Dan stares at my face. 'You, my friend, have a serious monobrow.'

I look at my reflection in the mirror on the perfume counter. He has a point.

'What do I do about it? Shave it?'

'Get it plucked.'

'You're kidding!'

'I'm serious. A little grooming never hurt.'

I stare resignedly back at Dan's face, and notice for the first time just how regular his eyebrows are.

'And I suppose you know just the place?'

2.50. p.m.

I'm sitting nervously in the reception area at Wax Worx, surrounded by giggling women, and waiting for the appointment that Dan's made for me. I flick idly through *Woman's Weekly* until Joanna, the girl Dan's recommended, comes out and calls me in. As with all of Dan's therapists, she's unusually attractive and, as usual, the first thing she does is asks me how Dan is.

'Well, I think he's finally managing to beat the bottle,' I tell her.
'Dan? Really? You'd never know.'

'Happens a lot to these celebrities, apparently. But I can't really say too much about it. For obvious reasons.'

'Amazing,' says Joanna, shaking her head in disbelief. 'Anyway, what can I do for you?'

I sit down in the treatment chair. 'Dan said, well, suggested, that I have a bit of work done to my eyebrow. Eyebrows.'

Joanna peers at my forehead. 'Ah, yes. I see what he means. There is a touch of the full moon about you.'

She stares closely at me for a moment, as if she's considering the best place to start, produces a serious-looking pair of tweezers, leans in, and proceeds to pluck.

Surprisingly, it hurts. And not just a little bit. It hurts more than anything I've ever done before. It makes the way I feel after a heavy session with Sam seem like a walk in the park, and it's all I can do not to cry, though the amount my eyes are watering, you wouldn't know that I wasn't.

Noticing my discomfort, Joanna tries to reassure me.

'You'll get used to it.'

'I don't want to get used to it. Ow!' I shout, as another single hair is pulled smartly out.

'Just try and relax.'

As far as I'm concerned that's impossible, given Joanna's rapid-fire tweezer action. Besides, if you have to try and relax, well, that just makes you more anxious, surely?

Finally, mercifully, Joanna stops plucking, and hands me a mirror. When I look at my forehead, which is a little red, I'm amazed at the difference. The results are, I have to say, quite spectacular.

'What do you think?'

'Amazing. I look younger, clearer, less…'

'Less like a werewolf?'

'Exactly.'

I stare in horror at the tweezers. 'I don't know how you women manage to put up with having your legs done. Or even, you know, your other bits.'

Joanna smiles. 'You should ask your friend Dan,' she says. 'He'll tell you how it feels.'

For a moment I just stare back at her, thinking she's joking, before I cotton on.

'You're kidding? Dan?' I point to my crotch. 'Down there?'

Joanna nods. 'It's very popular nowadays. I think the guys believe it makes them look, you know, bigger.'

And for the rest of the afternoon, I can't get the phrase 'last turkey in the shop' out of my mind.

6.35 p.m.

I'm a few minutes late by the time I meet Dan on the corner of Preston Street. As usual, he's dressed to impress, rather than appropriately given the somewhat nippy spring afternoon.

'Where the bloody hell have you been? I've been freezing my nuts off here.'

'I'm not surprised.'

'What?'

Dan slowly puts two and two together, and goes bright red.

'Bloody Joanna. I told her not to mention it.'

'Can I just ask you something?'

'Er…sure.'

'Okay. It's just…why the hell do you pay a woman to pour hot wax all over your tackle?'

Dan grins. 'You've just answered your own question, haven't you?'

'Pervert.'

'It's the fashion.'

'The fashion? Where? On nudist beaches?'

'I've told you. I have to look good on TV.'

'Well,' I tell him, 'if there's ever a programme where you need that particular part to look good, I'm changing channels.'

7.53 p.m.

I'm back at the Metropole Hotel, without Dan this time, for my second, and hopefully last ever, speed-dating night. My hair is Fudged to within an inch of its life, my new smile has been given an extra polish, and I'm dressed in my new Paul Smith suit—without a tie, as per Milo's recommendation. I feel a little awkward being here, as it's so close to Jane's return, but on reflection, it does seem to be the best way to see if I'm 'ready'.

Emily looks up from her table when I walk into the foyer, her marker pen poised above a sticky label.

'And you are?' she asks.

That memorable, eh? 'Ed…' I get as far as the first syllable of my name before I stop myself, wondering whether I should be using a false one, but by the time I've thought of a different one to 'Dan', she's written the two letters on my name tag, and is already sticking it onto my lapel.

'Well, Ed,' she says. 'Have fun in there.'

As we file into the room, I'm a little alarmed to see some familiar faces sitting expectantly at the tables. Admittedly it's been a couple of months, plenty of time for any relationships that may have sparked off at my first time here to have been through the date-split cycle, but I suddenly feel like I'm in danger of completely shattering any confidence I may have built up over the past few weeks. These women all rejected me once—what if they do it again?

But as we wait to go to our respective chairs, something definitely feels different. I may be wrong, but a few of my fellow daters seem to be regarding *me* with suspicion this time, and furthermore, I notice a couple of the girls are actually smiling from behind their clipboards. At me.

I'm just trying to process this information when I spot Melanie, the *Fatal Attraction* girl from last time, sat in the corner. Oh great—evidently she's back for another spot of cheering up. I position myself so I'll get to her last, take a deep breath, and wait for Emily to ring the bell.

And it goes well. The girls seem interested in me. They laugh at my jokes. 'You obviously work out,' someone says to me. 'I like your suit,' says another. I see a couple of them 'tick' me before my time is up, and one girl, Tina, even gives me a slip of paper with her phone number on it. In general, they all seem to be having a good time, and apart from one embarrassing incident when one of them tells me she loves gigs, and I think she means the Manchester United footballer, I have a good time too.

I'm on a high when I nervously take my seat in front of Melanie again, and wait for her to start laying into me. But this time, and to my astonishment, she starts off by smiling warmly at me.

I nearly blow it when I ask her what she likes to do with her spare time, and her answer takes me a little by surprise. I have to get her to explain.

'I'm sorry?' I say. 'Sleeping with strangers?'

Melanie's face runs through confusion, shock, and then realization, but then, fortunately, she laughs.

'No, Ed. I love to swim. Not swing.'

And I'm so amazed by the difference in her that it's a full minute—one third of our allotted time together—before I realize something very important, and it's something that causes me to sit up straight with pride. It's not that she doesn't remember me.

It's that she doesn't recognize me.

Sunday 10th April

1.04 p.m.

I'M SITTING AT THE bar, telling Dan about my evening. When I get to the part about Tina giving me her number, I have to stop him from ordering champagne.

'So what are you going to do?' he asks, staring in admiration at the scrap of paper on the table in front of me.

'What do you mean, "what am I going to do"? Nothing, of course. Have you forgotten why I'm doing all this?'

Dan shrugs. 'Nope, but I was hoping you had.'

'Jane's back in a week, Dan. My entire future happiness hangs on what she thinks when she sees me. I'm hardly going to want to jeopardize that, am I?'

'Which is exactly why you should call Tina. Go out with her.'

'You mean think of it as a dry run for when Jane gets back?'

Dan nods. 'Yup. Because you don't want Jane to smell the paint.'

I sniff the arm of my jacket. 'What on earth are you talking about?'

'When you see Jane for the first time. You don't want her to smell the paint.'

I'm still no clearer. 'What?'

'Like the Queen.'

'Have you been drinking?'

'The Queen thinks the world smells of paint.'

'You have been drinking.'

Dan emits a long-suffering sigh. 'Everywhere she visits has just been painted. You know—to look good for when she comes. And she knows it, because she can smell the paint. Same thing applies to you and Jane. You need to be comfortable in your new skin. Otherwise Jane will see straight through it.'

'Why? Surely I've proved things now. I don't repel women any more.'

'Maybe so. And perhaps you can even attract the odd one, and I mean that in both senses of the word "odd", but how about sustaining it past the initial attraction? If you can't manage that for an evening, how do you think you're going to do it for the rest of your life?'

Tuesday 12th April

7.44 p.m.

When I meet up with Dan in the Admiral Jim, he's looking more than a little cheesed off. What's more, and unusually for Dan, he's drinking beer and eating a hot dog.

'Careful. Those things will kill you.'

'Hark at you, mister healthy living convert.'

I make a face. 'Do you know what they put into them?'

'Don't tell me,' orders Dan. 'It's like women with breast implants. I don't want to think how they're made—I just want to enjoy the end result.' He holds the hot dog out towards me. 'Like a bite?'

'No thank you!'

'How about a beer then?' he says, waving his bottle in front of me. Dan rarely drinks beer, but when he does, it's only ever that expensive, cloudy, scented stuff brewed in some obscure Belgian monastery.

'You know I would. But not for another,' I consult my watch, 'four days and twelve hours, sadly.'

'Is that all you've got left?'

I nod, thankfully. 'My odyssey is nearly over.'

'Your odd what?'

'My journey of self-discovery. My mission to find the inner me.'

Dan takes a mouthful of beer. 'Your quest for a shag, you mean.'

'What's the matter with you? Bad day at the office?'

'You could say that.'

I catch Wendy's eye, signalling her to come over when she's ready. 'Do you want to tell me about it?'

Dan sighs. 'Well, today, after weeks of filming, where all we've found are crappy old toys and naff "antiques" that date from the early Formica period, we finally come across someone who's been left something half decent.'

'Which was?'

'I dunno. I'm not the antiques expert, am I? Some sort of crystal decanter thing that Digby practically got a hard-on about. Two hundred years old, apparently. Worth a small fortune.'

'Well, that's good news, isn't it?'

Dan grimaces. 'It would have been.'

'What do you mean, "would have been"?'

'If I hadn't dropped it. On camera.'

I have to stifle a laugh. 'How did you manage that?'

'Well, I was trying to be funny, you know, by pretending to drop it.'

'But instead, you "actually" dropped it?'

'That's about the size of it.'

'Ouch. So what's happened.'

'Well, firstly, we've had to recompense the couple. Secondly, of course, we can't put the programme out, so that's a whole two days' filming wasted, and thirdly...'

'Thirdly?'

'They've given me a warning. One more thing and I'm out. Banished to the wasteland that is free-to-air.'

'One *more* thing? What else have you done?'

'You know.' Dan blushes slightly. 'The thing with that chap's wife.'

'Ah, yes.' Dan had been caught trying to make a move on one of the bereaved couples' wives. 'Not the best career move, perhaps?'

'Yes, well, she was begging for it.'

'Dan, that's not a very nice thing to say. I mean, I know they call it their hour of need...'

'No, really. She was actually begging for it. Down on her knees, and everything.'

'And that's when her husband saw the two of you.'

'Exactly Didn't quite believe my "dropped contact lens" excuse.'

'Quite.'

'I tell you, sometimes it's hard being "TV's Dan Davis". Every time I meet someone they're expecting me to be this perfect person they've seen on television, with flawlessly scripted lines, whereas the reality is…' Dan stops talking, and downs the remainder of his beer.

'What's the reality, mate?'

Dan sighs. 'That sometimes I need my lines written for me. Maybe that's why my relationships don't last. Because they see through the gloss and realize that I'm pretty much just what it says on the tin.'

I put a reassuring hand on his shoulder. 'And there was me thinking it was because you never call them the next morning. Anyway, look on the bright side.'

'Don't you bloody start.'

'I'm serious. At least you've got something for *It'll Be All Right on the Night 207*, or whatever number they're up to now.'

Dan brightens slightly. 'I hadn't thought of that.'

When Wendy appears, I order my usual sparkling water, and buy Dan a refill.

'Five pounds fifty, please,' she says, placing the bottle down carefully on the bar. 'Four pounds of which is for Dan's beer, by the way.'

'Blimey,' I say. 'I thought it was brewed by monks?'

'Well, they've obviously got expensive habits,' she replies.

There's a pause, before Wendy and I collapse in a fit of childish laughter, filled only by the whooshing sound of her joke flying way over Dan's head.

Wednesday 13th April

7.09 p.m.
WE'VE ARRANGED TO MEET for drinks at Bar Bados, a Caribbean-themed bar-restaurant on Western Road. The place is quite busy already, and rather noisy, mainly due to the table full of Elvis impersonators, probably out on a stag do, in one corner.

I'm a little late, having had to unscrew the u-bend underneath my sink when one of my contact lenses fell down the plug hole, and peer anxiously around the gloomy interior until I spot Tina in one of the corner booths. I'm pleased, and not a little relieved, when she smiles and waves me over—last time I did this the person thought I was someone else.

'Hi, Ed,' she says.

I'm not sure whether I should kiss her hello or shake her hand, given that we've only previously spent a total of three minutes in each other's company. *She'll lead you*, Dan had said, but when Tina just sits there, smiling up at me, I realize I'm not getting any clues. I settle for sitting down opposite her, and against my better judgement, try to remember Dan's dating advice. Ah yes—start with a compliment.

'You look nice.'

'Thanks,' says Tina. 'So do you. I'm glad you called.'

'Well, I'm glad you gave me your number.'

Tina blushes slightly. 'I don't normally do that sort of thing. It's just that there was something about you. Something different to the guys who normally come to those things.'

'Oh yes?' I ask, fishing slightly. 'Which was?'

Tina regards me quizzically. 'I can't quite put my finger on it.'

'Maybe you will later.'

'I beg your pardon?'

'Put your finger on it…Oh, I see. No. Sorry. I mean, realize what it is that's different…Never mind.'

She's already got a drink, so I head to the bar and order myself a large glass of wine. When I sit back down opposite her. Tina smiles at me, and looks at her watch.

'Right. You've got three minutes.'

'Oh. Right. Well…'

'Only kidding. So, Ed. Tell me a little more about yourself.'

'Gosh. Where to start?' Probably not with the Jane stuff. 'There's not much to tell, really.'

'Go on.'

'No, honestly. There's really not much to tell.'

I talk a little about my job, careful not to give too much away, then try and turn the conversation round. 'What about you? What do you do?'

'Oh, I work with lager.'

I don't know quite how to process this. Is she telling me she works at a brewery, or is some kind of weird frozen beer sculptor?

'What?'

'LAGER. It's a charity. Lesbian and Gay Equal Rights.'

Ah. I'd forgotten for a moment that we lived in Be-right-on. 'That sounds…I don't know what I'm supposed to say about that. But you're not…Are you?'

Tina laughs. Fortunately. 'Oh no. It's just a job. But I do believe in equal rights for all. Don't you?'

'Oh yes. Absolutely.'

'None of this gender stereotyping, for example.'

'I couldn't agree more.'

'Great,' she says, holding out her empty glass. 'Now get me another drink, please.'

8.02 p.m.

'I'm a little hungry,' says Tina. 'I didn't get a chance to eat earlier. Shall we order some food?'

I can't believe that this 'early evening date' tactic of Dan's actually works. Deciding to follow the rest of his strategy, I look around at what other people are eating. Sadly, Caribbean cuisine doesn't seem to feature many spaghetti dishes.

'Here? Or shall we go for an Italian?'

Tina looks at me a little strangely. 'Italian? Why?'

'No reason,' I reply, picking up the menu sheepishly.

9.34 p.m.

The evening still seems to be going well. I'm having a pleasant time, Tina appears to be having a pleasant time, and as we chat over our food, I'm starting to see how this dating business can be fun. And it is fun, up until the point where we get on to past relationships. Tina tells me about the six or so boyfriends she's had since leaving college, and how she thought she'd give speed dating a try as obviously her work hasn't proved to be the best environment to meet single men. At least, not single men who aren't interested in other single men.

It's a little smoky in the bar, and my new lenses are starting to call out for a little more lubrication, which, of course, is making my eyes water. At the same time, I'm giving Tina an—admittedly abridged—version of what's happened with Jane and me, leaving out the fact that I've gone through this whole process to try to win her back, and deciding not to point out that Tina is, in fact, a trial run for Jane's imminent return.

I get to the bit about Jane leaving for Tibet and dab at my eyes, which are running quite freely now, with my napkin. When Tina suddenly puts her hand on mine, it's all I can do not to pull away in shock.

'You poor thing,' she says. 'If it's too upsetting for you, we can talk about something else.'

'No. That's fine. It's just I…' I consider telling her it's my new contact lenses, but then she might remove her hand.

Tina reaches up to my face and wipes away a tear that's running down my cheek.

'Don't worry,' she says. 'These things get easier with time.'

Funny. That's just what my optician said.

10.25 p.m.

We're arguing already, but in a nice way, struggling to hear each other above the noise in the bar.

'Tina, I asked you out. That means I'm paying.'

'But that's just reinforcing outmoded social conventions.'

'It's only right that I pay. After all, in caveman days, if we'd wanted to eat, I'd have hunted it down and killed it.'

Tina stares at her plate. 'A salad? Besides, we're not in caveman days any more.'

'Are we not?' I nod towards the stag do in the corner, where the Elvis impersonators are taking turns to climb on the table and sing. 'I'm worried we'll go deaf. And it sounds like some of them already are.'

Tina glances over at them without releasing her grip on the bill. 'They are making a bit of a din.'

'Is it Elvises? Or Elvi?'

Tina cups her hand to her ear. 'What?'

'I said, is it Elvises…'

Tina smiles. 'I heard you. I was making a joke. About the noise.'

'What's wrong with my nose?'

'No, I said…Ah. Touché.'

We have definitely had a good time, but not as much of a good time as the—well, whatever the collective term for a group of Elvis Presley look-alikes is, who are now all standing on the table, belting out 'Love Me Tender' at the tops of their voices.

'Shall we go?'

Tina just nods, we agree to split the bill, and head outside, strolling back along Western Road to where her car is parked. As Tina blips the door open, she turns to me, then surprises me by leaning in and kissing me on the mouth. Before I can even purse my lips in response, she breaks away.

'Thanks,' she says. 'Tonight was fun.'

I don't quite know how to react. I've not kissed another woman on the lips since Jane left, and to be honest, I hadn't kissed Jane on the lips for a while by then anyway, so in truth, this is one of the most exciting things that's happened to me in ages. I'm trying to work out what my response should be when Tina shivers in the chilly evening.

'Where do you live?'

I indicate back along past the restaurant. 'Oh, not far. Just about five minutes that way.'

'Jump in. I'll give you a lift.'

'No, that's OK. I don't mind walking.'

Tina gets into the driver's seat, then leans across and opens her passenger door. 'Come on,' she says. 'I won't bite. Unless you want me to.'

I don't know what to do. If I get into the car, who knows where that will lead. If I don't, I can just kiss this evening, and Tina, goodbye. Which of course, I'm supposed to, because after all, this is just a trial run for when Jane gets back. What I am sure of is that she's flirting with me. Big time. And in a guilty way, I like it.

After a moment's hesitation, and more because I'm cold than for any other reason, I get in.

'Buckle up,' she says, with a mischievous smile. 'Better to be safe than sorry.'

For the first time in ages, there's a parking spot right outside my front door. God, or more likely the devil, must be smiling down on me, so instead of having to double park and drop me off, Tina's able to pull her car into the space. We sit there awkwardly for a moment before I move to open my door.

'Thanks for the lift. I'd ask you in for a coffee, but…'

Tina stares straight ahead. 'Oh. I see.'

'No, it's not that. It's just that I don't have any coffee. I forgot to buy some. I've got tea…'

Tina looks at me for a few moments, as if she's weighing something up, then switches the engine off and unbuckles her seatbelt. 'Tea would be lovely. But…'

'But what?'

'But I'm not going to sleep with you tonight, Ed. I'm not that kind of girl.'

I'm stunned. 'Nor am I. I mean, I'm not that kind of boy. Man, I mean.'

Tina raises one eyebrow, 'Yeah, right.'

As we walk up my front steps, I try frantically to work out what Tina's 'I'm not going to sleep with you tonight' means. Is it simply to leave me in no doubt that we're going inside just for a cup of tea? Or does the 'tonight' part suggest something more, as in 'but I might another night'? For the first time, I envy Dan's simplistic approach.

When I show Tina inside, she takes one look around the lounge and whistles appreciatively. 'Nice place. And cool furniture.'

I have to stop myself from punching the air. 'Thanks.' And thanks, Dan. Or rather, thanks Alexis.

Tina sits down on the sofa, and I nip off into the kitchen, hurriedly removing my photos from the front of the fridge, then put the kettle on, before sticking my head back through the kitchen door.

'How do you take it?'

Tina makes a mock-horror face. 'I beg your pardon?'

'Your tea.'

'I know, Edward. I'm teasing you. Milk no sugar, please. And can I use your bathroom?'

I show Tina where the bathroom is, then head back into the kitchen, feeling pretty pleased with myself. As I make the tea, I begin to feel more relaxed. At least Tina's set out her position up front. There's going to be none of this first-date fumbling, wondering where it's going to lead, and I'll be able to emerge from this evening knowing that I've managed to go through the motions and entertain a woman on a date. After all, that's the whole point of this exercise, I remind myself.

When I walk back in with the mugs of tea, Tina's still in the bathroom, but this presents me with my second dilemma—do I sit next to her, or rather, take the safer option of the armchair? But what am I thinking? Of course it should be the armchair. I put Tina's mug down on the coffee table in front of where she's been sitting, and take mine over to the chair.

As I sit down with my tea, it occurs to me that I should probably put some music on. I rest my mug in its usual place on the arm of my chair and go to stand up, but I've forgotten that this isn't my old armchair, with wide, flat-topped armrests, but my new trendy leather armchair, with elegantly curved and inward-sloping armrests. What would therefore normally be a solid, secure place for a cup of hot, recently boiled liquid is now a precarious balance point, so much so that the second I let go of my mug it tips inwards, depositing its boiling contents straight into my lap.

With a yell, I leap up and out of the chair as the steaming liquid scalds my thighs, and its all I can do to undo my belt and drop my trousers, trying to stop the tea-sodden material from blistering my privates.

When Tina runs back into the room, having heard the commotion, she's greeted by the sight of me, trousers around my ankles, shuffling towards her. This would be bad enough on its own, but the fact that I'm repeating the phrase 'Fuck me!' at the top of my voice probably doesn't add to her sense of comfort and security at being alone in my flat with me.

As Tina rushes past me, grabs her handbag, and makes her escape, she doesn't even stop to close the front door behind her.

And at least I appreciate the nice cool breeze.

11.14 p.m.

I'm sitting round at Dan's, wearing a clean pair of trousers, holding very carefully onto my mug of tea, and telling him about my date.

'Well, look on the bright side,' he says, once he's eventually stopped laughing, which admittedly takes him a long, long time. 'At least you don't have to worry about telling her you can't see her again.'

'Maybe.'

But the truth is, I'm already experiencing a new feeling. Not hurt from missing Jane, and not pain from my daily torture sessions with Sam, but it hasn't taken me long to realize what this one is. Guilt. What was I thinking? In a few days my girlfriend, and yes, I think I can still use that word, is coming back from her 'holiday', and here's me flirting with another woman. Going out for a drink with another woman. Even inviting her back to my flat.

Dan takes one look at my glum expression. 'What's the matter with you?'

'What do you think? I could have been unfaithful to Jane, and now I'm going to have to tell her.'

'Whoa. Unfaithful? I thought you said that nothing happened.'

'It didn't. But I can't guarantee that it wouldn't have. Or that I didn't want it too.'

'Hold on,' says Dan. 'Those two things are quite different. And besides, do you think Jane's over there being faithful to you?'

'I don't know. I don't want to think about what she might be getting up to.'

'So why are you even going to bother telling her about what you didn't get up to tonight?'

'Because it's important to be honest.'

Dan shakes his head vigorously. 'I'll tell you something, Edward. Where relationships are concerned, honesty might be the best policy, but dishonesty comes a close second.'

'In your world, Dan, perhaps.'

'Besides, you did it for her.'

'And you think she'll understand that?'

'No. Which is precisely why you're not going to tell her. Instead, just look at the positives. You managed to entertain a girl for the evening, and so much so that she agreed to come back to your place for "coffee".'

'I suppose. Although that may have been only because she felt sorry for me.'

Dan shrugs. 'Even so. But sympathy votes only get you so far. This girl was obviously interested enough in you to go out with you, and even—up until you scared her off—to want to keep the evening going into extra time. What does that tell you?'

I don't answer him, but sip my tea contentedly, as I know exactly what it tells me.

It tells me that I'm nearly there.

Thursday 14th April

7 a.m.

I DON'T SLEEP MUCH, my mind buzzing with the events of the previous evening, and it's an effort to drag myself out of bed and into my somewhat looser tracksuit in time for Sam's knock on the door. She greets me with a 'Hey, partner', and we jog easily down to the promenade, picking the pace up between the piers.

It's a beautiful spring morning, with hardly anyone about, and Sam's pushing me hard—too hard for any real conversation, which for some reason I'm quite glad about. We do our usual seafront circuit before heading for the gym, and we're jogging up through Norfolk Square when suddenly Eddie comes bounding up towards me, yapping excitedly. I try to run a little faster, not wanting Billy to see me out jogging, but Eddie grabs hold of the leg of my tracksuit bottoms in his teeth, and I tumble onto the grass, narrowly avoiding a fresh pile of dog poo.

'Bloody dog,' I say.

Sam tries to hide a smile. 'Are you hurt?'

I do a quick check—all limbs seem to be functioning properly. 'I don't think so.'

As Sam holds out a hand to help me up, I look round for Billy, wondering why on earth Eddie's out on his own, but it's only when Eddie runs off towards the corner of the park that I see him, huddled underneath a bench. I pick myself up and sprint across to where Billy's lying. He looks a lot worse than normal, quite possibly due to the beating he's obviously taken, and Sam has to struggle not to heave as he's evidently soiled himself during the night. His face is bloody, and his breathing is way too shallow for my liking.

'Billy! Billy!' I shake his shoulder, but get the meekest of responses. 'Quick, Sam. Give me your mobile.'

As Sam reaches into her rucksack, Billy opens one blood-caked eyelid and a wave of recognition floods across his face.

'Edward,' he mumbles, then notices Sam. 'Whoosis?'

My guess is that his slurring is caused by the beating, and not by his usual liquid breakfast.

'Don't try and move, Billy. I'll get help.'

Sam looks horrified at Billy's bruised and battered face. 'You know him?'

'Yes. Well, I buy the odd *Big Issue* from him.'

Billy feebly waves a hand in my direction. 'Best customer,' he wheezes, before losing consciousness again.

Sam hands me her phone and I call 999, then put Billy into the recovery position and wait for the ambulance, which arrives surprisingly quickly. The driver, however, is less than sympathetic.

'Jesus. Bloody winos. What do you expect us to do with him? He stinks.'

I grab him by the shoulder and wheel him roughly around, taking both him and Sam by surprise. 'He's not a wino. He's a homeless person, which means he's still a person. And you'd probably smell a bit if you didn't have a home to go to, and a shower to wash in, or even any hot water. Try and show a little compassion, if you can't have the decency to show any respect.'

The ambulance man blushes and mumbles an apology, before he and his colleague lift Billy onto a stretcher and put him into the back of the ambulance. Eddie jumps in after him, only to be chased out by the angry driver.

'These homeless always have bloody dogs,' he says.

'Yes. Well,' I say, my anger subsiding, 'that's probably why they're called "homeless" and not "dogless".'

'Do you want to come with him?' he says to me.

'I'll get my car and follow,' I reply, grabbing hold of Eddie by his bandana. 'Sorry, Sam. Can we cut it short today?'

'Of course,' she says. 'I'll come with you.'

'What about your next client?'

'I'll cancel.'

I pick Eddie up, we jog round the corner to Dan's, and ring on his doorbell. When he eventually answers, all bleary-eyed, I thrust Eddie into his arms.

'Look after him. It's very important.'

'Huh?' says Dan, as Eddie licks his face. 'It's a dog.'

'Well, I'm sure you've entertained a few of those in your time,' I reply.

9.05 a.m.

We're in Accident and Emergency, waiting to see how Billy's doing. When the doctor finally comes out, Sam and I approach him anxiously.

'How is he?'

'Just bruising, perhaps a mild concussion. He's asleep now, but we'll keep him in overnight just to be sure.'

I breathe a sigh of relief. 'That's good news.'

'Are you Eddie? He's been asking for you.'

Sam nudges me. 'Eddie. I like it,' she whispers.

'No, I'm…It's a long story. But when he wakes up, tell him Eddie s fine. He's being looked after.'

The doctor looks from me to Sam. 'Does he have someone we could call?'

I shake my head. 'I'm not sure…'

'Perhaps they know him at the church drop-in centre?' suggests Sam.

The doctor nods. 'Is he religious, do you know?'

'Maybe,' I say, trying to remember whether I've ever heard Billy talk about religion, but as far as I know, all he worships is the bottle. 'I think he's more the spiritual type. Is there anything he needs?'

The doctor thinks for a moment. 'A change of clothes, perhaps?'

I reach into my wallet, and hand the doctor some notes. 'Could someone perhaps get him some? He's a very proud man and won't take charity, but if he wakes up and finds some stuff already there…'

The doctor smiles. 'I understand.'

9.21 a.m.

When I drop Sam off at her flat, she leans across and kisses me on the cheek. I can't stop myself from reaching up to touch the spot where her lips have landed.

'What was that for?'

'That was a lovely thing you did today, to stop and help like that. Really lovely. Most people would have just walked on past.'

'Well, you helped too. A real Sam-aritan.'

Sam groans. 'Is it too late to work on your sense of humour?'

'Anyway, I had to stop. For one thing, I was knackered. Besides, any excuse to get me out of the gym session.'

'Edward, I was trying to pay you a compliment. Don't throw it back at me.'

'Sorry, Sam. But I couldn't just let him lie there.'

'And that's the difference between you and so many other people.'

'Well, that's very nice of you to say so.'

Sam opens the car door and starts to get out, then pauses mid-way. 'Listen…'

'Yes?'

'That party tonight at your boss's house? I'd love to come.'

'Really?'

'Really. If you've not asked anyone else, that is.'

'Er…No.'

'Great. Well, pick me up at eight?'

'Eight it is.'

'I'll look forward to it,' she says, as she gets out and shuts the door behind her.

And as I watch Sam disappear into her flat, I realize that so will I.

12.02 p.m.

I'm in the office, preparing the invoices for the Go-Soft campaign, when Natasha finally appears. I can tell immediately that she's in a bad mood, so try and head it off.

'Good morning.'

Natasha glares at her watch, and then at me. 'Wrong on both those counts.'

She slams the door behind her, stomps over to her desk, and sits there staring at her PC. After ten minutes, I pluck up the courage to bring her a cup of coffee.

'Here you go.'

She looks up at me miserably. Even to my untrained eye, it looks like she's been crying.

'Thanks, Edward. Sorry.'

'For what?'

'For snapping at you earlier.'

'Is something wrong?'

I can tell for a moment that she's considering biting my head off. Something's clearly wrong, and I brace myself for her reaction to what's obviously the most inane question I could have asked. But things *have* changed in the Staff-IT office, because instead, and on top of the apology, she starts to explain.

'It's Terry. He's not coming to my party.'

This strikes me as the kind of thing a five year old might say. 'Why not? Did he give you a reason?'

Natasha sniffs. 'Some rubbish about his wife having another baby.'

'Ah.' In all the time I've worked for her, this is probably only the second conversation we've had about anything to do with her private life.

'It's just, well, I know you probably think I'm a heartless bitch…'

Natasha pauses, and I don't know whether this is one of those moments I'm meant to leap in and contradict her.

'Well, not completely heartless, exactly. I mean, not that you're a bitch, or anything…'

'It's just that sometimes I wonder what it's all about. This relationship lark. Why do the men I like always seem to feel threatened by me?'

'Possibly because you're actually a threatening woman?'

Natasha looks up sharply. 'Threatening? How so?'

I back away slightly. 'In that you make threats. Remember that guy who had the Ferrari?'

'Steve?'

'Yeah. You told him you'd pour paint stripper all over it if he didn't move in with you. And what about the one whose wife you challenged to a fight?'

'Peter?'

'He was a nice guy. Why didn't you see him again?'

Natasha blushes. 'What, apart from the injunction?'

'And then there was Martin. With the stutter.'

'He didn't have a stutter.'

'He does now.'

Natasha looks indignant. 'Yes, well, that was blown out of all proportion.'

'Again, the courts didn't seem to think so.'

'So tell me, Edward. Where do you think I'm going wrong?'

Gulp. I do a quick check for sharp objects within Natasha's reach. 'Maybe...maybe you're just setting your sights on the wrong types of men. They're married; possibly not completely happily in most cases but they value it, so when they've had their fun, and push comes to shove...'

Natasha stares at her untouched coffee for a few moments. 'Perhaps you're right, Edward. But what are the right types of men?'

'Well, them not having wives would possibly be a good start,' I suggest.

'Maybe.' She looks up at me and smiles hopefully. 'You're bound to know at least one single, good-looking guy, perhaps as a date for me? What about this friend of yours—Dan, isn't it? Why don't you bring him along tonight?'

At first this strikes me as ridiculous, firstly that Natasha is asking whether I know anyone I can set her up with, and secondly that she and Dan might get on, let alone get it on. Plus, the last thing I want is for Dan to try and have a 'crack' at Sam, especially in front of me. But as I think about it, I begin to realize that it's a brilliant idea. I'll earn some serious Brownie points with Natasha, she's bound to flirt outrageously with Dan all evening, which in turn will be the perfect diversionary tactic to keep him away from Sam.

'I'll see what I can do.'

7.45 p.m.

I'm in the Mini with Dan, who of course has leapt at the chance for a free night out, and we're on our way to pick up Sam for tonight's party at Natasha's. I'm dressed in Paul Smith again, but *with* a tie this time, and lightly doused in Guerlain's 'Vetiver', which may sound like a disease, but is actually the classiest aftershave known to man. And woman, apparently.

As I speed along the seafront, I can't help but smile to myself. As much as I hate to admit it, I do feel better driving this car than my old Volvo. Nought to sixty takes just nine point two seconds, as opposed to my old heap, which had a job even reaching sixty, let alone doing it in anything you'd want to measure with a stopwatch. I can park in spaces that don't have to be bus-length. I can overtake. I like the way it feels behind the wheel, and I like that I feel that I belong here too.

Dan catches sight of my inane grin. 'Told you,' he says. 'Cool car, eh?'

I glance across at him, before effortlessly accelerating past a bus. 'I am a Mini driver, and I'm proud.'

'Mate,' he says, 'if you were Minnie Driver, we wouldn't be talking now.'

When I ring on Sam's doorbell, I hear Oliver bark a few times, so I'm ready when he runs out and tries to jump up on me, but when Sam appears I'm certainly not prepared for her. She's wearing a classic little black dress, with shoes and handbag to match, a simple gold necklace, and diamond earrings that sparkle almost as much as her eyes. It's the first time I've seen her in anything other than a tracksuit or jeans, and as enjoyable as that has been, the sight of her this evening almost blows me away.

'Something wrong?' she asks, before pulling her coat on. 'Too over the top? Too little?'

'Yeah,' calls Dan from the car, where he's contorted awkwardly in the back seat. 'Like a woman can *ever* wear too little.'

'No. Not at all,' I say, ignoring him. 'You look, well, amazing, if I can say so.'

Sam blushes, and then rubs her fingers up and down the lapel of my suit. 'You scrub up pretty well yourself.'

I open the car door for her, and she says hello to Dan, who responds with a smile, his teeth shining out from the dark interior.

'Shift forward a bit, mate,' he says, as we head back through Brighton and up towards Dyke Road. 'There's not a lot of room in here.'

'Stop complaining. This was the car you advised me to buy, remember?'

By the time we get to Natasha's, her drive is full of expensive cars, at least a couple of them hers, but I manage to squeeze the Mini in between a couple of Porsches. As we get out of the car, we can hear music coming from the back of the house, a huge mock-Tudor mansion that I'm guessing wouldn't leave much change out of a couple of million. Sam stares open-mouthed at the place, whereas Dan, on the other hand, is a little more vocal.

'Bloody hell. Who did she sleep with to get this?'

Sam gives him an admonishing look. 'That's very sexist, Daniel. Why do you have to assume that she couldn't have earned it herself?'

I have to take Dan's side on this. 'Sorry, Sam. Natasha was married to a dot-com millionaire. When they split up, she got to keep the house.'

'Wow,' says Sam. 'What did he get to keep?'

'His testicles, I believe.'

The party is being held in a marquee that's probably as big as my entire flat, but takes up less than half of Natasha's back garden. We walk inside, helping ourselves to a glass of champagne from a passing waitress. Dan, true to form, takes two, winking at the girl as he does so.

After a few minutes, I feel a tap on my shoulder, and turn round to see Natasha wearing a gold, strapless evening dress. She air kisses me, and when she sees Sam, Natasha raises both her eyebrows.

'This is Sam,' I say. 'My, er…'

'Edward's date for the evening,' says Sam. 'Pleased to meet you, Natasha.'

'And this—' I say, turning to Dan, who's staring unashamedly at Natasha's cleavage.

'Must be Dan,' interrupts Natasha. 'It's very nice to meet you.'

Dan takes Natasha's outstretched hand and kisses it. 'The pleasure's all mine.'

I nudge Sam. 'That's true, according to all the women he's slept with.'

Natasha stares suggestively back at Dan. 'I find that hard to believe,' she says.

As the two of them size each other up, Sam and I almost have to recoil from the sparks. Dan switches effortlessly into charm mode, handing Natasha one of his glasses of champagne.

'Thanks for inviting me to your birthday party,' he says. 'Your thirtieth, isn't it?'

I'm amazed at the cheesiness of Dan's comment, and wait expectantly for Natasha to shoot him down. Instead, she laps it up.

'Edward,' she says. 'Why didn't you tell me you had such nice-looking friends?'

As she and Dan continue to flirt, I lean towards Sam, and whisper in my best David Attenborough impression.

'Observe, the mating ritual of the male and female of the species. Although I'm not sure exactly which species…'

It's clear that our presence in this foursome is two too many, so Sam and I excuse ourselves. Never one to do anything by halves, Natasha has hired a string quartet for the evening, and as they launch into a rousing rendition of 'Let's Twist Again', Sam grabs me by the hand.

'Can you twist, Edward?'

'I don't know. I don't think so.'

'Have you ever tried?'

'Er…no.'

'Well, how do you know you can't do something if you've never even tried it?'

Sam pulls me onto the dance floor, where a number of couples are trying gamely to follow the lead of the band, although their gyrations seem more suited to 'The Birdie Song'. Sam stands in front of me and tells me to follow her, but just as we're about to try, the music mercifully changes to something much slower.

'Oh well.' I start to walk off the floor, but Sam stops me.

'Where do you think you're going?'

'But the music...'

'Never mind,' she says, holding me close and leading me around the dance floor.

I have one hand on her shoulder, and the other on the small of her back, and can feel the sensual movement of her toned body beneath her thin silk dress. I can smell her perfume, the soft scent of her hair, and for a moment, just for a moment, wonder when was the last time I danced with Jane like this. I certainly can't recall when dancing with Jane made me feel this way. And worryingly, I can't actually remember the last time Jane and I danced.

As we move to the music, and I become more and more conscious of the soft firmness of her body pressed against mine, I feel a not-so-soft firmness of my own beginning to stir. *Quick*, I tell myself, *think of something else*. Normally whenever I've needed, shall we say, delaying tactics when I've been in bed with Jane, I've picked a football side at random and tried to remember all the players' names, but my mistake this evening is to pick the England World Cup squad from 1966: in goal, Gordon Banks, which I seem to remember is rhyming slang for something else. In defence—oh no—Alan Ball. Aargh!

Fortunately, just as I get to midfielder Nobby Stiles, and realize I couldn't possibly have made a worse choice of team, the music stops, to be replaced with the unmistakable sound of a champagne glass being tapped. Natasha steps up onto the podium in front of the band, and clears her throat.

'Well, I want to thank you all for coming,' she says, to a general murmur of appreciation. 'As some of you may know, tonight is a special night for me for two reasons. Firstly, because it's my fortieth birthday.' She pauses, obviously expecting to hear some mutterings of disbelief. When none come, she coughs awkwardly.

'Secondly, because it's also the twentieth anniversary of the day I started my company, which, at the risk of blowing my own trumpet…'

'That's not all she's been blowing,' I whisper to Sam.

'…has been doing rather well recently. In fact, business is booming. And that's why I have a rather important announcement to make. Someone special I want to introduce you to.'

As Natasha scans the crowd, I'm assuming she's looking for Terry. I haven't seen him at all this evening, but now I'm assuming that he's obviously left his wife holding the baby, so to speak, and come along. What on earth is she going to do—propose to him in front of everyone, or some other nonsense?

I'm fed up with this, and make my excuses to Sam, before heading off to find the toilet. But just as I'm walking back into the house, Natasha's voice, as it has done on so many occasions in the past, stops me in my tracks.

'Edward? There you are.'

I wave sheepishly, and just about manage to stop myself from cowering in the corner, as everyone turns to look at me.

'Just going to the toilet, boss,' I say, which gets a small laugh from the crowd.

Natasha grins. 'Well, cross your legs for a few minutes and come up here, will you?'

Trying to hide my embarrassment, I make my way towards where she's standing, and climb up on the podium next to her, struggling not to flinch when she puts her arm around me.

'As I was saying,' continues Natasha. 'The reason we're doing so well is all down to one person. My right-hand man. Edward.'

I blush. This isn't happening. I just want to curl up and die. Is she going to propose to *me?*

'Which is why,' she continues, 'I'd like to make him my partner.'

I stare at Natasha in shock, thinking for a moment that she *is* proposing to me, until I realize that, actually, this is one long-term relationship that I'm happy to take to the next level.

Natasha raises her champagne glass. 'So I'd like to make a toast. To what's going to be my last ever birthday. And to my new business partner, Edward.'

'To Edward,' comes the response, and a hundred glasses of champagne are raised in my direction.

As I look around the marquee, people I've never even seen before are applauding me. Dan is standing there open-mouthed. Sam is grinning wildly and clapping as loudly as she can. I mumble my thanks to Natasha, climb back down off the podium, and head back towards the two of them.

As Dan shakes me enthusiastically by the hand, Sam grabs me in a big hug.

'Partner, eh?' she says. 'I guess this means I'll be putting up my rate.'

'Yeah, well done,' says Dan. 'Partner in a two-person company. And it's only taken you, what, nine years?'

'Exactly,' I say. 'Who's the career person now, eh?'

As we head into the garden for some fresh air, Dan puts an arm around my shoulders.

'Lets just hope it's equal partners, eh?' he says, gazing admiringly back up at the house.

Sam looks at him strangely. 'Are there any other kind?'

12.02 a.m.

By midnight, we've danced, eaten, and danced some more. A few of the guests have started to make their way home, and Sam is getting tired, as am I. We have been up since before seven o'clock, I remind her.

'And have to be tomorrow,' she says. 'Our last session, don't forget.'

I look around for Natasha so we can say goodbye, but she's nowhere to be seen. Worryingly, nor is Dan.

'He's a big boy. He can look after himself,' I tell Sam, which is code for 'he's probably pulled, so that's the last we'll see of him'. 'But I ought to try and find Natasha. Just to say thanks.'

We can't seem to spot her anywhere, until one of the waiters tells us she was last seen heading towards the swimming pool, so Sam and I walk through the house, following the whiff of chlorine down into the basement. It's one of those impossible-to-do-lengths-in kidney-shaped pools, with a statue of Michelangelo's *David* between a pair of marble pillars at one end, and a large mosaic of two intertwined dolphins on the bottom.

'Mmm,' whispers Sam. 'Tasteful.'

Through what look like plastic palm trees in one corner, I eventually spot Dan. He's lying in the Jacuzzi, with a blissful look on his face.

'Typical,' I say under my breath. 'Talk about taking advantage of Natasha's hospitality.'

I'm just about to call out to him when Sam puts a finger on my lips and points towards David, who seems to have Natasha's dress draped over one of his arms.

'I think he might be the one who's being taken advantage of,' she says.

Confused, I peer back towards the Jacuzzi, where Dan still hasn't seen us, probably due to the fact that he's got his eyes shut. Suddenly, there's even more of a disturbance in the bubbling water, and Natasha's head surfaces from between Dan's legs. I suddenly feel unclean, like I've walked in on my parents kissing.

'Impressive,' whispers Sam.

'What is?'

'Natasha. She can stay underwater for a really long time.'

Natasha takes a deep breath and goes back under, causing Dan's face to change from blissful to ecstatic—an expression I'll take with me to my grave. We watch, perversely fascinated for a few seconds, until Natasha re-surfaces, and Dan decides to stand up. This is one image I can do without, so Sam and I sneak out through the door, giggling like children.

We retrieve the Mini and head back into Brighton, Sam dropping off into a doze and resting her head on my shoulder as I drive. I consider taking a longer route home to prolong the moment, but then worry that she might wake up suddenly and think I'm abducting her. When I eventually pull into her street, she stirs awake.

'Thank you for a lovely evening,' she says, trying hard to conceal a yawn. 'I'd invite you in for a coffee, but firstly you shouldn't be drinking the stuff, and secondly, we've both got to get up early.'

'No problem,' I say. 'I'll be off now, then.'

She smiles. 'So I'll see you in the morning?'

'As usual,' I reply, but with a touch of sadness. After all, from tomorrow, it won't be 'usual' any more.

As Sam gets out of the car, I hold out my hand, and she shakes it, rather formally.

'Thanks again,' she says. 'I had a really nice time.'

'Me too. Natasha throws a good party.'

'No, I mean I had a nice time with you, Edward. You're lovely company. I can't see how Jane can fail to be charmed.'

'You think so?'

Sam smiles again, and squeezes my arm. 'I know so.'

Friday 15th April

7.54 a.m.

THE MORNING SUN GLINTS off the sea as we jog down from the gym, turn right between the piers, and then as usual, pick up the pace along the seafront. For the first time, and in our very own Rocky/Apollo Creed moment, I manage to keep up with Sam on the final stretch, then out-sprint her to the bandstand.

As I dance around in celebration, my hands above my head, Sam chases after me and punches me playfully in the belly. I'm ready for her, and tense my stomach muscles to easily absorb the blow.

Sam raises her eyebrows. 'Well, you're done,' she pronounces, as if she's checking a pan of potatoes.

'Thanks. And I couldn't have done it without you.'

Sam shrugs. 'You're the one who did all the work, not me.'

'Yes, but I don't mean just for the physical side, if you'll excuse the phrase…'

She smiles. 'Don't mention it. Oh, and before I forget, I've got something for you.'

As she reaches into her rucksack, I suddenly feel a little awkward.

'There's no need,' I stammer. 'I mean, I haven't bought you anything…'

'No—this.' Sam holds out my front-door key. Not for the first time, I hope she mistakes my red face for effort. 'And actually, yes you have.'

'What do you mean?'

'An hour a day, five days a week, for three months, at forty pounds an hour…You've bought me quite a lot, actually.'

'Ah. Well, you're welcome.'

As I do a couple of unprompted stretches against the metal railings, Sam comes and leans next to me. 'So,' she says. 'Tomorrow's the big day?'

'Yup.'

'When does she arrive?'

'Early morning, I think.'

'You think?'

I nod. 'There's only one flight a day from Tibet, and that gets in at seven. Seven a.m., that is.'

Sam whistles. 'Early start.'

I smile. 'I'm used to those now.'

'Well, good luck, Edward. I hope you get what you want.'

'Thanks.'

'And remember to keep it up.'

'Pardon?'

'You know what I mean. The exercise.'

'Oh. Right.'

'And say hi to Dan for me.'

'Will do. Assuming he didn't drown in the Jacuzzi last night.'

'And I hope Billy gets better soon.'

'Yup. Me too.'

'And do thank Natasha for me. Great party.'

'OK. Sure.'

We stand in silence for a while, staring out at the sea, and then Sam looks at her watch.

'Well, time is money, and the world is full of fat people waiting for their thin selves to appear.'

I pretend to be hurt. 'You've already got someone else to replace me?'

She nods. 'Easy come, easy go. But…'

'But what?'

Sam leans in and gives me the briefest of hugs, before pecking me on the cheek. 'But you've got my number.'

With that she smiles, then jogs away along the seafront.

For a moment, I have an insane urge to run after her, but manage to stop myself.

After all, what on earth would I say if I caught her?

1.21 p.m.

Natasha doesn't appear in the office until lunchtime. Strangely, I haven't been able to raise Dan on his mobile either.

'Any messages?' she asks, before she's even sat down.

'Er…no.'

Natasha stares anxiously at her mobile, and then picks up the office phone to check for a dial tone. 'None at all?'

'No,' I say, thinking about Dan's usual modus operandi, and wondering how this will affect my recent promotion. 'Sorry.'

'Oh, well,' Natasha sighs, and puts the receiver back down. 'Did you have a good time last night?'

'Yes, thanks,' I say, grinning at her. 'Did you?'

She looks at me strangely. 'What do you mean by that?'

'Nothing,' I reply, innocently. 'I tried to find you to say goodbye. But I couldn't.'

'Oh?' says Natasha, the merest hint of redness creeping into her cheeks, before she goes on the offensive. 'You can't have looked very hard.'

'Evidently not,' I say, thinking *unlike Dan*, and glad that Sam and I left the pool room when we did. 'But Sam sends her thanks as well.'

'Ah yes,' says Natasha. 'Sam's lovely. Have you given up on Jane, then?'

'No,' I splutter. 'Sam's my personal trainer.'

'So I could see,' says Natasha. 'And with the emphasis on the word "personal", by the looks of things.'

I'm wondering how on earth to answer this, when something miraculous happens; the office phone rings, and when I pick it up, it's Dan. I decide to feign ignorance.

'Hello, Dan,' I say, noting Natasha's sudden interest. 'What happened to you last night? I looked everywhere for you.'

'Sorry, mate. I was...' Dan clears his throat, 'otherwise engaged.'

'You pulled, didn't you?'

'Might have done...'

Normally this would be the cue for Dan to regale me with last night's most intimate details. This time, however, he's unusually silent. 'Come on, what was she like?'

'Er...'

I can see Natasha listening in from her desk, so pretend that he's spilling the beans. 'Oh, no. Really? That bad? She didn't?'

As Dan starts to question my parentage, Natasha raps loudly on her desk.

'Edward. No personal phone calls in the office, please.'

I place a hand over the mouthpiece. 'That's rich. All you ever do is make personal phone calls. Anyway, mate,' I say back to Dan, 'did you call just to brag about your latest conquest?'

'No, I...Can I speak to Natasha please?'

I pretend to be surprised, enjoying the fact that Natasha is looking all flustered across from me.

'Natasha?' I look over and raise one eyebrow in her direction, and for the first time in nearly ten years I see Natasha go completely red—for reasons other than apoplectic rage, that is. 'Why? Oh, I see, the party. What's that? You want to thank her for having you.'

As Dan splutters down the telephone line, Natasha leaps up from her chair, her vulnerability lasting all of about half a second before she marches over and snatches the phone from me.

'Thank you, Edward.'

With a grin, I pick up my jacket and head out of the room.

1.42 p.m.

When I walk back into the office clutching a muesli bar and a banana, Natasha's sitting at her desk, flicking absentmindedly through a copy of the *Financial Times*.

I nod towards the paper. 'Anything interesting?'

Natasha looks up and notices my healthy lunch.

'Apparently Dunkin' Donuts are about to issue a profit warning.'

'Ha ha. Very funny.'

'Edward,' she says, folding the paper and slipping it into her briefcase. 'I've got something to tell you. About last night.'

'Really?' I say.

'Yes. Your friend Dan and I. Well, we…'

I'm not quite sure how much detail Natasha's about to go into, and as far as I'm concerned, any detail is too much. I hold up my hand to stop her.

'I know.'

She looks a little confused. 'How do you know?'

'One of the places Sam and I looked for you was in the pool.'

'Ah.' For only the second time in nearly ten years, but not the first time this afternoon, I enjoy the sight of Natasha turning scarlet. 'Well, anyway, he's just asked me out.'

'What?' Dan? Phoning a woman to ask her out *after* he's had sex with her? I try and hide my surprise, but fail miserably. 'On a date?'

'No, Edward. For a fight. Of course on a date.'

'Oh. Right. Are you going to go?'

'I'm not sure. What do you think I should do?' says Natasha, anxiously. 'I mean, he's quite a bit younger than me.'

'Hmm. Toy boy or not toy boy. That is the question.'

'Exactly. I mean, I like my men with a few lines. And I don't mean of the "chat up" variety.'

'Natasha, I can't advise you on this. He's my best friend, and you're my boss.'

Natasha smiles. 'Business partner. As of yesterday.'

'Yes, sorry. Business partner. But what do you want me to say—that you and Dan are perfect for each other? Or that you should run a mile, otherwise you'll only end up getting hurt again? Because, let's face it, it doesn't matter what I, or indeed anyone else, thinks.'

Natasha nods. 'You're right. I need to suck it and see.'

'I beg your pardon?'

'Sorry,' says Natasha. 'Perhaps not the most appropriate analogy. But it's something we used to say as kids.'

'Do I really want to know?'

'No, Edward. Nothing like that. It's when you're trying to guess the flavour of a boiled sweet, or you want to avoid the coffee-centred Revel in favour of the orange one.'

'Huh?'

'You may think you can tell what something's going to be like from the outside, but the only way to really find out is to…'

'Stick it in your mouth and try it?'

'Exactly,' says Natasha. 'Suck it and see.'

7.32 p.m.

I'm in the Admiral Jim with Dan, sipping what is, I hope, the last sparkling water I'll ever have to drink.

'So,' he asks, shifting nervously in his chair. 'What do you think? Did she say anything about me?'

'Well, her exact words were…' I stop myself, remembering last night's Jacuzzi scene a little too vividly. 'I think, to use language you can understand, she'd be "up for it".'

'Great.' Dan looks visibly relieved. I, on the other hand, don't quite know what to make of either his puppy-dog appearance, or the fact that he's asking *me* for advice about women. 'And she doesn't think the age difference is a problem?'

'Nah. She knows you're into antiques. But just be careful,' I tell him. 'She's not like your usual conquests.'

'I know that,' says Dan. 'Which is why I want to take it slow. Get to know her first.'

'Take it slow? The two of you were naked in a Jacuzzi within four hours of first meeting each other. Oh, hold on. That probably is a bit slow for you, isn't it?'

Dan grins guiltily. 'Maybe. Anyway. Speaking of important dates…'

I pretend to be confused for a moment, until Dan taps his laptop. 'Oh—you must mean tomorrow?'

'Look at you, Mr Cool. Do you want to do this or not?'

'Sorry. Yes,' I say. 'Please.'

'OK. Weight?' he says, tabbing through the spreadsheet.

I look at my watch. 'How long for?'

'No. How heavy are you now?'

'Twelve stone six.'

'Check. Trousers?'

'Check trousers?'

'No, dummy. Check, as in, well, checked. Off the list.'

'Ah. Sorry.'

'So. Trousers?'

'Yes. Got a pair on. Trendy combats.'

'No, I mean, waist?'

'What's a waste?'

Dan looks up in exasperation. 'Will you take this seriously, please?'

'Sorry. Thirty-four.'

'Check.'

'Can you stop saying check.'

'Sorry. Clothes?'

'Sorted.'

'Hair?'

'Cut. Styled.'

'Teeth?'

'White.'

'Smoking?'

'Thanks very much!'

'Glasses?'

I finish off my water. 'Empty.'

'Very funny. Car, flat...' Dan scans through the rest of the list, then clicks the laptop shut. 'I think we're finished.'

'Thank Christ for that. Can I have a proper drink now?'

Dan takes a sip of his beer. 'Not till tomorrow.'

'Spoilsport.'

'It's for your own good. So what's your plan?'

'My plan? Plan for what?'

'For when Jane gets back tomorrow?'

'Well, I haven't really thought about it.'

Dan slaps his forehead with his palm. 'Jesus. You've done all this work and you haven't even thought about what you're going to do when you see her again, or rather, when she sees you. "Be prepared", remember.'

'I didn't know you were in the Scouts.'

'I wasn't,' says Dan. 'I was in a few Guides, though. But I can't believe you haven't...'

'Of course I've thought about it, Dan. I've been thinking about very little else for the past few months.'

'So?'

'Well, I thought I'd go and surprise her at the airport.'

'Obviously,' says Dan. 'In the new car?'

'No, I thought I'd walk. Of course in the new car.'

'And then?'

'Maybe offer her a lift back home?'

Dan shakes his head. 'But it's not her home, is it? It's your home. She left it when she left you. This isn't just about you impressing her so she comes back.'

'It isn't?'

'Nope. You've got to make her feel that she's maybe got to impress you too. Otherwise…'

'Otherwise what?'

'Otherwise what's to stop her doing this all again?'

'What are you talking about?'

Dan puts his beer down. 'It's all about who has the power.'

'What do you mean?'

'In a relationship. The person who cares the least has all the power.'

'I still don't understand.'

'Well, say you were going out with someone.'

'I was. Am. And will be, come tomorrow, hopefully.'

'And she decided to leave you.'

'She already did.'

'No, I mean hypothetically.'

'Okay. Hypothetically.'

'Well, if you really cared about her, you'd be devastated, so she'd have all the power.'

'Well, I did, I was, and so she obviously does.'

'Right,' says Dan. 'But suppose you didn't care that much. If she was trying to make you do something, why on earth would she try to achieve it by leaving you? The effect of her going would be so much less.'

'But why would I be with her in the first place if I didn't care that much?'

'You're missing the point.'

'Well, please tell me what the point is.'

'Jane left you to make you change, right?'

'I suppose.'

'The reason you've put yourself through all this is because she had the power. Her actions have made you make this change.'

'Right…'

'So suppose when she comes back, she sees you, and by some miracle decides she wants you back. What you need to do is remain indifferent.'

I look back at Dan, astonished. 'You're saying that when she finally comes home, and if I manage to achieve the one thing I've been working towards night and day for the last three months, what I should actually do is play it all cool rather than pick her up and carry her in through the front door, which is probably what I'll want to do?'

Dan nods. 'Of course. It's important to set a precedent. Lay down some ground rules. Otherwise what's she going to do? The first sign of trouble, you start straining at the old waistband again and she'll be off to Outer Mongolia, because she knows that's what gets results. If, on the other hand, you can manage to give her the impression that you've done this for you, rather than for her, well, the shoe will be in your court.'

'What?'

'All I'm trying to say is, don't let her think that she's won.'

'But she will have won. I'll know it, she'll know it. She left me with some specific instructions and if I pass muster…'

'But there's the thing. You have to make her think that it's not just you on test. You're now this slimmer, fitter, better-looking love-god…'

'With a cool car, don't forget.'

'…so how does she measure up to you? Does plain old Jane deserve the new Edward Middleton.'

'So you're saying that in three months I've managed to leap-frog her in the attractiveness stakes? That now it's her who's trying to play out of her league?'

Dan laughs. 'Don't be ridiculous. But you have to make her think that. Don't let her assume that now she's back she's going to have it all her own way. I mean—do you just want the old Jane back?'

'Er…yes. No. I don't know. Well, not like it was in the last year or so.'

'Well take her back on your terms then. Tell her that if she comes back now it's for good. Or even better, make her feel that now it's her turn to win you back. Maybe she's put on weight while she's been away, or got a funny hairstyle, or lost an arm or something. You never know, you might see Jane and not fancy her!'

'Well, if she's lost an arm…'

'Edward, all I'm saying is that she may well have changed while she's been away milking yaks and whatever else it is they do in Tibet. You certainly have. Do you really think the two of you will still want the same things. And by that, I mean each other?'

He's right. And I can't pretend that this hasn't occurred to me. I've been working away single-mindedly for the past three months with one aim and one aim only—to get Jane back. But what Jane is it exactly that I want back? The Jane I met and fell in love with back at college? Or the Jane who thought I was so disgusting that she flew halfway around the world to get away from me? I suddenly wish I was drinking something stronger.

'I just feel I owe it to her to give her a chance.'

Dan raises one eyebrow. 'Now it's you who's giving her a chance, eh? Not the other way round?'

'You know what I mean. It's just that we've been through so much together. So much history, you know.'

'There's a reason why history's called history.'

'Huh?'

'Because it's in the past. Gone. Finished. Make some new stuff. Maybe even with someone new.'

'Dan, I can't even think about that. Not till I know how Jane feels about me. Or, more importantly, how I feel about Jane.'

'Tell me something,' says Dan. 'Isn't there a part of you that resents her for treating you the way she did? That wants to tell her that she's made her bed and has to lie in it?'

I nod. 'Of course there is. But there's also a part of me that wants to lie in it with her.'

'Ah,' says Dan. 'But that's not the part that should be making decisions.'

'You can talk.'

Dan drains the last of his beer. 'You know what I do when I have to make a difficult choice? Like between two women, for example?' he adds, unusually perceptively for him.

'Toss for it?'

Dan laughs. 'No—what I *actually* do is get a piece of paper, divide it into two columns, then write down all the good points of one of them on one side, and then do the same for the other one on the other side.'

I'm a little surprised that Dan should take such a practical approach. I didn't know he had it in him.

'What do you do then?'

He grins. 'Simple. I go out with the one who's the best in bed.'

8.44 p.m.

Wendy appears at our table, dressed in a pair of tight black jeans and a T-shirt to match.

'You off to a funeral?' says Dan, looking her up and down.

Wendy smiles sarcastically back at him. 'Yours, hopefully,' she replies.

'Ignore him, Wendy. You look very nice.'

'Thanks, Edward,' she says. 'Anyway, Danny-boy. What are you doing here so late on a Friday night? Not managed to find some poor unfortunate girl to lure back to your sleazy bachelor pad?'

'It's not sleazy,' protests Dan. 'And it's certainly not a "bachelor pad", as you so charmingly call it.'

'What is it then?'

'It's a loft.'

Wendy laughs. 'A loft?' she says, picking up our empty glasses. 'Isn't that where most people store their junk?'

I follow her to the bar, and we look back over towards Dan, who's checking his hair in the reflection of his Oakley's.

'He doesn't mean any harm' I say. 'He's just a little…'

'Retarded?' suggests Wendy.

I smile. 'Could be. I was going to say "insensitive", but you're probably closer.'

'Why on earth do you hang around with him?'

'Dan's not all bad. He's a good friend. And he's taught me a valuable lesson these past few months.'

'Really?'

'Yes. How not to behave towards women.'

'I can't imagine it's much fun going out with him,' agrees Wendy. 'He'd make a lousy boyfriend.'

'So tell me—any last-minute tips as to what makes a good boyfriend?'

'Hmm.' Wendy puffs out her cheeks. 'That's a hard one.'

'Is that the first thing?'

'No, cheeky. But I'm the wrong person to ask, aren't I?'

'Why? You're a woman.'

'Thanks for noticing. But why don't you tell me what you think? After all, you're the expert now.'

'Well, I'd hardly call myself an expert. But I think I have worked out where I was going wrong. Or rather, where Jane and I were going wrong.'

'Oh yes?'

'Well, the way I see it is this. Women spend all this effort on their make-up and hair to make themselves look as good as they possibly can. They can waste hours deciding what to wear before even venturing out as far as the corner shop. In some cases they spend a fortune on jewellery, watches, handbags, shoes; all accessories to make themselves look better.'

'So, what's your point?'

'Why then blow all that time and effort by walking around with a big, untrendy lump of a man hanging off your arm?'

Wendy laughs. 'You may be right.'

'But most women don't need wa-hey. They just want okay. Imagine the insecurity if you went out with a too-good-looking man. All the time you're worrying that other women are looking at your partner, wondering what on earth he's doing with you, and thinking how they can steal him off you. And what's worse, if it's someone like Dan, you know that he'll be thinking exactly the same thing—here I am with so-and-so but I'll just keep an eye out because you never know, I might spot someone better, and if I do…I think that really good-looking guys usually know they're really good-looking guys, and therefore think they can get away with murder. Not-so-good-looking guys just have to work that little bit harder at the "rest" of it, and that's what makes them better boyfriend material. Someone like Dan, well, you probably worry that he'll spend more time in the bathroom getting ready than you will.'

'You know,' she says, 'I hadn't thought of it that way round. If that's the case, then you're saying I should feel sorry for Dan, as from his point of view, it's actually a pain to be really good-looking. You're always going to worry that the girl you're with is feeling insecure, unsettled…'

'Precisely. When you go out with someone, you want them to complement you, not compete with you. Imagine how you'd feel as a woman, typically the glamorous side of the relationship, if every time you went out with your boyfriend you felt that people were looking at him, not you? It's as you said to me a while ago: what women want is someone who thinks *they're* special. Not someone who knows that *he's* the special one. And that's the way it's supposed to be. Like at the Oscars.'

'The Oscars?'

'All the women appear in the most fashionable dresses, in the latest designs, and a multitude of colours, trying to outdo one another on the red carpet. The men? They all wear the same thing. Why? Because that's what's supposed to happen. It's the way the world works. Women look beautiful, men just look. And most women are aware of this. They know they can't just log on to "He-Bay" or go down to "Boys R Us" and choose a finished model off the shelf, so instead, they pick a basic one and gradually shape them, making improvements until they reach that ideal balance—you know how women like a project. But occasionally, there comes a time when they realize they might be working on a lost cause. And that's what Jane had begun to wonder. Whether I was a lost cause.'

'Why?'

'Because I'd stopped responding.'

Dan chooses that moment to catch my eye, and indicates the lack of beer in his hand. As I pick up the drinks from the bar, Wendy leans over and kisses me on the cheek.

'I hope you get what you want after all this, Edward.'

'Thanks,' I say, starting to head back towards where Dan's sitting.

'And if things don't work out tomorrow with Jane…'

'Yes?'

Wendy just smiles.

9.32 p.m.

Dan's a little bit pissed by now. I, on the other hand, just need a piss, especially after all this water. When I get back from the toilet, he decides to give me the benefit of some more of his alcohol-induced wisdom.

'So, there's this guy…'

'What guy?'

'Any guy. Let's call him Edward, for argument's sake, and he's walking along the street, and he finds a magic lamp.'

'Are you telling a joke?'

'And he picks the lamp up, and because it's dirty, he gives it a rub.'

'Not likely in Brighton, mate. More likely to be a used syringe or an empty beer bottle.'

'And out comes this genie.'

'You are telling a joke.'

'Just listen. And so the genie says, "You have freed me from my prison."'

'He obviously hasn't seen Brighton yet.'

'"You have freed me from my prison",' continues Dan, '"so in return, I grant you one wish".'

'One? I thought it was usually three.'

'Are you going to let me finish this or are you just going to keep interrupting?'

'Sorry. Go on.'

'And so the guy thinks for a bit, and then says "Tell you what. I'm afraid of flying, but I've always wanted to visit America. Could you build a bridge across the Atlantic so I can drive there?" Well, the genie scratches his head, and says to the guy, "Do you realize just how complicated that would be? It's miles, and I'd need to make sure it was high enough for the ships to go under, and secure enough to resist the waves…It would take ages. Are you sure there's nothing else you want?"'

'And?'

'And so the guy thinks for a minute, and then replies, "Okay, there is one other thing. I've always wanted to understand women." And the genie looks back at him and says, "How many lanes wide did you want that bridge?"'

I sit there patiently while Dan finishes chortling to himself. 'You mean I'll never understand women?'

'None of us will. And shouldn't waste our time trying, mate.'

'So, I've been spending all this time trying to work out what it is exactly that women want, and then trying to mould myself into that person, when what I should have been doing is thinking about the specific woman I wanted, and trying to make myself attractive to her, instead of turning myself into some generic attractive-to-most-women clone like you? No offence.'

Dan shrugs. 'Well that's a good theory. Only trouble is that first of all you'd have had to decide whether that woman actually was Jane, and if it was then you'd have to see if you could work out exactly what it was she really wanted, and that's assuming a) that she knew herself, and b) that you could actually have found that out from her while she was in Tibet. And if it wasn't Jane, but someone else, well you would've had to have reached a certain level of attractiveness before you could have got close enough to her to then find out what it was she was looking for, and then moulded yourself to that.'

Strangely enough, the drunker Dan gets, the less he seems to talk rubbish. And after all this time, he's finally beginning to make sense to me.

'So have I just been wasting my time for these last three months? Why couldn't you have told me that at the beginning?'

Dan looks a little sheepish. 'Because I've only just worked it out. And besides, even you've got to think that it's all been worth it, hasn't it?'

'I'll let you know tomorrow.'

'You're back to at least that base level where you managed to attract Jane in the first place, right? So at the very least, you should be able to attract the likes of her, if not actually her, again.'

'I suppose so.'

Dan picks up his empty glass. 'Another?'

I check my watch. 'No thanks, mate. As appealing as one last glass of fizzy water might be, I think I better head on home. Big day tomorrow. Someone's got an important decision to make.'

Dan looks confused for a moment. 'You mean Jane, right?'

And it's only when I'm halfway home I realize that perhaps I should have corrected him.

Saturday 16th April

7.00 a.m.

THE ARRIVALS HALL AT Gatwick is teeming with people. Red-faced holiday-makers, some wearing souvenir sombreros, most carrying clinking bags of duty-free, swarm through customs and out towards the car parks, where they shiver in the biting spring wind, cursing the fact that there's another fifty weeks before they can head back to their sun loungers.

Jane's flight is on time, the notice board tells me, which means I've probably got about fifteen minutes to fight my way through to the front of the arrivals gate, where I'll hopefully be able to spot her as soon as she comes through.

Eventually she appears, pushing her trolley along the 'nothing to declare' channel, through the swing doors, and out into the main concourse. Her hair's a little lighter than when she left, maybe she's lost a little weight, but apart from that, she looks like the same Jane who left me three long months ago.

As she scans the crowds, searching for a route through, her gaze briefly meets mine, before moving away. Her face crinkles in puzzlement and she turns back towards me, eyes widening with surprise, before abandoning her luggage in the middle of the airport and rushing over to meet me.

Jane stares at me for a few seconds, lost for words, before bursting into tears. She kisses me hard, and tells me that it was all a stupid mistake, how much she's missed me, that she's sorry for the whole

Martin thing, and how unbelievably great I look. I take her into my arms, effortlessly hoisting her heavy suitcase with my new-found strength, and we pile into the Mini and drive off into the sunset.

Or that's how I imagine it would have happened, had I actually gone out to meet her from where I've been hiding behind the pillar next to the magazine rack in WH Smiths. Instead, when Jane appears through customs, I duck down behind my copy of *Health & Fitness*, pretty sure that she won't think of looking for me there.

As she makes her way past the entrance to Smiths, I sneak a peek at her over the top of my magazine. She looks great, radiant even, as if the last three months have done her the power of good, and I realize that it's important for me to be here to see this. To know that she's happy, healthy, and safe.

As I watch her stride confidently on her own through the busy airport, it occurs to me that I was wrong last night. I don't owe Jane a chance. I don't owe her anything, apart from an apology, maybe, for the last few years: for letting myself go; for making it seem like I'd stopped caring about myself; for not caring about her; and for not caring about us. And, more significantly, for not realizing what that meant.

Perhaps there'll be an opportunity to give her that apology, face-to-face, in time. But not here, not today. I don't need a reaction. I don't want revenge. I don't even require what I believe is known as 'closure'. And at the same time, I'm relieved that I'm not going to have to make a choice. After all, if I don't want her back, then there isn't a choice to make.

I wait until I'm sure she's a respectable distance away before leaving the safety of WH Smiths, then freeze as I feel a tap on my shoulder. Fortunately, it's only one of the assistants—I haven't paid for the magazine I'm absent-mindedly holding—so, red-faced, I hand it back. By the time I get to the walkway that links the airport to the car parks, Jane's already making her way towards the escalators that lead down to the Gatwick Express.

And the funny thing is, despite how hard the last three months have felt, how tough the training has seemed, and how difficult the dieting, not drinking, and giving up smoking has been, watching Jane walk out of the airport and out of my life is actually surprisingly easy.

7.50 a.m.

I race back home and change quickly into my workout gear, before heading off on my usual seafront loop. After about ten minutes I spot them in the distance, one a shambolic limping figure, and wince at the recollection of how similar that was to me just three short months ago. They're heading slowly in my direction, so I decide to sit in the nearest shelter and wait for them.

As they draw level, Sam's client collapses onto the bench next to me, breathing heavily. He must be about fifty, and at least that many pounds overweight, and I'm slightly jealous that he doesn't seem to be feeling sick, although I can almost hear his heart hammering through his chest. Mine is too, but it's nothing to do with my morning run.

When Sam sees me, she looks puzzled for a moment, before making the introductions.

'Lawrence, this is Edward. He's one of my success stories.' She looks at the two of us, sitting side-by-side. 'You two look like a "before" and "after" poster.'

It's turning into a warm morning, and perspiration glints off Sam's top lip as she talks. I have to resist the temptation to reach across and wipe it off for her.

'Which of us,' wheezes Lawrence, 'is which?'

Sam ignores him. 'Edward, haven't you got something important you should be doing?'

'Yes,' I say. 'Which is why I'm here. There's something I need to ask you.'

Sam looks nervously down at Lawrence, who's obviously grateful for the interruption. 'I'm kind of on somebody else's time right now.'

'Take all the time you need,' he gasps from his sprawled position on the bench. 'Please.'

'I won't be long,' I say, standing up and leading Sam away, out of Lawrence's earshot. 'I just wanted to check something.'

'Which was?'

'When you said to me a while ago that you'd never go out with a client.'

Sam frowns. 'Yes?'

'Well, yesterday was our last session, wasn't it?'

'I suppose so.'

'So, I'm not a client any more?'

Sam thinks about this for a moment or two, then leans forward and kisses me, but it's on the lips this time.

'I guess not,' she says, with a smile.

About the Author

MATT DUNN WAS BORN in Margate in 1966, but escaped to Spain, where he worked as a newspaper columnist and played a lot of tennis. After a stint in Brighton, he now lives in London.

Previously he has been a professional lifeguard, fitness-equipment salesman, and an IT headhunter, but he prefers writing for a living, so please keep buying his books.

Visit the author at www.mattdunn.co.uk.